COLD AS ICE

CHARLES SHEFFIELD

A TOM DOHERTY ASSOCIATES BOOK
NEW YORK

COLD AS ICE

Cover art by Vincent di Fate

A Tor Book
Published by Tom Doherty Associates, Inc.
175 Fifth Avenue
New York, N.Y. 10010

Tor® is a registered trademark of Tom Doherty Associates, Inc.

ISBN: 0-812-51163-8
Library of Congress Catalog Card Number: 92-85794

First edition: June 1992
First mass market printing: June 1993

Printed in the United States of America

0 9 8 7 6 5 4 3 2 1

CONTENTS

PROLOGUE

2067 A.D.: Rejoice! the War is Over

Every war begins with a first encounter, a first blow, a first casualty. That is the shot heard 'round the world.

But in every war there must also be a last victim. And the event that takes that victim can happen after the combat is officially ended.

The *Pelagic* was a deep-space freighter, hurriedly converted for passenger transport. Designed to creep ore-laden from asteroid mines to the great refineries in low orbit about Earth or Mars, the ship had a maximum acceleration of less than a quarter gravity. The Seeker that pursued her could sustain five gees, or boost briefly at a hundred.

The presence of the pursuer had been detected in a routine scan for Belt debris not listed in the data banks. Of the four people in the control room following the emergency call, only Vernor Perry, the navigation officer, had accepted what the Seeker's steady approach meant.

"I know we can't outrun it." Loring Sheer, the chief engineer, was still arguing. "Why should we *need* to? You heard the radio messages from Earth. The war is *over!*"

"Vern? What do you say to that?" Mimi Palance was the

captain, hurriedly appointed when the refugee ship left the mid-sized asteroid of Mandrake. She was a habitat designer, and she was having trouble in adjusting to the idea of space command.

Vernor Perry looked stupefied. He was the one who had called them to the control room. He knew more about Seekers than anyone else on board. He also knew that he was dead. All discussion was pointless.

"Vern!" said Palance again, in a sharper tone.

Perry roused himself. "It makes no difference if the war is over or not. Seekers are smart missiles, but they were built without a cancel mode. Once targeted, they can't be changed."

"But what makes you sure that *we* are the target?" asked the personnel officer. It was her first time in space since the war began, and Mary Vissuto was still bewildered by the sudden order to flee from Mandrake. "Why mightn't the target be another ship, or even a colony?"

"Probabilities." Perry pointed to a three-D display with the *Pelagic* as its moving center. "There's no other ship or artificial structure within five million kilometers. That Seeker is heading directly toward us. There's no reasonable chance that it's aiming for anything else."

"So what can we do to escape it?"

Perry shrugged.

"That's no answer, Vern," said Palance. And, sharply again when he did not reply, "Come on, man. We have four adults and fifteen children on board. I agree, we can't outrun a Seeker. But what about a course change?"

"Useless." *We're dead. Why are you bothering me?* "I tell you, a Seeker is *smart*. It's already observing us, with all of its sensors. If we change course, it will compute a revised contact trajectory. If we turn our power off, it will track us by our thermal signature. The *Pelagic* is hotter than any natural body in the Belt. It has to be, or we'd all be frozen."

"Then if we can't run away, can we hide? Suppose we head for an asteroid and park behind it."

"The Seeker will follow us. We can't run, and we can't hide." But even as he spoke, a flicker of an idea crossed Perry's frozen mind.

"What, Vern?" Mimi Palance had seen the change of expression.

"We may be able to hide—for just a while. Don't get your hopes up, though. We can't *escape*. But we might buy a little time." Perry went over to the control console and called up the banks of solar-system ephemerides.

"I thought you just said that we *couldn't* hide. So why are you looking at asteroids?" Loring Sheer had been trying to adjust to the idea of imminent death, but now the engineer was confused again.

"We can't hide behind *one*. What we need for breathing space is a *cluster*. I've got the computer looking for one we can reach before the Seeker reaches us." He checked the missile's progress. "Luckily, it's in no hurry—it knows we can't get away." He pressed the compute key. "Hold your breath."

"What are you calculating, Vern?" Mary Vissuto had been too busy on Mandrake with the children and with her own work to pay much attention to the celestial mechanics of the Belt.

"Asteroid groups. The asteroids move all the time relative to each other." And when Mary still showed no sign of understanding, "They move, you see, but the law of averages means that there have to be temporary clusters, continually forming and dissolving. The trick is to find one near enough to do us some good. Then we move over and snuggle up into the middle of the group."

He did not take time to explain the tricky part of what he was doing. The bodies of the Asteroid Belt ranged in size from Ceres, a giant by asteroid standards at seven hundred and fifty kilometers, down to free-falling mountains and on to the pea-sized and smaller pebbles. Everything from worlds to sand grains moved in its own complicated orbit, defined by the gravitational forces of sun and planets, by solar wind and radiation pressure, and by asteroid interactions.

Vern's first task was to choose reasonable size limits. He had on file the orbit parameters for every Belt body of more than fifty meters in diameter, and he had set the required number of bodies to one thousand, with a cluster radius of five hundred kilometers. If the computer could find nothing that matched those requirements, he would have to decrease the number of bodies in the cluster or increase the permitted cluster radius. Each of those options would make it more difficult for the *Pelagic* to hide. And the hiding place would be temporary, whatever he did. The Seeker would patiently search every body of a cluster until it again encountered the unique signature of the *Pelagic*.

The other two in the control room had not needed Perry's explanation to know what he was doing. Their eyes were fixed on the displays. "It's found some," said Palance as the computation ended. "Four of them!"

Perry shrugged. "Yeah, but look at the distances. We can forget the first three—the Seeker would catch us before we got there. It's number four, or nothing."

"That cluster's not even close to our present trajectory." Sheer was peering at the tabulation. "We'd have to burn all the fuel we've got to make that course change."

"You'll never find a better use for it." Mimi Palance had already made up her mind. "Vern, give me a flight path."

"Doing it." Perry was at the console. Hope was the biggest delusion, but what else was there to do? "Loring, make sure you're ready for full acceleration. I'm going to assume that you can squeeze out a quarter gee."

"You'll be lucky." But Loring Sheer was looking better as he hurried out. Something to do, *anything* to do. Even if he blew the engines apart, that was better than sitting around watching the approach of the Seeker.

"A quarter gee!" protested Mary Vissuto. "We haven't had a tenth of that since we left Mandrake. The cabins and galley aren't ready for it."

"They'd better be," said Perry. "In about two minutes. I'm programming for maximum thrust as soon as Sheer can give it to us."

"We'll never get things tied down in time." But Mary, too, was hurrying out, leaving Palance and Perry alone in the control room.

"So we go sit in the middle of the cluster." Perry spoke in a dry, controlled voice, as though they were discussing some academic problem of orbital rendezvous. At the same time, he was fine-tuning the trajectory, seeking a region where the cluster bodies were converging. "What then, Mimi? Loring and Mary still don't understand. They think this gives us a chance. It doesn't. It gives us a short reprieve. There's no way that the *Pelagic* can escape a Seeker."

"I know. We're going to die. I didn't accept that ten minutes ago, I do now. But I *don't* accept it for the children. They're special. We have to come up with an idea, Vern. And we have to do it quick. Get your brain in gear."

The control sequence took over. The engines fired. The *Pelagic* accelerated its ungainly bulk toward the random assembly of rock fragments that comprised the chosen cluster. Far behind, taking course changes in its stride and closing steadily on the bigger ship, the deadly needle of the Seeker followed every move.

When the group reconvened in the control room six hours later, Mimi had herself and the meeting under better control. She took no credit for that. Loring Sheer and

Mary Vissuto had come to grips with unpleasant reality, while Vern Perry was admitting that impending death did not remove the obligation to think.

"Vern." She nodded her head at the navigation officer. "Status summary, please."

"Our physical location has changed, but not our situation." Perry already had the displays he needed on file. "That's us." A blue point winked on the screen. "We're nicely tucked away behind a one-kilometer rock, and I'm going to keep us there. These fourteen other bodies"—more winking lights—"are available if we want to do some dodging. We're safe for twenty-four hours unless the Seeker changes its operating plan. I don't see why it should. Here it is." A red point of light appeared. "It knows where we are, and the Doppler from its radar signals shows that it's closing at a constant rate."

He turned from the console. "The bad news we already know. We can't run away, because we have no fuel left. Even if we could, the Seeker is fast enough to catch us and run rings round us."

"All right." Mimi Palance turned to Sheer. "The *Pelagic* is stuck here. What about other transport?"

"There's one lifeboat. We could all get into it, and we might even be able to fly somewhere before we ran out of air. But we wouldn't be given the chance. A Seeker can recognize a lifeboat as well as it can a ship, and it would see our drive go on. It would tackle the *Pelagic*, then come after us—or maybe the other way around. Either way, it would make no difference. We can't get anywhere using the lifeboat."

"So cross that one off." Mimi was aware of the clock. Any actions they might take were less likely to succeed as the Seeker came closer and the resolution of its sensors improved. "All right. Life support and habitats, that's my area. Not good. We have nine single-person pods. Self-contained life-support system on each one, but no thrust capability. Nine pods, and nineteen of us. Bad arithmetic. Mary? Ideas?"

"Nine of the children are two years old or less. Can you double up, put two to a pod?"

"No." Mimi Palance did not elaborate. She knew why that was impossible, as Mary should have known too. "If we put kids on the pods, only nine can go. And they have to be the youngest. They're the smallest, and the pods can keep them alive the longest. The bigger ones . . . stay here with us."

She paused and swallowed. The others could not look at her. They knew that although each of them had a child on board under two, Mimi Palance's only child was a boy approaching seven. He would stay with her on the *Pelagic*.

And die with her, thought Vernor Perry. *Just like the rest of us*. But all he said was, "Won't work."

"Why not? We can do a ballistic launch—throw them out of the *Pelagic*. No thrust from the pods for the Seeker to track. It will think they are bits of space junk associated with the cluster. I'm sure the Seeker doesn't have any better list of small rocks than we do, and there are thousands around here that we don't have in the data bank."

"That's not the problem." Perry hated to dash hopes, but there was no value to fantasy. "Sure, there would be no thrust to track, no deviation from free-fall to observe. But that's only one way that the Seeker hunts. The pods have to be kept above ambient temperature if you want the kids to survive. So the Seeker will find them in just the way it's going to find the *Pelagic*—because of a thermal signal far above background."

"Loring? Any comment? Any ideas?"

"No. Vern's right. The Seeker will detect and destroy the pods." The engineer was silent for a few seconds. "Unless . . ."

"Come on, Loring. Quick! We don't have time to dawdle."

"Well, this is half-baked. But we have liquid helium on board. Not a lot of it, but the I/R sensor detectors need cooling way down, and we use it for that. Suppose we put the kids inside the pods, as many of them as will fit, and then we blow a liquid-helium spray onto the *outside* of the pods. That could bring the skin temperature down to ambient, the same as the rest of the rocks in the cluster. It would take some calculation of latent heats and heat transfer, but I can hack that out pretty quick. And *then* we eject the pods from the *Pelagic* while we're in the shadow of one of the bigger asteroids . . . and hope the pods get far enough away before they heat up again because of the children inside. It's our best bet. Vern?"

"It's not our best bet, it's our *only* bet. We have to try it."

"But if you can do that for the life-support pods," said Mary Vissuto, "why not do it for the whole ship?"

"And then what?" Vern Perry was losing patience. "Even if we had enough liquid helium that we could spray the whole *Pelagic*—and we don't—we have no fuel to go anywhere. The Seeker wouldn't go away. It would sit and wait, and after a while our hull temperature would warm up again. It has to, or we'd all die of overheating. Then the Seeker would zap us. And when it realized what we had done to cool the ship, it might start looking around for other things that had been treated in the same way."

"But what will we do about the other children?" asked Mary Vissuto. It was as though she had not heard one word that Perry had said. "And what will happen to the rest of us?"

This time no one answered. If Mary still refused to look reality in the face, that was her problem.

The easy part was the desperate action. The nine pods were coated with an extra layer of thermal insulation, as much as could be installed and still permit the body heat of the infants within to dissipate. Ejection vectors were computed to make the pods seem as much as possible like ordinary members of the cluster. Finally the metabolism of the nine young children was reduced as far as Mimi Palance dared. No one had ever determined how long a child could survive in a pod, let alone with a reduced metabolic condition. Perhaps it was as well that no one knew.

When everything was ready, each pod would be thrown out into space at a preselected moment, chosen to optimize the masking effect of the natural bodies of the cluster. The pods shared no common destination, but all of them were targeted for the inner solar system. After nine days, when they should be safely beyond the Seeker's attention, each would begin to broadcast a distress signal.

As soon as the ninth life-support unit was ready, Vernor Perry placed an unconscious child inside it. He tenderly kissed the little boy good-bye. All of the children on the *Pelagic* were special, but to Vern this one was extra-special, Vern's own flesh and blood. He surveyed the cold anonymity of the pod and shuddered at the thought of his baby facing empty space, unnamed and unknown. With Mimi Palance's consent, he attached a little name card to the infant boy's shirt, then helped to prepare cards for the other eight babies.

He watched as they were launched, one by one. When the ninth pod was ejected with its precious cargo, Vern Perry muttered to himself, "The ark went upon the face of the waters. And the spirit of God moved over the vasty deep."

And then there was nothing more to be done. They could not run, they could not hide.

The hard part began.

Vern could not bear to stay with the other adults. He

went to where his older boy, Martin, was playing, and retreated with him to the navigation room.

The *Pelagic* had emerged from the shelter of the rocky asteroids as soon as the last pod was on its way. The Seeker was close enough now to show a visible image. It was a long, sharp-pointed cone, with a broad lip on its thick base. There had been no change in its behavior when the six-foot ovoids of the life-support units were launched.

Seated on Vern's knee, his eight-year-old son watched the Seeker with no fear and a good deal of curiosity. "I've never seen a ship like that before, Dad," he said. "Is it a Belt design?"

"Yes. It's called a Seeker. It's a . . . a weapons ship."

"Well, the war's over now. Thank goodness. Hey!" Martin could see everything that his father saw. "It's coming this way, isn't it?"

"Yes. How did you know?"

"Well, the picture looks the same size, but the scale bar on the display keeps changing."

"Quite true. You're a smart boy." *He is, too—super-smart. When he grows up—*

Vern choked off the thought and squeezed his eyes tight shut.

"Why is it getting closer to us?"

"It's coming to . . . to take us home." Vern opened his eyes again and peered at the other screen. There, diminished to a tiny dot, was pod number nine. It was still safely retreating. He stared and stared. It was all he had to hold on to.

"Back home to Mandrake, you mean? That's great." Martin was still gazing at the first screen. "Hey, look, Dad. The other ship's turning around."

The Seeker was rotating slowly on its axis, bringing about the end of its blunt cone to face the *Pelagic*.

Remote weapons system. Vern's analysis when he turned

again to the main screen was automatic. *So it doesn't intend to destroy us with impact.*

The Seeker's rotation was complete. Vern Perry was staring right down the emission venturi. But its image was a misty-eyed blur. He put his arms around his son.

Nine billion dead in four months. It's an unthinkable number, when every loss could be as painful as this.

"Dad, quit that!" The boy was laughing. "You're *squashing* me. See, the end's opening up."

"It's all right, Martin. Everything's going to be all right."

"Dad, look. *Dad!*"

As space around the *Pelagic* bloomed yellow and crimson, the Great War claimed its last casualties. But Vernor Perry did not see it happen. He was holding his beloved son close. His eyes were closed, and the agony in his heart had nothing to do with his own fate.

His final thought was a prayer for the end of all such sorrow.

INTERLUDE

This is the size-distribution law of the Asteroid Belt: For every body of given diameter, D, there will be ten bodies with diameter d = D/3.

Corollary: *As the body you are searching for becomes smaller, the problem of distinguishing it from others of similar size becomes rapidly more difficult.*

Conclusion: *Personal survival pods, each a couple of meters long, will be lost in a swarm of natural objects, more numerous within the Belt than grains of sand on a beach. Visual search techniques in such an environment will be useless.*

· Solution: *Although the sky in and beyond the solar system glimmers and glows with visible light from stars, planets, diffuse and luminous gas clouds, novas, supernovas, and galaxies, other regions of the electromagnetic spectrum are far less busy. Choose carefully. At the right wavelength for observation, Earth shines brighter than a thousand suns.*

The designers of search-and-rescue systems choose very carefully. The available signal energy must be radiated in many directions, travel millions or hundreds of millions of kilometers, and fill an immense volume. The amounts of power available for distress calls are usually just a few watts. No matter. The radio energy needed for signal detection and location is truly minute; the total microwave power received at the solar system's largest radio telescope would not carry a crawling fly up a windowpane.

SAR systems are designed to detect and triangulate a crippled survival pod operating on its last dribble of power. From a single one-minute fix, a ship or pod's position and velocity can be computed. A rescue vehicle will be chosen, and a matching trajectory defined.

What SAR systems cannot do—because no one ever anticipated such a need—is to operate efficiently when wartime battle communications swamp every channel. And when war ends, emergency needs for reconstruction are no less demanding.

The last urgent and one-time call from the Pelagic, *giving trajectories for nine small objects, goes unheeded.*

The pods drift through space. The sedated infants within them dream on. Their sun-centered orbits carry them steadily closer to the monitored zone of the Inner System, but they move at a snail's pace, too slow for the internal resources of the pods. Life-support systems, intended for at most a few weeks' use, begin to fail. The pods' own calls for help continue, but they, too, weaken, merging into the galactic radio hiss that fills all of space.

Months pass. The pods drift on, interplanetary flotsam borne on sluggish tides of radiation pressure and the changing currents of gravitational force.

No one knows that they exist.

1

2092 A.D.:
Black Smoker

Nell Cotter had visualized the sequence precisely during the final minutes before the hatch was closed: a slow fading of light, a gradual extinction that would grow ever fainter as they descended, never quite bleeding away completely.

And had she got it wrong! Here was reality, a few seconds of cloudy green filled with drifting motes of white. A sudden school of darting silverfish all around them, and then, moments later, no trace of diffused sunlight. Only darkness, absolute and implacable. Scary.

But reporting personal discomfort was not what she was paid to do. "We are now moving through the three-hundred-meter level," she said calmly. "That little cluster of shrimp was probably the last life we'll see for a while. All external light has disappeared."

She spoke into her main microphone, the one that Jon Perry could hear, but after that, she automatically went on subvocalizing for the private record. *Don't need to say the depth. One of the cameras is trained on the instrument panel. Can hardly see it though, it's so dim in here.* She glanced at the other two video recorders. *Getting nothing from outside. We need action, or all of this sequence will be edited out.*

The third camera showed Jon Perry at the submersible's controls, leaning back, totally relaxed, even bored.

Cold fish, as cold-blooded as anything outside. Well, I was warned. The Ice Man. Wonder if Mr. Personality does any better when he knows he's on camera. "Dr. Perry, would you narrate while we're descending? I could do it, but I'd only be parroting what you told me earlier."

"Sure." He displayed no more emotion, dropping in this hollow glass shell through black depths, than she had seen him do on the ocean's surface. He turned his face toward the camera. "We will be making an unpowered descent for the next sixteen hundred meters. That will take approximately ten minutes and put us onto the eastern edge of the Pacific Antarctic Ridge, about forty-five south, a hundred and ten west. The coast of South America and the Arenas Base are fourteen hundred kilometers east. We are already into the stable temperature regime, with the water at a constant four degrees Celsius. It will stay that way for another thousand meters. The only change we'll notice until we reach the seabed is in the outside pressure. It adds ten tons of load to each square meter of the *Spindrift*'s surface for every ten meters that we descend. If you listen closely, you can hear the vessel's structure adjusting to the outside force. At the moment, the pressure on the hull is about a thousand tons per square meter."

A thousand tons! Thank you, Jon Perry. I could have gone all day without needing to know that. Nell stared around at the transparent goldfish bowl of the submersible. On the surface, the three-meter globe of the *Spindrift* had seemed substantial enough; now it felt as flimsy and as fragile as a soap bubble. If it were to shatter under the enormous outside pressure . . .

She felt a twinge of discomfort in her bladder but pushed awareness of it into the back of her mind.

Is he going to talk his damned statistics all the way down? No one on Earth or anywhere else will want to watch. A pox on you, Glyn Sefaris. Promise me a "quick and easy" assignment, so I'll agree to come here unprepared. And give me this. (And better be sure to edit that out, before Glyn gets his editorial look.)

It was a party trick, elevated to a practical technique. Nell could keep up her own stream-of-consciousness commentary on the subvocal recorder installed in her larynx and still monitor and direct the course of the video program. The final show would be a mixture of on-the-spot and voice-over comments. Continuous time-markers on cameras and microphones ensured that she would have no difficulty in coordinating, editing, and splicing the different tracks. As she paused, Jon Perry wound up the string of statistics and was moving on.

". . . at which point I will begin using our lights. We could do it now—we have plenty of power—but it's not worth it, because the only thing we're likely to see are a few deep-water fish, all of them well-known benthic forms."

"Not well known to me or to the viewers, Dr. Perry." Nell jumped in on her public mike. The thrust of the show was supposed to be about the seafloor hydrothermal vents and the life forms around them, but final subject matter was irrelevant if viewers turned off before you ever got there. "Can we take a look?"

He shrugged and turned back to the control panel. Nell watched his fingers flicker across a precise sequence of keys.

Beautifully shaped hands. Make sure we show plenty of footage of them. Nice sexy voice, too, if I could get more animation into it. Talks old, no juice. Check his age when we get back—twenty-eight to thirty, for a guess. Check background, too. I know next to nothing about him. How long has he been playing deep-sea diver?

The darkness around them was suddenly illuminated by three broad beams of green light, each beginning twenty meters from the *Spindrift* and pointed back toward it.

"Free-swimming light sources," said Perry, anticipating Nell's question. "Half a meter long, two-kilowatt continuous cold light, or pulsed at a megawatt. We have half a dozen of them. They normally travel attached to the base of the *Spindrift*, but they can be released and controlled from here."

"Why not just shine beams out from the submersible?"

"Too much back-scatter. The light that's reflected toward us from an outgoing beam would spoil the picture. Better to send the free-swimmers out and shine light back this way."

"They're radio-controlled?"

He gave her a glance that might have been amused, but it was probably contemptuous. He knew she'd been sent here half-briefed as well as she did. "Radio's no use under water. Lasers would do, but focused ultrasonics are better. They travel farther and don't interfere with what we see."

Which at the moment happens to be nothing. Nell stared out into three empty cones of brightness. *Not one hint of fish. Amazing, I can see everywhere. The* Spindrift *admits light completely from all directions. Even the chairs are transparent.* "Progress in ceramic materials since the war, Miss Cotter." Perry had patted the side of the clear globe as they were first boarding. "We can make everything in the submersible as transparent as the best glass . . . except the crew, of course. We're working on that." (*Joke!*) "And so strong that the *Spindrift* could descend to the deepest part of the Marianas Trench."

To which, thank God, they were not going. The hydrothermal vents lay at what Jon Perry described as a "modest" depth of a couple of thousand meters.

Which means that we're going more than a mile straight down. Two thousand tons of force on every square meter of the hull. Smash in this Christmas ornament, and no one would ever find the broken shell. Or its contents. God, I hate the deep sea—and I never knew it before. Feel like I have to go to the bathroom. Hope I don't pee in my pants (and be sure to edit that out, too, when I get back).

Still they were descending, through cold, lifeless water. Jon Perry had his free-swimmers on autopilot, their lighthouse beams creating cones of green, fading in the distance. Over to the left, Nell finally caught a glimpse of movement. Something dark, something faint, a wisp of smoke at the limit of vision.

"Dr. Perry, I see a big object swimming. Over on your side."

But he was shaking his head. "Not swimming. That's the first sign of what we came down here to look at. You're seeing the top of the plume from the smoker. Look at the water temperature."

Nell—and the camera—looked. It was eight degrees above freezing, warmer than it ought to be. They were descending into the region of the hydrothermal vent. A feathery plume of darker water—like up-flowing oil—was the first sign of the vent's proximity.

Jon Perry had listened well when she briefed him before the descent. He picked up his cue now without a hint from her. "From this point, the water as we descend will become hotter and hotter, all the way to the entry chimney of Hotpot—a crack in the seafloor, the hydrothermal vent that leads right to Earth's hot interior. Actually, this is both the newest and the hottest of the known vents. Those in the Galapagos Rift are deeper, and they have been studied for a long time: Mussel Bed and Rose Garden, Clambake and Garden of Eden. But even the hottest of them, the 'black smokers,' don't run over three-fifty Celsius. Hotpot here tops out at over four-twenty, a super black smoker. If it weren't for the *pressure* down here, this would all be superheated steam . . ."

And if it weren't for the calmness *down here, this would all look damned good on camera. Beautiful clear eyes, total technical confidence. Pale complexion, because he spends too much time in the dark. Editing color balance will take care of that easy enough. But you need a few pins sticking into you, Jon Perry. We have to liven you up. Because let's face it, what you're saying to our vast but shrinking audience is* bloody dull stuff.

And Nell's experienced ear and eye told her that it was getting worse. Given that the average audience member had an attention span shorter than the time it took to blink. And given that there was not much to look at outside anyway. As they descended farther, the water was becoming steadily more turbid. The lights stopped a few yards beyond the glassy wall of the *Spindrift*, and in those few yards she could see *nothing*.

"There are live organisms thriving down here," Perry was saying, "at temperatures far above the usual boiling point of water—temperatures that would kill a human being in a few seconds. But even that's not the most interesting thing about the black smokers. Every creature on the land surface of the earth or in the upper levels of the oceans depends on the sun for its existence. Plants trap the energy of sunlight, animals eat plants, and animals eat each other. So it all comes back to sunlight and solar energy. But the animals that form colonies around the black smokers don't rely on the sun at all. Their life cycle starts with bacteria that are *chemosynthetic*, not *photosynthetic*. They depend on chemical energy, breaking down sulfur-based compounds and using the energy from that to power processes within their cells. If the sun were to go out completely, all life on the surface of the earth would vanish. But it might be centuries before life down here even *noticed*. It would go on as usual, energized by the earth's own minerals and internal heat . . ."

Pictures. Nell stared desperately at the roiling darkness

out beyond the *Spindrift*. *Great God of the Boob Tube, give me pictures. I've recorded enough talking-head material in the past five minutes for an hour's program.*

It was duller than her worst fears. And she knew what was coming next, because Jon Perry had told her even before they left the surface. They were going to scoop up exciting things like clams and mini-crabs and tube worms and sulfur-munching bacteria from the seabed around Hotpot, with the aid of the *Spindrift*'s remote handling arms. And they were going to push the creatures into the viewers' disgusted or bored faces.

I told you, Glyn, I didn't need this bloody job. I should have stayed in bed.

But before Nell had finished that subvocal thought, Jon Perry had moved. He was sitting up straight in his seat, and his face suddenly had an *expression* on it. A live, interested look, like a real human being. He had stopped speaking in mid-sentence, and he was ignoring the cameras. Nell felt a movement of the *Spindrift*, an upward bobbing that she had last experienced when the submersible was on the surface.

"What's happening?"

He did not reply, did not look at her. But he jerked his head toward the instrument panel, which told Nell nothing. She saw only dozens of dials and digital readouts, most of them unlabeled and unintelligible.

What *was* intelligible was the sudden disappearance of every scrap of outside illumination. The free-swimmers' lights had vanished. Nell Cotter and Jon Perry sat at the center of a jet-black globe, dim-lit from within. She saw a streak of dark movement outside—opaque liquid swirling around them. It was followed by another and more violent rocking of the *Spindrift*. The vessel tilted far to one side, until Nell was thrown across to collide with Jon Perry.

"Pressure wave." He finally spoke. "A big one. We have to get away from here. The *Spindrift* was designed for uniform external pressure. It can't take much of this." His voice was calm, but his hands were skipping across the controls at unbelievable speed.

Nell gasped. Something had reached out in the darkness, grabbing and holding her at her waist, chest, and shoulders in soft, cool tentacles.

"It's all right." Perry had heard her indrawn breath. "That's only the restraining harness. It operates automatically if we exceed a ten-degree tilt."

Which we should never do, except when we're bobbing around on the surface. Nell remembered at least that much of her briefing. *What's wrong with the attitude stabilizers? They're supposed to keep us level.*

"I saw the temperature rising," Perry went on calmly, "faster than it ought to, but I didn't know how to interpret it. We arrived here at just the wrong time."

"But what's *happening*?" Nell could feel all of her weight transfer to the harness on her right side. The *Spindrift* had rolled through ninety degrees.

"Undersea eruption. Seafloor quake. The area around the smokers is seismically active, and it chose now to release built-up compressions."

Nell heard a low, pained moaning. *The seabed, crying out in agony? No. It's the* Spindrift, *groaning because the hull is overstressed. Can't take much of this, Perry says. So when the ship's had all that it can take—*

The submersible shuddered and spun. Nell no longer had any sense of direction. The seafloor could be right beneath her feet—or directly over her head. Jon Perry was still busy at the controls. And, incredibly, he was talking in the same lecturer's voice as before. *Narrating* his comments, as though they were still making a video documentary.

"It is necessary that we leave the eruption zone at once, but it's no use to head straight up toward the surface. The pressure waves fan up and out from the seabed fracture zone to fill a wedge-shaped volume, broadest at the top. We must travel *laterally* and *down* to take us out of the active zone. That's what I'm doing now. It's going to be touch and go, because we've already had two pressure pulses that exceed the hull's nominal maximum tolerance. Hold tight. Here comes another one."

The *Spindrift* groaned again, a sound like creaking timbers. Nell glanced around. Outside there was nothing but turbid black water at killing pressure. How could Perry have any idea of where he was going? She could see no instruments that told direction or attitude. Yet his dim-lit fingers were never still. He was making continuous adjustments to *something*. Nell could hear another noise behind her: the whirring of electric motors, driving the *Spindrift*'s propulsion system at maximum thrust.

Does he know what he's doing? Or is he trying anything, just at random?

The submersible shuddered and changed direction again, so violently that Nell was convinced that it must be the end. The hull moaned, surely ready to collapse. But in that same moment, Jon Perry was lifting his hands clear of the controls.

"Are we—" Nell didn't know how to finish the question. *Are we doomed*? didn't seem likely to receive a useful answer.

"Almost. Almost clear. Another few seconds."

The front of the submersible was admitting a faint, faded glow. The water ahead was clearer, no longer filled with dense, suspended solids ejected by the seafloor eruption. Nell could see one of the free-swimmer light sources, leading the way to safety like a pilot fish. The *Spindrift* rolled slightly, responding to a faint, final tremor from behind. And then Nell could feel no evidence of movement, although the sound of the motors continued from behind. Her restraining harness released and slipped away, retracting into the seat.

"We're right out of it. All clear." Perry slapped his hand on the panel in front of them. Able to see his profile for the first time in what seemed like hours, Nell found that he was grinning like a madman.

Nell wasn't. *Look at that! The crazy bastard, he acts like he loved it.*

"Are you all right, Miss Cotter?"

Nell gulped, trying to clear her throat for anything more than subvocal rage. Before she could say a word, he was turning to face her, his expression changing from excitement to concern.

"I'm afraid I'll have to take us back to the surface. I'm really sorry about your show. I realize that we didn't get the materials I promised you, but there's no way we could examine Hotpot today. It's too dangerous. Anyway, there'll be so much *ejecta* from the vent that we wouldn't be able to see a thing for hours. We can come back another day."

Nell looked at the cameras. Still in position. Still working. They would have recorded everything: the eruption, the abyssal darkness, the *Spindrift* tossed and stressed by forces that had come close to shattering the little vessel.

Relief and excitement washed away tension. Nell wanted to laugh hysterically. *He's apologizing! He brings us back from the brink of death, then he worries because he didn't get me camera shots of his godawful slime-worms. And he must get his kicks from danger, because he was grinning like a loony a second ago, and not a sign of perspiration. And here I am, sweating like a pig in a sauna.*

"Dr. Perry." A maniacal laugh came gurgling up from her throat. *Edit that out.* "You don't need to say you're sorry. We didn't get the show we expected—we got something a whole lot better. You promised chemosynthesis and photosynthesis and sulfur-chewing clams. You delivered a *seaquake*, an eruption with us in the middle of it. And a recording of everything. The viewers will love it."

He's surprised—at the idea that someone might prefer high drama to tube worms? But now Nell could not control her own grin. To be sure that you were dead, and then to know you had survived . . . there was no feeling like it. In that moment of greatest satisfaction, she saw a red alarm winking on the control panel. She pointed to it without speaking.

"Oh, that's all right. Nothing to do with our onboard status. The ship is fine." He leaned over to activate a small display screen, angled so that Nell could not read it. "That signal shows that the *Spindrift* has received a message from the surface."

"I thought that was hard to do."

"It's damned hard. It takes a tight-focused sonic beam to find us, and an even tighter one to send a signal. Lots of energy waste. That's why it's done so seldom." He was frowning. "It must be for you."

"I'm sure it's not."

"Well, I can't believe it's for me. There's nothing in my projects so urgent it can't wait until we return to the surface. But here it comes."

Nell watched as he read the contents of the screen. She saw his expression change again.

Bye-bye, Ice Man. I don't know what this is, but it's something that sure frightens or upsets Jon Perry. He's excited by physical danger, and it doesn't worry him—but he's sure worried now.

"What is it? Is the message for me?"

Jon Perry was shaking his head. "It's for me. I'm sorry, Miss Cotter, but we have to head for the surface at top speed. The undersecretary's office called, and they say there's a major problem."

"With our descent? I hope it hasn't caused trouble."

"It has nothing to do with today's descent. There's a problem with my project to explore the life forms around the hydrothermal vents—the thing I've spent the past six years working on."

"What sort of problem?"

"That's what has me worried. They say to return *at once*, it's most urgent. But they don't say *why*."

2

The Fight at the Edge of the Universe

All it took was one touch of the finger.

Camille Hamilton depressed the right-hand key. A prerecorded instruction sequence was initiated. The main computer at DOS Center set up individual commands, and sixty thousand lasers rifled them out across the solar system.

Now there was nothing to do but wait. It would require almost an hour for the light-speed commands to reach the most distant of the individual waiting telescopes, and another hour before confirming data could be received at DOS Center that those instruments were swinging into precise alignment with the target. Three more hours before the whole network of telescopes, cross-talking continuously to each other about attitudes and orbits, would settle into a final and stable configuration.

Camille reflected, for the thousandth time, that "observing" with the Distributed Observation System didn't offer the real-time pleasures of olden-day astronomy. Galileo and Herschel and Lord Rosse had enjoyed the results of their efforts at once—assuming you agreed that "enjoyment" could include perching on an exposed platform twenty feet or more above the ground in subfreezing temperatures, peering through soupy skies at an object that might become obscured by cloud at the crucial moment.

The first confirming message was arriving, showing that the closest telescope of the DOS had already received and was obeying its target command. Camille hardly glanced at it. All of the finicky components of the system were orbiting on the other side of the sun, more than a billion kilometers away. She would not learn their status for another hour and a half. Meanwhile, she pulled the previous display onto the main screen for another look.

"Playing God, I see. As usual." The voice from behind came at the same moment as the physical contact. David Lammerman had drifted silently into the room and was right behind Camille. He was hovering over her, massaging her shoulders and the trapezius muscles running in toward her neck.

Or *pretending* to.

Camille was sure that what he was really doing was testing—and disapproving of—the thinness of the fat layer between bone and skin. If she ever followed his diet advice, she'd be as *zaftig* as a Rubens' model.

David sniffed disapproval, stopped his prodding and leaned to peer over her shoulder at the full-screen image of the Andromeda galaxy. "Hey, that's not a simulation. It's a real shot. Pretty damned good."

"Good? Bit picky, aren't we? I'd say it's more like *perfect*." Camille had been waiting for that important second opinion before she allowed herself to feel the full glow of satisfaction. "Every test shows that we're spot-on in focus, and we're close to diffraction-limited resolution. The last group of telescopes came on-line about five hours ago. It turns out that the mirrors weren't damaged at all—it was just the predictive algorithms in the local computers that needed a wash and brush-up. Watch now. I'm going to do a high-res zoom."

David dutifully watched, dazzled as usual by the speed and precision of her system control. The field shifted, closing in on one of Andromeda's spiral arms. A cloud of stars rapidly resolved to points, then went spilling off the edge of the field of view until only one yellow dwarf 'burned at the center. The zoom continued, homing in on a bright fleck of light snuggled close to its parent star. That grew in turn, finally to display a visible disk on which continents formed dark, clotted smudges on a grey-blue background.

"I picked a close target—M31, two million light-years— for media impact. Then I set up a computer scan for a Sol type. That planet is about the same distance from its primary as Earth is from the sun. Spectroscopic analysis says we're looking at a high-oxygen atmosphere. That's water, too, in the blue areas. Think there's anybody up there, staring back this way?"

"If there is, I hope he gets better observing time than we will as soon as people see that picture. Here. Put yourself around the outside of this." David Lammerman was carrying two containers of soup in his left hand. He held one out to Camille.

She took it reluctantly. He was *always* trying to feed her. He had the best of intentions, but when she was working she could never develop any interest in food. Everyone told her that she was over-thin, that she needed to build herself up. It was futile to explain to all of them that her skinny blond fragility was as illusive as her childlike appearance, that she had never been sick in her life, that her body was as tough and durable as steel wire—though David, surely, had other evidence of that.

"Once they see this image, the honeymoon's over," he went on. He squeezed into the chair at Camille's side. Two meters tall and powerfully built, he outmassed her by a factor of three. He emptied his pint of soup in three quick gulps, while she hid hers from him behind a monitor. He at once retrieved it, opened the top, and handed it back.

"Too good?" she took a dutiful sip. "The images, I mean . . . not the soup."

"Far too good. As soon as they realize that everything's up and running, we'll be squeezed out of the schedule. All of our time will go to some grey eminence who hasn't had an idea in her head for fifty years."

He didn't want or need a reply. He and Camille had grumbled through it all before. It was the age-old complaint of aspiring young astronomers. You did the dog work, the years of repairing, cleaning, and calibrating the instruments, while planning observational programs to tackle the most fundamental problems of astronomy; and as soon as everything was perfect, your elders and supposed betters came in, commandeered the prime observing time, and dribbled it away on out-of-date and discredited theories.

At twenty-four, David Lammerman was good, and he knew it. He was impatient. He was not consoled by the thought that his turn would come someday. And at twenty-seven, Camille Hamilton was beginning to wonder if hers ever would. She had already been at DOS Center two years longer than David, and he knew her powers even if no one else seemed to.

"Quit, then." She could read his mind, peering at him over the top of the soup carton. "I'll take your observing time."

"I'll bet you would. You try to do that already." He smiled at her and rubbed his hand through his bushy mop of tight-curled blond hair. Camille noticed how handsome and healthy he looked. Healthy in mind *and* body. She knew both, better than she was ready to admit to anyone.

There was irony in that thought. During three years of working together, often around the clock and always sharing the same cramped living quarters—and after the first three months, the same bed—she and David had never once had a real argument. They told each other everything. She would have trusted him with anything that she owned, including her life. But she was not ready to make a commitment.

David couldn't understand that. She didn't understand it herself. Was it because of Tim Kaiser, David Lammerman's predecessor at DOS Center? She and Tim had been lovers, too, for a little while. But the tensions between them had grown high. When Tim finally announced that he knew she was having affairs with half a dozen others at the center, that he could stand her rejection no longer, and that he was taking an assignment back on Earth, Camille had felt true sorrow . . . and vast relief.

Don't let that happen again.

"We won't have more than a day or two." David's voice intruded on her thoughts. "Then they'll realize that the whole of DOS is performing to spec. So we'd better make the most of it. Andromeda's all right for the media, but let's get on with some real targets. Something a decent distance away."

And here it comes, thought Camille. She would have preferred to avoid David's look, but she forced herself to swivel her chair and face him.

"I already did that. DOS is set for a target eleven billion light-years out." She hurried on, knowing that her next words would halt his nod of approval. "It's going to observe the proto-stellar cloud that I found on last year's test run."

"Star formation! That's low energy, and it's useless science. We shouldn't waste a millisecond on crap like that."

"Just because your own interests happen to be quasars—

"*Intense energy sources*—that's where you learn something *new*. Not in proto-stellar clouds. It's a crime to take the whole capability of DOS and piss it away for twenty-four hours on something you could see just as well close-up using a different instrument—"

"Bullshit! You know that's not true as well as I do. If we're ever going to understand the anomalous fusion cross sections we measure right here in our own solar system, we need DOS. We have to look at stellar fusion and star formation way back in time, before supernovas did element seeding and changed the rules of the game. We have to look ten and eleven and twelve billion light-years out."

Even while Camille argued as hotly as David—and *enjoyed* it, that was the amazing thing—she suspected that it was a waste of time. They had recognized for years that this day was coming. While the Distributed Observation System was performing sporadically or not at all, creeping back into operation after its partial destruction during the war, she and David had sneaked in ample observing time in pursuit of their own separate interests. But with the return of DOS to full service—and they could not hide that fact—guest observers would swarm in from all over the system. They would demand access. Their programs would have priority over the needs of a couple of recent graduates. She and David, both cocky and opinionated, would be forced to fight over scraps and slivers of observing time.

And they would fight. They agreed on the *distance* of good targets, but on nothing else. He was interested in observations of a certain class of quasars as a tool to answer cosmological questions. She found cosmology too speculative, too akin to theology. The questions she wanted to answer on fusion processes would lead to new experiments in the Vesta labs, and they in turn would suggest new observations. In her view, physics experiments and DOS observations should feed on each other through the intermediary of computer models and drive each other along.

But the information flow from David's work, in her opinion, was all one-way.

"You don't have any method of finding out when you're *wrong*," she had said to him often enough. "It's the curse of astronomy. You have no way to perform an *experiment*, here or in the Belt, and then say, 'Well, this result shows that my theory is nothing but piffle, but it also suggests this different theory that I can test.'"

Camille stood up. It was the old argument. She did not want to sit and repeat it when there were more productive things to do.

"Where are you going?" He stood up too.

"It will be at least five hours before observations begin to come in. I'm going to take another look at the Super-DOS configurations."

It was not wholly a lie. Only a week ago she and David had finished their design for a coordinated space-borne array of five hundred thousand orbiting telescopes, ranging in distance all the way from Jupiter to Mercury. They had agreed that it was the next logical step in exploring the edge of the universe. And they had further agreed that although the orbit computation and the dynamic control of the array presented formidable problems, the main hurdle was not technical. It would be—and wasn't that the story of every major observing instrument ever built?—*financial*.

Until today, SuperDOS had been a paper dream. And maybe it still was. What Camille really wanted to do was to read the incoming-message files to DOS Center. The super-sharp images of M31 and the Earth-type planet within its spiral arm had already been sent, beamed out to the Jovian system and in to Mars and Earth. It was the response to those images, to the proof that DOS's first integrated test had been a whopping success, that would tell if SuperDOS, ten times as big, could become more than a dream in Camille and David's lifetime. And those responses should be coming in right now.

David trailed behind her as she left the DOS observation chamber and headed for Communications. She could tell from the look on his face that he hadn't got everything off his chest.

"So you jumped in and grabbed your turn without telling me," he said. "You took advantage of the fact that I was off duty. You *deliberately* didn't tell me. Pretty shitty thing to do."

"Don't give me that." Camille glanced back at him over her shoulder, but she floated right on across the zero-gee hub of DOS Center. She was not going to pretend a guilt she didn't feel. "Suppose DOS had come into full operation on *your* shift and I hadn't happened to be around. What would you have done?"

She could hear his breathing and feel his presence, drifting along a few feet behind her. He did not answer at once, but silence was all the reply she needed.

"I'll tell you. You would have trained DOS on one of your stupid, bloody, high-red-shift quasars," she went on. "And when I came on duty, you'd have told me what you'd done, and then *I'd* have had to lump it—and for a lot longer than a day, too. Your low light levels need longer exposure times."

"You seem to think everybody's like you." But David's tone lacked conviction. When it came to his sacred experiments, he was no different from Camille. Absolution, not permission. You grabbed observing time now, took the flak later.

"*You* certainly are like me," said Camille mildly. "That's why I'm so fond of you."

She was declaring a truce. They had reached the entrance of Communications. The chamber was empty, but that was normal. DOS Center still ran on a skeleton staff; there were just nine technicians and maintenance personnel, including David and Camille, for a facility that would house over two hundred when the Distributed Observation System was going full bore.

The incoming-message unit was flashing blue to indicate the arrival of an "Urgent" received signal. All of the on-site staff had learned to ignore it, and the blaring station-wide siren had long ago been disconnected. The ideas of urgency on Earth and Ganymede seldom coincided with the priorities of DOS Center.

"Let's see how well they like our pictures." Camille scanned the display of incoming messages. "Wait a minute, though. This first one has nothing to do with DOS. It's personal. For you, and it's from Earth. From Husvik. Do you have high-up friends at the capital that you've never told me about?"

She was making conversation, not expecting an answer. Personal messages were just that. You didn't ask about them. And anyway, David had no secrets from her. But his reaction was shocking. He froze and stood motionless, biting his lower lip.

"Sorry." She stepped away from the console. "Read it here if you want to, or take a private screen. I'll wait outside until you're finished."

And that was the next surprise. The offer to leave was made as a formality, but almost always it was waived. Even private messages to DOS Center were never *that* private, because when you lived in each other's pockets for a few years, the number of secrets dwindled away to nothing. And David's messages in particular were never shielded from Camille.

But now he was nodding.

"If you would. Leave, I mean. For a few minutes. I'd like to read it here."

That left her with no choice. Camille was desperate to learn how the images from the full DOS—the result of five years of effort out here in the middle of nowhere—were being received around the system. But she would have to wait. Personal messages always took priority.

She went outside the chamber and hovered at the door. All of her plans for observations, not to mention the future of SuperDOS, depended on the reactions she received in the next day or two. And David was just as involved, just as dependent. How could his personal message be more important than the future of their work? Hell, he didn't even know what the message was *about* when he said he wanted to take it; all he knew was its point of origin. That information meant something to him, but it told Camille nothing. The last time she had seen a census, over two million people were living in Husvik, and the population of South Georgia Island was still growing as Earth's climate warmed.

She itched to sneak back in and take a look, but she couldn't quite bring herself to do it. David had been too upset, too obviously worried. Instead, she waited impatiently at the door.

He was occupied for maybe ten minutes, which felt like hours to Camille. When he emerged, any annoyance with him evaporated. All of his cheerful assertiveness was gone, replaced by a painful hesitancy. He stared at Camille as though he had never seen her before.

"Er . . . mmm. You said you'd like to have my observing time. Didn't you? Well, I guess—now I suppose—" Even his speech was affected. The know-it-all, super-confident David had been transformed to a tongue-tied, awkward klutz. "I guess that it's all yours then. For now."

"David, what's wrong? Can I help?"

"Uh-uh." He shook his blond mop and did not look at her. "I have to . . . to go to Earth. Soon as possible. Got to get on the first ship. Soon as I can."

"But *why*? You shouldn't leave. The next few days here at DOS are going to be critical."

She didn't want to say that. She wanted to say, "David, sweetheart, tell me. I have a *right* to know, whatever it is." But before she could speak again, he nodded, turned, and headed back for the hub. Camille started to follow, then changed her mind. She went into the communications chamber and across to the outgoing-message screen.

Reading someone else's personal message without permission was even worse than standing around while that person read it. But surely this was a real emergency. David had been asked—ordered—to do something that he certainly didn't want to do. And maybe he had sent a message back that was *not* marked "Personal."

She scanned the outgoing messages. There was nothing from David, personal or otherwise. So he was not even putting up an argument.

And what about the *cost*? A minimum-time trip to Earth was expensive. David had never seemed to have much money. So who would be paying for his transportation?

Yielding to temptation, Camille went across to the incoming screen. It showed the recent arrival of dozens of messages, but no personal ones. She sat down at the console and queried the data bank for information on all personal messages received at DOS Center within the past twelve hours.

There was just one. It had been of the Read-and-Erase type, which scrolled once across the screen and was obliterated from the computer record as soon as the recipient signed off.

Camille gave up. She began to review the incoming, congratulatory messages about the DOS results, and the eager requests for scheduling by guest observers. It took every scrap of concentration for her to register even their general content. At what should have been the most exciting time at DOS Center since the end of the Great War a quarter of a century ago, a far-off hand had been able to reach in and disrupt everything.

Her mind repeated the same thing over and over again. Someone wanted David Lammerman back on Earth; someone was in a position to make it happen, whether David wanted to go or not. And for whatever strange reason, *someone* was no more willing than David to divulge his or her identity.

Twelve hours later, Camille was at the computer again. Part of her mind was locked into detailed fusion calculations. The process felt automatic, a hindbrain function. The rest of her, the deepest inner core, was elsewhere.

David was going to Earth. More than that, he was going for reasons that he had not discussed, would not discuss—*could not discuss?*—with Camille.

What now of her complacent belief that she knew David better than anyone else in the system? She knew his family background, his education, his likes and dislikes, his fantasies and phobias. And she didn't know him at all. Didn't understand why he was upset, why he was going to Earth, why he wouldn't talk about it. Was it—could it be—another woman? Even if it were, what right had she to be jealous, she who had held on so firmly to her own independence?

Amid her emotional turmoil, the calculations went on and on in a complex dance between woman and machine. No one was there to observe the odd partnership and the way that the roles of the two shifted, minute by minute, into an unfathomable kind of oneness.

3

The Sun King

By the time that he was twenty years old, Jon Perry had become convinced of two great truths: Life in the water world of the deep oceans made sense; it was logical and predictable and calm. And life in the world of air, on the surface or above it, was none of those things; it was random, baffling, and bizarre.

Now he had new proofs of that. One of them walked half a dozen paces in front of him. He stared at the back of Nell Cotter's red-dyed head, gleaming in the benign December sun, and puzzled over the mystery of her presence. She had no right to be there. Not after what had happened in the deeps of the Pacific Antarctic Ridge.

As the *Spindrift* had returned to the surface, neither of them had found more than a few words for the other. He was worried and perplexed by the sudden order to return to surface base without explanation, while she had been badly shaken by the shock of the seaquake, two kilometers down. She did not have Jon's confidence in the *Spindrift*, or in his powers as pilot and navigator. To him, the episode of the seafloor eruption was clear in memory but already remote in feeling, an experience seen through a glass that screened emotion. To Nell Cotter, the episode had been direct, new, and terrifying. Her euphoria when she realized that she was not going to die in the depths only emphasized that point.

At the surface she had insisted that she had recorded everything that she needed. The taping of the video show was complete. When they parted at the jetty of the floating base, there had been no expectation on Jon's part that he would see her again. He had gone forward to make his report. And there he had encountered a typical piece of Admin irrationality. He was told that he was to head at once for Arenas, and the office of the undersecretary.

Why? No one in the administrative offices of the base would or could say. That was baffling and disturbing enough.

And the *undersecretary*? What did a high-level politician have to do with Jon Perry, with hydrothermal vents and the study of benthic life forms? Absolutely nothing, according to the pinhead lieutenant who had given him his flight papers. But the man could provide no more information.

Jon had slowly walked the length of the thousand-meter floating deck to the short, sloping runway and the waiting aircraft. And there, mystifyingly, Nell Cotter had appeared ten yards ahead of him. She was strolling along in the middle of a group of four mid-level staff members, laughing an easy, swinging laugh as relaxed as her walk. There was no sign that she had been through anything traumatic. Her ability to bounce back—or to fake it—was amazing. But she certainly had no right to be heading for the aircraft. It belonged to the Global Ocean Monitor System, and only GOMS staff members were permitted aboard. He knew for certain that she had no connection with the group.

But five minutes later they were flying east at Mach six,

and Nell Cotter was walking along the aisle to sit next to him.

She laughed at his question. "I didn't exactly *invite* myself. I just talked a little about the show. Then I showed them this"—she tapped the midget videocamera—"and explained that the work's not finished while the cameras are still rolling."

"You told people you had to travel to Arenas *with me* to do your show? But that's a lie. The taping is over. You can't use *me* as an excuse to board."

She reached across and placed a hand on his arm. "Hey, don't get excited." *Whatever happened to the Ice Man?* "I'm due in Stanley tomorrow to meet the show's producer. If I'd gone commercial, it would have taken eighteen hours by surface skimmer and I'd have been a wreck when I got there. Who needs that? And it's not as though I'm squeezing somebody out of a place." She waved at the aircraft's interior, where half of the forty seats were unoccupied, then leaned forward so she could turn and look into his eyes. "Come on, Dr. Perry—or may I call you Jon? All I've done is hitch a ride. Lighten up and let me buy you a drink."

"Alcohol is forbidden on GOMS installations. As are all other drugs."

"Then I'll buy you one in Arenas."

"I'm sorry." Jon turned his head from her direct gaze and stared out of the window, to where the afternoon sun was transforming the krill farms to a golden lacework on the southern horizon. "I won't have time for anything like that. Upon arrival I have an immediate appointment with Undersecretary Posada." He felt ashamed the moment he said it. It was true enough, but he was hiding from her behind a meeting that he had not expected, did not understand, and did not want to attend.

If he had hoped to rebuff her, the effort was a failure.

She was leaning closer and he could smell a faint, flowery perfume.

"*After* you've seen him, then, I'll buy you a drink. From what I've heard of Manuel Posada, you'll need one if you spend more than two minutes with him." Her face was inches from his, her right hand still resting on his forearm. "Actually, I've got a much better idea. Before I was given this assignment, I had expected to cover another event today—in Arenas. We're going to be there in time, so we could go to it together. It's a posh Inner Circle dinner to honor Cyrus Mobarak, ten thousand pesos a head."

"I don't have ten thousand pesos . . . I don't have one thousand. And I'm to report at once to the undersecretary as soon as we land."

"He'll never know the difference if you show up tomorrow instead of today. And don't worry about paying. I'll get press tickets. Two of them."

"They wouldn't let me in. I'm not the press."

Sweetheart, where have you been all your life? Two kilometers down? (And that's probably not far from the truth.) "Jon, they'll never know *who* you are unless you tell 'em. You'll be with me, I'll do the talking. And I owe you an evening out, don't I, for your putting up with me all day, and saving my life like that?"

Jon stared into her innocent brown eyes and wondered how she did it. She proposed implausible sequences of events but made them seem perfectly natural. He was summoned to the capital for a meeting, one that sounded ominous at best. So Nell Cotter blithely suggested that he ignore an order from his boss's boss's boss and trot off for a fun evening on the town. He shuddered, and at the same time, he was fascinated. He had never in his life encountered anyone remotely like Nell. He wanted to go to dinner with her, desperately, and for reasons that went far beyond the idea of hearing Cyrus Mobarak: the Sun King, the legend. Jon took a deep breath.

"I can't do that, Miss Cotter." *I'm crazy. I'm throwing away the chance of a lifetime.*

"Nell. People who've sweated and shivered together can't be formal." *Except that you didn't sweat or shiver, when I was ready to scream. Don't say no to me, Jon Perry. I won't take that for an answer.* "You have to call me Nell. And you have to come."

"I can't do it. Nell. The dinner, I mean. Word will have been sent to the undersecretary's office that I'm on the way. They'll be expecting me. Otherwise . . . well, otherwise I'd like to go with you. *Love* to go. And I'd like to hear Cyrus Mobarak. Do you believe the stories about them?—the Inner Circle, I mean."

"Not all. But what I do believe are quite sufficient. There'll still be time, you know, after you see Posada. The dinner isn't until eight. We'll be landing at four."

"You're assuming that he'll see me as soon as I call. But it doesn't work that way. *I* have to be fitted into *his* schedule, not the other way around."

"So I'll cross my fingers for you." She leaned contentedly back in the seat, crossing not her fingers, but her legs. "It always works. You'll see. You'll have your meeting with him and be a free man again before eight. And then we'll go to the Inner Circle dinner and have some fun."

Nell Cotter was wrong. But so was Jon Perry.

Even before the war, GOMS had been run on quasi-military lines. That had never changed. The floating bases, scattered across the oceans of the world, still had the attitude and ambience of military field operations. There might be rigid lines of command, some inefficiency, and a good deal of unnecessary or wasted effort, but things got done. Equipment was serviced. Machinery worked. Schedules were met.

- By contrast, the Administrative Center of the Global

Ocean Monitor System ran like the headquarters of a peacetime army. With no end product, bureaucracy was more important than results. Delay was irrelevant, efficiency had no meaning.

Jon had spent his working life in the world of the floating bases. It was a shock to report to Admin Center by five o'clock and learn that no one knew who he was or had any information about his arrival. Undersecretary Posada was busy and could not be disturbed. There was no Jon Perry on the appointments calendar, today or in the future. Posada's assistants had already left and would not return until nine the next morning. No one was available to authorize a call back to the floating base.

Jon was given—reluctantly—a chit that would allow him to stay overnight at an Admin Center facility. He was warned that any service other than dinner and breakfast would have to be paid for personally. By six-thirty he had arrived at the spartan GOMS dormitory, to find the building packed with people. The manager informed him that with the climate change, Arenas was booming as never before, that every building was full to overflowing for the Midsummer Festival, and that Jon's chit meant nothing. If he could find nowhere else, he might be given a bedroll and a place on the dining-room floor—after all the meals were served, of course, and after the clean-up staff had done its work. Say, about one A.M.

Jon called Nell Cotter, who was staying down by the strait. Her number did not answer. He left a message that he was on the way over, went outside onto the hilly streets, and walked south toward the water.

Some elements of Arenas had not changed with the new prosperity. Every square meter of soil was riotous with summer flowers, and the air was balmy with their evening perfume. At latitude fifty-three south, the December sky would cloud over but not darken for another three or four hours.

After six years of solitude and open ocean, Jon found the flowers and crowded streets as alien as another planet. Even the skuas, petrels, and terns were gone. He searched the sky for them, but they had flown far south for the summer, to reap a rich harvest around the diminishing icecap.

Strangest of all were the children. There were no children on the floating bases, but here they were everywhere, playing games on each street corner, scuttling across sidewalks under his feet, or rolling uncontrolled down the hill on homemade carts and scooters. He avoided them unconsciously, his thoughts far away. It was one thing to be ignored at your home base, where you were free to set your own schedule and work on your own scientific projects. It was another to be dragged fifteen hundred kilometers without explanation and then be treated in a way that made it clear that you were a total nonentity. He became gloomier and more irritated with every step. Something bad was going to happen to him. He knew it. But he could not guess what it might be.

By the time he reached the address that Nell had given him, he was in no mood for dinners of the rich and famous. Not at ten thousand pesos per head, not at any number of pesos.

When he called from the lobby, he was ready to tell her that he had changed his mind, he was not going out for dinner. She offered him no opportunity.

"Great. Sixth floor. Come on up." And she was gone.

She had told him where she was staying, but it was like no hotel he had ever seen. The building was a graceful high-rise structure, far more inviting than the Admin dormitory. There was no guest registration, no sign of porters or staff. The elevators seemed designed only for freight. When he emerged onto the sixth floor, he found himself in a great windowless room divided into square cubicles by waist-high partitions. Some of the cubicles were bright-lit and glassed in from floor to ceiling. Others were dark and held nothing but rows of grey-painted cabinets. People seemed to be hurrying everywhere at random. He stared around in confusion until he caught sight of Nell four partitions away, leaning over a bank of television sets.

She had already changed from the green jump suit she had worn in the *Spindrift* to an off-the-shoulder gown of the same color. She had also done something mysterious to her hair, sweeping it up to reveal the graceful curve of her neck. When he reached her side, she straightened and gave him a head-to-toe instant scrutiny.

"Standard size should do it. Come on."

She took his hand. He allowed himself to be towed along through a chessboard of partitions and on through a pair of double doors.

"There you are." She waved an arm at a score of tall cupboards along one wall. "Just help yourself."

She saw his puzzled expression. "Look, I'm not picky, and what you're wearing right now is fine with me—personally. But we're going to a *formal dinner*, for God's sake. If you don't want to be stopped at the door and asked questions, you have to change. It's dinner jackets and gowns tonight."

"I don't have a dinner jacket, not here or on the base."

"I thought you might not. Why do you think I told you to come over?" She flung open the door of one of the cupboards. "Take your pick. All sizes, colors, and styles. All centuries, too."

It was dawning on Jon. "This is a *studio*."

"Of course it is. My job. Remember, I have a job? They do plays and period pieces here, too. You could go dressed as anything from a twelfth-century Franciscan friar to Peter Pan, but we want you to fade into the background, so we'll match your plumage to the typical ten-thousand-peso-a-dinner millionaire." She reached in and pulled out a hanger. "Better let me help, I think. Why don't you try this for a start?"

It took a long time. Jon would have settled for the first suit picked out, but she insisted that the drape across the shoulders was not quite right. "Rich people *do* wear clothes that don't fit, I know. But hydrothermal-vent specialists *posing* as rich people don't." She adjusted the bow tie and installed a tiny videorecorder in his buttonhole. "The final touch. Camera instead of camellia, so there'll be no doubt as to what you do. Who knows? Maybe you'll get some priceless footage." Nell stepped back and surveyed the result. "How do you feel?"

"Strange." Jon hardly recognized himself in the all-around mirrors. She had done something peculiar to his hair, greying and thickening it around his temples and ears and trimming it at the front.

"You look great. We'll walk over. By the time we get there, you'll be adjusted to your fine feathers. Let's go."

The trek back up the hill in the deepening twilight was a revelation. Other pedestrians gave them one look and moved out of the way. Even the children on the little carts veered aside.

"The protective aura of wealth." Nell had taken his arm and was looking straight ahead, ignoring the people around them. "Even fake wealth."

"I thought this sort of thing was supposed to have ended with the war."

"Spoken like a true scientist. That's one of the lessons of history. It *never* ends, and it never will. Not as long as people are people." She squeezed his arm and stared haughtily down her nose at a man who was slow in getting out of their way.

The meeting hall itself stood on a western slope, facing over the strait and toward the distant ocean. A dozen men in uniform hovered around the entrance. They watched closely until the tickets that Nell produced were verified. Jon stood by, nervously fingering his slick lapels.

"I thought we were in real trouble," he said softly when they were finally admitted. "All those guards."

"Not for us." She squeezed his arm again. "Lighten up, dear."

"For who, then?"

"There's been talk around the studios that Bounders might be coming here in force to cause trouble. An Inner Circle dinner would be one of their natural targets."

"But that's ridiculous. Outward Bound needs the Mobies. Cyrus Mobarak ought to be a Bounder hero."

"He ought to be, and for all I know, he is. But Security doesn't have the sense to understand that, so they're hunting for Bounders behind every garbage can." She tugged at his arm. "Don't go that way, dearie. We're tolerated because they want publicity, and we'll even be fed. But you don't get to sit with the *real* Inner Circle."

The dining room contained ten round tables, each one holding place settings for eight. Nell led the way to a small, bare bench, half-hidden from the main floor and offering a good camera view of the head table on its dais. A man and two women were setting up cameras on the bench. Nell nodded to them, and they gave Jon an incurious glance before they went back to work.

Cyrus Mobarak was already at the head table, chatting with a woman in uniform on his immediate left. Jon Perry studied him as the service of the meal began. He found the examination oddly unsatisfying. Mobarak was in his middle-to-late forties. Seated, he appeared to be short and strongly built, with a thick neck that bulged against the blue-and-white wing collar. His suit was plain grey, lacking medals, decorations, or jewelry. His nose was prominent. He bore a thick shock of greying hair, and his brow ridges overhung pale, vacant-seeming eyes. He ate lightly, pecking at most of the dishes that were served, and he seemed to listen and nod a lot more than he spoke. By contrast with the glittering, bejeweled, and medal-laden audience of Inner Circle members, he was unimpressive.

"Well, what did you expect?" asked Nell when Perry commented on how *normal* Mobarak looked. "A ten-foot giant covered with red hair? It was one of the early discoveries and big disappointments of my career. Great men—and great women—mostly don't look different from anyone else. My job would be a lot easier if they did."

"But *they*—" Jon jerked his head toward the audience.

"—are not great people." Nell was leaning close. "It's heresy to suggest it, especially in this room, but the Inner Circle are only *wealth*, just old wealth and nothing more. The woman next to Cyrus Mobarak has the brain of a clam, and she got her high-level job through family influence. I've never spoken to Mobarak, but I'll bet he isn't here because it's where he'd most like to be. He's here because he needs their *money* for his projects. You'll see Mr. Wizard at work in a few minutes."

The meal was ending. The uniformed woman to Mobarak's left had risen, and the hall fell silent.

"Good evening." She smiled around the room, careful to include the press table for a long moment. "My name is Dolores Gelbman, and I am energy coordinator for the Pacific Rim. My friends, ladies and gentlemen of the Inner Circle, tonight I have been granted an unusual privilege. It will be my pleasure to introduce to you our honored guest, Cyrus Mobarak. But before I ask him to address you, I would first like to say a few words about his work and what it means to all of us." She lifted a couple of sheets of paper and took a glance at them. "Humans were relying on fusion energy long before they knew it. Our sun, that mighty solar furnace, is itself nothing more than a giant fusion reactor, changing hydrogen and deuter-rerum"— she stumbled over the word and dipped her head briefly to consult her hand-held notes—"*deuterium* to helium and oxygen and . . . other things. But it was not until a hundred and fifty years ago that we achieved the first controlled fusion. And it was not until the nineteen fifties that fusion with net energy production became possible."

Jon Perry started and turned to Nell. "That's all wrong!"

"I know." She was smiling. "Somebody as dumb as her wrote it, and she can't even read it properly. She has no idea that it's rubbish. But sssh! Enjoy. If *you* don't like what she's saying, think how Mobarak must feel. Look at him."

Cyrus Mobarak was leaning back in his seat, elbows on the table and hands set fingertip to fingertip as Dolores Gelbman went on with her speech. He seemed perfectly calm, perfectly relaxed, enjoying the occasion. It took a few more minutes before Perry realized what he was doing.

He leaned across to Nell. "He's *counting*. Counting her factual errors, ticking them off on his fingers. See, there's another one, she said *neutrons* and she meant *neutrinos*. That's half a dozen so far. He's going to tear her to pieces when she gets done."

"Like to make a bet? He'd probably love to, but he's far too smart for that. He knows who he has to manipulate, and how to do it. Wait and see."

"—until the end of the war," Dolores Gelbman was saying, "when our industry was destroyed, much of our land rendered uninhabitable, and our energy production devastated. And at that moment of greatest need, riding in to Earth from the Belt like a savior knight in shining armor, came Cyrus Mobarak. Ready to make the secrets of the compact, ultra-efficient fusion devices that he had invented freely available to all who needed them, here or in the Outer System. During the past quarter of a century, the name of Cyrus Mobarak has become *synonymous* with fusion energy. By his efforts, it has been developed to the point where no other power source can compete with it for efficiency, cost, or safety. And so it is my privilege tonight, on behalf of the Inner Circle, to present Earth's highest technology award, for pioneer work in the systematic development of safe fusion power, to Cyrus Mobarak. The man whom I am pleased to dub . . . the *Sun King*."

"Listen to her," hissed Jon. "She says 'Sun King' as though she just made it up. It's been used throughout the solar system for fifteen years!"

But Cyrus Mobarak was rising to shake Gelbman's hand, smiling as though the name she had given him was totally new and surprising.

"Thank you, Coordinator Gelbman, for your kind words. And thank you everyone, for the honor of this award." He nodded toward the wrapped package, half a meter high, on the table in front of him. "And thank you even more for giving me the honor of addressing you tonight."

"Told you," whispered Nell. "He *is* a great man, but he's a real smoothie, too. Someday I'm going to catch him with his pants down."

"You're going to *what*?"

"Catch him with an expression on his face that he didn't calculate and plan. Not tonight, though. He'll wrap 'em around his little finger. Watch him."

Mobarak was shaking his head ruefully. "To my mind, the many honors lavished upon me are unearned. Plasma theory and detailed fusion computations have always been too difficult for me. I've never been more than a tinkerer, playing around and having fun, and now and then finding something that seems to work. So if a group of *scientists* gives me an award, I feel uncomfortable. I always think of what Charles Babbage said about the British Royal Society: 'An organization that exists to hold elaborate dinners and to give each other gold medals.' But when I am given an award by *real* people such as yourselves, people who work in the real world and understand its needs and priorities, why, then I am overcome by a sense of well-being and a totally unreasonable feeling of pride. Pride which, I must now confess, is all too likely to come before a fall."

There were knowing laughs from some of the audience and a few cries of "Never!" and "You can do it!"

Mobarak paused and stared around the hall. "I gather that despite my best efforts at secrecy, some of you must already have heard of my dream. If that is the case, I hope that some of you may even be interested enough to want to take part in it as direct supporters, when the opportunity presents itself. But I have to warn you, by this time next year there is a good chance that the name of Cyrus Mobarak will be the laughingstock of the whole system. And if that happens, I hope that those of you who have been so nice to me when I have seemed near the top will be just as kind when I am down at the bottom."

There were more audience calls of "Count me in!" and "You never had a failure yet!"

"True enough." Mobarak held up a hand. "But there is a first time for everything, including failure. And we are getting ahead of ourselves. Tonight it was never my plan to hold out the promise of a grand new project"— ("Except that you'll notice he's done just that," whispered Nell. "He could sign them up now if he wanted to.") —"but rather to thank you for, and to accept—with real gratitude—this award."

He pulled the tall package across the table toward him and with the help of Dolores Gelbman removed the wrappings. A glittering set of nested cylinders was revealed, surrounding a central torus and an array of helical pipes.

"Now where have I seen something like this before?" Mobarak was grinning. "For anyone who does not recognize it, here we have a model of the Mobarak AL-3—what most people call the 'Moby Mini.' The smallest, and the most popular, of my fusion plants." He studied it for a moment. "Thirty megawatts of energy, one like this would produce. And this is a beautifully made model. At a reduced scale of—what?—about four to one?"

"Exactly four to one." Dolores Gelbman turned the model around so that the press table could have a good view of both it and herself.

"And with all of its parts in proportion." Mobarak was leaning over, peering at the interior. "It's just perfect." He frowned. "Wait a minute, though. It's *not* perfect. This is a *fake*—it can't produce energy!"

There were a few titters from the audience, the self-conscious sound of people laughing at a joke they do not understand.

"We can't have that, can we? A Moby that doesn't produce energy." Cyrus Mobarak paused, then stooped to reach down under the table. "What we need is something more like *this*."

With the help of two uniformed men who appeared from the side of the room, he lifted a package and placed it on the table. With the wrapping removed, it proved to be an oddly distorted version of the Moby Mini, with an out-of-proportion central torus and a set of double helices beyond it. Everyone watched in silence as Mobarak turned a control on the side of the machine. He nodded to another man over by the far wall. The room lights slowly dimmed. As they did so, a vibrating whistle came from the machine on the table, followed by the sputter of an electrical discharge. The last room light faded. The hall was illuminated by a growing blue within the central torus.

"Ladies and gentlemen." Cyrus Mobarak, dimly visible behind the blue glow, raised his voice. "May I present to you, for the first time to any group, the Moby Midget. The system's first tabletop fusion reactor. Sixty kilos total mass, external dimensions as you see them, energy capacity eight megawatts. And, as you will also see, perfectly safe."

The glow was still brightening. The blue-lit face and hovering hands above it were those of a magician, drawing power from the air by primordial incantation. The audience gasped as Mobarak's hands, one on each side of the torus, suddenly plunged into the flaring plasma at the center. The glow was instantly quenched, and the lights in the hall just as quickly came back on. Cyrus Mobarak stood behind his tabletop fusion reactor, casual and relaxed. As the members of the Inner Circle rose to their feet, he stepped off the dais and moved down among them, shaking hands and slapping backs.

"And that, kiddies," said Nell quietly, "concludes our show for this evening. What did I tell you? He didn't put a foot wrong. Now I know why it was so easy to get press tickets. Mobarak *wanted* this whole thing to receive maximum coverage."

Jon Perry was sitting in a daze. He lacked Nell's exposure and early immunization to wealth and fame, and most of all, to simple charisma. "He's a genius. An absolute genius. What did he mean when he talked about being laughed at a year from now?"

"I don't know." Nell's eyes were on Cyrus Mobarak, who every few seconds glanced across to the press table. "But it has to be a monstrous new project, big enough for even the Sun King to talk about being a laughingstock. Don't worry, we'll find out what he's planning. I'll call Glyn Sefaris, and he'll set our staff onto it over in Husvik. Mobarak's home base is there."

"No one's going to laugh at Mobarak, whatever he does. What makes you so sure that your staff *can* find out?"

"Because the Sun King would never have thrown it at us—the press—if he had any real interest in keeping it secret. You'll notice that none of us caught even a sniff of the tabletop fusion reactor before tonight's unveiling. It surprised me as much as it did anybody."

Nell tucked Jon's arm in hers and began to steer him into the crowd. "Come on, let's see if we can get a word with Mr. Wizard before he's dragged away to better things. I've a feeling that he's very receptive to press attention just now. We're *meant to* explore and learn what his new project is, so who knows? Maybe if we're lucky enough, or clever enough, we'll find out tonight."

4

Starseed

Nell Cotter and Wilsa Sheer came from different backgrounds. They had never met, or even lived on the same planet. They were a billion kilometers apart. And yet, were Nell transported to Wilsa's side, she would have had no difficulty in recognizing the other woman's feelings. She had experienced them herself, just twenty-four hours earlier.

Wilsa, pleasurably nervous, sat alone in a small submersible cruising turbulent ocean depths. No glimmer of light penetrated from distant sunlight. The submersible's eyes were a combination of radar and ultrasonics, providing a flat, low-contrast image that faded away to uniform grey a dozen kilometers from the ship.

The voice of Tristan Morgan was just as grey and flat, sounding far-off and thin, though the words were spoken right into Wilsa's ear. "All right so far, but now you'll have to descend. See that vortex cloud, right ahead? You want to steer clear of it. And you'll have to go *down*. The upper region has convection currents too strong for the *Leda*, and the cloud top will extend upward for thousands of kilometers. Set yourself into a thirty-degree down-glide. Aim to the left side of the cloud and hold your heading for fifteen minutes. You'll be moving in the same sense as cloud rotation. Any circulation will speed you up. When you come around and out, there should be three or four Von Neumanns right in front of you."

"Check." Wilsa's hands felt huge and clumsy, like monstrous gauntlets, as she slowly operated the *Leda*'s control levers. The submersible tilted and began the long slide downward. Another faint voice was chanting numbers, matching a red readout in the upper left corner of the image display. It reported isobaric depth in kilometers: "One-three-one-two. One-three-one-three, One-three-one-four." Thirteen hundred kilometers below the planet's upper cloud layers. The pressure would exceed a hundred standard atmospheres. It was no longer cold. The submersible flew through a helium-hydrogen mixture bubbling at nearly three hundred degrees Celsius. A little deeper and the heat around the ship would melt lead.

The swirling cloud was towering closer on Wilsa's right. She stared hypnotized into its jagged, broadening helix: orange and umber turbulence, transformed by the synesthetic imaging system to a sickly, mottled yellow, rising up forever. The thunderhead was stately, black-centered, and threatening. Flickers of lightning ran around its perimeter and lit the dark interior of the submersible with random pulses of intense green.

Wilsa gazed into its deadly heart. As she did so, another voice spoke unbidden from the secret depths of her mind. Its imperative banished every other thought. The broad, royal theme that it proclaimed rose irresistibly from a low E-flat, arching up to take command of her brain.

The melody of Jupiter itself. Her piloting of the submersible became unconscious as she allowed the theme to grow, shaping and reshaping in long, *cantabile* phrases while the *Leda* slid around and beneath the cloud base. She exulted as the tune soared higher, rising as majestic as the helical cloud in front of her. Like the starting point for all of her compositions, its arrival came as a complete surprise. Two minutes earlier she could have offered no hint of form, tempo, or key—or even predicted that anything creative was on the way. Everything else in a composition could be produced by thought and hard work, but melody remained aloof, beyond conscious control. And this one, she knew already, was a beauty.

"That will do." Tristan Morgan's voice entered from a million miles outside, touching but not breaking the creative spell. "I know you've decided you can fly blind-folded, but bring it out now."

"Okay." The rolling cloud vanished behind as Wilsa changed course; it was replaced by streaks that ran across the whole field of view. *East-west.* She recalled Tristan Morgan's earlier warning: "Don't forget that the small-scale shear is all east-west. And don't forget that any one of those little pencil lines holds enough energy to tear the ship in two."

But the black, broken striations on the horizon carried another message. They initiated a persistent little sawtooth of a tune, running as an *ostinato* counterpoint to the earlier theme. Wilsa wove the two together, feeling out the harmony. Then, as an experiment, she transposed the whole thing to the key of G Major. Not so good. She had been right the first time. E-flat was much better.

"One-three-two-two," said the depth monitor suddenly.

"Wilsa, your brain's on autopilot again." Tristan's voice was sharp. "Stop the turn and look half-left. You'll see three Von Neumanns—no, make that two. The other one's got a full cargo and it's starting to ascend. If you don't hurry, you'll miss it."

"I'm not sleeping. I'm *working*." But as she snapped back her answer and tucked the nascent composition safely away in the back of her mind—there was no danger that she would forget it—Wilsa was scanning the atmosphere ahead for her first sight of a Jovian Von Neumann.

There. And not far from it, a second one. But the third that Tristan had mentioned was already far above, rising through the atmosphere on the smoky column of its Moby drive. In twenty minutes it would pass through the colorless layers of ammonium hydrosulfate to reach the base of blue-white ammonia clouds. Fifteen minutes more and the Von Neumann would be at full thrust, striving upward to break the great planet's gravitational bonds.

The other two were quietly harvesting. Monstrous intake venturis, hundreds of meters across, sucked Jupiter's atmosphere into their broad, beetle-shaped interiors. Hydrogen was vented at the rear, except for the tiny amount needed to supply the Moby fusion drive. Traces of sulfur, nitrogen, phosphorus, and metals were separated and hoarded, awaiting the time when enough of those raw materials had been collected. Then the Von Neumann would create an exact copy of itself, and release it.

Helium, a quarter of the mass of the Jovian atmosphere, remained to be processed. Most of it, like the dross of a mining operation, was of no interest. The precious nugget was the isotope helium-3, ten thousand times as rare as helium-4. The Von Neumanns painstakingly separated the two components, vented the common isotope and stored the lighter molecules in liquid form. When a hundred tons had been collected, the storage tanks would be full and the Von Neumann ready to begin its long ascent to planetary escape.

But that triumphant exit was not the event that Wilsa had come to witness. Anomalous signals had been arriving at Hebe Station, orbiting Jupiter half a million kilometers above the highest cloud layers. Tristan Morgan had pinpointed the signals as deriving from one of the Von Neumanns now ahead of the *Leda*. As the submersible closed on the beetle-backed collection vehicle, Wilsa could see the source of the problem. Intense heat—presumably a lightning bolt—had fused and deformed one set of intake venturis and storage tanks. The Von Neumann rode lopsided, a pale exhaust of escaping hydrogen hissing out of its base.

Wilsa steered the *Leda* to within a hundred meters and matched their paths. The Von Neumann was descending at a rate of about a kilometer a minute. She focused the imaging systems on the crippled side.

"Pretty bad." Tristan Morgan was inspecting the damage. "In fact, worse than I thought. With that loss of hydrogen, we could fly as far as the upper edge of the atmosphere, replacing as we went. But it would never make escape velocity."

"What can we do?"

"Not a thing. Unless it reaches orbit, there's no way to perform repairs. We have to write this one off."

Wilsa stared out at the doomed machine. Suddenly it seemed to be alive and suffering, despite Tristan's assurance that it was of very restricted function and intelligence. "You mean we just leave it here crippled, and it floats around forever?"

"That won't happen. It will keep sinking down to greater pressures and temperatures. Look at the depth gauge. You're at one-three-two-seven now. By the time the Von Neumann reaches six or seven thousand kilometers, the temperature will be up over two thousand Celsius. It will melt and disperse, and its elements will go back into the planetary pool."

His voice was casual, but Wilsa could not help contemplating a more personal vision. How did he *know* that the temperature would keep rising, and know that the Von Neumann had no feelings? Suppose that it was self-aware. And suppose that it was doomed to remain functioning and to drop forever, through increasingly dense layers.

She told herself that it could not be forever. Seventeen

thousand kilometers down, according to Tristan Morgan, Jupiter had pressures of three million Earth atmospheres, and hydrogen changed from a gaseous to a metallic form. No matter what happened at higher altitudes, the Von Neumann could not survive that transition.

Music began again inside Wilsa's head, grave and cadenced. A C-minor dirge. Pavane for a dead Von Neumann. It built for a full ten minutes, until it was interrupted by Tristan Morgan's thin, far-off voice.

"Unless you're proposing to ride all the way down together, I suggest a little action. You're at thirteen-thirty-seven. Want to return to a higher level, and cruise some more? Or do you want to come all the way back? I ought to mention that you've had a call from your agent."

"Magnus? What did he say?"

"No message. He's still on Ganymede, and he wants you to return his call. At once."

"Damn that man. Why does he always think he has to *talk* to me, instead of leaving word telling what he wants?" Wilsa lifted the gauntlets, allowing the automatic control system of the *Leda* to take over and cruise at constant isobaric depth. "All right. Bring me back. And *slowly* this time."

"No can do. Not set up that way. Hold tight."

The transition was painfully abrupt. One moment Wilsa was staring out of the *Leda*'s port at Jupiter's roiling interior. The next moment she was sitting stunned in the control chair on Hebe Station, blinking her eyes at the bright lights. The headset had slipped upward by itself, and the gauntlets had relaxed their hold on her hands and forearms.

"So. Did you get what you hoped you would?"

Tristan Morgan was bending over her. He did not match the cool, distant voice that had reached her over the headset. The man in person was tall, bright-eyed and intense, with bulging chipmunk cheeks and a broad smile.

Like everyone else in the Jovian system, he had ideas of personal space that did not match the preference of an individual raised in the Belt.

Wilsa leaned away from him by habit, although she did not feel at all uncomfortable. "I got more than I hoped for, a lot more."

"I thought you seemed a bit far-gone some of the time down there. New material?"

"New, and first-rate. At least the themes. I still have a lot more working-out to do. Jupiter is a wonderfully stimulating environment. Pity I didn't make a trip before, when I was working on the suite."

"Change it. There's still time."

"Maybe." Wilsa stood up, went across to one of the ports and stared out. The banded orange-and-brown face of Jupiter loomed large, spread across fifteen degrees of the sky of Hebe Station. She gazed upon the monster planet and called into her mind the feeling of the budding new composition.

She shook her head. "Maybe, but no."

"Not as good as you thought at first?"

"Better. That's not the problem. It's a question of *scale*. Being down there makes you think big."

"People always miss the point with Jupiter. They know that it's three hundred and twenty times Earth mass, but that's the wrong number to use. The volume of the Jupiter atmosphere, from the upper clouds down to the metallic hydrogen interface, is *half a million* times as big as Earth's biosphere. *That's* the comparison to make."

"You get it right when you're flying through it. If I tried to incorporate my new themes and ideas into the suite, they would *distort* it, no matter how good they turn out to be. They just don't fit."

"Like Beethoven, wanting to make the *Grosse Fuge* the last movement of the B-flat string quartet? It never works when they play it that way, because it's such a brute. It's out of proportion."

"That's *exactly* what I mean."

In talking with Wilsa, Tristan Morgan had at first insisted that he knew nothing about music and was not interested in it. She had believed him when she arrived on Ganymede and ran into him at a concert reception. But as time went on, he had lost credibility. For one thing, he somehow managed to be at every musical event that she attended. For another, he seemed to be on friendly terms with everyone on Ganymede who played, wrote, or cared about music.

It had taken Magnus Klein, monitoring everything that might affect Wilsa's life and career, to put his finger on the obvious and to disapprove of it. "How old is Morgan?"

"He's thirty-three. What does that have to do with anything?"

"He loves music, and with anyone else he'd admit it. He's chasing after you, you know."

"But *why?*" Wilsa was intrigued by Tristan, more than she was willing to admit.

Magnus raised a bushy eyebrow. "That's a dumb question. Because you fascinate him, that's why. But you have him *intimidated*. He knows that you're seven years younger, and yet no matter what he does, he'll always be your musical inferior. He'll never have your critical ability, or your memory, or a thousandth of your creativity."

"Oh, nonsense. I couldn't intimidate anyone. He's just *shy*."

She didn't understand Magnus's skeptical shrug. Wilsa's talent had been recognized early by the Belt's foundling education system. Before she was three years old, she had been assigned to live in a music crèche, where everyone was a musical prodigy in outsider terms—and the word "prodigy" was never mentioned. Perfect pitch was taken for granted—it was as natural as having two ears—and the teachers *expected* you to read music before you could read words.

Surrounded by her peers, Wilsa thought herself perfectly ordinary. At twelve years old, her unusual talent for composition was discovered and encouraged; but by that time, Bach and Mozart and Beethoven and Stravinsky had become her constant companions. Comparing herself with the immortals, she knew she was nothing.

It had taken another ten years, plus concert exposure to the "real" world, for her to learn that although she might be nothing, one day she could be something. And two more years to appreciate that musical talents were not the only important ones, perhaps not the *most* important ones.

In the days after her conversation with Magnus, Wilsa had watched and listened. She decided that, as usual when it came to people and motivation, he was right. Tristan Morgan was confident and relaxed and talkative with everyone and about everything—except when he was face-to-face with Wilsa. Then it was hard to force more than a few words out of him.

She hated that. It offended her self-image. With time to spare while Magnus Klein haggled contracts, Wilsa had reversed the roles for the past week. She had pursued Tristan, tracking him to his meetings on Ganymede, eating at the same times and places he did, and at last having the inspiration to sit down in front of him and ask about Project *Starseed*.

And then the words had poured out. He told her of the grand design, more than a century old, to send an unmanned, fusion-powered ship to the stars. "We changed the name, and the old-timers would have boggled at our technology, but they'd have been right at home with the physics. We fuse a helium-3/deuterium mixture—"

But when he wanted to give her details, she had outmaneuvered him. She had, she said, at least a week free. Why not let her *see* things, rather than just hearing about them?

He seemed hesitant again. She had to coax him along. First she persuaded him to take her to a small deuterium-separation facility right there on Ganymede, and then to the main one on a big ice fragment beyond Callisto. From that point it seemed natural for them to travel inward, together with a load of deuterium, to the construction program on the orbiting *Starseed* base and watch the Von Neumanns soar up to dock, discharge their helium-3 cargo and drop back to repeat the cycle. The final step had been the visit she had wangled to Hebe Station.

The vicarious cruise in the *Leda* through Jupiter's depths, to watch the Von Neumanns mining for fusion fuels within Jupiter's cloud layers, had been part of the same strategy. The music that flooded into her head while she did it had been a long shot, a bonus benefit. New stimulation usually led to new composition, but there were no guarantees.

Her plan had worked. Tristan would at last speak freely to her. He would even offer comments on music, on *other* people's music. The only thing he would *not* do was to discuss *her* works. Wilsa realized that she wanted that more than anything, but she had not yet understood why it was important . . . although she had noticed that it pleased her rather than distressed her when Tristan Morgan stood, as he was standing now, two feet closer than Belt politeness permitted.

She turned from the port, stretching arms and shoulders that had been too long in one position. He moved to her side, towering over her. He had a lanky, lean build, and one of the first things that she had noticed about him was his hands and their long, pale, flexible fingers. She coveted them through the eyes of a professional keyboard player. He could probably span a twelfth with no difficulty. Her own coffee-colored little hands struggled to play a ninth.

She visualized a keyboard, and in the same moment realized that she had forgotten all about her agent's call. "Did you tell Magnus when I'd be able to get back to him?"

"No. He was being pushy, so I told him you weren't here, that you were a thousand kilometers away, down in the guts of Jupiter. He didn't like that at all. Probably thinks his precious ten percent might be in danger."

So the disdain between the two ran both ways. Wilsa sighed and scanned the chamber. "Can I put in a call to him from here?"

"Sure. I've got it set up for Call Back. Press the send button and you'll have a direct circuit to Klein on Ganymede." He looked across at a chronometer. "You should do it soon, though, while the geometry's good. No relay station is needed if you act now, and there's less than a four-second, round-trip travel time for signals."

Wilsa pressed the button at once. The time to pick-up somehow seemed less than four seconds. Magnus Klein must have been sitting right by his receiver.

"WhereyoubeenforGodsake?" said a grating voice. "Get your butt over here."

"Why? What happened?"

A longer delay. "What do you think happened? What I *said* would happen. We're signed—for your *Galileian Suite*. System premier performance nine days from now. *That's* what I've been doing while you were goofing off. Hurry up back."

"What terms?" asked Wilsa. But while she was waiting for her words to laser out to Ganymede and the reply to return to Hebe Station, Tristan Morgan was shaking his head. "What a *bastard*."

"A bastard doesn't do anything except have the wrong parents."

"Worse than a bastard, then. Why do you let a jerk like

Magnus Klein push you around? He's just taking advantage—"

"Eighty thousand for the first performance," broke in the harsh voice from the speaker. "Option for four more at thirty thousand per—which I'm sure we'll get. We keep recording rights for all but the first performance. I figured you'd be better on the second or third night. We split broadcast royalties with them for the premier."

"*That's* why." Wilsa patted the speaker and made no attempt to lower her voice as she went on. "Magnus is a real tough son of a bitch. He told me he'd get that, but I didn't believe him."

She winked at Tristan and waited through another four-second silence.

"Well, you damn well should have," said the voice, louder and angrier than ever. "I always deliver what I say. I told you, I know these guys better than they know themselves. Hell, I was *raised* here. So you get your ass back to Ganymede. Sharpish, or I'll be an even *tougher* son of a bitch."

The line went dead and the Connect light blinked out. Wilsa shrugged. "The Master's Voice."

"You're going to take orders from that little monster?"

"He's half a head taller than I am. Tristan, I have to go. As soon as possible. I've got a concert in nine days, including the first performance of my new suite. It's my biggest chance anywhere outside the Belt halls, and my reputation in the whole Jovian system will be on the line. I have to practice 'til I *bleed*."

She did her best to sound worried, and reluctant to leave. But deep inside, she was bubbling over. She had poured her heart into the *Galileian Suite* for over a year, *slaved* over it, living on Vesta but dreaming of the chance to give the first performance out on the big Jovian satellites. Ganymede of course for preference, but she would have settled for Callisto.

It had been a wild dream. Now—in only nine days—it would be reality. On Ganymede. *Nine days!* Wilsa shivered, and decided that she was more worried than she was willing to admit.

While Wilsa exulted and trembled, four hundred million kilometers away Camille Hamilton waited and worried. Through the two weeks since David Lammerman had left DOS Center for Earth, she had been braced for a blow that never came.

The first full tests of the Distributed Observation System had been mind-blowing. Camille and David's hard work on calibration had paid off, and the system exceeded specifications. The best images were already showing city-like features on a planet in the Large Magellanic Cloud. Other images had revealed thousands of mysterious reflecting spheres, each perfectly round and the size of Earth's moon, orbiting a star in one of the Virgo cluster's prominent galaxies. That oddity alone was worth the whole price of DOS.

The press certainly thought so. It had gone wild, clamoring for more. The schedule for DOS use, with its plan for availability to guest observers—who would squeeze Camille's personal use of the telescope system to a minimum—should have been sent to DOS Center days, even weeks, ago.

Instead, nothing had arrived. Queries from Camille to headquarters had been met with vague answers: The project was under review; basic management decisions had to be made. She fidgeted and fretted. With DOS so obviously a success, why did anything *need* to be reviewed? The instrument was ready for users.

While Camille waited, she carried on with her own observations, setting up a computer-controlled program to examine low-intensity fusion targets twelve billion light-years away. But even that did not bring satisfaction. She was wondering all the while if she would ever be allowed enough DOS time to complete her task.

The terse message that David Lammerman was returning from Earth came as a relief, even if it also made her a bit miffed. He'd told Camille, maybe with a little prompting from her, how much he would miss her when he was away. And then she had heard nothing from him after his departure.

Not even a form message to say that he had arrived safely on Earth. Of course she would certainly have heard about it on the news programs if he *hadn't*. But damn it, it was the *principle* of the thing . . .

Now David was coming back, as he had departed, on one of the high-acceleration passenger ships that were turning solar-system travel into a simple problem of linear trajectories. Camille decided that she would ignore him, as he had chosen to ignore her. She would stay at work and not meet the ship when it docked.

In the final couple of minutes, she changed her mind. She would go and *tell* him that he was a thoughtless jerk and that she had every right to be annoyed with him. She went drifting over to the periphery of DOS Center and arrived at the dock just in time to confront him as he was emerging from quarantine.

"So." She stood, hands on hips, in the classical ham-video pose of the slighted lover. "You finally decided to drop in."

He turned. She saw his anguished face and slumped shoulders, and all thought of accusation vanished.

"David. Are you sick?" Except that he was never sick. And he had a crushed, beaten look that was more than physical.

He shook his head. He did not speak as they traveled back through the hub and arrived at last at their living quarters.

She had forgotten how crowded the room was with the two of them present. David's great limbs sprawled across three-quarters of the available space. He sighed as he relaxed into his favorite seat, but still he showed no desire to talk.

Camille dropped into his lap and put her arms around his neck. "Well? So what was Earth like?" She kept her voice light, as though nothing was wrong. "It doesn't seem to have agreed with you."

She had been raised on Mars herself and had gone to Earth only twice for short visits. But it hadn't been that bad, nowhere near as awful as it was described.

He sighed again and rubbed at his tangled blond hair. "I was told . . . something. Something I'm not supposed to know. That's why they took me there."

"What was it?" Camille relaxed a little. She could pry it out of him, whatever it was. She knew how. She stroked his cheek, with its fuzz of downy hair—David still needed to depilate only once a week. "Come on, David. A secret's safe with me."

"I promised not to tell anyone. That's why I couldn't send you any messages."

"Well, when you promised whoever it was, did you really think you weren't going to tell me?"

"No." He leaned his face into her stroking hand. "I knew I would." He gave her a wan smile. "You'd worm it out of me, wouldn't you? I'll tell you. Anyway, you'd learn it directly in another week or two."

"Learn *what*, for God's sake?" If he was trying to soften a blow, he was certainly failing. "David, don't do this."

"Learn that we're out. You and me." His eyes wandered the familiar room. "We're off DOS."

"That's ridiculous." She sat up straight and placed her hands flat on his chest. "Who told you a stupid thing like that?"

"I can't say. I promised—really promised this time—

that I wouldn't." There was the awkward, cowed look again, the hesitant voice that she had heard when he was first summoned to Earth. "But I know it's true. I saw the documents. We're off DOS."

"But DOS is a *success*, a big one. It's doing *better* than anyone expected. And a lot of the credit for that has to go to us. We did years of good, solid work."

"Success has nothing to do with it. Or maybe it does, and that makes things worse. Camille, something happened at the top of the pyramid. Right at the top. At that level, you and I don't matter. We don't even *exist*. There's going to be a complete change in the use of DOS for the next two years. No extra-galactic targets. Concentration on nearby stellar systems. Stars and planets, a hundred light-years away, or even less."

"That's preposterous. DOS was never designed for local work. You can use it for that, sure, but no one in his right mind would. Who needs to see something a few meters across, fifty light-years away?"

"You don't have to persuade *me*." His voice was unsteady. "Hey, I said all that when I was on Earth. I was told that it makes no difference. The Outward Bound group has been gaining influence, making more noise, finding support in high levels of government. The DOS decision was made to keep them happy."

"By whom?"

"By the only people who matter. Those who control DOS funding. It's not just Outward Bound. There are other politics behind it, have to be."

"It's totally *illogical*."

"So? What's logic got to do with it? When politics comes in the door, logic goes out the window."

Camille wanted to curse and scream. She had enough sense and self-control to realize that it would do no good at all. No matter how bad the news, you didn't help anything by attacking the messenger . . . even if you had no idea of why he had been singled out as the bearer of the news.

It was time for logic, not for shouting matches.

"David, think for a minute. It's not as bad as it sounds. In fact, things may even be *better* this way. If they're going to be crazy enough to revamp the program for close targets, DOS will eat them up. There just aren't that many stellar systems within a hundred light-years. We'll find gaps in the observing schedule. You and I know how to reprogram DOS quicker than anyone, and no one else in the system has any idea of how fast we can do it. We'll take advantage of open slots and still explore the edge of the universe."

He lifted her effortlessly from his lap and placed her on a chair, went to a bunk and sprawled there. His eyes closed. "You weren't listening, love." His voice was gloomy and distant. "I didn't say that *our experiments* were off DOS—we knew that was likely to be the case as soon as the astronomy superstars came to use the facilities. I said that *we* are off DOS. You and me. Camille and David. They'll bring in a new staff, one that specializes in observation programs of near-stellar systems. That's the real message I had to go to Earth to get."

"But damn it, what happens to *us*?"

"That's the worst news of all." He opened his eyes and stared miserably at the ceiling. "We have to go. Within a couple of weeks, we have to be out of DOS Center. I was told that it will be at least two years before we can have any hope of getting back in."

5

The Bat Cave

To the colonists and explorers creeping outward past the Belt in the third decade of the twenty-first century, Ganymede was the plum of the Jovian system. The largest of Jupiter's four Galileian satellites, it was also the biggest moon in the solar system, planet-sized with its radius of 2650 kilometers. There was plenty of Ganymede real estate to explore, shape, and develop.

Ganymede's low density offered a gravity only one-seventh that of Earth's, a factor most appealing to the low-gee Belters. And, finally, Ganymede had volatiles in abundance; ammonia and methane and—most precious of all—water. Half of Ganymede was fresh water and water-ice, the latter covering almost all of the frigid, cracked surface. A human wandering in a suit could split off a chunk of ice, thaw it, and safely drink the slightly sulfurous result.

There was only one snag. Jupiter loomed in the sky, a million kilometers away. *Jupiter pluvius*: Jupiter, the bringer of rain. But this rain was no cooling balm from heaven. It was an endless sleet of high-energy protons, gathered from the solar wind, accelerated by the demon of

Jupiter's magnetic field, and delivered as a murderous hail into Ganymede's frozen surface. A human wanderer, garbed in a suit offering ample protection on Moon or Mars, would cook and die on Ganymede in a few hours.

The colonists had taken the problem in their stride. After all, the proton rain was far worse on little watery Europa, closer to Jupiter and visible in Ganymede's sky as a disk half the size again of Earth's moon. It was worse yet on sulfur-spitting Io, innermost of the four Galileian satellites.

Ganymede would do nicely. The whole solid interior of the moon was available and safe; all it needed was a little work. A handful of Von Neumanns in the form of tunneling robots was developed, dropped off, and left to replicate and do their thing for a few years, while the humans went away and redesigned their suits.

The new suit models that they returned with carried woven-in threads of high-temperature superconductors. Every charged particle followed the magnetic field lines and traveled harmlessly around and past the suit's surface. The human inside was safe and snug. It was often claimed, in the tall stories that human males apparently could not live without, that the occupant could tell which way he was facing on the surface of Ganymede from the force exerted by diverted protons on the protecting suit.

Whoppers like that could survive, because most settlers never dreamed of going near the surface. Why should they? The outside was ice and cold and dreary rock. All of the life and action was in the burrows and the sub-Ganymedean chambers, ever-expanding and complexly interlocked.

And it never occurred to the colonists to think of their home as alien, or sterile, or hostile. When the Great War broke out between Earth and Mars and Belt, the inhabitants of Ganymede had stayed clear of it, watched in horror as three-quarters of humanity perished, and thanked whatever gods might be that they were snug inside safe, civilized Ganymede.

By the time that Wilsa Sheer received the call from her agent and flew out from Vesta, the war had been over for a quarter of a century and the inversion of native perspective was complete. The idea of living on ravaged, war-ruined Earth, with its dead hemisphere and crushing gravity, was repugnant. The notion of Mars or Moon, dust-grimed and arid, was little better. And the thought of living *anywhere* on an open surface, prey to falling bomb or random hurricane or tidal wave or solar flare, was worst of all.

Rustum Battachariya, thirty-seven years old, was a true child of Ganymede. He had never ascended to the naked surface. Although he was head of Passenger Transport Schedules for the Outer System from Jupiter to the Oort Cloud, he had never visited another planet or satellite. He saw no reason to. Every amenity of life was available in his chambers or within a few minutes of it. From his cave, seven kilometers beneath the surface, he had rapid access to every open library file and data source of the solar system. And to his office, when occasion demanded, any person of importance could find a way.

"You will not see my travel records there, because of course I do not travel." Battachariya spoke to Inspector-General Gobel in the patient, kindly tone of one addressing a small child. "Travel is no more than a distraction. It is a means by which deficient intellects provide themselves with the illusion of progress where there is none."

Magrit Knudsen bit her lip to remain straight-faced. Battachariya resented Yarrow Gobel's presence, as he resented every visitor to his private domain. He knew that the man had to travel constantly, all over the system, to do his work as inspector-general. He was being deliberately distracting and provocative.

But Battachariya was wasting his time. The inspector-general was a match for him. Gobel was a thin-lipped, red-bearded man, losing his hair, and totally devoid of any sign of imagination or humor. He made it clear that he was interested in numbers, and only numbers. Numbers spoke for themselves. He ignored explanations and justifications and obfuscations, and he was not swayed by personalities.

Magrit knew from experience that Gobel was good at his job. Make that superb. She watched him warily when he pored over the stack of reports. If he asked questions, they were always pointed, often subtle, and usually damning. She breathed easier when he returned to the study of the Transport Department schedules, reviewing them, item by item, with the patient and unwavering persistence of a tortoise.

Bat versus turtle. Magrit resisted the urge to become involved. As a cabinet-level official, she had no reason to be here. She should stay aloof and let Battachariya fend for himself.

She thought of the early days. It had not always been this way. She had inherited Bat a dozen years ago, when he had been a junior scheduling analyst and she had just received her first promotion, to Transportation Department branch chief. Advice from the outgoing branch head had been offered on her first day: "Get rid of Battachariya. He's trouble. He's indolent, and gluttonous, and arrogant, and pompous, and it's impossible to control him."

Which had filled Magrit with the urge to say, "Fine. So why didn't *you* do something about it in the two years you had him?" But her predecessor was moving up in the system, and Magrit Knudsen already had a kernel of shrewd political sense.

She had watched Battachariya for the next few weeks and decided that the advice she had been offered was quite appropriate. Bat, at twenty-five years old, massed over five hundred pounds. To Magrit's eye, he appeared more huge and unkempt at every meeting. She heard others call him in his presence "The Fat Bat," and "Blubber-Bat." The terms were appropriate, but he ignored them. He treated their originators with disdain. He ate sweetmeats constantly; his clothes were all-black and three sizes too small for him; his appearance was slovenly; and his office, at the deepest level of Ganymede burrows, was a true bat cave. It held such an insane jumble of papers and computers and ineffable bric-a-brac from all over the system that Magrit was sure he would never be able to find anything that he needed in order to do his job.

Fire the man!

There was only one problem. Magrit had never fired anyone. She didn't know how to. She was too inexperienced to realize that you got rid of a person you didn't want by transfer to another department.

And so in her first three months as branch chief, she had found herself in the bizarre and unhappy position of *defending* Rustum Battachariya in staff meetings. "Sure he's fat, and he doesn't wash as often as I do, or have many social graces. But his private life is his affair, not mine or yours. He's competent, he's quiet, and he does his job well. That's what matters."

Of course she could not keep the psychology crew away from Bat, whose strange and solitary disposition was a magnet to them. In that arena, however, he proved more than able to look after himself. From his thirteenth year, he had "wasted his time" in the solar system's Super-Puzzle Network. Twelve years had taught "Megachirops" (his puzzler code name) to be endlessly alert for logical traps and infinitely devious in setting them.

The psych crew and their poorly disguised hidden agendas didn't stand a chance.

"You mass five hundred and thirty pounds. How do you feel about the potential effect of this on your survival?"

"Sanguine. I employ the best-known prophylaxes for life extension, including interior symbiotes. By the standards of any human of one hundred, or even fifty, years ago, I am disgustingly healthy. My life-style is also consistent with longevity. Compare, if you will, my survival expectancy with your own. And in making that comparison, do not omit the travel that you undertake to perform your profession. Travel has its inevitable risks, you know. Factor in the life-shortening effect of changes in circadian rhythms, implied by that same travel; and do not ignore the mental stress endemic in your work. When your analysis is complete, you will find that I am likely to outlive you by a decade or more."

They did the calculations and were horrified to learn that Bat was right. They tried again.

"You have a high regard for your own intellect. Why do you have no interest in handing your intellectual gifts on to the next generation?"

"*Another* sex question! Do psychologists think of nothing else? But I will answer you. In the first place, you make an invalid assumption. My sperm was donated to the central bank nine years ago, and remains available today. It will be available for use centuries hence—but not, as you suggest, for the *next* generation, since I have given instructions that my sperm must remain frozen until fifty years after my death. You see, by the time that I was sixteen years old, I had realized something that many never learn: Human breeding patterns are based on a shocking logical error, one set in place long before there was any understanding of genetics. Most children result from the fusion of *fresh* sperm and ova. When they are born, their parents are still alive and *still young*—too young for lifetime achievements to be assessed, or for fatal flaws to have appeared. Do you want in the solar system the offspring of an Attila, or of a Hitler? Is it not more logical to wait until a man or woman's life is over, when an objective evaluation of virtues and vices can be made? The potential value to the human race of any man or woman is contained *only in their genes*, not in their bodies. And that genetic material—sperm or ova—can be frozen indefinitely. It is quite unimportant that the parental bodies exist when their children are born, and from most points of view, it is better if they do not."

The psych crew was in retreat, but its members tried one more question of revealing subtlety.

"Rustum Battachariya, you live a solitary and introverted existence. Have you ever considered suicide?"

Bat thought for a few moments. "Frequently. But only for others."

The psychs fled the field, to argue whether that was a yes or no answer. They did not return.

And during the next three months, Magrit discovered a great secret: What she had been saying about Bat was true, and more than true. Rustum Battachariya carried in his great round cannonball head every detail of every passenger transport system throughout the whole solar system. He loved games (provided they involved no physical exertion) and Megachirops' Super-Puzzle Network experience had made Bat expert in everything from chess to double-acrostic sonnets to hidden ciphers. In his view, complex transport scheduling was just another variety of puzzle.

One day Magrit had gone to him as her last resort. She had a set of wildly conflicting requirements, a desired schedule that she and all of the department analysts had beaten out their brains on, with no result.

Bat glared at the offending document. He was sitting on his specially made seat, like a great rolling ball of black-clad flesh that would have sagged and sunk in higher gravity. "A few moments of cerebration are in order, Madam Knudsen. And of silence." He blew out his cheeks, grunted, and half-closed his eyes.

While he was thinking, Magrit roamed the office, finally

picking up one of the more perplexing objects that littered it.

"You are holding an infrared communications beacon." Battachariya must have eyes in the back of his head, because she was standing on the side of the chamber behind his chair. "Developed on Pallas, and the smallest one ever made. Be careful with it. There are only three other copies, all in the Ceres Museum."

He had been scribbling on a scrap of paper, but now his fat, dimpled fingers went running across a keyboard, while at the same time he dictated verbal inputs to the computer.

"Here." He sniffed, held out the paper, and indicated the output display. "You might see if that is satisfactory."

Magrit had looked at the screen with no special hope. It took a minute or two for her to realize that she was seeing a simple and economical solution to her problem, one that met all of the scheduling constraints.

"It's *perfect*."

She was still holding the communications beacon. Bat took it gently from her hands. "It was trivial. But this device reminds me of something else." He spoke with—for him—unusual diffidence. "According to the passenger rosters, you will be visiting Ceres in two weeks?"

"I guess so. I'm supposed to attend a meeting of transportation heads."

"Then I wonder if you might do me a big personal favor. A Palladian genome-stripper is being held at the Ceres Museum, awaiting my collection instructions. It is an item developed by Belt scientists in the final days of the war. It masses less than half a kilo, and it is of course inactivated. But it is also fragile, and I have some reluctance to entrust it to orthodox transfer methods."

He paused.

"I'll bring it back to you, sure I will. Just let them know I'll be coming for it."

(Magrit had resisted the temptation to repeat to Battachariya the conversation she had overheard a few days earlier, between him and one of her other analysts: "The only reason you never travel anywhere, Fat-Butt, is 'cause you can't pack all the blubber into a standard suit."

"That is intolerable slander." Battachariya was unperturbed. "Why should I endure a peripatetic existence when you and my other witless minions are available to serve my needs?")

Magrit Knudsen had received the genome-stripper permit from Battachariya and carried the solution of the scheduling problem away in triumph. Every branch head in the department had sworn that it couldn't be done. She knew that at the next staff meeting she would have something *real* with which to fight off attacks on Battachariya. At that moment she had decided—with relief—that she could drop any thought of firing him.

And now, twelve years later, Magrit watched Bat interact with Gobel and reminded herself that he no longer *needed* her defense for anything. He was the acknowledged master of all tricky transportation problems, capable of levels of subtlety that left newcomers gasping.

Except that such skill meant not a thing to the inspector-general. Yarrow Gobel followed his own audit agenda. He had plowed right through the authorizations and expenditures for Battachariya's work on transport planning, ignoring all jibes or distractions. Apparently he had found nothing out of line there, since that heap had been checked off and placed to one side, but now a final thick stack was being placed in front of him.

Magrit winced. The stack contained Battachariya's discretionary account. Or what, in her mind, she thought of as his *indiscretionary* account. It showed the items of expenditure for which no budget had been allocated. It had not been audited for nearly five years. It was, when Magrit Knudsen descended to the reality level, the reason she had come here. She had approved every item on that list, at least in principle. Her signature was on them. In practice, she had no idea of what most of them were, but she could guess.

That was apparently not true for Inspector-General Gobel. He was frowning in perplexity at the tables of expenditures and at the entries that sat beside each.

Finally he raised his head and stared at Rustum Battachariya. "Most of these purchases and requisitions do not correspond to anything on the chart of accounts for the Transportation Department. They appear to be for—" the expression on his face changed, to one that Magrit had never seen before "—for *Great War relics*, and for *war records*."

It was not an explicit question, so Bat chose to be awkward again and treat it as a statement. He stared very hard at the inspector-general's face and said nothing. There was a long silence, until Magrit could not resist jumping in.

"There is a supplementary list of approved expenditures specific to Coordinator Battachariya's department. I'm sure that all of the items you are looking at are covered by that set."

Gobel turned his chilly attention to her. "Then it should be obvious to you that I need that list. And I also require the memoranda that show how such an anomaly came into existence."

"The list is on the computer here. The original memoranda are over in my office. I can go along and get them if you like. Naturally, we are cooperating fully."

He nodded slowly. "I am sure you are. But while you are finding the memoranda, Mr. Battachariya and I will review the materials described in these documents. *In detail*."

The two men stared at each other, ignoring Magrit. She sighed and headed out of Bat's office toward the suspension tube that would carry her five hundred meters up to the main department. How much explanation would be necessary—or sufficient—to satisfy Gobel? Some of those data and equipment requests had seemed strange even to Magrit's tolerant eyes. Only Bat could justify them. All Magrit could do was to look for her written records and hope that they were accurate enough and complete enough to satisfy a nitpicker like the inspector-general.

The discretionary account went back such a long way. Long ago, even before she brought the genome-stripper back from Ceres, Magrit had learned that there were other deeps within the brooding mind of the Great Bat. His office might appear to her and others as a random junk heap, but to him every item in it had its own place, value, and significance.

Half of Bat Cave was devoted to relics of the Great War. Battachariya was a war buff, although of a curious kind. The general Ganymedean view of the war was that it had been a disaster of enormous cost, but also that it had served as a pivotal event necessary before the move from Earth-centered to system-centered human psychology could take place.

Bat cared nothing for nostalgia, philosophy, or historical imperatives. He saw the war differently. Although the Inner System had suffered far more casualties, in his mind it was the Belt that had sustained the greater, and perhaps irretrievable, loss. The war had arrived at a time when Belt technology was bursting out toward a period of incredible fertility of invention. All of that had been blown to bits. Many Belt discoveries had been destroyed, along with their creators. But not all of them were necessarily lost forever. Bat was convinced that their secrets might yield to careful analysis and systematic search. It was the puzzle to exceed all puzzles.

Through the branch, he had made tiny investments in old records, ones that Magrit could justify, if necessary, as evidence of former patterns of passenger movement around the Belt. He had studied the faded printouts in the seclusion of Bat Cave and finally requested that a certain orbit be close-scanned for objects of specific description. Magrit had approved the search. The wreckage of the Belt freighter located there contained design procedures and samples of an unknown class of bonding adhesives, superior to anything currently available.

Magrit Knudsen had been praised for the discovery. She had refused credit and made sure that the true source of the accomplishment was acknowledged. Bat was a department hero—for a few days; then his arrogance and pomposity again became too much for most people to stand.

On Battachariya's second data request, the department had been a little more generous with funds. The subsequent search had yielded no new invention, but the Ceres Museum had paid handsomely for the little antique Von Neumann. It was the original model, used in the mining of the Trojan asteroids before Fishel's Law and Epitaph— *"Smart is Dumb*: It is unwise to build too much intelligence into a self-replicating machine"—became accepted dogma. Everyone thought that the particular Von Neumann model had been exterminated, but this one was still functioning after forty years of drifting in space. The museum put it on display . . . in a triple-sealed, inert enclosure. Deprived of raw materials, the Von Neumann was not judged dangerous.

By Battachariya's fourth success, no one questioned his hobby, or the anomaly of Great War-related expenditures within a transportation department. If anyone had, an economic analysis would have shown investments repaid by discoveries a hundred times over.

But the departmental memoranda were another matter. Looking at the scanty file as she returned through the suspension tube, Magrit had the feeling that Bat's war-relic activities had been not so much approved and planned as simply *grown*. She was too experienced to let nervousness show, but the last steps back into Bat Cave were not easy ones. She paused on the threshold, looking around the chamber and trying to see it through the inspector-general's probing eyes. The granular paneled walls and ceiling, the recessed solar-spectrum lighting, and the soft but impenetrable grey floor did not draw her attention. What Magrit sought were items and emphases exclusively Battachariyan.

She stared along the narrow, ugly chamber that formed both living quarters and office. The Bat Cave was only three meters high and four wide, but it was at least thirty deep. The useful width was diminished by bookcases and file cabinets that ran along both the right and left walls. They carried thousands of unbound sheaves of dusty printouts, the results of Belt Sweeper surveys, all placed apparently at random.

At the far end there was a small, well-equipped kitchen and the great mound of Battachariya's bed. To reach that point, a visitor must pass through a central corridor wide enough to admit Bat's own bulk. That corridor was flanked by tables and benches covered with a chaos of gadgets and machinery, many of them incomplete or fused to uselessness.

It was a unique collection, a cornucopia of Great War relics and debris. The one thing missing—Magrit could see it clearly now, as she had not seen it for years—was any evidence of *passenger transport schedules*. Evidence, in fact, of Bat's official duties. Yarrow Gobel's gimlet eye, no matter how sharp, could not see inside Battachariya's head, where those schedules were securely tucked away. What he could see was evidence of diverted attention, lax supervision, misuse of department funds . . .

Magrit had left the two men sitting at the table where Gobel had stacked the transport requisition reports. She had expected to find them sitting there still. The reports had apparently not been moved, but Bat was halfway along the room. Gobel was at his side, peering into some sort of viewfinder.

"I have the records you requested." Magrit tried to sense the atmosphere as she advanced into the room. She failed. Bat was as impassive as ever, and Gobel's turtle face did not seem built to show human expression. He took his eye at last from the viewfinder and turned to face her.

"Thank you." And now Gobel was suddenly giving off an emotion that Magrit Knudsen could read. Annoyance. He took the folder she proffered and placed it under his arm. "With your permission, Administrator Knudsen, I will take this with me for review and return it to you tomorrow." He walked past Magrit, heading for the door.

"But the review of the supplementary list—"

"—is in my hands." Gobel turned back to Battachariya. "Eight o'clock?"

"Choose the time for your convenience. I will certainly be here."

"Then eight o'clock." Gobel was gone, without a word to Magrit.

"What have you been *saying* to him?" She turned to Bat. "When I left, he was just unsympathetic, but now he's *mad* at you."

"That is untrue." Bat was easing the viewfinder back into its case. His moonlike, swarthy face wore a rare look of gratification. "He is not angry with me, not in the slightest. It was your return that provoked his animosity."

"All I did was bring him the memos he asked for."

"True. It was not *what* you brought that caused annoyance. It was the simple fact of your return." Battachariya had moved to a pile of listings, and he removed one. "Since the inspector-general has left for the moment, may I bring another matter to your attention?"

Bat's sideways mental leaps always lost Magrit. Today he seemed more obscure than usual. She stared blankly at the listing that he handed her. It reported on a Sweeper survey of parts of the Belt. The search had been completed two years ago, but the results had only recently been forwarded to Bat from the Ceres data banks.

"Is this something Gobel asked you about?"

"Not at all. The inspector-general knows nothing of it. I was reviewing this survey before his arrival interrupted my work. Now I wish to draw your attention to this item."

His pudgy finger jabbed at a dozen lines of written description halfway down the page. "Read that. Carefully."

Magrit read. One of the Sweepers, the machines responsible for continuous surveillance of potential hazards to navigation as far out as Uranus, had located and examined a man-made object. It was a piece of a deep-space ore freighter, the *Pelagic*, which had been converted for passenger transport near the end of the war. The vessel had been attacked and disintegrated. The Sweeper had found one small fragment, which happened to include an intact flight recorder. A querying of the recorder showed that the *Pelagic* was a Belt vessel carrying a total of ten passengers and crew at the time of the ship's destruction. The nature of the damage and the weapon that inflicted it were described.

Magrit read it through twice. "So a Sweeper found a bit of space debris left over from the war. What about it? There must be millions of them."

"There are indeed. The Sweeper recorded the approximate position and velocity for future tracking, but it did not recover the fragment from orbit, nor did it destroy it. I would like your permission for recovery to be initiated at once, and the flight recorder sent here."

"What will it cost?"

"That estimate is not yet available. But it will be significant, since the position is poorly known."

It was wrong for a supervisor to lose her temper *visibly*

with someone who worked for her. Except sometimes. Except like now, when nobody else was here.

"Bat, I don't know why I bother. Where's your goddamned sense? You have the inspector-general breathing down your neck and aching to find something he can stick you with. He hasn't seen one thing in writing that says you ought to have any interest in war relics. So while he's actually poring over your records, you want to stick some new fund request right up his nose. What do you propose to tell him when he comes back tomorrow to go over your requisitions?"

Arrogant was right. Pompous was right. But add *crazy*, too, because Battachariya was smiling at her serenely. "Inspector-General Gobel will not return here tomorrow."

"He sure said he would."

"No. He said that he would return your file tomorrow, and see me at eight o'clock. That is eight o'clock *tonight*. For dinner. I have promised goulash, which, as you know, is a specialty of mine. As for the list that so concerns you, he examined it while you were gone and pronounced himself fully satisfied."

In the inverted world of Bat Cave, where subordinates did what they liked and logic hung by its heels from the ceiling, you took an incorruptible, tunnel-visioned inspector-general and seduced him with promises of goulash.

But Bat was continuing. "Yarrow Gobel is, as should have been apparent to you from the expression on his face when he first saw the items on the discretionary account, a Great War *aficionado*. Far more so than I. He is convinced that the Belt was in the final days developing a secret weapon, a device that would have won the war for them had not something gone dreadfully awry. I will, of course, mention to him over dinner the fragment of the *Pelagic* and my interest in recovering it." He tapped the sheet he was holding. "And given his predilection, it is inconceivable that he will disapprove funding when I show the evidence and explain its possible significance."

Magrit went across to Bat's huge padded chair and plunked herself down in the middle of it. Bat had to be a genius or an idiot. The trouble was, he thought he was a genius. And so did she. "You might start by explaining its significance to *me*. I'm the one who has to find the cash. And I don't see any reason to spend one cent on dragging back a lump of a ship that was blown apart twenty-five years ago."

"That can only be because you did not read the report as carefully as I requested. Rather than asking you to peruse it yet again, I will summarize the salient facts. First, the *Pelagic* was a Belt vessel. Not merely *made* in the Belt, but operated for the Belt during the war. To confirm that fact, I checked Inner System records. There is no evidence that the *Pelagic* was ever captured or controlled by the Inner System.

"Second, the damage report on the remaining fragment of the *Pelagic* leaves no doubt as to the weapon that inflicted it. The *Pelagic* was destroyed by a particular type of smart missile known as a Seeker."

"I've heard of it. Thousands of ships were wiped out by Seekers."

"They were indeed. *Inner System* ships. The Seeker was a Belt weapon." Battachariya moved to Magrit's side and gently laid the listing in her lap. His arrogance and pomposity had vanished, subordinated to intense curiosity. "So a Belt ship was blown apart by a Belt weapon. The *Pelagic* was destroyed *by its own side*. Why?"

The Great Bat was not the only one with an evening meeting. As the cabinet-level officer in charge of transportation, Magrit Knudsen could not afford to stay away from the evening's General Assembly meeting, although she was already tired. She left the Bat Cave at six-fifteen, allowing herself just forty-five minutes to eat, shower, change, and review her position on the main issue before the Assembly.

Further development of one of the Galileian satellites, particularly on the scale proposed, would change traffic patterns all around Jupiter. Irrevocably. How could that be justified? Not easily. She felt herself tilting toward opposition of the project, but she wanted to hear all of the evidence before she made up her mind.

There were others in the General Assembly, though, to whom evidence mattered not at all. *Snakes*, she thought as she gulped down a few mouthfuls of soup and a handful of crackers. Empire builders, who would publicly oppose development but promote and lobby for it strongly in private. Snakes and *wolves*. Tonight's meeting would be packed with them, because development projects brought them out in packs, scenting profits. She glared at her face in the mirror and brushed her long black hair harder than necessary. Snakes and wolves and *pigs*. They didn't give a damn what happened to the Jovian system thirty years from now, as long as the hogs could roll in the money today. She could name a dozen of them who were sure to be there tonight.

And, like it or not, she had to work with them. It was that, or give up and let them have their way.

Magrit thought of Rustum Battachariya and his goulash. The meal was sure to be delicious. Bat was as much a gourmet as he was a gourmand. No handful of crackers for *his* dinner.

As usual when she came away from a meeting with Bat, she was half irritated and half envious. He didn't care about promotions. He had no interest in political infighting or power struggles. If he were given a line position at Cabinet level, he would not survive for two days. But tonight he was the one who would be working his way through four or five portions of goulash, lounging in the

Bat Cave and showing off all his toys to Inspector-General Yarrow Gobel while Magrit was sitting and nodding politely at people whose company she hated.

She checked her appearance, checked the time, and headed over to the assembly hall. Battachariya lived a peaceful, intellectual, stress-free life, doing just what he wanted to do and refusing to consider anything else. Now and then Magrit thought it might be nice to change jobs with him.

Now and then. About once a year. The idea lasted at most for an hour.

She quickened her pace. Her juices were already stirring. Magrit couldn't wait to meet those greedy sons of bitches and jump into the middle of the hassle over the Europan development project.

6

An Offer You Can't Refuse

By the end of the week, Jon Perry had seen too much of Arenas. His meeting at the Admin Center of the Global Ocean Monitor Service had been scheduled, postponed, confirmed, and postponed again. Three times he had appeared with an appointment at Manuel Posada's office, only to learn from anonymous underlings that the under-secretary of GOMS was detained "indefinitely." Twice Jon had been bumped by "the imperatives of highest authority," whatever that meant.

After the fourth day and fifth aborted meeting, he had moved from puzzled to seething. By design or by accident, someone was telling him that he was of negligible importance.

He left GOMS HQ in a foul mood at five P.M., when everyone except the guards at the door had gone. They were itching to leave, too, for it was opening night in Arenas for the Midsummer Festival, and the streets were already packed with musicians, floats, and noisy celebrants.

Jon was in no mood to participate, and in his plain dark-green uniform he felt conspicuous among the vivid, flower-bedecked costumes. The buildings of the city thinned out to the west and he headed that way, toward the smoky orange eye of the sun. Before it finally dipped to the horizon he had walked to the crest of the line of hills, over the brow, and all the way down the gentle western slopes to the seawall. He reached the embankment, a hundred feet above turbulent water, and stared down at the white-caps in Otway Bay. As he watched, the surface broke to a glittering line of foam.

He had wanted solitude and had expected to find nothing more than sea and sky; but he had arrived when the management team of Plankton Unlimited was assembling to head out to the krill farms. They were in a wild mood, even for professional jokers. As he watched, a score of them started to play follow-the-leader, swimming nose to tail, faster and faster, hurtling toward the sharp-edged rocks before turning at the last moment. Once all of them disappeared for half a minute, to emerge in a giant cascade of spray and blown spume. They had changed underwater from the serial motion of the chase to the parallel efforts of a chorus line. Four hundred tons of gleeful, muscular mammal rose in a perfect arc high into the air, turned, and smashed back in unison into the sea. The thrown water glowed with phosphorescence. Ten seconds later, twenty black heads bobbed up, bowed, and began a stately pirouetting dance in matched pairs.

The baleens were putting on a show—but for whom? Jon had watched them and waved to them a hundred times from the *Spindrift*, but there was no way they could know that one of their friends from the submersible was on the seawall. They were doing it for nobody. For sheer joy.

He found himself grinning down at the cavorting black bodies and the waving flukes. Maybe he should be feeling lucky, not peeved. Nell Cotter had left Arenas for Stanley three days earlier, but she had told him that he could stay at the studios for as long as he liked. Suppose that she had *not* done that? His GOMS dormitory permit had been good for one night and one day's meals. As far as anyone at the Admin Center knew, he was sleeping out on the sidewalks and starving to death among the flowers. It was no thanks to them that he was living in a luxury unknown on the floating bases.

The only real thing to be annoyed at was the waste of time. He had never thought to bring work to Arenas, never dreamed that he would have the time for it. Meanwhile, his office desk was piled with unread papers and unreduced smoker observations from earlier descents.

When he turned to go home it was quite dark. Jon allowed the rising southern constellations to guide him back east until the moon rose. It was close to the half, and bright enough for him to pick out the stark-black saber-cut of the Armageddon defense line across its mottled northern face.

The night was warm, and Jon had no reason to hurry. It was close to midnight when he reached the top of the hill and the first of the buildings. Now the moon had to compete with the gaudy lights of Arenas. The party was far from over. Jon was a mile outside the town and a thousand feet above it, but already he could hear the marching bands.

The main thoroughfare of Arenas descended in a huge double curve, turning north as though heading for the airport, then twisting all the way back to the south and finally turning again to run east to the great piers and jetties that flanked the Strait of Magellan. The slope of the road had been carefully chosen by its construction engineers. Never more than a degree or so, it presented no problem for even the most delicate and ungainly of the mobile floats.

Jon did not follow the broad, curving avenue, with its gleaming spheres of bioluminescence. Instead, he descended one of the darker and steeper crossing streets.

These streets headed straight for the shore and were restricted to pedestrian traffic.

One of the guards on duty at the GOMS Admin Center had told him that this year's festival would be the biggest ever, with more than two hundred floats. When Jon reached the main street, he could easily believe it. There were moving behemoths visible in both directions as far as the eye could see.

The huge-wheeled figure of a sleeping giant came rumbling by at no more than two miles an hour. "Earth Mother!" droned a cavernous, amplified voice. "Bow down to the Great Earth Mother. Number one-seventy-eight." Pink smoke rose from the nostrils, white smoke jetted from the gigantic jutting nipples. Half a dozen near-naked women danced on the bare belly in the glowing red light issuing from the deep navel. They were carrying a gigantic phallus, striped red and white like a barber's pole. The men and women on both sides of the road cheered and made obscene gestures. As the giant passed them along the avenue, they entered their scores for Entry 178 on their electronic cards and waited for the next float to arrive.

Entry 179 did not use wheels. It was a re-creation of an apatosaurus, forty feet high and eighty feet long. The beast padded along smoothly on four vast articulated legs, beautifully matched in their movements. Although a dozen men and women rode on the broad grey back, the model's control was too precise to be anything but a single person operating from within its interior. The head on its immense neck swung out and swooped over the crowd, passing no more than three or four feet above Jon. He could see glittering red-rimmed eyes dipping down at him, and a quiet voice from the three-foot maw said, "Number one-seventy-nine. Remember one-seventy-nine." The number was painted on the great body in letters eight feet high.

Then there was a long wait, enough for the float that finally appeared to be greeted with hoots and jeers. It had obviously been having problems. The internal mechanism was squeaking, and the head-high outer lip had a crude and amateurish look, a contrast to the polished perfection of previous entries. The driver was visible in an open and unfinished box in the center, a skinny, dark-haired man crouched worried over the controls. The float bore the number "65" on its side, and it should have passed this point in the route hours ago. Now it was moving fast, trying to catch up. The effort was hopeless, because there was no way that the entries ahead would offer passing room.

The float was a miniature solar system installed on a carousel. Ten six-foot open baskets rotated on long metal arms, and inside each basket sat the living emblem of a planet. Mercury came past the audience first: a man—or was it a woman?—dressed in the garb of an ancient messenger. The face was hidden by a glittering visor, and nothing could be seen but a silver apron, two bare brown legs, and waving arms clothed in silver mesh. Venus was certainly a woman, never a doubt about that. She was naked, painted all over in gold but shrouded by long, cloudy-white tresses. Earth was her sister, clad in filmy blue-white drapes.

Mars was a muscular, red-painted male, as bare as Venus but in his case, totally exposed. From their reaction, the crowd preferred him to the women. They were warming to Entry 65, with its shaky, homemade look. The basket for the Asteroid Belt received the biggest cheer so far. Inside it sat not one person, but a dozen riotous dwarfs, brawling, waving, mooning the crowd, blowing farts, and fighting to stand on each other's head for better visibility.

The basket for Jupiter was just swinging into sight when the whole structure made a sudden lurching right turn.

The crowd booed as Mars came back into view, waving his arms wildly to keep his balance, followed by Earth, flat on her back in her basket. The driver had made a spur-of-the-moment decision to leave the main avenue and take the float down one of the narrower streets. The strategy was clear enough: The float would catch up with the procession on the southbound leg, closer to the strait and the final rallying point, and try to regain its original position in the parade.

And it was clear to Jon at least that the decision was a disastrous one. He had walked the narrow, dim-lit crossing street and he knew how steep it was. While the bystanders were still jeering and waving at the departing Sixty-five, he sprinted across the avenue in pursuit. The float was picking up speed fast, in spite of a screeching from its wheels as loud as any of the marching bands.

The driver had realized his mistake. The brakes were on, but they were not enough to stop the vehicle, not even to slow it. The long arms, designed to operate horizontally, came gyrating crazily above Jon's head as he approached the float's rear. The baskets were missing the buildings on each side of the street by only a couple of feet. The driver knew that he was in desperate trouble, but he was helpless. All he could manage to do was to hold the vehicle in an exact line down the center of the street as its speed increased.

Faster and faster. Control would hold for another twenty seconds at most. Jon was running alongside now, flat out. The street was rough-paved but he hardly noticed. His feet scarcely seemed to touch ground, his balance adjusted without effort to the uneven road. He stared ahead to the main avenue. He could see a dense pack of spectators there, and a shape like a gigantic green grasshopper moving just beyond them. If Number 65 held to its present path, the juggernaut it had become would roll over hundreds in the unsuspecting crowd, then plunge through the middle of the parade itself.

The smooth side of the float was head-high, too tall for Jon to scale as he ran. He waited until an unbalanced arm swung over him, then leaped and grabbed it one-handed. He caught a glimpse of the gilded Venus, breasts bare, her tresses torn away, crouched helpless in the bottom of her basket. And then he was swinging hand-over-hand inward along the metal arm, toward the center of the carousel.

The air was thick with black smoke, and his nostrils filled with an unpleasant smell of burning plastics. The overloaded brakes were on fire . . . and failing. As Jon reached the open control cockpit, the float shuddered and began to pick up speed.

It was no time for half measures or courtesies.

Jon thrust the skinny driver out of the way without a word. The man fell to the flat body of the carousel. Jon ignored him. He turned the wheel, angling the float to graze the wall of the building on the left. One of the metal arms crashed into it first, along with the basket and its contents—Uranus? A bearded figure in glittering thaumaturgic robes fell into the street. Then the left front wheel scraped along the wall, twisted, and broke off.

The float listed steeply. The steering wheel jerked and turned in Jon's hands. He held it against a half-ton torque, dragging it back to the right. At last the heavy mechanism responded. The crippled vehicle lurched back toward the right-hand wall. Another turning arm smashed into a building. A basket and its human contents—the Belt this time, with its dozen cursing dwarves—went spinning away and out of sight. The right wheel hit, harder and more directly. The impact bounced the float back toward the center of the narrow street.

With both front wheels gone, the vehicle skated forward until it reached a break in the pavement. The forward edge dug in with a scream of twisting metal, and the float canted to forty-five degrees. There was a moment when Jon thought that the whole machine was going to turn over, but it collapsed backward and hit the roadway in a jangle of broken parts.

It settled motionless. And caught fire.

Burning insulation added to the smoke of cindered brakes. Jon glanced around. The driver had rolled away over the side. The people in the remaining baskets were swarming out of them, dropping to the floor of the carousel and jumping down to the street.

Only one basket was still occupied. Mercury. The radial metal arm was bent low, and the basket hung over the densest smoke. Jon ran across to it. The floor of the carousel was hot beneath his feet.

He swung up into the open basket and bent over the unconscious Mercury. He pulled off the figure's visor and found himself looking at a young woman. She had no obvious injuries. He lowered her feet-first onto the carousel and heard her moan of pain. In spite of the silver mesh and the apron, she was going to have burns from contact with the hot metal. Jon could do nothing about that. Choking on foul black smoke, he followed her from the basket, dragged her to the edge of the float, tipped her over, and jumped free. He lifted her again and carried her twenty yards down the hill toward the avenue.

And there he paused. The world steadied, came into different focus, and speeded up to normal.

The crashing of the float against the walls and pavement had finally drawn attention from the main parade. Scores of people were hurrying up the hill. At his feet Mercury was beginning to sit up, and she put a hand down to her seared bare leg. She did not seem to be badly hurt.

What about the others in the baskets? He could not see uphill past the smoke of the burning carousel, but those who had escaped to the downhill side were up and moving about.

Jon walked across to a shaded wall and stood with his back to it. He breathed deep and rubbed his smoke-irritated eyes. In just a few minutes, the worst part—for him—would begin. He was no longer useful, because others with better medical training than he would be arriving; but he would have to explain what he had done—over and over, to the parade organizers and the float operators and the Arenas police. And then to the press . . . and to the passersby . . . . and to who knew how many others?

How could he explain to them that he *did not know* what he had done? As always in an emergency, another part of him seemed to take over his actions. They would ask him how he was feeling, how it had been for him when he was chasing the float. How could they understand that the incident already seemed as though it had happened to someone else? He *remembered* everything, but it was seen through the wrong end of the telescope. Every detail was clear, yet distant.

He turned to look down the hill. Maybe it didn't have to be like that. The people hurrying up toward him had their attention on the burning float and its injured crew. They took no notice of the soberly dressed individual quietly leaning against a shadowed wall.

Jon waited for a minute longer, until a score of people had passed him; then he walked quietly down the street to the main thoroughfare. The floats were still passing there, gaudy and enormous. People were cheering as though nothing had happened on the hill behind.

He merged into the crowd and felt vast relief.

It was two o'clock before Jon arrived at the studio building, exhausted but hungrier than he had been in months.

That was no problem. No worries *here* about being late for

dinner. He washed the smoke and grime from his face, inspected the seared palms of his hands, and went into the deserted canteen. He helped himself to sushi, plums, and bean curd, and took them to a table.

He had to admit it. After years on the floating bases, the life-style of Arenas was a shock. He had thought at first that it was unique to the studios, but now he suspected that it was true everywhere: no set hours for meals, 'round-the-clock noise, and dress odd enough that *everyone* seemed to be in theatrical costume.

Now that he thought about it, he realized that no one in Arenas had ever asked for his identification. And that was the least of it. Tonight he had limped home with torn and smoke-blackened clothing, seared black face and hands, and scorched hair, past hundreds of people. Every moment he had expected to be stopped and questioned. And no one had taken the slightest bit of notice. In this world, his disheveled appearance was still drab enough to excite no attention.

He went back for a second helping of food. As he ate, nodding wearily over his plate, it occurred to him that there was a lesson here that he ought to be applying elsewhere. To be effective in Arenas, he had to operate differently. Studio-style. *Nell Cotter* style.

Even at GOMS HQ?

Hell, why not? He could not see that he had anything to lose.

He had been told to return to the GOMS Administrative Center at nine in the morning. He slept until ten, then visited the studio's costume department. The uniform he picked out was impressive in its suggestive but nonspecific authority. He added a short cloak and a stiff bell-shaped cap with a white peak, studied himself in the mirror, and cringed.

It was the hat that did it. He looked like a military refugee from an overblown operatic production.

He set off through the drizzly and near-deserted morning streets of Arenas and found that the few people whom he did pass took no notice of him. They looked blanched and weary in the pale light. Everyone was still recovering from the opening night of the Midsummer Festival.

The guards at the GOMS Admin Center were in no better shape. They nodded as Jon marched past them with a quiet "Good morning." He reached the top floor and the office of the undersecretary and walked in without knocking.

"I have an appointment. Is Posada here?" No title.

"Is he expecting you?" The receptionist eyed the uniform uncertainly.

"Yes." No explanation. Jon walked on past her toward the frosted glass door with the inset of ruby letters: MANUEL POSADA.

"Your name?" asked the receptionist as he was opening the door.

"Perry." He spoke haughtily over his shoulder as he went through. "You'll find me on the appointments list."

The inner office was huge, skylighted, and filled with spiky potted plants. They formed an aisle that led to a conference table, beyond which was a monstrous desk of southern redwood. Behind the desk, and dwarfed by it, a short, black-haired man sat staring at a terminal and muttering under his breath. It was at least fifteen seconds before he swiveled the chair and scanned Jon from head to foot.

"Yes?" The voice was unexpectedly deep and forceful.

Jon looked at the wizened prune face and the cold, dark eyes and knew that the run was over. He was a junior research specialist in the office of an undersecretary. He removed his ridiculous hat and slipped off the cloak. "I'm

Jon Perry. I was flown here from PacAnt Base Fourteen to see you."

"Were you now? And do you usually dress like the head pimp of the Ruritanian Navy?"

"No. Just to get in here."

"Which you did. Guards, they're a damned waste of money. They don't do shit. You could have wandered in and shot me." Posada did not seem concerned. He nodded Jon to a chair and stood up. "Sit down. You were supposed to be here five days ago."

"I was, sir. I couldn't get onto your schedule."

"You're on it now. For ten minutes. Did anyone in PacAnt tell you why you're here?"

"No, sir. They said they couldn't."

"Craven bastards. *Didn't want to* sounds more like it. Let's get the bad news out of the way." Posada was facing away from Jon, pulling dead yellow leaves off the base of a spiny bush. "You don't have a research project anymore, Perry. Five days ago the funding for your PacAnt Fourteen submersible activities was zeroed out."

He swung around. "I didn't initiate the action. It came from way up, above secretary level. I tell you that not because I'm passing the buck, but so you'll know it's a waste of time arguing the decision with me. But I'll answer questions."

Questions. Jon had no questions, only shock and a bitter, deep anger. Zeroed out. Submersible activities canceled. The hydrothermal-vent program that had been his passion since he finished formal training was gone, cut off by the stroke of a bureaucrat's pen. No wonder he had been treated as a nonentity at GOMS headquarters.

"You're using up your time." The deep voice broke into his trance. "Do you have questions?"

"I thought I was doing a really good job."

"That's not a question. You were, according to all reports." Posada waved to the terminal on his desk.

"First-rate. Read your evaluations if you want to . . . but not on my time."

"Are any other submersible projects being canceled?"

"No."

"So why me and my project?"

For the first time, Posada's face carried a hint of sympathy. "If it makes you feel better, the decision was no criticism of you at all. Your project was a casualty of a dirty shore-politics squeeze. More questions?"

"If my work is canceled, what happens to me?"

"That's what I mean by politics. That's why I had you flown here. You've had the bad news. Now let's talk, and I'll tell you how you might come out of this as well off as before. Better, if you play it right. GOMS HQ has had a request concerning a Europan hydrothermal vent."

"European?" The name summoned images of a blighted northern continent, where filter-masked bounty hunters tracked escaped teratomas across the dark ash.

"*Europan.* The smallest of Jupiter's major satellites."

"I know that."

"Don't act insulted. A lot of PacAnt staff wouldn't know the moon from their own backside unless you put it a thousand meters down in the ocean. So you know that the sea on Europa has submarine hydrothermal vents, just like Earth's?"

"Not like Earth's. A lot lower temperature."

"Right. Any other differences?"

"The Europan smokers are not very interesting, because they're lifeless. Like the whole Europan ocean."

"*Wrong.* Not anymore. Or *maybe* not anymore. Did you ever hear of a Dr. Hilda Brandt?"

"No."

"Nor had I. But she's a big wheel in the Jovian system. Among other things, she's the director of Europan research activities. Six weeks ago she filed a restricted report with GOMS, announcing that life had possibly been discovered around a Europan hydrothermal vent. *Native* life." Posada cocked his dark head. "Do you believe that?"

"I don't see why not." The technical question finally forced Jon's brain to begin working. "It would have a chemical energy base, probably sulfur, like the vents here on Earth. That close to Jupiter, there's plenty of electro-magnetic and tidal energy to stir up the interior. The idea that there *might* be life on Europa has been around for over a century. But what does Brandt mean, *possibly* discovered?"

"They don't possess the sophisticated water-submersibles that we have on Earth, so they've had to work with primitive divers and indirect evidence. Ever hear of Shelley Solbourne?"

"Certainly." Jon wondered what was coming next. He remembered Shelley—only too well. Talented, hard-working, and super-ambitious, she had suffered the mis-fortune of being born beyond the north-equator margin. She had arrived in southern hemisphere civilization as a perennially discontented student, complaining that her birthplace had deprived her of the life to which her talents entitled her. Ten years of job advancement and profes-sional success ought to have worked the chip off her back. They never had. It had been two years since her volcanic outburst at Jon, but he would never forget it.

All he had done was to point out to her that *his* start in life had been no better than hers. Nor had that of millions of other infants, growing up rootless, homeless, and parentless in the immediate postwar period. Southern hemisphere or northern, the number of kids who had had to find their own way to survival and education on a devastated Earth was uncountable. Jon's earliest memories happened to be of the southern hemisphere, which had not suffered "much" in the war (less than half of its population had been annihilated)—but he had no more idea than

Shelley of where he was born, or when. If he had living relatives, he did not know who they were.

He had been trying to give her reassurance, telling her that whatever she felt, there was a group of fellow sufferers who would give her support and sympathy. But she had taken it as an attack.

"What are you telling me? That I have to live like a peasant and put up with shit like this"—she swung her arm around, to show the austere furnishings of PacAnt 14—*forever*? Well, you can do that if you're fuck-face stupid enough. I deserve a better life. If you're ass enough to settle for a fish's existence, piddling around underwater for the next fifty years, then you can have it. You can have my share, too. All of it."

"*Clock's still running, Dr. Perry.*" Posada cut in on Jon's recollections.

"Sorry. Yes, I know Shelley. Very well. She's on PacAnt Nine, up toward the Galapagos Islands."

"*Was*, Dr. Perry. She *was* on PacAnt Nine. She quit a year ago and headed out for the Jovian system. She's the one who came up with evidence of Europan life."

"Then it has to be taken seriously. Shelley Solbourne did the genome mapping for a dozen different hydrothermal life forms. She was one of PacAnt Nine's absolutely top people."

"It *is* taken seriously. That's the reason Dr. Brandt contacted GOMS HQ. She's requesting the use of one of our deep submersibles to explore one particular Europan vent and confirm by direct observation that native life forms are present there."

"The *Spindrift*?" Light was dawning in Jon's head.

"You got it. And there's more. Brandt requested a submersible, and the decision was made—made higher up than me, as I said—to loan her the *Spindrift*. But the Europan science staff has no experience with manned deep-ocean exploration. So Brandt requested a Terran operator, too." Posada sat down opposite Jon, and he was actually smiling. "A first-rate operator, one who knows all about hydrothermal-vent life forms. And one who happens to be available right now."

"Why not Shelley Solbourne? She's already there."

"Not anymore. She did well for herself and came back to Earth a wealthy woman a few months ago. She bought a big villa in Dunedin, and she says she has no interest in leaving Earth again. So she's out. And I'm afraid you're in. Your name has already been mentioned and your credentials approved by Hilda Brandt. See what I mean about dirty political squeeze plays?"

Nell Cotter was still over at Stanley, impossible to reach. Jon desperately wanted her advice. He could have called one of his colleagues back on the PacAnt floating base, but they were as innocent of this sort of thing as he was. They lacked Nell's nerve and shore smarts.

He kept trying. It took over twenty-four hours, and when he finally contacted her, it was early afternoon. She was formally dressed and at some sort of party. He could see bright-clad people in the background and hear dance music.

She listened to his story in silence. At the end, when he said that he rather liked Undersecretary Posada, she shook her head.

"Poison, sweetie, pure poison. Don't believe him for a second when he tells you orders are coming from higher up and he can't do a thing about 'em. Posada *runs* GOMS. He keeps the whole organization, top to bottom, inside his head. Did he know exactly who you were when you walked in unannounced? Thought so. The secretary—the guy above Posada—is just an Inner Circle figurehead, doesn't know oceans from motions." She studied Jon's blistered face. "Mind telling me how you got burned? You must have found a way of celebrating Midsummer Festival that's new to me." And then, when he had given her a terse description of the runaway float, "So *you* were the hero! Everyone in Arenas went mad trying to find you—'specially our people. In video, you just can't do Hamlet without the prince. Don't worry, I won't tell. And anyway, it's yesterday's news."

"But what should I do—about Posada's proposition?"

"My dear, that isn't a *proposition*. It's rape. You do what anyone does when being raped. You relax—just long enough for him to think he has you. Then you kick his balls off. Anyway, you really want to go. I can tell you do by the look on your face. You *want* to wander around that damned Europan ocean. So what do you have to lose? You should go back right now and tell Posada you'll take the job."

"And how do I kick his balls off? He wants me to leave Earth and head for Ganymede in just three days."

"We'll work on that when I get back. I'll be in Arenas tomorrow morning. But I have to run now. You go tell Posada the good news."

Nell cut the connection and walked thoughtfully back to her table. Glyn Sefaris had arrived in her absence, barely too late for the reception. He had taken the place next to hers.

"Trouble?" He was snub-nosed and boyish, with a close-cut cap of hair and a puckish face and manner. You had to look closely to see the fine wrinkles on the apple cheeks.

"Not for me." She smiled at him in a superior way. "What would you say if I told you that I know who stopped the rogue float the night before last?"

"I'd say, 'Well, fuck it, you're a day too late. No news value now.' *Do* you know?"

"I do. It was Jon Perry. You worked with his footage on

the underwater-vent sequence." She was sipping dark beer, watching him closely. "Remember?"

"I do indeed. Enjoyed his shots. Pretty boy. Wouldn't mind a little of that myself."

"How did his show go?"

"*Your* show, dearie. Extremely well. Of course, I had to work it over a bit. Cut out a lot of the talky crap about chemosynthesis and photosynthesis, splice in some older material showing horrible-looking wriggly worms, add shots of the pressure gauges running up past maximum. Nice drama. Lucky touch, running into that undersea eruption."

"If you want to call it luck."

"I do. In fact, from a dramatic point of view, there was only one thing wrong with it." He was smiling seraphically. "If only the *Spindrift*'s hull had collapsed under the force of the pressure wave and the video recording had had to be recovered from the bottom of the sea . . ."

"Get screwed, Glyn."

"I should be so lucky."

"But the show's ratings were good?"

"Better than good." He glanced at her warily. "All right, Nell. What's the pitch?"

"How would you like to send your highest-rating star reporter on another assignment?"

"News value?"

"I'd bet on it. But don't ask me what it is, because I don't know yet. I'd have to be away for a while, and it would cost."

"Numbers, dearie. I'm not Croesus. I need numbers. How long, and why would it cost?"

"Weeks at least, probably more. I'd be going all the way out to the Jovian system. To Ganymede and Europa, maybe other places." She held up her hand. "I know. But don't cancel the play before you see the script. Let me talk for a minute."

She talked for much longer than that, while Glyn Sefaris maintained a surprising silence. When she finished, he held that silence for another thirty seconds, pursing his lips and drumming his fingers on the table.

"Jon Perry again," he said at last. "Let's get one detail out of the way. Are you screwing him?"

"No."

"Not yet, you mean. Better not wait too long—others are standing in line."

"I have no intention of seducing Jon Perry, or of being seduced by him." (Below table level, Nell crossed her fingers.)

"But you're certainly *interested* in him."

"Glyn, you don't understand. Perry is a man whom things happen to, and he comes through them without blinking. Back in PacAnt, he's called the Ice Man. I didn't understand why until we hit the seaquake. Then he wasn't scared—he *enjoyed* it. And look at what happened in the Arenas festival. He saw what was happening to that float when no one else did, saved it, and walked away as calm as you please. You admit that he looks good, and I think he has news value. Can't you see this making an exciting show, wandering the wilds of the Jupiter system?"

"Don't press too hard, darling. It puts horrid frown lines on that lovely face."

"But what do you *say*?"

"I say you're a first-rate reporter. You're pushy when you're after a story, but not so pushy that you turn people off. And you have one great gift that can't be taught and that you did nothing to earn—you have a nose for *action*. You're a person that things 'happen to,' just like Perry."

"So you agree I should—"

"*But*"—he held up his hand to cut her off in mid-sentence—"you have one weakness. You like to tuck poor helpless males under your mother wing and protect them."

"Jon Perry is as far from being a poor helpless male as you can get."

"That's what you say. Every time. Remember Roballo?"

"The only thing I did with Pablo Roballo—"

"The only thing you *didn't* do with him—but let's not get into sordid detail. Just don't fall like that again. It's not good for you. If you go with Perry, watch those wild, runaway hormones. When will you leave?"

Nell, her mouth already open to continue the argument, changed direction. "You mean you *approve*?"

"When could I ever deny you anything? I said, when will you leave?"

"In three days."

"Then I'd better start the paperwork now." He stood up, glancing around the dining room. The place was empty except for a few other couples, deep in their own business discussions.

"By the way." Sefaris turned back to Nell. "One other thing. Remember when you came here after you covered the Inner Circle's dinner for Cyrus Mobarak, and you asked me to put somebody onto finding out about a big new project that he'd mentioned? Well, it took a little while, but I got feedback this afternoon. It's real, and it might have big story potential. It's for huge fusion installations—no surprise there. But if he gets approval, they won't be for use on Earth. They'll be placed out on Europa. How about that?"

Glyn Sefaris savored the look on Nell's face for a second before he left the dining room. It wasn't easy to surprise her. He knew she wanted to ask him questions, but he had just told her all he knew about the new Mobarak project. If she wanted more, she would have to dig it out for herself.

There was just one thing he had not told Nell, and he was not sure that he was going to, at least not until she was well on the way to the Jovian system. Earlier in the day he had read an incoming news clip from Arenas. The travel recorder from the runaway carousel float at the Midsummer Festival had been examined by security police, and its accuracy was now being questioned.

The recorder showed that the vehicle had reached a speed of more than fifty miles an hour during its wild downhill rush.

Faster than a world-class sprinter. Far faster, according to Glyn Sefaris's research service, than any human could ever run, under any conditions.

7

Let's Make a World

It was the saddest job imaginable, like abandoning your half-grown children. Camille sat alone at the terminal in a trance state, closing files, shutting down experiments, putting programs in mothballs. In another hour she would be finished; nothing at DOS Center would remain of her and her work.

So good-bye, NGC 3344. Her spectroscopic probing of low cross-section helium fusion at the center of that perfect spiral galaxy had to end. Good-bye, SGC 11324. She would have no more observations of that dark mystery three billion light-years from Sol.

And good-bye now to her special babies: galaxies so far away that even DOS could not resolve their centers to individual stars.

Camille erased the program sequences for four of them. At the fifth, she paused. The observational program for this experiment in the far infrared had only just begun. She was using multimillimeter wavelengths to study fusion processes of the heavier elements as they built their way from carbon to iron. The early results from this galaxy, seven billion light-years out, were already showing intriguing anomalies. She had a thin scatter of data points far from what theory predicted.

Did she *have* to erase this experiment? In principle, she did. Those were her instructions. But suppose she just dropped it into background mode on the DOS sequencing algorithm? Then her observations would be made only in dead time, when no other observer was asking for use of the telescope array. No one would miss it, or probably even notice.

It was a dreadful way to perform an experiment, with no guarantee that results would ever be obtained. But it was the way that she and David had been forced to operate during the whole period while DOS was being checked out. She had learned how to deal with data gaps and incomplete recording sequences.

And suppose that someone found out what she had done? Well, she would be banned from future use of DOS—and no worse off than she was now.

Camille placed her experiment at the bottom of the DOS priority list and gave it an innocuous name, one that a casual reader would assume was part of the telescope array's own diagnostic routines. She set up an off-site tap with her own ID so that she could query the relevant DOS data bank remotely. Then she signed off the system, feeling like a criminal.

But an *unrepentant* one.

She left the DOS control chamber and headed back to the living quarters. David had to be told what she had done, and he should have a chance to do the same thing for one of his own pets. The canceling of the DOS deep probes had produced at least one beneficial side effect; she and David had nothing left to fight over. They were being extra-nice to each other. Camille had, with enormous self-control, managed to avoid further prying into his trip to Earth.

"Want to know what a hardened criminal looks like?"

she started to say to his broad back as she floated into the chamber.

She cut herself off just before she reached the incriminating word. David Lammerman was not alone. She could see a pair of feet sticking out from beyond the little table.

The newcomer's face had been shielded from view by the bank of supply cupboards. As she moved past David, Camille saw a jutting nose, prominent brow ridges, and a thick shock of grey hair. She recognized that strong profile at once. Anyone who worked in fusion, even if it was in abstract science rather than commerce, knew him from a hundred cartoons.

She stared at Cyrus Mobarak too hard to be polite, while he casually turned and smiled. The pale, vacant eyes warmed and lit his whole face. He held out a manicured hand.

"Dr. Camille Hamilton. It is a pleasure to meet you. I know your work, of course."

Which was a mystery as big as the Sun King's presence at DOS Center. Camille had no false modesty about her own worth and competence. At what she did, she was the best. But *what* she did was abstruse and little-known theory, far from the sort of thing that Cyrus Mobarak cared about; none of her own delusions of grandeur could convince her that, like him, she was a household name around the system.

She turned to David and saw on his face the same awkward expression that it had worn when he had been summoned for the meeting on Earth. He was twisting his thick fingers around each other. His shoulders were stiff, his lips were tight, and he showed no sign of wanting to introduce the Sun King to her.

Camille grasped Mobarak's outstretched hand instinctively and received a businesslike handshake in return. His hand was small, dry, and unusually warm. Or was her own unnaturally cold after that long session of sitting at the DOS computer?

"What in the world are you doing on DOS Center?"

It was hardly a diplomatic greeting, but Mobarak took it in stride.

"I am on my way from Earth to the Jupiter system. I very much want to talk to you, Dr. Hamilton, but would you excuse me for just a couple of minutes first? I need to send a message over the communications net."

He eased past her and left the room before she could respond. She turned to David feeling something between confusion and accusation.

"That's ridiculous. DOS Center isn't on a reasonable flight path from Earth to the Jovian system, not for another six months. How do you know Mobarak, and why did you bring him here? And why did he walk out the moment he met me?" Questions spilled out of Camille before David could even try to answer. "He's the one who made you go to Earth, isn't he, the one who told you we were going to be dumped out of the DOS program? Why did he do that . . . and what have you been telling him about me?"

With Mobarak out of the room, the tense, constipated expression on David's face eased a little.

"Nothing he couldn't have told me. He seemed to know all about Camille Hamilton before I ever arrived on Earth."

"How?"

"Don't know. Maybe . . . maybe from that man who was here before me." David didn't want to mention the name, had never mentioned the name. "Didn't he go to work on Earth?"

"My God. Tim Kaiser. He did. He went to Earth to work on fusion projects." Camille had a new worry. If Mobarak's ideas about her had come from poor lovelorn and jealous Tim, convinced of Camille's casual carnality . . .

"But how do *you* know Mobarak? You never met Tim Kaiser."

"True." David didn't just look uncomfortable now, he looked *ill*—and he was as physically tough as Camille. She had never seen him sick for a moment.

"I don't know Tim Kaiser." The words were being pulled out of him. "I don't want to. You understand that. But I do know Cyrus Mobarak." The twisted smile was out of place on his plump, good-natured face. "You might say that I have always known Cyrus Mobarak. Or maybe you'd say that I've never known him."

The stiffness left David's shoulders, and he seemed to shrink into his seat with a great exploding sigh of escaping breath. "He's my *father*, Camille. My real, biological, goddamned father."

She stared at him in disbelief. She realized that other people had known relatives, even if she didn't. But *Mobarak* as David's father . . .

"*You never told me that.*"

"Of course I didn't. I didn't want you to know . . . didn't want anyone to know."

"But David *Lammerman* . . ."

"Lammerman was my mother's name. She and Mobarak lived together—for just six months, after the war—when he first arrived on Earth from the Belt."

"And he *disowned* you?"

"No. She disowned *him*. She didn't want me to mention his name. Ever. I didn't. But she mentioned it often enough. She told me that he was a horrible man, nothing like the pleasant person that he pretended to be. I believed her—I was only a kid. I can see now how irrational and bitter she was, but I didn't know it *then*.

"She died when I was seventeen, and she left me broke. But I wouldn't ask *him* for anything, not to save my life.

He came to see me a month after she died. He was too much for me to handle. You know, I couldn't even get up the nerve to ask him to *leave*, and I really wanted to. He told me that there was a bank account to pay for my education, whether I liked it or not. He would not try to force other money onto me or interfere with my life in any way, and he kept his word until last month, when he called out of the blue and asked me to come to Earth. He paid for my trip, and he told me the news, that our work on DOS was going to be canceled, that we'd have to get out of here."

David's burst of words ended. Camille nodded. It made sense, in an oddly distorted way. The rejected—or rejecting—son, in the presence of the larger-than-life father. Cyrus Mobarak was still too much for David to handle.

And yet it made no sense at all. What else had David kept from her?

"David, I don't understand. Why would Cyrus Mobarak summon you all the way to Earth just to tell you what we would hear anyway in a few weeks? There's *no way* they could keep the cancellation of the DOS deep-probe program a secret. A hundred other experimenters are affected as well as ourselves. The whole DOS scientist community was buzzing with the news less than a week after you got back here."

He shrugged but said nothing. Recounting his relationship to Cyrus Mobarak had apparently drained him. Camille did not push further. Instead, she returned to her worries about Cyrus Mobarak's reason for being here, and David's miserable condition. If Mobarak were going to try to push David around, he'd have to take Camille Hamilton on first. And she was getting madder and madder. The pair of them sat for five minutes in uncomfortable silence until Mobarak returned.

"Well, Dr. Hamilton?" He was cheerfully unaware of

the atmosphere in the room, or pretended to be. "What do you think of my proposal?"

Camille frowned at him in perplexity. He picked up on it in a fraction of a second, flashing a glance at Lammerman.

David shook his head but did not speak.

"No? Then I suppose I'd better have a try." Mobarak came back to the table, settled opposite Camille, and steepled his fingertips. She again noticed his tiny, neat hands—totally different from David's great paws. David's height and massive build must have come from his mother's side.

"I'd heard a lot about you from Tim Kaiser," Mobarak went on. "You might not like some of it too well. Kaiser tells me that you're donkey-headed and determined, so once you get your teeth into a problem, you never give up."

"You don't solve a difficult scientific problem if you give up easily, Mr. Mobarak." *And when you grow up grubby and penniless on Mars, you get nothing—not even your next meal—if you give up easily.* Camille had acquired her education as she had her dinners: the hard way. Persistence was nothing more than a childhood survival trait carried on into adult life. But she was damned if she'd weep on Mobarak's shoulder to tell him that things hadn't always been easy.

"But Tim says that although you're stubborn," Mobarak continued, "you're sometimes impulsive, too. Even when you're wrong, it's a waste of time trying to push you around. Don't worry, I won't try it—people say the same thing about me. But Tim also insists that you're the best damned theorist in fusion processes that he's ever met. He says that you seem to know what's going on in fusion stability, even in complicated situations, without having to think about it. When the computer models give answers that you don't like, you look for errors in the programs."

"No." Camille could handle this at least without starting a fight. "He's wrong. I calculate *everything*, and I don't trust intuition. It's just that I've found some geometric shortcuts, ways to visualize complex interactions for quick results. Like a fusion version of Feynman diagrams."

"Even better." Mobarak smiled with what appeared to be genuine delight. "I'm just an experimenter, so I've learned to mistrust theorist intuition, too. It's usually no better than an extrapolation of solved cases."

Camille was beginning to understand why they called him the Sun King. She had assumed that it was for his development of the Mobies and his mastery of practical commercial fusion. But you could make just as good a case for the name based on his warmth and personal charm. The vacant eyes were not at all empty now, and she could feel his interest in her pouring across the table. It was impossible to hold her anger against him.

Poor David! How could a youngster have possibly handled that force?

"Now," Mobarak was continuing, "I've been saying all these personal things about you. But that's not why I'm here. May I take a few more minutes of your time and explain the reason? You see, I have a problem. I'm hoping to start work soon on the biggest project of my career, and I need help. You'll see why when I tell you what I want to do. And if what I say next sounds grandiose, it's because it *feels* grandiose—even to me.

"I want to add something major to the solar system. I want, in fact, to give humanity a whole new habitable planet." He took a split second to study her reaction and then swept on. "Europa. You probably know at least as much about Europa as I do, but I'd like to offer my own summary. I'll keep it short. Please interrupt me if you disagree with anything I say."

Camille noticed that despite his polite words, he began at once, without waiting for permission. She knew a good deal about Europa, so she had a chance to evaluate Mobarak's technique. He used a simple, down-to-earth style, talking neither up nor down to his listener but watching her face intently for signs of boredom or confusion. The description that he offered was spare and logical, with a manageable minimum of numbers. And he seemed to have his facts right.

Europa: second closest of Jupiter's four Galileian satellites, orbiting less than seven hundred thousand kilometers out. Sandblasted on its surface by an even more intense rain of high-energy particles than struck Ganymede, Europa shared with Earth, and with Earth alone in the solar system, one unusual feature: a water ocean. In Europa's case, the ocean lay beneath kilometers of ice.

The ice on Europa was a protective blanket, varying in thickness but continuous over the surface except at one point: the side perpetually facing away from Jupiter. At this Jovian antipode, the small landmass of Mount Ararat jutted through, just far enough to provide a space landing site and a base of surface operations.

Europa's weak surface gravity permitted the rise of Mount Ararat all the way from an ocean bed that averaged fifty kilometers deep and, in places, plunged to over a hundred. Small on a planetary scale, Europa nevertheless had as large a body of liquid water as any in the solar system; and unlike Earth's oceans, it was *fresh* water. The leeching of minerals from land surfaces, always adding salinity and minerals to the waters of Terra, had never taken place on Europa.

Fresh, and cold, and more than a billion cubic kilometers in volume, Europa's ocean was lifeless, and useless, because of the thickness of its icy shield.

"But not necessarily always so." Mobarak was keeping

his promise to be brief. "If the ice were melted away from below until it was just a couple of meters thick, it would still shield Europa's ocean from hard radiation as well as ever. And below a thin ice layer there would be more than enough light to permit plants to grow—the right varieties already exist. So do the nutrient upwellings. It's all a question of energy supply, and detailed heat-balance calculation and control.

"I plan to provide that extra energy. I'm designing a series of fusion reactors bigger than anything we've ever seen before. The ocean of Europa has all the hydrogen for fusion that we could ask for."

"You can get the hydrogen, but you'll never get the permits." Camille had been invited to interrupt, and she decided that it was time to do so. David certainly would not—he was staring at his father with the helpless, hypnotized look of a rabbit facing a python. "The Jovian General Assembly set the Europan ocean aside for deep submarine experiments thirty years ago. If you change the environment, you'll ruin all that scientific work."

"Permits will be a problem, certainly. And we have to keep the scientists happy." Mobarak was nodding agreement, but Camille read in his manner a suggestion that permits would be no problem at all.

The scientists on Europa would somehow prove to be right out of luck. In the General Assembly, the right wheels had already been greased.

"Well, there's a bigger problem than that," she said. "You may have been too busy to see the announcement, but the scientific grapevine has been full of it. Supposedly there's been a discovery of life on Europa—*native* life, down on the seabed. If that's true, we'll see a hold on all developments there for an indefinite period."

But again he was nodding, calm and reasonable. "I heard that, too. If it's true, of course it will make a big difference. But I'd heard that so far it's all based on indirect evidence. We'll have to wait and see. Meanwhile—"

He paused.

"Meanwhile, let me be frank with you. I'm going on the assumption that the benefits of the project to develop Europa will be judged by the Jovian General Assembly to outweigh all possible disadvantages. And that's why I am here. I know you've been wondering, because you can't see DOS Center on any rational Earth-Jupiter flight path.

"And maybe these days I'm not feeling rational. I said I'm designing the fusion plants, and that statement is quite true. But it's also true that I'm running into terrible difficulties of stability, something I've never met on the smaller Mobarak fusion units. These will be Moby monsters. I can't do everything by small experiments and scaling. I need a theoretician to help me. A *top* theoretician.

"I need *you*, Dr. Hamilton. You will be without a job here in a few days, so the timing couldn't be better. There's nothing that would make me happier than for you to come with me to Europa. David, too—that goes without saying—if he'd agree." Mobarak shot an oddly pleading look at Lammerman, and Camille had a sudden insight that the relationship between the two men was nothing like as simple as it seemed. Was she no more than the bait to catch David?

"I'd love to have you," he went on. "Both of you. And think of the *opportunity*, of what you'll be able to tell your children and grandchildren." He smiled, and the old, golden Mobarak was back full force. "How many people in the history of humanity can say they made a whole new world?"

8

The Galileian Suite

The high-acceleration drive had been a direct result of the Great War, a classical spin-off of weapons development. Many scholars argued that if the high-gee drive had been available before the war began, the biggest-ever trauma of the human species might have been avoided.

Their logic was simple and plausible: Prewar travel from Earth to the Outer System had been painfully slow. A trip to the Belt or to Jupiter, even with the best of gravity swing-bys to assist the low-thrust ion engines, had taken years. Tourist travel was quite unthinkable. The worlds of the solar system were far apart physically, and so they had grown far apart culturally and socially.

But postwar travel, even with the high-thrust drive restricted to one gee for reasons of economy, had collapsed the scale of the solar system. With continuous acceleration, travel times grow only as the *square root* of distance. A trip from Earth to the Belt is not much longer than a trip to Mars. Jupiter is a week away, Saturn hardly more, even distant Neptune a fraction over two weeks. A unified system is again possible.

If such unity had been feasible *before* the war, said the students of technology's effects on history . . .

But perhaps they were indulging in no more than wishful thinking. For with travel made easy, *psychological* distance defined the new metric of the solar system. Local surroundings, local calendars, local day length—they all meant far more than absolute location. Easy travel might bridge the physical gap, but local environments guaranteed a steadily increasing social separation. And at the most basic level, the habitable worlds were just too different from each other.

Jon Perry and Nell Cotter had directly experienced the wide gap between worlds—psychological, social, and environmental—while arrowing from Earth to Ganymede in an interplanetary transit vehicle. The ITV was built for efficiency, not for comfort. It had no observation ports. The two passengers had embarked in Earth geosynchronous orbit, where Sol was a fiery white ball. Less than a week later they left the sealed box of the ITV for the surface of Ganymede, to find the sun dwindled to a fifth of its usual diameter, the tiny blazing disk insignificant. In Sol's place, the broad sprawling face of Jupiter, fifteen hundred times as big, hovered motionless above their suited bodies.

Nell had mixed feelings when they disembarked. She had *needed* to get out of the ship, because she had been going crazy, boxed for seven days into a three-meter space with no way of escaping. It was all very well for Glyn Sefaris to make cracks before she left about an "interplanetary love cruise" for her and Jon Perry. A great idea, and Jon had shown signs in the final hectic day on Earth that he was ready for it as soon as they had a moment's spare time. But fat chance! Not with a bored ship's captain, flying a simple ITV trajectory that was hardly more than a straight line joining planetary destination, and hanging around her so close she could count his nose hairs. The ship had no privacy of any kind!

The *Spindrift* had traveled with them. The submersible, which from the inside had seemed so small, now bulked huge. It had preempted most of the usual living space, and Jon's repeated advice to her—"Relax, we'll soon be there"—had made things worse. He was *used* to living in such a squeeze, and the ITV actually had a lot more space inside than any submersible. But Nell needed air, and space, and the breeze on her face.

Which unfortunately she was not going to get, not for quite a while. She stared around at the rugged surface of Ganymede as she was decanted from the ITV, then spoke into her subvocal recorder. *Well, my mistake. I was told "rock and cold and ice," and I said, "Right—just like Antarctica." But my brain betrayed me. This is a lot starker, a lot less benign. No rain or snow to eat away at inclines, no atmosphere to blur and soften edges. I can see ice all right, lots of it. But some of it isn't water-ice. It's frozen carbon dioxide and ammonia, bound to a solid form by cold beyond anything that Antarctica experiences, even in the deepest of bleak July midwinters. I'm feeling peculiar, too. Ready to float up, up, and away. Gravity here must be even less than on the moon.*

And there was other strangeness. Over to the left, gleaming at the foreshortened horizon in the eerie half-twilight, there was a great gash in the surface. It was the scar left by a stony meteorite, hitting Ganymede at close to grazing incidence. Logic told Nell that it had happened long, long ago, maybe a billion years in the past. But the outline of the furrow was so crisp, so sharp, that it looked as though it was new-formed this morning.

And maybe another one just like it could arrive right now.

Nell scanned the sky with her video camera. Another body was visible up there, moving to transit the ruddy face of Jupiter. *Europa, it must be. That's where we're going—or at least Jon is. I still have to find a way to get myself there with him. And it looks* big, *much bigger than I expected. As big as the moon from Earth.*

Europa, like Jupiter, was at half phase. It was hard to believe that the fiery spark of Sol, way off to Nell's left, could throw enough light to illuminate the whole of the planet looming over her head. She zoomed in on the frosty half-moon image of Europa and suddenly noticed the blinking light on the side of her camera. The smart circuits inside it were warning her that something was interfering with their delicate electronics. It took a few moments more for Nell to realize what the interference must be. A hail of invisible but deadly particles was whipping at her and being diverted by her suit, but the camera had no protection. Those high-speed protons were searing its inside circuits, and it had not been designed for use under such conditions.

Nell worried that the camera might be destroyed. Then she had a much worse thought. *The particles are just millimeters away from my skin, held off by the suit's field. But suppose the suit failed? I wouldn't know it, not until I was fried and it was too late to do anything about it.*

The people around her obviously shared none of her concerns. Over the suit's communications unit, itself an oddly modified design to permit signals to enter and leave while keeping out marauding high-energy protons, she could hear the unconcerned banter of the surface crew as they unloaded the *Spindrift* and moved the ITV beneath a protective cowl. They were swapping insults, in no hurry to run below to the safety of Ganymede's interior. Except for the skintight suits and the bizarre surroundings, they could have been a dockside team casually unloading cargo in Arenas.

Jon Perry was not speaking to anyone. Nell knew why. *I have him pegged now. He's the perfect Ice Man only when it's external danger that's involved. When it's internal worries,*

*or dealing with people, he's no calmer than I am. Less calm.
He's worrying about how he'll impress Hilda Brandt.*

"Come on," said a stranger's voice in Nell's ear. The
ITV was safe under cover, and the new arrivals were
finally being addressed directly. Half a dozen Ganymede
surface workers had moved the *Spindrift*, and now they led
Nell and Jon in the same direction. Nell found herself
staring at a great shaft in the surface, a near-vertical tunnel
that had started life as another meteorite-impact crater. It
held a gigantic elevator and formed one of the many entry
points to the endless kilometers of Ganymede's internal
caverns. A car stood waiting at the top, the *Spindrift*
already positioned within it.

Nell followed Jon inside the car and soon heard a thrum
of pulsed magnetic fields. The vehicle slid into downward
motion, slow-moving and in tune with the low accelera-
tions of Ganymede's gravity.

Two workers were traveling down with them; the rest
had stayed behind to tackle another job on the surface.
Nell and Jon followed their guides' example, removing
their surface suits in the elevator as soon as the inflowing
warm air reached its normal interior pressure. No one
spoke. Nell did not feel like using her subvocal recorder,
though she did record pictures of the *Spindrift* and of their
descent. Her camera seemed to have survived the murderous particle flux at the surface. She would know for sure
when she reviewed the images.

They reached destination level and stepped out. And at
last, for the first time in a week, Nell felt comfortable.
Except for the absence of windows and the unnaturally low
gravity, she could have been in the basement level of a
building in Stanley or Dunedin. In her mind she had
continued the barren waste of Ganymede's surface down
into the interior, expecting something bleak, gloomy, and
forbidding. What she saw was a bright-lit room whose
walls flamed with color and life. And there were plants

everywhere, from familiar forms seen blooming anywhere on the streets of Arenas to alien exotics, whose long, arching stems could have developed only on a world where gravity offered no more than a weak restraint to form.

The travelers were expected—or at least Jon was. He was scarcely out of the elevator before a woman was stepping forward to greet him.

"Dr. Jon Perry? Welcome to Ganymede. I am Hilda Brandt."

Nell, ignored, automatically pointed her camera and added her subvocal capsule description. *Dr. Hilda Brandt. Not at all what I was expecting. She's pretty old. Close to seventy, for a guess. Brown hair, bright brown eyes, very dark complexion. Dumpy build, dressed for comfort, not for style. Looks easygoing and—what's the word I want?—motherly. Hard to see her as the top scientist for Europa, or as any sort of scientist at all. But that's just me showing my prejudices. Scientists are supposed to be intense, and serious, and focused. How come they never are?*

Jon had stepped back into the elevator and was showing Hilda Brandt the main features of the newly arrived submersible. His manner remained stiff and formal. Nell, standing apart, studied both of them. There was something odd about the way they were positioned, but it took a few moments before she caught it.

Jon Perry had brought from Earth the superior submarine that Dr. Brandt had requested. The Jovian system had sophisticated submersibles for exploring the atmosphere of Jupiter, but nothing specially designed for water. Hilda Brandt ought to be interested in knowing exactly what the *Spindrift* would do. Yet she was facing *Perry*, and all of her attention seemed to be on him. She didn't even glance at the *Spindrift*. Not once.

And her expression was . . . what?

Nell puzzled over it. *Friendly? That certainly. Possessive? Closer. As though she's ready to eat Jon up. Acquisitive.*

That's better yet, as though she can hardly bear to keep her hands off him. My God, I bet that's it! She wants to grab him. Dirty old woman! But I feel the same way about him myself, and I hope I'll still feel it when I'm her age. (Edit! And back to business!)

Hilda Brandt was shaking her head firmly. Nell forced her attention to what the woman was saying.

"A very delicate environment, perhaps the most delicate of any body in the solar system. Certainly, we want you to explore the Europan seabed. After all, that's why you came out from Earth. But the movements of the submersible must take place under tight control. No random wandering through the Europan ocean." She smiled. Her brown eyes sparkled, and she put her hand on Jon's forearm. "I'm sorry to have to say that, because if you're anything like the scientists who work for me, wandering off the beaten track is the thing you most enjoy. But my job is to protect Europa."

She kept her hand on Jon's arm and began moving away from the *Spindrift*, slowly, yet firmly enough to leave no doubt in anyone's mind that she was not going to spend more time in looking at the submersible. And whatever she was doing to Jon, it was working. Judging by the complacent expression on his face, he was completely sold. On the way down in the elevator, he had not been able to relax, but Nell could tell that he was relaxed now. After less than five minutes' exposure to Hilda Brandt, he was totally at ease with her.

Maybe Dr. Brandt can teach me a trick or two. But hey, how do I finagle my way to Europa? Jon, you thoughtless swine, you didn't even bother to introduce me.

Hilda Brandt had already left the entrance chamber and was leading Jon along a horizontal corridor that seemed to stretch away forever. Nell moved quietly up behind them and poked Jon in the back. He turned, and got the message. He motioned Nell forward to walk by his side.

"Dr. Brandt, this is Nell Cotter. She came with me from Earth. She has accompanied me on my most recent descents in the *Spindrift*."

It was a good way to put it, even if "descents" stretched singular to plural. But Hilda Brandt didn't buy it.

"Accompanied you as a *scientist*?" she said at once. The brown eyes scanned Nell's clothes and figure, and when they reached her face, they seemed more shrewd than kindly. Nell began to revise her ideas about the woman.

"As a . . . recorder," Jon began, and was saved more explanation by another voice from a door on their left.

"Hilda? Got a minute?"

A tall, thin man in his early thirties bobbed out into the corridor. His eyes were as bright as Hilda Brandt's, but he lacked her easy manner. He didn't just *look* at Nell and Jon—he stared at them with open curiosity, then turned expectantly to Brandt. "Dr. Jon Perry," she said at once. "And Nell Cotter."

She had caught and remembered Nell's name on first hearing. Hilda Brandt's sharpness went up another notch in Nell's evaluation.

"They arrived from Earth just a few minutes ago." Brandt turned to Jon and Nell. "Let me introduce Tristan Morgan, of Project *Starseed*."

"And of Ganymede," said Morgan. "Born here, but lived mostly somewhere else. Dr. Brandt and I are old friends and allies. Do you know about *Starseed*?" He had the subject-switching, hyperkinetic manner of someone who would not be able to sit still for more than a couple of minutes.

"Whether they do or not, Tristan," said Hilda Brandt firmly, "you're not going to talk about it now." She turned back to Jon and Nell. "Tristan is ready at all times to tell anyone, willing or otherwise, more than they ever wanted to know about Project *Starseed*."

"The unmanned interstellar probe?" asked Nell. "With

the helium-3/deuterium fusion drive? I can't understand why you don't just use a Moby." She was rewarded with a surprised and appreciative stare from Hilda Brandt. No need to explain that Nell had edited hours of documentary footage about *Starseed*, unwillingly, as one of her first assignments for Glyn Sefaris.

"Don't encourage him." Brandt laughed. "Otherwise we'll never get away. What do you want from me now, Tristan? You asked if I had a minute, and that's about what I do have."

Tristan Morgan gave her a look of wounded innocence. "I was going to do you a big favor. You know that Wilsa Sheer's in the Jovian system? Well, I took her to Hebe Station, then down for a remote cruise through the Jupiter atmosphere. Drove her agent wild when he found out, but she loved it. And she's doing me a favor in return. Tonight at seven-fifty she's giving the system's first performance of her new commissioned work, *The Galileian Suite*—and she's arranged for me to get free tickets. Three of 'em. I'm offering you one!"

Without thinking, Nell had turned on her camera. He was an oddly intense young man, and words came squirting out of Tristan Morgan as though his inside was at ten atmospheres' pressure. Wilsa Sheer? The name was vaguely familiar to Nell, but as just that—a name. She had seen it somewhere on a news clip.

Hilda Brandt was shaking her head. "I'd like to, Tristan, really I would. But I'm on a tight timetable to get back to Europa, and I came here only long enough to meet Dr. Perry"—she smiled at Jon, a repeat of the maternal, possessive smile that Nell had noticed earlier—"and see his famous submersible. And now I have to run."

"Wilsa Sheer," said Jon unexpectedly. "The keyboard player? I've got half a dozen of her recordings, back in my PacAnt collection. She's *really* good, as good as Fechmann. I've watched to see if she ever gives performances on Earth, but I don't think she does. If you won't be able to stay and hear her, Dr. Brandt, you'll be missing a treat."

He spoke to Hilda Brandt, but he was staring at Tristan Morgan in a way that was hard to misinterpret.

"Of course you can come along," said Tristan with hardly a pause. "I've got two spare tickets now. You're right, she's usually in the Belt and she's never been to Earth. In fact, this is her first visit to the Jovian system." His eyes lit with a new thought. "You know, it's funny that you should mention Fechmann, because just the other day I was listening to Wilsa Sheer playing Fechmann's keyboard arrangement of the finale of a Mozart quartet—the K.464. Do you know it?"

"I have Fechmann's own recording of it. A Major, right? The way he handles the polyphony!"

"Exactly! But Wilsa changes the emphasis, and it works even better."

Hilda Brandt caught Nell's eye and smiled indulgently. *Boys will be boys.* "So you were with Jon Perry on his most recent descent." She spoke across the two men, who were far off in their own discussion of pseudo-fugal forms, revealing a side of Jon Perry that Nell had not encountered before. "Wasn't that the one where the submersible encountered an eruption at depth and went beyond its pressure tolerances? It must have been frightening."

"It was to me, but not to Jon. Nothing scares him." It might not be an olive branch that Hilda Brandt was holding out to her, but it was close. And it gave her an opportunity to prove that she knew something—learned for the program, but who was to know that?—about underwater exploration and hydrothermal-vent life forms.

It could be the best chance that she would ever have. Nell moved closer to Hilda Brandt and began to make her pitch.

Jon Perry loved life on the PacAnt floating base, but even he would admit that it had its limitations. The outside environment changed all the time, a constant delight as the huge segmented pontoon moved across Earth's oceans, through sun and rain and flat calms and howling storms. Yet within that varying environment, Jon dealt all the time with the same fixed group of people: PacAnt 14's staff, and now and again his counterparts on some other floating base. For some reason, work in PacAnt seemed to attract few amateur musicians. So although Jon listened to a lot of recorded music, alone, he had few people to talk with about it—and certainly no one as knowledgeable and enthusiastic as Tristan Morgan. He already knew that he would miss Tristan when he went back to Earth.

And Jon had found even less opportunity to hear live music performances. In six years with PacAnt 14, he had been able to go to only half a dozen concerts. Not one of them had been given in anything of the scale of the Grand Concert Hall of Ganymede.

In fact, Jon was not sure that *any* hall on Earth, prewar or postwar, could compete with what he was seeing now.

He stared around at the stragglers of the audience settling into their seats and decided that low gravity provided most of the disconcerting effect. In a field only one-seventh of Earth's, walls could soar to ridiculous heights, while the fluted cross-members in the distant ceiling were to an Earthling's eye of an unnatural delicacy and fragility. The whole chamber had been excavated from Ganymede's interior on a lavish scale; it was three or four hundred feet high and more than that across. The seats were well-separated but built in layered banks so that some of the audience were down beneath Jon's feet. He could see them through the thin web of glassy fibers that supported the tier where he, Tristan Morgan, and Nell Cotter were sitting. It was like occupying a precarious seat in open space, except that any fall here would be slow, controllable, and unlikely to do serious damage.

One thing at least was common to Earth concerts. With

the music scheduled to begin in seconds, there was a last bustle in the audience and a final rash of throat-clearing. Jon glanced again at the program. The concert would begin conventionally enough, with a Bach keyboard work, the Fantasia and Fugue in A Minor. It would follow with Schubert's posthumous Sonata in B-flat, and conclude with *The Galileian Suite*. Wilsa Sheer was living dangerously, inviting comparison of her new composition with two of the great keyboard works of history.

There was no curtain, but the designers of the hall had done something very clever with lights and mirrors. At one moment, the stage seemed bare. The next moment, Wilsa Sheer was sitting at the open piano, her profile to the audience.

She began at once, after only the briefest glance and smile toward her listeners. Jon caught a flash of white teeth in a dark-brown face. Then Wilsa Sheer was bending over the keyboard. The music started, and he immersed himself in it.

She played the Bach with more independence of fingering than he had ever heard before; it was as though each digit formed a separate instrument. Yet every articulate voice fitted the others with musicality and balance. And as the Fantasia and Fugue came to its close, she did something very strange. She went at once, without any break to permit audience applause, into the opening chords of the Schubert. The two works, only a semitone apart in key signature but far apart in almost every other way, should not have fitted. But they did. Polyphonic perfection was succeeded by a dream of melody and daring harmonic progressions, as naturally and inevitably as the change of Earth's seasons.

At the end of the long allegro finale of the Schubert, Jon came out of his daze and looked about.

Did the audience know what it was hearing? There was applause, but it was not overwhelming. He suspected that many there, like the audience at most première performances, had come only for the new work—and not to *hear* it, but only to be seen to be present at an event.

He glanced to his right. His condemnation might apply to most, but not to his neighbor. Tristan Morgan was applauding wildly. He nodded at Jon.

"Great, eh? Isn't she wonderful!"

"Absolutely fabulous." But was Tristan talking about Wilsa Sheer, or her performance? "She's the best I've ever heard."

Morgan grinned at Jon. "Then just you wait. You ain't heard nothin' yet."

On stage, another mysterious transformation was taking place. Wilsa Sheer did not seem to have moved, but the piano had vanished from before her. Its place was taken by a two-keyboard synthesizer, which slowly rose higher above the stage. Soon the audience could see Wilsa Sheer's legs, clad in tight-fitting blue trousers. The synthesizer and performer continued to rise. Finally a third keyboard was revealed, at the level of the performer's feet.

And Jon, along with the rest of the audience, saw Wilsa Sheer's bare brown feet for the first time. He gasped. Her toes ran the whole length of her feet, right to the ankle. Jon watched in fascination as she flexed and spread them wide apart, spanning eleven or twelve inches from toe-tip to toe-tip on each foot.

He turned again to Tristan Morgan. "She's been modified. I didn't know that."

Morgan nodded casually. "Most Belters are. It's a big asset in really low gravity. But that's not important—it's what Wilsa *does* with it that's different. You'll see."

She was turning to face the audience, and spoke to them for the first time. "Ladies and gentlemen. *The Galileian Suite: Io, Europa, Ganymede, and Callisto.*"

Again she began without delay. The music for "Io" was fast, throbbing and energetic, with syncopated concussion in the deep bass and flashes of fire in the treble. The synthesizer had to work overtime in the variety of orchestral colors that it was called on to produce. The way that those sounds could infallibly suggest to a human ear and brain the pulsing, sulfurous Hades of Io was baffling. But it was there, in all its volcanic fury.

"Europa," by contrast, was cool mystery: four atonal floating themes that lazily interwove and finally resolved to a solid harmonic result. "Ganymede" began as a vigorous, extraverted march, which surrendered in its middle section to the noblest of melodies—an anthem for the capital of the Jovian system, Jon decided, if one was ever needed or wanted—before returning to the march, louder, a third higher, and at doubled tempo. "Callisto," the fourth movement, breathed the feeble sighs of some ancient immortal, a Tithonus undying but consumed by his own vast age. Jon could feel in those slow, painful dissonances the eons-old surface of the cracked and cratered outermost moon. The final pianissimo chords faded into each other, like echoes that would go on forever, softer and softer, never quite dying.

When Wilsa Sheer lifted her hands from the keyboards, the applause began slowly, and grew hesitantly. Jon shared the confusion. It was a strange and less-than-satisfying end to the new suite. He realized that after the first few moments he had been oblivious to Wilsa Sheer's modified body. He had seen fingers and toes working, in precise coordination, but the music was all that mattered.

He leaned over to Tristan Morgan and Nell Cotter. "Odd. I'm not sure what to make of it. Nor is the audience."

"And I'm with them," said Nell. "Is it a masterpiece, or what?"

"It is," said Morgan. "But not yet. Wait a few minutes longer."

"But it's over." Except that even as Jon said it, Wilsa

Sheer spoke to interrupt the applause. "And as a concert encore: 'Amalthea.'"

"That's cheating!" whispered Jon. "It's not a Galileian satellite."

"Shhh!" said Tristan Morgan. "Do you think people don't know that, here in the Jovian system?"

Jon settled back, wondering what Wilsa Sheer could possibly offer as music for tiny Amalthea, an irregular lump of rock only a couple of hundred kilometers across, scooting around far inside the orbit of Io. He was surprised when the music began with a brief reprise of themes from the four main movements of *The Galileian Suite*. Was she *inviting* the audience to think of the last movement of Beethoven's Choral Symphony, which started with a similar recapitulation? If so, it was an extremely risky comparison.

And then a very familiar tune entered, in five-four time, and added itself slyly to the "Ganymede" march. Suddenly Jon knew exactly what was going on. The new theme was "Mars," from Gustav Holst's *The Planets*. And "Amalthea" was going to be a *quodlibet*—a musical mixture, taking material from anywhere and everywhere and throwing it all together into the creative melting pot.

The complexity of the music increased. Jon caught other snatches of *The Planets*, a dazzling fragment of the finale of Mozart's *Jupiter* Symphony, a hint of the "Venusberg" music from *Tannhäuser*. The themes melded into a whirligig of sound, a miraculous tangle that seemed impossible to produce and coordinate with twenty, or even thirty, digits. And then everything steadied and settled into a triumphant restatement of the anthem from "Ganymede," moving to an inevitable conclusion while the other themes spun around it in demonic counterpoint.

This time the end came decisively. The audience had no doubt of its arrival, or of their enthusiasm.

As the applause rose in volume, Jon had a sudden

insight. Wilsa Sheer had described "Amalthea" as a concert encore, but *The Galileian Suite* would never be played without it. Her sense of musical form had not led her astray. That "cheating" fifth movement formed the necessary and natural conclusion, and after today, it would be played following "Callisto" without a break.

But now Jon was absolutely sure that most people did not realize what they had just heard. He was quite sure that *he* didn't, that he had missed at least half of the musical allusions. Soon Tristan Morgan leaned over and confirmed it.

"You ought to see the 'Amalthea' score. I have, and I'm still trying to fathom it. The themes aren't just *stated*, the way you hear them. They also appear inverted, and mirrored, and in half-time and double-time, in ways that you'd never know unless you saw them on paper."

Wilsa Sheer had stood up and was moving forward to acknowledge the applause. Jon Perry had his first good look at her. Her music might be titanic, but she was a tiny, full-figured woman, brown-skinned and smiling. Her relief that the suite had been well-received showed on her face, still flushed with exertion. *She* must know that it was wonderful, that it would be played a century from now—but how many masterpieces had been booed on their first performance?

Jon stared at her again. He found himself leaning across to Tristan Morgan, while the volume of the applause soared ever higher. "Is there any chance of going backstage to meet Wilsa Sheer?" He was astonished by the words. He hadn't been intending to say that. "I'd love to congratulate her," he went on. "In person."

Nell Cotter trailed after the other two, feeling totally left out. She *liked* music very well, and she listened to as much of it as she could find time for. But it wasn't as big a deal to her as it obviously was with Jon Perry and Tristan Morgan. And in any case, half of Nell's mind during the concert had still been on Hilda Brandt.

Had Nell sold the research director on the idea that she ought to accompany Jon to Europa, as she had accompanied him all the way to the Jovian system? Nell did not know. Brandt remained quite unreadable. And Glyn Sefaris would have no sympathy if Nell came all this way and then couldn't find the trick to get herself to Europa. Sefaris expected reporters to do whatever they had to do to cover an assignment.

With those thoughts running in her head, Nell hadn't been overwhelmed by *The Galileian Suite* in the way that Jon obviously had been. But Tristan Morgan seemed to find Jon's request to meet the composer the most natural thing in the world. "We can certainly give it a shot," he said. "I have friends who ought to let us backstage, and I want to congratulate Wilsa myself. Let's wait a few minutes, though, until things quiet down."

From Tristan's tone, what he felt for Wilsa Sheer was far more than admiration. Now he was leading the way along a corridor to the right of the concert hall. The audience was dispersing, but it was in no hurry. Tristan was going against the traffic, and it was ten more minutes before he was nodding to a woman in a formal gown, standing at the entrance to the cluster of rooms behind the stage.

"Is Wilsa in her room?"

The woman shook her head. "Hasn't even got there yet. She's still walking around, trying to settle the adrenalin." She glanced at Jon and Nell. "Go on in, Tristan, if all of you are together. I don't think she'll mind."

Nell was last again as they started down another corridor, where she paused to take a video clip of the backstage area. She was well behind Jon and Tristan when they came up to Wilsa Sheer, leaning alone against a broad white column. Nell heard the introduction and Jon's muttered comment about how wonderful the new suite sounded, even on first hearing. But she could not see his face, or the faces of the other two, until she came at last to stand by their side.

She moved next to Tristan Morgan. And stood baffled.

Jon Perry had walked forward until he towered over Wilsa Sheer. They were facing each other squarely, no more than a foot apart. Wilsa had to tilt her head far back to stare into his eyes. Neither said a word, but some current of feeling was flowing between the couple, strong enough to isolate them from Nell and Tristan.

Nell opened her mouth to speak. And closed it in shock. For the two faces wore an identical expression: an expression that Nell Cotter, worldly-wise traveler and seasoned reporter *par excellence*, had never seen before in her whole life.

9

Bat Games

Like Jon Perry, Nell Cotter, Tristan Morgan, and four thousand Ganymede concert-goers, Rustum Battachariya had also attended the system première of *The Galileian Suite*. But no one would ever have located Bat in the audience. The idea of sitting in a concert hall, surrounded by other people, appalled him.

Not, of course, that he was agoraphobic or upset by crowds. Certainly not. He merely preferred his own company to that of anyone else's. Like any rational being.

And so Bat had attended the performance in his own way: through piped-in sound and video signals to Bat Cave, with the kitchen close at hand and plenty of nibbles even closer. He had greatly enjoyed Wilsa Sheer's new composition, far more he was sure than the unfortunates in the concert hall, who were obliged to sit on top of each other and breathe each other's air. And if he had sensed during the hectic gallop of "Amalthea" that there was something in it beyond his grasp, and no one was next to him with whom he could compare notes? Well, that offered its own pleasure, like a cunning cipher that would yield to future attack.

He was in excellent spirits when the concert ended—not for him the crush of people struggling through narrow exits—and he settled down for a session of hard work.

Alone, as anyone would choose to be alone for work. The only question was whether that tired final word should be applied to what, in Bat's mind at least, was going to be undiluted pleasure.

The flight recorder of the *Pelagic* had been found. The expenditures for search and recovery had been blessed, as Bat had known they would be blessed, by Inspector-General Gobel. The only condition was that Yarrow Gobel be informed of the results and permitted to wander periodically through the Great War treasures of Bat Cave.

And now the flight recorder, addressed to Rustum Battachariya and carefully shipped from the central warehouse in the Belt, sat before him. He had already connected it to his computer system. As he queried the recorder, he reviewed mentally the related items. Every piece of data had to be assigned its own credibility quotient, according to the first Battachariyan rule of data analysis: *"There is no such thing as reliable information or data, only different degrees of uncertainty and unreliability."*

The most certain element:

• The Great War ended on July 25, 2067. Even Bat was forced to admit that this was as close to a certainty as life was going to produce.

And then, in no particular order of unreliability, since Bat had not yet attached his own probability factors:

• The *Pelagic* had been destroyed by a Seeker missile. The weapons signature of a Seeker was unambiguous, like nothing else in the armaments of the Great War.

• The Seeker missile was used exclusively by the Belt. There were no records of Seeker-missile capture or use by Inner System forces.

• The *Pelagic* was a Belt ship. There were no records that it had been captured by Inner System forces.

• The *Pelagic* had been destroyed, according to the flight recorder, on July 29, 2067. That was *after* the official cease-fire. Bat had never heard of a later casualty; but there had been other postwar deaths, simply because some weapons could not be recalled after launch. The *Pelagic* was unusual only in that it was destroyed four full days after the war's end.

• According to the flight recorder, the *Pelagic*'s last departure point had been a small and insignificant asteroid known as Mandrake.

• Mandrake had been devastated during the final days of the Great War. Little remained of the one-time settlement there, and none of its data files had survived.

• The flight recorder showed a manifest of nineteen people on board at the ship's departure from Mandrake, and no cargo other than general supplies.

• The flight recorder also indicated that the *Pelagic* had attempted evasive action from the Seeker, but had run out of fuel well before its destruction.

And, finally, Bat had a handful of statements, or conclusions, that in his mind provided at least some element of mystery:

• The *Pelagic*, a Belt ship, had been destroyed by a Seeker missile. This was the point that had originally aroused his interest, and it remained no less of an oddity.

• The records of the Inner System showed no evidence of any Great War attack on Mandrake. Bat admitted that this was weak proof of anything. A smart Inner System destroyer missile, suitably programmed, could have been the attacker, and itself have been destroyed before its final war activities could be reported.

• A few hours before the Seeker attack, the flight recorder showed a decrease of onboard personnel from nineteen to ten people. It also indicated the launch of nine survival pods.

Was that everything? Bat squatted on his mounded

chair, spooned his way through the last of a two-liter container of rum-and-butter ice cream, and frowned over his pittance of information. There was one additional will-o'-the-wisp, an item so vague and subjective that it might never yield to formal analysis. It was no more than this: The world lines of the passengers on the *Pelagic* felt too incomplete. They were mere short segments, blocked off at beginning and end. Bat was unable to learn who the passengers were or what they had been doing *before* they left Mandrake, and the Seeker had annihilated all knowledge of them past the moment of their death.

This was the point where Magrit Knudsen or anyone else on her staff would probably have given up. Bat was just starting. Many of his Great War investigations had begun with much less than this.

The Ceres Museum was the central repository of all wartime Belt data. It should possess a full backup of files from Mandrake, or show where the original Mandrake duplicates were now maintained.

Bat initiated a call sequence to Ceres, then changed his mind. The Ganymede-Ceres communication geometry was bad, and would be bad for the next year because of orbital configuration. He would have to wait almost an hour for a reply. Maybe he could do it locally. Ganymede ought to have at least summary files of the same information.

He set up his linkages. And found, within minutes, that they led nowhere. The Ganymede file showed that all backup data for Mandrake had been stored on Pallas. But the Pallas inventory file revealed in turn that all of those backup records had themselves been purged near the end of the war.

Purged, for undocumented reasons.

Dead end.

Bat grunted. He had reached the point where Magrit *definitely* would have said, "The hell with it," and abandoned the chase. But Bat had a long way to go before he would admit defeat.

He returned to ponder one of his data elements: The *Pelagic* had been out of fuel before the survival pods were launched. The pods would therefore have been ejected ballistically, which in turn meant a low-velocity escape from the ship. A pure ballistic launch, without drive, made sense for other reasons. The Seeker would surely have destroyed any powered craft leaving the *Pelagic*.

But a ballistic launch, with its low relative velocity, had other implications. The nine survival pods at the time of their launch must have shared, to a close approximation, the velocity components of the *Pelagic* itself. And the parent vessel's inertial position and speed had been monitored by the flight recorder until the ship's moment of final destruction.

Suppose that the survival pods had not been destroyed? Then they would have continued from their time of release as free-orbiting bodies, moving under the gravitational influence of the major bodies of the solar system. It would be an elementary but computer-intensive task to propagate the spreading locus of those free-fall trajectories forward through time. At any given moment, the possible positions and velocities of the survival pods would occupy a region of phase space, large in everyday terms, but minute compared with the set of all speeds and positions possible for bodies moving within the solar system.

Bat called up the necessary programs and fed in the initial orbital elements from the flight recorder. He asked for an estimated computation time, and grimaced at the result. He could not expect an answer for hours.

There was one other useful thing to do while he waited. Although the Pallas backup records for events on Mandrake had been purged at the end of the war, the decision to make that purge, and its implementation, would not have been made by machine. It must have involved human action. One or more of those humans might still be alive, and able to tell why a data purge had been ordered.

The big problem was in tracking down the people. Wartime personnel records for the Belt were also stored on Ceres. And for them, no summary file existed on Ganymede. Bat would have to go to the source, which meant that he was back to the inevitable hour-long communication delays between the Belt and the Jovian system. He carefully constructed his inquiry, seeking to make it so self-contained that time would not be wasted with return queries from the Belt's retrieval systems.

It took longer than he expected, but it never occurred to Bat to quit. He was enjoying himself. When he heard the sound of the door of Bat Cave sliding open, his only feeling was one of irritation at an uncalled-for disturbance.

He turned, expecting Magrit Knudsen. For the past eight years she had been the only person to visit him without an appointment.

It was not Magrit. A man stood on the threshold, scanning the room as though he had no idea that he was intruding.

Bat scowled at him. "Although your face is not unfamiliar to me, I must point out that these are private quarters. Your presence is uninvited. I ask you to leave. At once."

Cyrus Mobarak nodded affably. "Since you know me, and I obviously know you, introductions do not seem to be called for."

"They are as uncalled-for as your presence. Leave, if you please. Immediately."

"Suppose that Cyrus Mobarak agrees to go—but Torquemada asks if he may remain."

Bat froze. "You purport to be Torquemada?"

"I *am* Torquemada."

"Prove it."

"I can cite twenty years of Super-Puzzle rivalry between Torquemada and Megachirops."

"Meaningless. Anyone could research the leading problem setters and solvers of the Puzzle Network."

"Then how about this: There are fourteen published solutions of Grew's Labyrinth."

"That is no better. I know them all. So do a score of others."

"And if I could show you a fifteenth form, published nowhere?"

That produced a pause.

"Do so . . . if you can." Bat pushed a pad across to Cyrus Mobarak.

"I can, but not on something so small." Mobarak nodded to the wall-size display screen. "Can that be annotated at full resolution?"

"At any preferred scale."

"Do you have the published solutions of Grew's Labyrinth available in storage?"

Rather than answering, Bat bent over his keyboard. After thirty seconds, the display filled with fourteen distinct curvilinear patterns, each one tangled and reentrant. "The known forms."

"Very good. If I might move them around a little . . ."

Bat held out the keyboard. Mobarak took it and was busy for a minute or so, rearranging the position of each figure on the great screen.

"The fourteen," he said. He raised a bushy eyebrow at Bat, who nodded. "And now . . ."

Mobarak drew in seventeen complexly curved lines, running among and joining the fourteen separate figures. "Behold, a fifteenth."

"Ahhh." Bat stared for only a few seconds before he sighed out a long, admiring breath. "A super labyrinth. It contains as subunits all the known forms. Most satisfying. How did you find it?"

Mobarak laughed. Bat's question was an inside joke of the Super-Puzzle Network, the cliché question that all non-puzzlers asked: "How do you come up with those weird solutions?"

"This time I can actually give you an answer," Mobarak said. "There's an analogous situation in the theory of finite groups—a monster group that contains many smaller ones as subgroups."

"And at a less elevated plane of inquiry, how did you find *me*?"

"With *Megachiroptera* as the formal name of the suborder of great bats, Megachirops is a poor choice of identifier for any bat who really seeks to remain hidden."

"Ah." Bat shrugged. "An admitted folly on my part. Such conceits had their appeal to the mind of a fourteen-year-old, but you are right. I should have changed my code name." He gestured to a chair at the other side of the room. "Although I am honored to meet Torquemada, I must admit that I would have preferred you at a distance, as an esteemed rival on the network."

"I understand." Mobarak sat down far away, respecting Bat's need for personal space. "I came here only because I have a problem. One that I cannot discuss over public channels, and one that I don't know how to solve."

"If it defeats Torquemada, why am I likely to do better?"

"Because you have information that I lack about activities in the Jovian system." Cyrus Mobarak leaned back in his seat. He had difficulty in keeping his manner casual, but he sensed that his usual style of intense personal interaction would be a disaster with Rustum Battachariya. "You and I have never met, but I assume that you have heard of me through standard channels. That is not vanity on my part. I am a public figure."

"I know of you . . . or at least I know such parts of the public figure as you choose to make public." Battachariya was sitting perfectly still, his close-cropped head as black, round, and expressionless as a cannonball.

"Then you will not be surprised to learn that although I have done my best to make friends around the system, I have by my actions also made *enemies*. Not because I sought to, but because my inventions have blighted the hopes and plans of others."

"The universe does not guarantee equality, either in talent or in opportunities. You must have a great deal of experience in dealing with such adversaries. Far more experience than I."

"I do indeed. *If I know who they are*. But in this case, I do not know. I have a secret enemy, someone who lives in the Jovian system. I can detect the effects of that animosity, but I am unable to trace its source. But you, with your access to Jovian records, and your skill as a puzzle-solver . . ."

"Spare my blushes." Bat looked as incapable of facial erythema as an obsidian statue. "I assume that you are willing to provide me with the clues that you mention?"

"That is why I am here. But it will take a little while to tell my story."

"The night is young." Bat rose from his seat and went padding across to the kitchen, a great black-shrouded sack of flesh surmounted by a face that frowned now only with pleasurable anticipation. "I rely on you, as Torquemada, not to waste my time with trifles." He began to empty packets of orange jujubes, peppermint bonbons, and chocolates into a large ceramic bowl. "And for a *satisfactory puzzle*? Why, with adequate nourishment for the brain, no time to the end of the universe can be too much."

10

Outward Bound

Time, thought Nell. Here was the oddest thing about subjective time. When you were running along in the studio-production routine of meetings and splicing and editing, time *shrank*. At the end of the week, you had no idea of where the days had gone. But if you went somewhere new, to a place you had never been before, and worked with a whole different group of people, then— time *stretched*.

Like now. She had been on Ganymede for less than a day. Already it felt like forever.

She stared at the watch handed to her the previous evening, and wondered what time it was. The wristwatch showed four-fifty. But Ganymede, like the rest of the Outer System, had changed after the war to SDT: Standard Decimal Time. She would have to drill that time-keeping method into her head until it seemed natural. A twenty-four-hour Earth day was equal to ten standard decimal hours, each of one hundred decimal minutes, each minute of a hundred decimal seconds. So the decimal second was a little bit shorter than the second that Nell was used to. There were 100,000 decimal seconds in an Earth day, rather than the usual 86,400 seconds.

Fine. She herself had never found anything wrong with the old nondecimal twenty-four-hour/sixty-minute/sixty-second system, although the Ganymedeans mocked it as being as old-fashioned as fathoms, feet, fortnights, and furlongs. But meanwhile, just what the hell *was* the time? Her appointment with Hilda Brandt had been made for eleven—but eleven on *Earth*'s timekeeping system.

Nell did the conversion as she checked her appearance in the mirror. (Simple clothes, no makeup. Just the one plain brooch on her blouse. She should have had the sense to prepare herself this way before the first time she met Brandt.) Four-fifty Ganymede time meant four and a half decimal hours, which was a bit less than half the day of ten decimal hours. So it was still morning, and four-and-a-half tenths—nine-twentieths—of the way through the day. Nine-twentieths of twenty-four. A bit before eleven o'clock in the old Earth measure.

Which meant that she was close to being late. And late was the same in *any* system of measurement.

Nell hurried along the corridor from her sleeping quarters, making slower progress than she desired because she could not find an efficient low-gravity gait. She was off the floor too long between steps, and if she tried to speed up, she simply lifted higher and went slower. The maintenance machines knew. They froze at her approach, although they carried on their work as usual around everyone else. The Ganymedeans whom she passed didn't freeze. They just watched, and grinned at her efforts.

She finally reached the elevator leading toward the surface and jumped aboard, wishing that she felt more like grinning herself.

At the moment, she felt betrayed. Logic told her that the feeling was nonsense. Jon Perry had not *asked* her to come with him to the Jovian system. It had not been his idea at all. She had forced herself on him, explaining that Glyn Sefaris wanted to do a program about the Galileian satellites. It had taken another effort to persuade Jon that since they were both going, it made sense for them to travel on the same transit vehicle. And yesterday she'd had to push him to introduce her to Hilda Brandt.

He had promised her nothing, made no commitment to her. He owed her not one thing, except perhaps to return the trivial favor of her providing him with a place to stay while he was in Arenas.

So just what was upsetting her so much about the obvious way that Jon Perry and Wilsa Sheer had been bowled over by each other? She liked Jon. She admitted that. Liked him a lot. But did she like him *that* much? And in *that* way?

Glyn Sefaris, in his passing reference to Nell's old affair with Pablo Roballo, had been giving her a warning: "You have a job to do. Don't let your personal feelings get in the way of it—the way you did before." Did she need that warning? Nell resented even the suggestion. Her job required that she stay physically close to Jon Perry, but that didn't mean she had to be *emotionally* close. She would find a way to go to Europa with Jon, but that was only to fulfill her assignment. And the need to reach Europa made her imminent meeting with Hilda Brandt more important than any self-indulgent notions of personal rejection.

Nell pushed aside her memory of Jon's quiet confidence in an emergency, of beautiful hands skipping across controls with uncanny speed and accuracy, of eyes that lit up with enthusiasm whenever he talked of the mystery and wonder of the deep ocean. It was the wrong time for *that* sort of thinking. She had reached the Assembly Suite, where she was to meet the Europan research director.

Hilda Brandt had told her to go right along to the end of it, where Brandt would be found tucked away in the private-dining area. Nell glanced at her wristwatch again.

Four fifty-six. Which meant in Earth time that it was eleven—eleven? She struggled to do the conversion in her head, and failed. Damn all decimal times. Why the devil didn't they give her a watch with *both* timekeeping systems on it?

But she knew the answer to that. As long as you were allowed to use the old, you would never change to the new. People were people, here on Ganymede just as much as on Earth. That was why the Ganymedeans themselves had not managed to introduce a time system based on their own day-night cycle of a little more than an Earth week, matching the moon's revolution around Jupiter. Maybe in another generation they would force themselves to do that, too, and throw away all the old watches.

Hilda Brandt was there as promised, sitting staring at a fist-sized woolly pink ball on the table in front of her. Nell had the incongruous thought that the woman was *knitting*, until she saw that the ball was moving.

Brandt looked as motherly and good-natured as ever, her hair drawn back from her temples and her bright brown eyes peering at the round object as it crawled along the tabletop. She glanced up as Nell approached and chuckled at the expression on her face.

"No, Nell Cotter, it's not alive. Not quite. And it's perfectly harmless. This is a form of Von Neumann they use on Callisto for the collection of surface metals. Vanadium, this one is after, and it must be disappointed with the tabletop. I'm being asked to test it on Europa."

"I thought Europa's surface was all water-ice, except for Mount Ararat." Nell was delighted to move the conversation at once to the inner moon. "How can there be metals?"

"Oh, metals don't *stay* on the surface. They gradually sink down into the ice, because Jupiter's field induces eddy currents that keep them warm. In a few million years they finish up on the Europan seabed. But there's a steady resupply from meteorite impact—all sizes from dust specks to big boulders. Anything bigger than gravel sinks and is gone in the first second because of impact heat, so this little dear isn't designed to swallow anything more than a couple of millimeters across. But you'd be surprised at how much it can snuffle up over a few months."

"So you'll approve the Von Neumann's use on Europa?"

"Oh, no." Hilda Brandt was firm and matter-of-fact. Nell sensed a lot of strength beneath the easygoing exterior. "As I said, it's not quite alive, but there are live components to it. That makes it too big a risk of contamination. The whole point of Europa is that there must be *no* transfer of living materials. We are keeping it as a perfectly sterile world. A pristine planet." She smiled again. "But this one is awfully nice and cuddly. Here, feel it."

She passed the warm ball across to Nell, who took it gingerly. The woolly tendrils ran across the surface of her hand, pronounced her vanadium-free, and settled quietly into her palm. If Hilda Brandt would not accept the risk of contamination by this little Von Neumann, how must she be feeling about the discovery of *native* life on Europa? But maybe protection of that life was the main reason Brandt was so worried about contamination . . .

Life on Europa. Nell stroked the furry little pink ball—could it make a popular pet back on Earth?—and returned to her own worries. *Never mind life on Europa, what about getting Nell Cotter on Europa?*

"What did you decide, Dr. Brandt?" No point in putting it off.

Hilda Brandt could have had no doubt of what Nell meant, but she stared at her in surprise. "Didn't Dr. Perry tell you? I met with him first thing this morning. The submersible that he brought from Earth cannot be shipped to Europa for another few days, not until changes are made to remove any danger of contamination from it. But a primitive Jovian submersible that we already used for travel on Europa is ready for use again, and it is big enough to hold two people. There is no reason why another person should not go with Dr. Perry on his familiarization visit."

It was going to be yes! Nell felt her anxieties wash away.

But Hilda Brandt was continuing. "However, since a readily available vessel will initially be used, and since no serious exploration can be done with that vessel, your experience on the *Spindrift* is not relevant. Dr. Perry requested that Wilsa Sheer go with him, instead of you, on the first trip to Europa. And since after her concert she now has celebrity status with the General Assembly, in the interests of public relations I did not object. I'm sorry. I can't think why Dr. Perry didn't tell you this before he left."

Don't kill the messenger. It was the oldest rule for dealing with bad news, but the hardest to apply. Nell felt shock and anger. Hilda Brandt was not the cause, but she was *there*. Nell had an urge to pick a fight with the woman.

And Hilda Brandt knew it. Her expression of concern made things worse.

"I'm sorry," she said again. "I thought that you and he would already have discussed all this. Never mind. When the *Spindrift* is shipped to Europa, and the *real* exploration begins—"

Nell wasn't sure of how she was going to reply. Not politely, that was certain. Fortunately she was saved by the unexpected and noisy arrival of Tristan Morgan, clattering into the dining area—unexpected to Nell, for it would be a little while before she realized that people did not "accidentally" drop in on meetings in the private suites of the General Assembly.

Tristan looked as bad as Nell felt. He gave her a

troubled nod. "Hilda—"he began. And then, "Miss Cotter! Do you know what's happened?"

"I do now."

"Did he mention anything about this to you?"

"I haven't even seen him since last night. Did she tell you?"

"No. I thought I'd be seeing her this afternoon, but she just left a message for me to say that she was going. She sounded excited, bubbling over at the idea of visiting another world. She wants to compare it with deep-cruising Jupiter."

Maybe Jon had left a message for Nell. She hadn't thought to look. Maybe there was even another explanation. Maybe she had not simply been dumped as a clinging nuisance in favor of Wilsa Sheer.

Maybe.

She and Tristan stared at each other, recognizing fellow victims, until Hilda Brandt said at last, "They'll be gone for only a couple of days. Then we'll sort this out. Tristan, you're all the time looking for more publicity for *Starseed*. Nell Cotter is a reporter, you know, and I hear she's a first-rate one. If you have the afternoon free—"

"I do *now*."

"—then you ought to show your work to Miss Cotter. I'm sure she has cameras with her."

Always, and everywhere. Nell lifted her work bag and showed them the multiple recorders. The subvocal mike was in position, too, but Nell never advertised that. And she didn't admit the presence of the micro-video concealed in the brooch on her blouse.

Tristan, from the look of him, wanted nothing less than Nell's company. But he had already admitted that his afternoon was free. Finally he nodded at her. "Last night you said that *Starseed* will use a helium-3/deuterium drive rather than a Moby. So you're not starting from scratch. How much do you know?"

Confession time. "I edited a documentary on your project three or four years ago. That—what I remember of it—is all I know."

"Fine. Let's go teach you something substantial." Tristan Morgan sighed, but his old energetic manner was beginning to creep back. "Get your skates on—we'll be moving fast."

Run away, run away. Away from rejection. Nell nodded, while Hilda Brandt looked on benevolently.

"Don't let him rush you," she said to Nell. "He considers that anything he knows must be easy, so he goes twice as fast as he ought to. Next time I see you, I hope you have a useful program in the bag. Be nice to her, Tristan."

She said *bag*, thought Nell as they left. But she was staring at my *brooch*. *I don't think I'd like to get into an argument with Hilda Brandt.*

To run all the way out to the Jovian system, then to return weeks later with nothing more than a documentary about Project *Starseed;* Glyn Sefaris would skin her alive. Worse yet, he would be *amused.* She could hear him now: "How are the mighty fallen!"

Nell couldn't stand that. No matter how much Tristan loved his pet project, there had to be *something* more newsworthy than *Starseed* somewhere in the Jovian system. She would have to keep her eyes open.

The afternoon did not start well. Tristan rushed her over to a lab close to the Ganymede surface, sat her in front of a screen, and played a recording.

She endured it for ten minutes, while dozens of pictures of Saturn, Uranus, Neptune, and Persephone, along with all of their moons, rolled by to the accompaniment of a woefully adenoidal voice-over.

"Tristan, I don't *watch* shows, I *make* shows. What's the point of all this?"

"Sorry. This is designed to point out that more than half of the useful resources of the solar system are beyond the orbit of Jupiter. We're not yet to the good stuff, but it's coming now."

They were beyond the known planets of the solar system, cruising from body to body in the Oort Cloud.

"Courtesy of DOS," said Tristan, overriding the spoken commentary. "A few weeks ago we didn't have anything like these pictures. Comets in the making, though I'm sure we'll get to most of them long before they start to fall into the solar system, and use them for something else. That one's about thirty kilometers across. According to the spectroscope, it's pure volatiles. DOS could spot something on its surface the size of a mouse. Of course, if there *is* life in the Cloud, it would be microscopic. And hidden away inside."

Useless for a program. Nell was adding comments automatically, although she was not recording any video. *The only thing worth having on record is Tristan Morgan's intensity. That would come across—if he had anything worth hearing.*

". . . and when we reach the edge of the Cloud, what then?" The adenoidal voice-over was back. "Well, then we are still less than a quarter of the way to our nearest stellar neighbors. So let us examine the nearer stars . . ."

Nell was reaching the limit of her tolerance. But so, apparently, was Tristan.

"I know, dull stuff." He switched off. "It's all very useful for a hundred years from now, but what you saw at the *beginning* is a lot more important to us. The Outer System, beyond Jupiter. That's where the action's going to be. The old Inner System—Earth, Mars, even the Belt worlds—that's all dead."

Just the words to include in a show that would have its

largest audiences on Earth and Mars. But strange words, too, from a man whose life work was supposedly devoted to the unmanned probes that would explore the stars, the same stars that he had casually dismissed as dull stuff.

"Not everyone on Earth is mindless jelly, Tristan, even if we do have our fair share of deadheads." Nell had to follow her hunch. She quietly turned on her video recorder. "I wanted to ask you, how come you and Hilda Brandt seem to be such good friends?"

"What makes you think we are?" But there was a knowing gleam in his eyes.

"Well, for one thing, you said you were. Last night you said you were friends and allies. And the way you dropped in on her this morning during our meeting."

"Dropped in?" The caution was replaced by indignation. "I never did. You don't 'drop in' on Hilda's private meetings. Not if you want to come away with your head on your shoulders. She made an appointment with me—told me to be there at four-eighty. Come to think of it, I never did find out why. I was too wrapped up with Wilsa's running off to Europa."

But I know, thought Nell. *You were scheduled to arrive just after I did, so Hilda Brandt could send us off to console each other. But I don't know why, either.*

"You did say you were allies, though."

"Yes." Caution and evangelical zeal struggled on Tristan's face. Caution lost—easily. "We *are* allies, though most people wouldn't realize it. You just said that not everybody on Earth is the same. I accept that, and I apologize for the stupid remark. But I'm sure that if you say 'Jovian system' to people back on Earth, you'll find that they think *we're* the same."

"I'm afraid you're right."

"Well, they're *wrong*. There are conservative stick-in-the-mudders here, the same as there are on every planet.

They don't care that someday we'll run out of Jovian-system resources."

"But you're not one of them."

"Of course I'm not." Tristan was full of passionate conviction. "We *have* to keep pushing out, pushing on. We *have* to explore and develop the Outer System, all the way to the Cloud. If we don't, we'll find ourselves sitting on overpopulated worn-out worlds, like Earth was before the war took some of the pressure off you."

It was not the first time that Nell had heard the suggestion that the Great War had been *good* for Earth, because it had wiped out three-quarters of the people and given the planet a breathing space. If you said it fast, "nine billion dead" didn't sound as unthinkable as it was.

"I don't see how that ties you to Hilda Brandt. Isn't she committed to the exact opposite of what you want? To *preventing* the development of Europa?"

"She is. But she's a clever woman. She sees that the best way to make sure that Europa remains unspoiled is to offer *other worlds* for the developers. New worlds, Saturn's moons and beyond. And that puts the two of us on the same side of the argument." He glanced around the room, although there was no way that anyone could possibly have entered. He lowered his voice. "We're both members of Outward Bound!"

How old was he? Thirty-three, maybe. Older than Nell. But she looked into Tristan's bright eyes, bubbling over with naive enthusiasm, and felt the weight of centuries upon her. *I'd hate to have him as my co-conspirator. He speaks as though Outward Bound is a big secret, when it's one of the best-known organizations in the solar system.*

"You've heard of it?" he was asking.

"Many times. There are Bounders, even on Earth."

"But not the way there are here." Tristan hesitated. "Actually, there's a meeting tonight. Hilda Brandt won't be able to make it, but if you'd like to go . . . you

wouldn't be allowed to take those cameras in, of course."
He gestured to her work bag.

"Of course." *Not these cameras. Hasn't he ever heard of micros? Such innocence, he should be a priest. But there's something underneath all this, I swear it, if only I can find a way to dig down far enough. Don't laugh at me yet, Glyn Sefaris.*

"I'd love to attend, Tristan. Just tell me when and where."

In agreeing to go to the Outward Bound meeting, Nell had no particular end in mind. She was simply following the first rule of video reporting: *Go take a look.*

But Tristan was making a big deal of it. He wound them through a maze of darkened and little-used corridors, in which Nell became totally lost, and came at last to a paneled door. He gave her a little lapel pin that identified her as a nonmember but an approved guest, and showed her the special way to attach it. Finally he rapped a syncopated sequence on the panel.

Nell wanted to laugh. Shouldn't there be an eye-level slot that slid to one side and a husky voice growling, "Okay, gimme de passwoid?"

But instead, the door was opened by a fresh-faced twenty-year-old who gave Nell one quick look, then said breathlessly, "Tristan, you're late. D'you have your stuff ready? You're on first. Let's go!"

He whipped Tristan away to the far end of the long hall, leaving Nell to her own devices. So much for maximum security. She was carrying three cameras, two of them designed to elude any normal body scan, but here a search was not even attempted.

Not that she was much inclined to switch on a camera.

Nell inspected the meeting room. There were forty to fifty people present, a few of them sitting in the first two rows of seats, but most still standing in the aisles. All but four of them were males. She edged her way to the periphery of a group of eight containing two of the four women.

"Less than *one half of one percent* of the budget." A gangling beanstalk of a youth who sported an unsuccessful attempt at a beard on the very tip of his chin was speaking in a loud voice. "*That's* the problem. The rest is squandered on social programs—and when did a social program ever *solve* anything?"

"But it's *always* been that way, right through history," said a stocky, fair-haired man on Nell's right. "Research never gets enough funding. It's no different now than it ever was. We have to take that as a fact and find a way to live with it."

"'Those who cannot remember the past are condemned to repeat it,'" said one of the women. "That's what Santayana said, and he was right. People like us have managed to get things done in the past, and always without enough funding."

"That's all very well." The skinny, unkempt man who had spoken first gave her a superior look. "But I can improve on Santayana: 'Those who remember the past *too well* will never learn to do anything new.' *That's* what's wrong with our General Assembly. They say, humans have managed very well without star travel. Why do we need it, they say, when we have problems still to solve right here on Ganymede? They don't realize that star travel is the tool—the *only* tool—that can solve those problems."

He smirked at Nell, inviting her admiration for his insight, while others around the group chimed in with their opinions. She automatically smiled back at him, busy with her own thoughts.

They're all not so much listening as waiting for their turn to speak. And they're all so young—not necessarily in age but in outlook. Even the man at the front there with Tristan, trying to bring the meeting to order. He has to be at least ten years older than I am, but look at him. He's as awkward and self-conscious as an eight-year-old. And nobody's taking any notice of him.

"I don't think we've met."

Nell turned in surprise to find that the lanky, straggle-beard youth had moved to her side and was grinning down at her. It took her a second or so to identify his expression—and to control her own.

She was being *propositioned*, for God's sake. And as ineptly as she had ever seen it done.

"Do you come here often?" His smile was almost condescending.

Never in the mating season. But she didn't have the heart to slaughter the innocent. She gestured at her pin. "No. It's actually my first time. I'm just a visitor."

"Oh . . ." He peered at her lapel with the squinting concentration of the purblind. "Well. Maybe after the meeting is over—"

". . . for the *third time*." The man at the front had finally found out how to work the sound system, and it boomed through the hall loud enough to make other speech impossible. "So if those in the aisles will *please* take their seats. We have a lot of important business tonight."

Saved by the chair. Nell gave the scarecrow a vague noncommittal nod and moved to take the last available seat in a row. As the man on the podium rambled on, she studied the audience. In less than five minutes she had formed her impression of the Ganymedean Outward Bound. These people were a perfect example of what Glyn Sefaris described as "single-issue voters," driven by one overpowering interest.

Except that it would also be a mistake to dismiss this group. Nell took another look around the room. Single-issue advocates they certainly were. But they had youth, they had intelligence, and they had endless focused energy. Single-issue voters, and single-issue workers. "Fanatics" might be a better word for them. How many other cells of Outward Bound were meeting today, all through the solar system? Anyone who *did* remember history would recall that it was people just like this who changed the universe; who started revolutions, bloody or intellectual; who died on the battlegrounds, stormed the Bastille, or turned accepted scientific wisdom on its head.

"*Starseed*." Tristan's voice brought Nell's attention back to the platform. He was standing at the microphone.

"Let's start with the propulsion system. That's where the remaining problems are. First graphic, if you please." He began a whirlwind progress report, flashing up a too-rapid sequence of spacecraft schematics and talking just as fast. If Nell was not lost, it was only because she had seen much of the design when she was editing the documentary. It was a bulb-nosed, plunger-tailed rocket whose midsection was girdled by two clusters of spheres. The only difference she could see from the earlier design was that now the nose of the rocket was a lot bigger. She turned on her hidden camera and added subvocally a simplified commentary.

Those rings of spheres held the fuel. A thin stream of a helium-3/deuterium mixture was fed from them to the cup-shaped tail, where it was fused at stellar temperatures to create three fusion byproducts: charged particles, radiation, and neutrinos. The particles were gripped by a magnetic field and steered by the Lorentz force to emerge from the back of the rocket as a precisely collimated beam. Radiation was reflected from the inner face of the cup with equal efficiency and precision, and exited just as well collimated. The neutrinos alone could not be harnessed by any available technology. Spreading out at light-speed in a ghostly sphere, they provided in front of the rocket the evanescent and only evidence that *Starseed* was approaching.

"We could hold the exhaust beam tight for light-years," Tristan was saying. "We don't do that, because we don't want to fry any interstellar neighbors by accident. Let me wrap this up with a few words about the current schedule. The propulsion system is twenty-eight months from completion. The communication and navigation systems, a year and a half. Propellant will be no problem; we already have ample helium-3 and deuterium in storage. We have enough mirror matter for a dozen missions. So the big item before *Starseed* is finished will be systems integration. And *then* . . ." he paused. ". . . and then we make the *big* decision. Questions?"

"We'll take them in a little while," said the chairman. "Before that, we have some urgent new business. *Cyrus Mobarak.*" There was hissing from the audience. "I don't have to tell you what he means to Outward Bound. We've worried about him for the past two years, but now *we*—in this room—have more direct reason to worry. He's *here*—on Ganymede. And that's bad news. He *says* he's here to push for the big Europan fusion project, but he won't stop at that. He'll try to push the Mobies into every project in the whole Jovian system. You know how much money he has, and how much influence. So this is the word for tonight: *Cyrus Mobarak is the enemy.* We have to work to learn what he is doing and then stop him. Who has suggestions?"

A dozen hands were raised, and a babble of eager voices sounded from the audience. Nell was recording, but she hardly noticed them. Time was still stretching. The rush of new experience, new people, and new environments had continued. It had been enough to throw her off balance and to make her miss the most obvious thing of all about Outward Bound.

This group was smart and energetic—and utterly naive. Nell's very presence proved that. Any rational group would not have allowed her through the door. And it was not simply a naivety that came from lack of experience. Jon Perry—*curse the man, off on Europa without her!*—didn't have much experience of Nell's world, either; but he had a natural sense of balance that would keep him out of the worst kinds of trouble. Not so these people. Here was the cannon fodder, the young men and women who would give their lives for the cause. They would be the ones to storm the fort, to advance through the mine field, to fight and die on the wire.

But revolutions did not succeed without older heads. Where was Franklin, where was Lenin, where was Ho Chi Minh? Where were the masterminds, the *generals* of Outward Bound?

Nell did not know. She did know one thing: Kindly, motherly, *shrewd* Hilda Brandt, Tristan's "ally" and fellow member of Outward Bound, did not belong in this group at all. She would be out of place here, as out of her natural element as Nell Cotter piloting a Europan submersible.

11

The Service of the Sun King

Camille Hamilton was twenty-seven years old, blond, and according to most people, thin enough for elegance and too thin for health. She massed maybe fifty kilos. Rustum Battachariya was thirty-seven, black, and who knew how many times as heavy as Camille. Five? Six? Don't ask Bat; scales were for masochists, grocers, and the outside of fish.

The two had never met. And yet on at least one subject they were in perfect agreement: Work, real work, was best done *alone*.

"*All work is one man's work.*" Camille approved the notion, written two hundred years earlier, as much as she deplored the assumption built into its expression.

She was working now, in a solitude that even Bat would envy. She was on Abacus, a Jovian station that orbited Callisto. The artificial moon of a moon, Abacus was not the *main* computing facility of the Jupiter system. With computers everywhere, a "main computing center" was as meaningless as a human body having a main cell. Abacus could not even prove that it was the most powerful or the largest facility in the net. All of the linked computer elements of Abacus were Von Neumanns, and no one knew how many times they had replicated and added the resultant offspring to the net.

But Abacus was certainly the *least-restricted* facility. It had no protected programs, no passwords, no locked files. Anyone could go there, log on, and stay as long as she liked, with access to vast computing power.

Which meant, thanks to the perversity of human nature, that almost no one did. People needed to feel that their ideas were unique, their data secret and valuable, their programs exclusive.

Upon her arrival on Abacus, Camille had asked for a system status report. How many others were present and running?

Answer: "Seventeen programs are currently running. And no one is present."

So Camille was the only human on the station. That suited her very well. The task that Cyrus Mobarak had handed her was turning into a real brain-buster. He had implied, back on DOS Center, that a problem with the Europan fusion project was the stability of monster Mobies.

It was, but it was not the only or the worst problem. Camille had studied the design of the gigantic new Mobies, and she had been astonished at Mobarak's understanding of fusion processes. He seemed to do with ease what she could do only after enormous, focused effort. That had not discouraged her. She knew from her own work that experience in a field finally provided an ability to survey the landscape as a whole, to map broad outlines, and to know almost viscerally what would work.

"*Knowledge comes, but wisdom lingers.*" Following the general lines of thought suggested by Cyrus Mobarak, she could, with a few weeks of effort, provide the added factors to ensure Moby-monster stability. And at the end of it, she would see those hills and valleys for herself.

But that was turning out to be the beginning of the

story, not the end. When a Moby generated heat, it had to get rid of it. Out in space, no problem. The whole universe was available as a radiation sink. But beneath the Europan ice shield, another way of heat dissipation was needed.

Still no problem. Massive heat exchangers attached to every Moby would do the trick and accomplish the primary goal of warming the waters of Europa and thinning the surface ice layer to a few meters. That was intrinsic to Mobarak's grand design.

But now came the *real* problem. The power level provided by the new Mobies was highly sensitive to the temperature and purity of the coolant passing through their heat exchangers. The coolant temperature depended on the position, efficiency, and currents generated by *other* Mobies scattered through the interior ocean of Europa. There were going to be eight hundred of them. So the power produced by any one Moby depended on the power produced by the others. What Cyrus Mobarak had tossed to Camille as a single, isolated problem of fusion theory turned into a nightmare of eight hundred interlocking problems: nonlinear, time-dependent, and requiring a simultaneous solution of three-dimensional equations of hydrodynamic flow and heat diffusion—a juicy, unique monster of a problem.

It was time to talk to Cyrus Mobarak. Maybe he knew all of this, but if not, he needed to.

Camille opened a line and asked for a connection, hoping that he was still in the Jovian system. That would keep signal times down to a few seconds.

She waited and waited, wondering what was happening. If he were in the Jovian system or out of it, some type of feedback should have been provided minutes ago. When Mobarak's urbane and smiling face appeared at last on the screen, she leaned forward eagerly.

And swore.

"Stuff it! What level are you?"

The blinking red spot in the middle of the forehead said that she was talking to a Fax, an expert system of Mobarak's, designed to answer as he would. She waited impatiently for the facsimile's answer.

"I am Level Three. Do you wish to proceed?"

"For information transmission only. The data and my final question must go to Mobarak himself."

"Noted. Continue."

Camille swallowed her irritation and laid out the problem: how far she had gone, what was still unresolved. She did not bother to mention the value of her accomplishments. They spoke for themselves, and Cyrus Mobarak would recognize them.

"The big question," she concluded, "isn't physics, or governing equations, or computational power. It's *boundary conditions*. I need to know more about the geography of Europa. I need the ocean depth and the seabed temperature at every point, particularly those where the Mobies will be located. I need to know the present thickness of the ice layer. I need to know the water impurities introduced by existing upwellings. And I need the surface albedo at every wavelength. Without those, I can't specify the problem well enough. And those data are not in the files here, nor on Ganymede. How do I get them? That's all."

The Fax nodded politely. "Noted. If you wish, you can of course insist upon waiting for Cyrus Mobarak's personal response. However, I should warn you that his answer may not be provided to you for one day or more. In addition, I contain sufficient detail to know what he will say to you."

Camille hesitated. She could insist on an answer from Mobarak. She could also push for contact with a higher-level Fax, which might itself take a while. Or she could take this Fax's word. And, unlike humans, no Fax exceeded its own level of competence.

"Go on." She waited impatiently for the reply.

"You have the capability needed to obtain answers to your questions. Therefore, you should do so. If necessary, by proceeding to Europa and obtaining data directly."

"But I have no ship. And Europa is a controlled environment!"

"A ship can be made available to you with Cyrus Mobarak's authorization. Cyrus Mobarak cannot, however, guarantee you access to Europa."

"So how do I manage it?"

"I lack that information. Can I be of additional service?"

Camille swore, but only to herself. It was pointless to be rude to a Fax, or to try to argue with it. Even the highest-level Fax could not change its mind without additional data.

"If David Lammerman is still on Ganymede, connect me with him."

There was another delay. It was a task too menial for a Level Three, and Camille suspected that she had been passed on to a less complete simulation.

"David?" The image that finally appeared on the screen in front of her was smiling broadly. "What are *you* grinning at? That is you, isn't it, and not a damned Fax?"

"That's sure not *your* Fax I'm seeing." His smile did not waver. "I can tell it's the real Camille Hamilton, as grouchy as ever. I'm smiling because I'm glad to see you. I guess it's *wrong* to be pleased to see somebody. Where are you, sourpuss?"

Camille knew that David had not been near Mobarak for a while. He was too relaxed. There was no sense of a man looking over his shoulder, no feeling of Don Giovanni waiting for the stony tread of the *Commendatore*.

"Sorry, David. I'm still on Abacus, computing my life away. But I'm going through a frustrating time with you-know-who."

Camille could tell to the split second when her words reached him. His smile vanished and was replaced by uncertainty. "Then I doubt that I'll be able to help you."

"I don't want you to *talk* to him or anything like that. I just want you to listen and give me an opinion. I'm stuck." She began to outline the problem with the Europan Mobies, not waiting for David's approval. "So you see," she concluded, "the Fax says that I can have the use of a ship. But what good is that? It also says it can't get me permission to go to Europa. You know him a lot better than I do. What do you think he expects me to do?"

"I really don't know him, not personally." *And I never will*, said David's bitter expression. "But I've studied him from a distance for a long time. He has some good points, I guess. One of them is deciding how much authority to give people who work for him, and letting them have it. What Mobarak's giving you is actually a vote of confidence. He thinks you can solve your problem without him. So he's letting you. But don't think that means the solution will be *easy*, or even that he knows how he would handle it himself. The only sure thing is that he expects *you* to handle it."

"But I don't know *how*. The information I need isn't available here!"

"I heard you the first time." David's smile was back, but now it was rueful. "That's pure Mobarak. What you need is on Europa. So Cyrus Mobarak expects you to get permission to visit. He expects you to go there. And he expects you to solve your problem—without his help."

David did not say that it would be easy. He did not say that he could do it himself. He suggested only that Camille could do so. It was that expression of confidence, more than anything, that made her feel she had to try. She would be ashamed to go back to David and say not that she had failed, but that she had never made the effort.

She sighed and returned to her terminal. The general

data banks on Abacus provided information on the Jovian system, including the names of the office and the individuals who controlled access to Europa and other worlds. Camille had no experience in such matters, but by the time she had data on the screen she had decided her working procedure.

It was always easier to try for the top, as she had tried for Cyrus Mobarak, and to be bounced as appropriate down to a lower level of authority. But if she *began* at the top and received a refusal, that would be the end. No one lower in the chain would reverse a top-level decision. What she had to do was to begin at the lowest level. If she were told yes, she would take that answer and run with it. If she were told no, she would say that she had other information to offer and ask again at a more senior level in the hierarchy. The whole thing might take days, but she was used to problems that took a long time to solve.

She entered her name, the topic, and her general request into the system and filed them with the Europan entry-control office.

The response was slow. She expected that, particularly if the query were serviced at Europa, which was another four hundred thousand kilometers closer to Jupiter than Ganymede. Any reply had an absolute minimum three-second feedback delay from her present location. She spent the time in rehearsing an opening speech to a none-too-smart first-level Fax.

And suddenly found herself facing a woman whose forehead showed no sign of the blinking red spot of Fax identification. More than that, although the woman was dressed casually in a bulky and faded sweater, pinned to it was the stabilized metallic-hydrogen emblem of the senior Jovian executive service.

"Yes, Dr. Hamilton?" The woman was old, in her sixties at least, and only her enzyme-stabilized brown hair suggested any attempt to deny it. She was peering at

Camille with bright, intensely curious eyes. "I am Hilda Brandt. What can I do for you?"

Camille's cunningly crafted speech, designed to wring instant access to Europa from a low-level Fax, went into oblivion along with the rest of her thoughts. Dr. Hilda Brandt. Not just *a* human—*the* human, the one person who had final say on all travel to the watery world of Europa. But at least her expression was benevolent.

Camille gave up any idea of Machiavellian cunning. She organized her thoughts, crossed her fingers, and launched into an honest and full—but also terse and organized—account of her activities for the past couple of weeks. "So you see," she concluded, "without on-site measurements, at the very least for the actual Moby sites, I'm stuck. I can't possibly produce a reliable solution."

Hilda Brandt had been listening with her head cocked to one side. When Camille finished, she nodded. "You make a very clear case. But you know—or maybe you don't know—I'm the last person to come to with a request like the one you're making. I'm opposed to *any* idea of terraforming Europa. I want it held in its pristine condition."

Which was just what Camille had been fearing. She nodded. It was all over. Down and out in the first minute. "I'm sorry to hear that. If anything could persuade you to change your mind—"

Hilda Brandt was holding up her hand. "My dear child." She used the phrase with the sincerity of literal truth. "You are in full retreat before there has even been a declaration of war. I was going to say, I want Europa to stay just as it is, but that decision is unfortunately not mine. Yesterday the General Assembly on Ganymede passed a resolution *approving* the Mobarak proposal. I will of course fight it—there are at least four more votes before it becomes Jovian law—but in the meantime, I must be a realist. If the Mobarak project is finally approved, I want it performed *right*, without unpleasant technological surprises. And that means that the project analyses must be as thoughtful and complete as possible."

She smiled at Camille, with no trace of animosity. "You will receive permission to travel to Europa. You may observe for as long as you wish from orbit, or land for access to local records at the Mount Ararat base. You may also, if you choose, examine the ice surface beyond Mount Ararat. You will not, of course, be allowed to cruise the interior ocean, but otherwise your visiting permit will be unrestricted. I am sorry that I cannot be there to greet you, but I have continuing business on Ganymede for the next few days, opposing the new resolution. I look forward to meeting you after that."

And she was gone. Camille found herself, mouth open, ready to argue her case with a blank screen.

Instead, she lolled back in her chair. *She had won.* Instantly, and against all her expectations.

Camille wanted to call David back and boast of her triumph, but she didn't have the gall to do that. She would call him back, certainly, for a mutual gloat. But she would tell him the truth: that she had talked with Hilda Brandt; that she was going to Europa; that she had, in fact, achieved just what she set out to do. But that she had absolutely no idea of *why* she had succeeded.

Paradigms for changing times.

New discoveries have always forced changes in perspective, slowly but irreversibly. To the eighteenth century, the System of the World laid down by Isaac Newton was, above all else, calculable, a great machine moving rationally through absolute space and time like an orrery of exquisite clockwork. By the middle of the nineteenth century, the leitmotiv for science had changed. It became the era of expanding worlds and shrinking humanity. Earth had been dethroned as the center of the universe, to become a tiny mote, one among multiple millions, on a stage that constantly expanded from planets to stars to galaxies. At the same time, mankind descended from a being in God's own image to an upstart animal, a bewildered player newly arrived on a scene where other actors had been in position for billions of years. The blow to the species' ego inflicted by evolutionary theory was immense.

The first quarter of the twentieth century learned to accept the diminished view of Earth and of humanity's role, but science soon found forced upon it a new paradigm: the disappearance of the absolute. In place of final knowledge came uncertainty, relativity, undecidability, incomputability.

After a traumatic seventy-five years, scientists at last came to terms with that vanishing concept of complete knowledge . . . and found themselves facing another drastic change in viewpoint. A seed planted before 1900 and dormant for a hundred years began to sprout. Soon after the beginning of the twenty-first century, a principle enunciated by an Italian economist, Vilfredo Pareto, arose to provide the underlying scientific dogma of the new age: "Whenever a number of like items are grouped together, a small percent of them will account for almost all of the group's significance." Pareto's principle, reformulated and strengthened, explained that most of nature worked only to hold the status quo, to inhibit change. Marginal forces—small force differences—controlled the behavior of the universe.

To children of the late twenty-first century, the struggle to develop the mathematical tools appropriate to the new scientific world view was just history. The paradoxes of the calculus of small differences, with their tangled substrate of divergent series and asymptotic expansions, were no different to them than were earlier logical worries over differentials, limits, generalized functions, action at a distance, and renormalization. What remained were the polished tools and the main principle: The natural scientific underpinning of the world is balance. The universe exists only as a delicate matching of immense forces. Change, and life itself, are the result of minuscule imbalances.

Examples could be seen everywhere. The activity of the sun resulted from a never-ending internal battle of gravitation and radiation pressure. Every surface variation, from sunspots to gigantic solar flares, was the manifestation of some brief advantage of one of those forces, evidence that the balance had temporarily broken down. Galactic stability was no more than the delicate matching of rotational kinetic energy and gravitational potential energy, creating and maintaining spiral arms and central hubs and dark-matter halos.

Life itself was not exempt from the principle. It had learned the lesson early. Successful species sat on the narrow line between exact replication, which permitted no adaptation to a changing environment, and too-imperfect replication, which resulted in large error rates and nonviable offspring. Sex was no more than an ingenious attempt to solve the problem, by permitting generational variability within the constraints of the exact duplication of genetic material. Within every cell of every organism the same struggle went on, a fine balance between uncontrolled combustion, which would kill, and the too-slow enzymatic release of energy, which in a competitive world was just as fatal.

The Pareto principle had been in place for a long time. Its viewpoint was not something that twenty-first-century scientists thought about, because it had been built into them, by their teachers, by their reading, by their whole scientific environment. Science was balance. The principles of balance governed everything, from subnuclear processes to galactic evolution.

Camille Hamilton was a scientist. She had the mental equipment to be a scientist, and a first-rate one, in any era where society permitted it (a woman, and attractive: two strikes against her through most of history). But like all save a handful of the very greatest, Camille saw science through the philosophical eyes of her own times.

The curious thing was that although Camille's childhood and adolescence on Mars had been one long struggle against poverty and neglect, she had never tried to view that experience in terms of general principles. Of course the ideas of struggle, balance, and delicate advantage had to apply to *people*. But it did not occur to Camille that there must be other unseen elementals within the solar system, men and women who fought each other to a standstill while they battled constantly for small advantage.

And certainly it never occurred to her that in that war of titans, a slight misalignment or a minor imbalance could accidentally wipe out a being as insignificant as Camille Hamilton with a force as deadly and impersonal as the greatest solar flare.

12

The Word for World is Ocean

Jon Perry and Wilsa Sheer sat side by side, gazed down at the approaching surface, and saw two different worlds.

. . . Europa is small, a minor planet with a diameter less than Earth's moon and a mass only two-thirds as great—

—*but Europa is vast, eighty times as massive as my home-world, Ceres, and with fifteen times the surface area* . . .

. . . Europa's gravitational field is puny, small enough for easy ballistic launch, so small that the same vehicle can be used to travel to the moon and to land upon it—

—*but Europa reaches out and pulls a transit vehicle with a giant's hand, so forcefully that the rockets are already working when landfall is many minutes away. Escape velocity is whole kilometers per second* . . .

. . . Europa's surface offers nothing of value: no metals, no minerals, no fuels—

—*but Europa's surface is a treasure house of the most precious volatile of all: water* . . .

. . . Europa is a drab, lifeless ball, devoid of the breathing cover of atmosphere—frozen, sterile, and inhospitable—

—No way. *Europa is a* womb, *ready and waiting to*

*welcome and nurture life, including millions, or billions, of
humans* . . .

They stared at each other and recognized what should
have been obvious in the first moment of their first
meeting: They came from backgrounds so different that
communication between them was almost a delusion.
They were about the same age, and both were war
orphans, but meeting as a Belter and an Earther they could
find little else in common. It would take weeks, or
months, of talk before they could understand each other's
perspective.

The odd thing to Jon was that they were certainly going
to take those weeks or months.

It worried him. He liked things to be logical—even
emotional things. And nothing resembling logic applied to
his reaction to Wilsa. When he first stood before her,
face-to-face, he had experienced a sensation that was easy
enough to describe: It was like the dreamy glaze of
nitrogen narcosis, with all of that condition's odd certainty
that the world was a safe and wonderful place. What was
not easy—what he could not do at all—was to explain it.

Was it some disguised form of sex, some aberration of
hidden pheromones? He didn't think so. He might be an
innocent in Nell Cotter's worldly eyes—she had as good as
told him that—but he was far from virginal. He'd had
partners enough. He and Shelley Solbourne had even
enjoyed—most of the time—a two-month explosive affair,
until their final argument. Anyway, the PacAnt floating
bases, with their veiled threats of psychological treatment
for anyone who declined to lead an active sex life, tended
to force physical relationships upon even the naturally
celibate.

Which Jon certainly wasn't. He and Nell Cotter had
been on the brink—almost-lovers, lovers in all but
opportunity—when he met Wilsa. His desire for Nell was
still there, as strong as ever. But suddenly, in an abrupt

shift of viewpoint, it had seemed more important that he interact with *Wilsa* than to do anything else. He hardly remembered asking Hilda Brandt if Wilsa could travel to Europa with him.

Had he done so? Or had the suggestion come from elsewhere? It didn't matter. The need to spend time with Wilsa, to understand her, to *learn* her, transcended details. The more he thought about it, the more he was sure that this compulsion had no physical basis. He recognized that Wilsa was good-looking, sexy, and probably highly sensual with the right partner; but that partner was not himself. He felt no stir of sexual attraction to her, and the lack of feeling was obviously mutual.

What the hell was going on?

He stared down. The transit vehicle was following a direct-descent path, unconcerned with Earth obsessions of reentry trajectories and atmospheric braking. They were homing straight in on the Jovian antipodes of Europa. The sun behind them was at the zenith, turning the moon beneath to a glittering network of bright-colored ice plains separated by stellations of rough-edged cracks and nets of long, dark fissures. And such colors! Jon had expected muted tones, like those in the space images he had seen of Europa. The sparkling landscape below must be a short-lived anomaly, a combination of illumination and look angles. Trace elements, tiny refractive spicules of metal suspended within the top few millimeters of ice, were catching the sunlight at just the right inclination.

Mount Ararat was visible directly below. Europa's only land surface consisted of four small connected peaks stretching in a knobby line over a dozen kilometers of surface. Even the highest hill was no more than a rounded nubble in an endless frozen plain. Encroaching ice nipped at the low points of the sawtooth ridge, almost dividing the knolls into separate islands of black rock.

Igneous rocks, said a remote corner of Jon's mind. They

must be. Or could nature find a role for sedimentary processes even on Europa, despite the absence of atmosphere, of rivers, of weathering, of life? Or *was* there life? That was the key question, the whole purpose of his trip. But somehow the frosty visage of the moon below spoke to him of a dead world.

The descending vehicle had located its approach beacon and was following the signal. The sole Europan spaceport sat like a shallow circular cup near the peak of Mount Ararat's principal upthrust, in a crater formed at least in part by meteorite impact. Humans had merely improved on nature, smoothing the bottom to a perfect plane and adding gantries, antennas, hoists and slides. And, of course, the proton shields. Europa was subject to a particle flux even more intense than that at Ganymede.

Jon gave the Europan spaceport its share of attention, but his main focus was still on the surrounding ice plains. He was seeking Blowhole, the access point to the Europan ocean. It should lie twenty kilometers off the rim of Mount Ararat. Blowhole was an artificially created and maintained vertical cylinder of open water through which the *Spindrift* would eventually descend—down, down, down, past a kilometer and a half of encircling ice and on into the stygian unknown, for exploration of the fifty-kilometer-and-more Europan deeps.

He could see no sign of Blowhole. It must be too small to be visible during a descent from space to Mount Ararat. He knew that Blowhole was maintained by a man-made thermal source at the lower ice-water interface, in combination with natural upward convection and the use of repeater pumps. With every upward meter, the warmed waters of Blowhole lost heat to the surrounding ice. The liquid column narrowed until at its top it was only twenty or thirty meters across, just wide enough to admit submersibles and service vehicles.

"Look!" Wilsa's grip on his arm brought Jon out of his

musings. A beam of the purest monochromatic blue had speared out from the center of the spaceport's smooth cup and caught them in its cone of light.

"Final descent pattern," said Jon. Reluctantly he brought his mind away from Blowhole and the Europan interior. "Don't worry, we'll be all right. From this point, the ship will be controlled directly from Mount Ararat."

That earned a flash of dark eyes. He realized belatedly that although space was new to him, Wilsa had probably made a thousand controlled descents.

"I know that! I said to *look*, Jon. At the pattern. Can't you see it?"

And he could, once it was pointed out to him. The sun was right overhead. The descending vehicle was arrowing toward a circular target, with the bright blue of Mount Ararat's upturned control laser as its bull's-eye. Beyond it glistened the refractive ice of Europa, a series of frost-touched rainbow rings. His mind's eye added another component: Farther yet, beyond Europa's horizon but full-lit by the sun, the cloudy globe of Jupiter would be glimmering in colors of ocher and umber and burnt sienna.

That was what *he* saw and imagined. But Wilsa had an open-mouthed, wide-eyed expression on her face—almost a look of terror.

What did *she* see? She had started humming to herself, almost too softly for him to hear.

Wilsa had caught sight of the rounded quadruple peaks of Mount Ararat at the same moment as Jon. She saw not igneous rocks, but the terrifying, upthrust fist of an imprisoned frost-giant, caught at the very instant when his four iron knuckles came smashing through the glassy shield of Niflheim's wall. The moment had frozen in time, but in another second he would escape, straddle the world beneath, steady himself, reach far up into space . . .

The blow of the fist had shattered the world below into concentric circles. Chromatic rings spread across the planet. Those outgoing ripples of color in turn set up musical resonances. A melodic fragment expanded and took shape inside her. She began the conscious, near-sensual process of thematic development.

That she and Jon held widely divergent views of the approaching world of Europa did not worry her, or even arouse much interest. Anyone with a talent for polyphony knew that two themes, totally different in style, mood, and content, could coexist in perfect harmony. She saw, as Jon probably did not, that both of them were right about Europa.

Even the strange bond between the two of them, created at their first meeting, did not worry her. So much of her internal world would not yield to logical analysis. Take the themes that were drifting even now inside her head. They surely would not have appeared without the multihued panorama of Europa, Mount Ararat, and the bright shaft of the landing laser. But how could an impact on one sense stir the creative impulse in another? *The synesthesia of inspiration*: That was something she had never seen explained, scarcely heard discussed. And yet it happened, again and again. Visual inputs could transmute and then emerge from the crucible of the mind as golden music; architecture could give birth to great sonnets; music could inspire immortal words.

Wilsa drifted on toward Europa, her soul singing. The final planet-fall at the Mount Ararat spaceport came as no more than an annoying interruption.

Jon had heard Hilda Brandt talk of an uncontaminated Europa and had wondered how she—or anyone—could hope to keep it that way.

Now he knew. The only access to the untouched interior of the world was through Blowhole, with the surface elsewhere protected by an unbroken breastplate of ice. And to reach Blowhole, any living thing would have to do what he and Wilsa had just done: travel across twenty kilometers of open ice from Mount Ararat, in a temperature so cold that escaping air would freeze and drift down as tiny flakes of oxygen and nitrogen.

But suppose that by some miracle of hardiness, a living organism were to escape the settlement on Mount Ararat, survive the cold, and drift out toward Blowhole? Then it would have to endure an even deadlier attack. The particle flux on Europa's surface was lethal to any unsuited creature. The outside of the suits that Jon and Wilsa were wearing needed no human-designed sterilization program. Nature had provided.

With such safeguards, there was only one threat to the sanctity of Europa's interior ocean: the submersibles that might descend into it. And those were protected by a small but vigilant staff.

In the first two minutes, Jon had recognized the female and two males assigned to receive them at Mount Ararat spaceport and accompany them across the ice to Blowhole. He had not recognized them *individually*, of course, but as a familiar type. They were matter-of-fact, knowledgeable, casual, and impersonal. They were Jon himself, transported across a billion kilometers of space.

Or rather, they were Jon as he had been before his beloved hydrothermal-vent project had been axed. After that, he had been thrown away, first into the political mixer of Arenas, then out across the solar system with Nell Cotter. He was not sure how much of the old Jon still survived.

The staff of Mount Ararat recognized Jon, too. He might be their savior, by confirming the existence of native Europan life forms and protecting the world from a development they did not want. But even if he could not do that, he was someone who shared their language of science and technology.

They did not know at all, though, what to make of Wilsa. Famous she might be throughout the Belt, and now on Ganymede, but her reputation had not carried as far as the Europan scientific community. No one reacted to her name. They registered only her naive comments and questions. Jon was amused to note that after the first few minutes they addressed all their explanations of mechanisms and procedures to him.

"When you're inside, you'll be hermetically sealed off from the exterior." One of the men, his muscles bulging beneath his tight suit in a way that made nonsense of the low-gravity environment, had opened the top of the submersible and was pointing within. "You'll have your own air and food, even your own water supply. It sounds silly, I know, with water all around you, but we don't want any danger of mixing and contamination. If water has a way to get in, pee might find a way out. Oh, and don't forget that the ship doesn't have a particle-flux shield. You mustn't take your suits off until you're at least a few meters under water. At that point, you'll be safe. All right, let's take a look at the controls."

He climbed inside, gesturing to Jon and Wilsa to follow. Wilsa went first, up the three steps that led to the snug elliptical interior. Jon trailed behind to take a last look around. He had stood like this in central Antarctica, back on Earth, and had been overwhelmed by the thought that beneath his feet lay a mile and more of ice. If he walked for a hundred days in any direction, that would still be true. Here he had that same mile of ice beneath his feet— although below it lay not land, but more miles of water; and he could walk not for a hundred days, but *forever*. Except for the insignificant pimple of Mount Ararat, Europa's icy girdle was complete and unbroken.

Jon looked up, searching for Jupiter. Then he realized that he would never see its looming presence here. The king of the Outer System remained forever on the far side of Europa, holding the moon so that Mount Ararat faced always away from the great planet. But even after sunset, and without Jupiter's reflected sunlight, it was not dark. Ganymede and Callisto were visible in the sky to provide a sinister twilight. They showed the long, smoothed ramp leading from the submersible to Blowhole, to open water that sat like a black, staring-eye pupil a hundred meters away.

Jon finally managed to make his legs work, and climbed the steps.

"Of course, you're used to those terrific water submersibles you have back on Earth." The man had waited for Jon before he began his gruff explanation. "I doubt if you've ever seen anything as primitive as the *Danae* here. But everything works. The controls and dials will just be somewhat unfamiliar and take a little getting used to. Sit down, and I'll run you through checkout. We'll go really slow at first. Don't be afraid to tell me if you want anything repeated. Use "Sandstrom" as your info ID— that's me, I'm Buzz Sandstrom—to get you into the system."

Jon nodded and began to move to the pilot's seat. Before he could get there, Wilsa pushed ahead of him and set her hands on the *Danae*'s controls.

"Level-One check," she said. And then her fingers were traveling across the console of keys and switches at a speed that even Jon—PacAnt's fastest, four years in a row—was not sure he could have beaten even on his own familiar equipment. Displays flickered and raced, audio beeped, tiny warning lights flashed on and off.

"Clear on One," said Wilsa in a cheerful, witless voice. "Hold your hats. Beginning Level Two."

The second and more complex phase of the checkout began. And ended even more rapidly.

"Clear on Two." Wilsa turned to beam at Sandstrom. "Ready for operation. I guess we can go anytime."

"*Well*." The man gave Jon and Wilsa a black glare through his suit visor. "Well, I guess you damn well can." He climbed out of the *Danae* submersible without another word or a backward look.

The sealing cover came crashing down like an accusing voice aimed right at Jon. It said, "*You bastard. Why didn't you tell me you brought a hotshot Jovian pilot with you? Then I wouldn't have made an ass of myself.*"

"Wilsa. How the devil were you able to—"

"Sorry." But she didn't look it, not at all. "They said that this submersible was like the ones used to monitor the Von Neumanns down in Jupiter's atmosphere. I didn't realize until I saw the control board that it would be *identical*. I don't think they've changed a switch. This one is direct control, and I piloted using a remote. But direct is easier."

"Well, you didn't have to show off like that. Now Sandstrom thinks I set him up."

"That's right." Wilsa was smiling. "That's what you get for cutting me out of the conversation. I have feelings, too, you know. I don't like it when people talk *around* me, as though I'm some sort of animated pumpkin, just because I'm not a trained scientist. Do you want to take over now?"

"No." Jon wasn't angry. Not quite. "You be my guest. But just remember one thing. This is *real*. If you're stupid enough to smash into a rock face or take us too deep for the hull, you won't find yourself safe on Hebe Station when it's over. You'll be dead. Now go ahead."

Jon had three reasons for saying that. First, Wilsa had shown no inclination to move from the pilot's seat; second, he liked the role of observer of this new world; and third, he wanted to see how well she could *perform*. She had extraordinary physical coordination; he had known that since the first minute of her concert on Ganymede. The dazzling and independent finger speed of two minutes ago had confirmed it.

But checkout was one thing, routine and standardized. Piloting was another. How would Wilsa handle the hundred little decisions that had to be made in submarine cruising? He could take over if she got into trouble, but he was ornery enough to avoid doing that unless he really had to. Let her stew and find out for herself that there was more to piloting than ten-finger—or twenty-digit—exercises.

But before he became too cocky, he needed to confirm a few facts for himself about the *Danae*. This wasn't the *Spindrift*, designed to wander the deepest of Earth's oceans and with a hull strengthened accordingly. The *Spindrift* was rated to stand fifteen hundred Earth atmospheres, more than enough to allow it to plumb Europa's farthermost seabed; but the *Danae*, quickly converted from Jovian atmospheric use, didn't have that strength. The plan, after they returned to the surface, was to modify it to withstand full oceanic pressure, but for the moment its hull was rated at only a meager couple of thousand tons per square meter.

Jon called the Europan depth profiles onto his observer screen. This was a small, light world, lacking Earth's dense metallic core, but if you went deep enough, you would still meet huge pressures. And in Europa's ocean, you *could* go deep—a hundred kilometers and more if the bathymetry charts were accurate. He would visit that abyss eventually and be the first being to explore the deep Europan seabed directly.

Not today, though. He read off the tabulated values. They shouldn't go below fifteen kilometers in the *Danae*. Fifteen was deep enough to reach a couple of the shallow hydrothermal vents but not to visit the one he really cared about; Scaldino was forty-seven kilometers down, where the water pressure was six hundred atmospheres and the seafloor temperature might rise to within a few degrees of blood heat. For Europa, that was a superheated black smoker, the equivalent of Earth's Hotpot.

So today stay above ten kilometers for safety and forget any idea of real work. Hilda Brandt had been right. This could be no more than an exercise in familiarization and sight-seeing.

Jon felt a vibration in his seat, stared out of the curved, transparent screen in front of them, and realized that the sight-seeing had already begun. The *Danae* was being guided steadily forward along the grooved downward ramp that led into Blowhole. Already the observation screen was dipping below surface level. Jon had a last glimpse of Europa's icy plain, with the four rounded hills of Mount Ararat rising gently in the background; then dark water was lapping at the smooth sides. The stars, visible through the transparent roof of the submersible, were the last to go. They became quivering pools of light, slowly fading as the depth increased and then vanishing instantly as the *Danae*'s searchlights went on.

The ship was sinking steadily at five or six meters a second. Jon was convinced of that, even without consulting a readout. This was one of the things that he had wanted to test. Back in PacAnt, he had a reputation for possessing his own private inertial navigation system, an internal sense that told him whether he was rising or falling underwater, and how fast. He scanned the dials to confirm his feeling. Five-point-five meters a second. It was nice to know that his absolute positional sense worked just as well on Europa.

He glanced at Wilsa, gave the control board a more thorough inspection, and relaxed. The *Danae* had its own warning systems to tell if they went too deep, or were heading for a solid shelf of rock or ice. It was at least smart enough to keep them out of life-threatening trouble.

But they weren't going to need those built-in safeguards. Wilsa, annoying as it might be to Jon, was as competent as she was confident. She was making instinctively timed sweeps of the main indicators of the environment, both inside and outside the submersible: power level and power reserve; submersible speed, depth, and pressure; internal and external temperature; water turbidity; air supply rate; and air composition. At the same time she had an eye on the ultrasonics that gave the distance in all directions to the nearest solid objects.

A natural.

"Well? Satisfied?" She wasn't even looking at him, but she was smiling as though she had seen his expression. "In a few more seconds we'll reach the lower limit of Blowhole. We'll be under the ice shield proper."

So she could read his mind. He had been all set to give *her* that same information. But at least she had been forced to read it from the instruments. He had *known* it, from some internal resource.

"What do we do then?" Wilsa went on. She was scowling at the screen, where the forward lights showed a vertical ice face maybe forty meters away.

"Don't ask *me*." Jon leaned back in his seat. He could be awkward, too. "You're the pilot. I'm just the passenger. Take us wherever you like."

He closed his eyes to prove his lack of concern and interest, and knew, without a doubt, that Wilsa was staring across at him now, with raised eyebrows and pursed lips.

Maybe that was the difference between Wilsa and everyone else, man or woman, whom he had ever met. He *knew* her and she *knew* him, at some deep-down level, without a word spoken.

And yet there was no matching *physical* bond . . .

Jon's thoughts switched suddenly and uncomfortably to

Nell. She would be as mad as hell with him for not bringing her. And it would do no good at all to say that he'd been missing her. She wouldn't waste one moment before telling him off the next time they met. "*Actions*," she'd say, "not *words*—that's what makes a video show. You can *stuff* your *explanations*."

Then she'd *really* chew him up and spit him out.

She and he were like a pair of chaotically out-of-synch pistons, working against each other with no coordination, wasting energy, canceling forces, missing each other's cycle.

But here was the mystery, another place where logic could not go: Behind the mental mismatch with Nell Cotter lay some hidden power source, a physical fire that he and Wilsa Sheer, sitting by his side, would never share.

13

Sneak Attack

"I believe that for the first time in our acquaintance, I have caught Rustum Battachariya in an error."

Yarrow Gobel had been standing at the waist-high counter that separated the kitchen from the rest of Bat Cave. Now the inspector-general turned and went wandering off along the length of the room, finally pausing to pick up and marvel at the meter-wide helmet of a combined survival-and-assault suit—one of the Great War's most spectacular failures, a device that had performed neither of its intended functions and had killed almost all of its wearers.

Bat, busy with half a dozen covered pots and pans, confined his response to a noncommittal grunt.

"You have told me several times," went on Gobel, his voice echoing along the great cluttered room, "that there is nothing of old Earth that you would wish to have here on Ganymede. Forests, mountains, lakes, grassy plains, blue sky, green expanses of ocean, birds, butterflies, flowers, mist and rain and snow—you yearn for none of those."

"Quite right." Bat removed the pressure lid of a sauce-pan, frowned down at the contents, tasted them with a ceramic spoon, and replaced the seal. "I have truffles, I have mushrooms. I have garlic and saffron and fennel and capers, native-grown. Earth has nothing to offer me."

Gobel strolled back, to lean again on the counter and watch Bat's cooking rituals. "I am sure that you are sincere in what you say. But still, there is one natural feature of Earth that you would like. One thing that Earth people have, and take for granted, and are even perhaps unaware of, but which you desire." He paused, waiting for Bat's skeptical frown. "You wish that you had, here on Ganymede, the *air pressure* of Earth."

Bat gave a startled glance down at the stove, with its array of closed pans. He nodded. "Say no more. I admit my guilt. It is one of nature's mysteries why humans, who certainly did not *evolve* with a diet of cooked food, should find a water boiling point of one hundred degrees Celsius ideal for the purposes of cuisine. But it is so." He gestured with the spoon at his cooking vessels. "I am glad to see that you, if no one else, understand my predicament. If I cook with open pans, water at Ganymede ambient pressure has its boiling point thirty degrees too low. If I close them and cook under pressure, I cannot taste and stir as often as I should, and continuous tasting is essential in the culinary arts. That and stirring lie at the heart of subtle flavors and textures. The chefs of Earth are uniquely fortunate.

"However, we do what we can." He began to remove lids and hurriedly transfer the contents of the pans to heated serving dishes. "Five more minutes—of concentrated *silent* effort—then I leave it to you to tell me whether or not I have succeeded."

"There has not yet been a failure." Yarrow Gobel took the hint and walked away along the length of Bat Cave.

Bat returned to his labors. Yarrow Gobel did not know it, but tonight's dinner, regardless of the quality of the food, would not be a pleasant occasion.

For Bat was finally ready to admit defeat. Through the inspector-general, he had obtained sufficient funds to identify everyone who had worked on the Pallas data banks and been in Pallas at the end of the war. Many had died in the final battle, and most of the others were dead now—it had happened a quarter of a century ago—but Bat had personally contacted and interviewed every survivor. No one could tell him anything about a purge of data involving the asteroid Mandrake. No one recalled even the name of the converted ore-freighter *Pelagic*.

Bat's other bright idea had also ended in failure. The calculations had taken forever, but he had finally received trajectories for survival pods ballistically launched from the *Pelagic* before the Seeker destroyed it. All of the pods had been headed toward the Inner System, with Mars as the closest world and the logical place for distress-signal detection.

There had certainly been no shortage of distress signals. The war was just over, and vehicles crippled in the final disastrous battles were strewn across space from Earth to the Belt.

And the records of those distress calls and emergency pickups had not been lost. They were kept in the Ceres files. Bat had examined them all, checking ship ID's and pod positions and survivor profiles. He had found nothing unusual, nothing to suggest that one or more of those rescued from space could have been in a pod sent out from the *Pelagic*. He had carried forward the computations and search for a full two months beyond the end of the war, to a time when the limited oxygen, water, and food supplies of any pod would long since have run out. And he had found nothing. The survivor pods, wherever they had gone, could have contained no survivors.

Tonight Yarrow Gobel would be expecting a progress report. He had kept his side of the bargain: support, in return for occasional visits to Bat Cave for dinner and Great War discussions. But there was nothing to report. There had been no progress.

Bat began carrying filled dishes to the waiting table. "Two more minutes."

"What's this?" Gobel was down at the far end of the room, examining a flat box about a foot across. "It looks new."

"It is new, and unexpected. A loan from the Ceres Museum, in appreciation of a little work that I did to trace a missing exhibit. The box contains the control disk for the *Pinwheel*. It is all that was ever found of the forty-vessel Mars fleet that took part in the Battle of Psyche. The package arrived when I was already preparing dinner, so I have had no opportunity to examine it. According to the label, the disk is in excellent condition, still perhaps capable of being read. Take a look . . . if you are interested."

The last phrase was Bat's attempt at irony. The inspector-general was obsessed by every aspect of the Great War, and his interest in the *Pinwheel*'s disk was guaranteed. Bat, arranging dishes on the table, heard the immediate rustle of stiff wrapping, followed by the creak of a lid and a faint snapping sound.

"Bring it with you to the table," he said. "*Quickly*, if you please." There was a rare urgency in his voice. "This sauce is most delicate. Any delay could ruin its bouquet."

There was no reply. No sound of approaching footsteps. Bat, sauce boat in his hands and poised above the dish, gave an annoyed glance down the room. One of the reasons that he could tolerate Yarrow Gobel's visits was that the inspector-general possessed, most unexpectedly, a sensitive palate and an appreciation for fine food.

Gobel stood bending over the open box. His face was not visible, but there was something odd about the man's total stillness. Bat set down the sauce boat, gave the laden table a regretful look, and started toward the other end of the room.

Halfway there, he paused. The association of events was

too clear to ignore. The unexpected package. Its opening by Yarrow Gobel. And now, the silence and frozen posture.

"Inspector?" Bat came no closer, but he moved sideways and crouched so that he could get a look at the downturned face.

Gobel was moving again, letting the open box in his hands fall to the floor. Bat felt a sense of relief that vanished at once when he saw the other man's face. It was blank, utterly lacking in expression.

"Where am I?" The words were puzzled, delivered in the bewildered voice of a child. "What happened?"

"You are quite safe." Bat retreated a couple of steps. The top of the box was still ajar. "Sit down on that chair, over to your right. Do you know who you are?"

"Of course I do." The voice was stronger. "I'm Yarrow Gobel. Who are you?"

"I am Rustum Battachariya. Please sit down." Bat had reached his communications console and now he was speaking into it. "*An emergency. At once, and in suits. No, I cannot tell you if there is still a danger, to me or to anyone else. But I have to assume that there might be.*" He turned again to the inspector-general. "Now, Yarrow Gobel, I want you to do just as I tell you. First, *sit down*, and don't move. We're going to have a visitor in just a moment."

"Yes, sir." Gobel finally sat down and stared around curiously at the cluttered contents of Bat Cave. "This is a very strange place."

"You don't remember being here before?"

"Oh, I never have. I'm sure of that. Why am I here now—and not in school?"

Eight hours later, Bat slid the cave door closed, headed for his favorite chair, and sank quivering into it.

It had been a night of multiple indignities. He could enumerate at least four of them.

First: Someone had had the temerity to invade the sanctity of Bat Cave with what could only be regarded as a dangerous weapon. Admittedly, the medical staff of Ganymede had found no physical damage to Yarrow Gobel. They had identified the synthetic neurotransmitter released from the package and were now working on the molecule that had piggybacked that transmitter into the inspector-general and across the blood-brain barrier. They also insisted that over time—say, five or six months—Gobel should recover his memories and his adult mind, and no longer be the eight-year-old child who had greeted them tonight in Bat Cave.

But the offense had not stopped there.

Second: Bat himself had been dragged protesting from the cave and subjected to a demeaning battery of physical and mental tests. That had ended only when, to prove his memory of recent events, he had recited a few parts of the private data file of his chief tormentor.

Third: To divert attention from himself, Bat had been obliged to offer a deliberate lie. He had told the security officers that the box had been intended for inspection by Yarrow Gobel. Gobel himself was in no position to disagree, and no one could be found on Ganymede who admitted to delivering, or even to having heard of, the package. But it was a lie nonetheless, and therefore unworthy of Rustum Battachariya.

Fourth: Bat's peace of mind had been permanently affected. For years he had thought of the cave as a totally safe retreat. Now that was no longer the case. Should he then run away? But if so, to where? He could think of nowhere safer than the cave, nowhere whose exits, entrances, blind spots and hideaways he knew better. At the same time, if he stayed in Bat Cave he had to admit that he might be a sitting—literally—target for a new attack.

Bat stared around at his home of many years, noted the dining table, and added a fifth offense against his person: sacrilege. A culinary masterpiece had been ruined, before he or Yarrow Gobel had taken a single bite. If only he had told the inspector-general to wait until after dinner before opening the package . . . but then Bat would more than likely have been close enough to share its contents.

It was time to cease brooding and start thinking. Who, and why?

First, the target of the attack. Presumably Bat himself, but not necessarily so. Yarrow Gobel's visit was no secret; who knew how many people Gobel himself had told of it? And Gobel had arrived a little late, soon after the package was popped into Bat Cave by a delivery Von Neumann. If the inspector-general had been on time, he would have taken the package anyway because Bat was cooking; and knowing Gobel's interests, the man would surely have opened it.

So the target could be Bat, or Gobel, or *both* of them. But Bat's instincts insisted that someone was after him. If they got Gobel too, they didn't mind.

Why?

There were only two plausible motives, because Bat was engaged in only two new activities: He was feeling his way backward in time toward the passengers and cargo of the ill-fated *Pelagic*, seeking the reason for its flight from Mandrake and its destruction by one of the Belt's own weapons. And he was trying to find, within the Jovian system, a secret adversary of Cyrus Mobarak.

Bat was beginning to get ideas about the second problem, but no one else should know about that. He had spoken of the matter to no one, and Mobarak himself had promised strict secrecy.

That did not, of course, mean that Mobarak had provided it. The Battachariyan first rule of data analysis had a corollary: "There is no such thing as a reliable person, only different degrees of unreliability." And as a corollary of that: "*Everyone* has an agenda."

So perhaps Mobarak had talked, or been even more directly involved. But that was not the likely explanation. The line of thought that spoke most plausibly to Bat involved the *Pelagic*. Which was a real irony, since he had that very night been ready to give up the hunt as hopeless and pointless.

But if someone were so keen to keep knowledge of past events hidden that they would attack him directly . . .

Bat sat hunched on his chair, a black cowl drawn around his newly shaven skull. Good so far, but he was missing something important.

The attack itself. It had been . . . half-hearted. A box of that size could hold enough explosive to vaporize Bat, Gobel, and everything in Bat Cave. Instead, a weapon had been used that was neither fatal nor physically harmful. Not even, according to the medics, permanent in its mental damage.

Bat raised himself from the padded seat and ambled across to his communications terminal. He canceled all funding requests for anything connected with the *Pelagic* or with the period close to the end of the Great War. He generated two memoranda to Magrit Knudsen, one making it clear that his recent investigations of the Great War had been fruitless, the other stating that he could waste no more time or funding on them. Finally he purged from his files all information about the *Pelagic*, Mandrake, the Pallas data banks, and survival-pod trajectories.

And then he dropped into the "Megachirops" file, hidden by seven layers of intrinsic pointers and designed to resist the most ingenious, powerful, and persistent ferret. All of his *Pelagic* files were already copied there, and heavily read-and-write protected.

Bat was not finished with the *Pelagic*. Not anymore. If nothing else, he owed that to Yarrow Gobel.

But it was time to go deep, deep underground.

14

Camille Takes
a Test

Money and influence, influence and money; with them you could walk on water, breathe vacuum, raise the dead—even get a priority high-drive ship from Abacus to Europa, when all of the standard manifests showed there was nothing available for weeks.

In her twenty-seven years of existence, Camille Hamilton had never possessed either money or influence. She'd never even realized that such power *existed*.

But now she sure liked the feel of it.

She flourished at the scheduler her unlimited credit rating from Cyrus Mobarak and her stamp of approval from Hilda Brandt, and watched the walls of bureaucracy come tumbling down.

Traveling to Europa in service to *both* Mobarak and Brandt? That's a first. "But certainly, ma'am, a ship can be made available to you in three days—no, make that two days."

One day, if Camille could accept the discomforts of a single-passenger ship. And if she was ready to travel *now*? Then how about eight hours—would that be soon enough for her needs?

If it hadn't been such a power trip, it would have been embarrassing. And, of course, when the ship schedule was approved and the vessel was on its way, Camille was suddenly not ready to leave. A surprise signal had beamed in to her personal ID on Abacus, coming all the way from DOS Center.

It seemed that her hidden experiment, the one she had left in deep-background mode, was producing results, and they were odd enough that the DOS computers, even assisted by her Level-Three Fax, did not know what to make of them. Nor did Camille. She took a quick look, saw that the far infrared observation program was picking up data spikes that matched no signature in the book, and decided that she was as mystified as her Fax. What the world needed was a Level-*Six* Fax—smarter and more complete than a person was herself.

She dumped the data just as it came in onto a high-density storage device. It could go with her to Europa, and on the way she'd do some honest-to-God data analysis.

That's when the ship arrived, and she had her second shock. She had agreed to a single-passenger ship, expecting it to fly out to Abacus on autopilot. Then she'd take it on to Europa herself.

But no. That wouldn't do for the high-level Belt potentate who apparently had pull with both Cyrus Mobarak *and* Hilda Brandt. There had to be a special service.

So the ship arrived with its own, quite unnecessary, crew: Pilot Husky, matching the name—big, breezy, all torso and teeth. Ready, Camille was sure after the first few words, to do anything that she needed or wanted. It gave her an idea of the sort of trip that some of the high officials in the Jovian General Assembly preferred.

It wouldn't have been so bad, maybe, if Pilot Husky had been a man.

Camille clutched her data pack to her chest, wriggled away from a too-friendly arm that tried to help her aboard, and headed into the cabin. "How long is the trip to Europa?" she asked over her shoulder.

Husky laughed. "As long as you want it. Six hours, or sixty."

And after they reached Europa? The pilot would still be around, an unwanted extra pair of hands, and no doubt other body parts as well. Camille nodded at the port, where Callisto's scarred surface filled four-fifths of the sky. "I need to pick up a few things. Any problem if we drop in for a quick stop before the main trip?"

"Not with me. I'll add it to the programmed flight plan. My wish is your command."

So take a space walk. Except that none of this was the pilot's fault. Husky was only doing what she was expected to do and paid to do. Camille made up her mind. Pilot Husky could do one more thing to earn her salary.

During the fifteen-minute hop from Abacus to the Callistan spaceport she invented a quick list of personal items that she would need on Europa. After they touched down and were sitting snug at their mooring, she went across to the hatch, stood there, and looked doubtful.

It took only a few seconds.

"Problems? Anything I can do to help?" Husky was at her side, their shoulders touching.

"It's nothing much, only that I don't know my way around this spaceport." Camille tried to look frail and helpless, but suspected that she managed only one out of two. "It might take me a long time before I can find what I need. And all I want are these few little things."

Camille held out the scribbled list and watched, thirty seconds later, as Pilot Husky grinned a farewell and headed off across the surface toward the spaceport building complex.

It took another five minutes, and one more invocation of the magic names of Mobarak and Brandt, before Camille was cleared for takeoff.

She felt bad about what she had done to Husky. But not very.

When she wanted a sleep-in pilot-companion, she'd damn well ask for one.

The trip to Europa was more like nine hours than the six on the flight plan that Pilot Husky had filed. But even with the extra time, Camille had no chance to examine the infrared data sent to her from DOS. There were too many other things on her activity list. She had to get ready for her main task: Moby-fitting a world.

She notified the Mount Ararat spaceport of her entry into Europa's sphere of influence but indicated no intention to land. Not yet. First she wanted to take a look at the world below. She dropped the ship to fifty kilometers, placed it into a precessing orbit that would eventually carry her over the entire surface, and settled down for a session of observation.

Donkey-headed she might be. Of all of Cyrus Mobarak's fine words to her back on DOS Center, that was naturally the phrase that came again and again to her mind. Impulsive, too? He'd accused her of that. At times, without a doubt. Camille tried to imagine Pilot Husky's face when she returned to find both ship and Camille gone.

So donkey-headed *and* impulsive. But when it came to straight thinking and the solid, hard grind needed to get a job done, she wouldn't take second place to anyone in the system. She adjusted focus and set to work.

The globe below had two noticeably different types of terrain. One was dark and rough, mottled with the faint splotches of old impact craters of all sizes. The other was brighter and more uniform, but crisscrossed by long, narrow ice ridges. These ridges were hundreds of kilometers long, but only a few tens of meters high. They were also piled one on another in a tangled, reticulate pattern, like strands of thread randomly added to a ball.

Both types of Europan terrain had one thing in common. They looked very smooth from a distance, but travel across them on the surface would be hell.

Camille understood now the lack of interest in detailed surface maps of Europa. They would be useless. She imagined driving across the terrain on the ground. Your path would be interrupted every few kilometers by sharp drops, fissures, or vertical walls of ice. No one would do much ground travel on Europa, except close to Mount Ararat or in a few other places where the going happened to be unusually smooth and easy.

Detailed surface maps were a waste of time for another reason, too. The systems of fissures in the ice were prominent enough, and easy to map from orbit. But what about their permanence? They must move around slowly, under tidal forces. Only the seabed, far out of sight beneath the frigid shell, should be unchanging over long periods.

After four hours of observation she had seen enough. Camille made a decision. All of the Moby siting would have to be done in terms of seabed locations. Another "detail" job that Mobarak hadn't bothered to mention, and one that implied access to Europa's hidden ocean, access that Hilda Brandt had specifically denied to Camille.

However, those seabed maps might be available in Europa's data banks, and so might other information on ice depth and upwellings that Camille needed. One thing was sure: orbiting, she would never get what she wanted.

She called down for landing permission. On the next orbit, a blue communication beam reached up, took over control of the ship, and routed it for a gentle touchdown at the center of the Mount Ararat spaceport. "A flux-diversion suit must be worn before you exit," said a firm voice from the ship's control console at the moment of contact. "The external environment is presently unprotected. A ground vehicle is waiting."

Camille was already wearing her suit. She headed for the hatch, then at the last moment turned back and grabbed the DOS experiment records. She stuffed them into an interior suit pocket. There might be no chance to look at them for a while, but she didn't want them lost. Someone else might help themselves to this ship and take it away as easily as she had.

Her first ground view of the surface belied the impression from orbit. She stepped out onto a smooth plain of rock, concave and sloping up to a circular lip maybe a kilometer away. There was no sign anywhere of broken, icy ridges. As she climbed into the empty ground vehicle, she realized why. She was at the exact center of the smooth bowl of the spaceport; the rest of the moon lay hidden beyond its wall.

No matter, she would see it soon enough.

Within two minutes she learned that she was wrong about that. The ground car registered her presence and trundled off, but it did not head up the slope to the rim of the modified crater. Instead it rolled along for maybe half a kilometer past a jumble of deserted staging areas and bright-painted storage tanks, then started down a descending tunnel in the rocky wall. "Flux-diversion suits may now be removed," said the same emotionless voice. "Ambient radiation levels are satisfactory."

Camille puzzled over the absence of checkpoints. With all of the Europan worry about contamination, she had expected to be met, questioned, and maybe even examined. But there was less red tape for this arrival than for an arrival on Ganymede.

The answer came to her as she was removing her suit. Control here was guaranteed by planetary structure. Solid Ganymede was riddled with caverns and tunnels and elevator tubes, and it had hundreds of possible entry points to its interior. But Europa had just one spaceport, and just one settlement. With the reception vehicles preprogrammed, every visitor could be funneled through a single entry channel. Unless you were crazy enough to head away on foot from your arriving ship, you could not get anywhere but here.

And the absence of people waiting to meet her made sense for quite a different reason. Mount Ararat was a *research* establishment, and few scientists or engineers were interested in policies and procedures. Camille knew that attitude very well, and she sympathized with it. Anyone who had to spend time worrying about new arrivals would do so grudgingly, considering it time stolen from his or her own theories or experiments.

Except that the man who was waiting at the car's final stopping point seemed to deny her speculations. He was short, solid, and muscular, with the battered face of an unsuccessful thug. But there was a definite smile on that scarred face—not exactly of welcome, but of—what? Almost of *relief*? No matter. Anything was better than the accommodating leer of Pilot Husky.

"My name's Buzz Sandstrom. I'm deputy director of Mount Ararat Base." The man offered a hand that swallowed Camille's.

"Camille Hamilton."

Sandstrom nodded. "I expect that you're tired after your trip. I suggest you start with food and a rest." He led the way further along the tunnel. The walls became smoother, and soon Camille saw that there were metal doors set into it, but the floor and ceiling remained bare and undecorated rock. Camille nodded to herself in approval. A research station *ought* to look like this, simple and functional, a place for hard work and plenty of it.

They went on and on, until Sandstrom finally entered a small cubicle containing a cot, table, and single chair. "All yours. Make yourself at home. I'm sure you're keen to join your buddies right away, but just now that's not possible."

He caught Camille's puzzled glance and misinterpreted it. "They're still in the submersible, below the ice. Don't worry, they're quite safe. They have enough supplies to stay down in the water for weeks if they want to."

Buddies. Submersibles. Trips below the ice.

"*Who* is down in the water?" Camille sensed a screw-up.

"Jon Perry and Wilsa Sheer. No one told us she was a qualified Jovian pilot. Do you know what those two jokers did to me?" Buzz Sandstrom wore an expression of remembered irritation.

"Wait a minute." Camille couldn't let it go any further. "I know Wilsa Sheer's name, she's famous. But I've never even *heard* of Jon Perry."

"But aren't you part of the same . . ." Sandstrom stared at Camille. "The arrival record shows that you came here with approval from Dr. Brandt, just like the other two."

Camille fished the printed stamp from her pocket and held it out. Buzz Sandstrom examined it.

"This is okay." He handed it back. "So you *are* approved. Are there *two* groups checking for native life forms? No one told me that."

A *major* screw-up. "I'm not here to look for native life forms."

"What! Then why *are* you here?"

"To gather information. Of seabed depths. Of ice thicknesses." The deputy director's face was changing as Camille plowed on, but there could be no stopping now. "And water turbidity. And temperatures. I need all those before I know where to place the big Mobies. It's all part of the Europan transformation project."

She held out her other ace, the unlimited credit approval from Cyrus Mobarak. But as she had feared, on Europa the value of every card had been changed. Sandstrom took one quick look at the credit slip and seemed ready to spit in Camille's face.

"You mean you're working for *Cyrus Mobarak*? I don't know why you dare show yourself here. That bastard! He's trying to ruin everything for us, all the work that we've done for all these years. Let me have another look at that entry permit from Dr. Brandt."

Camille silently handed over her approval stamp and watched as Sandstrom gave it a much more careful scrutiny.

"I don't get it. This is *genuine*." He stared at Camille. "Are you a friend of Dr. Brandt's?"

"She gave me her approval, directly and personally, to come to Europa." It didn't seem the moment for a strictly accurate answer about the degree of friendship.

"Well, I can't think why. But she sure as hell didn't give you permission to go down Blowhole and start screwing up the interior." Sandstrom slapped the stamp back into Camille's hand. "I didn't look for it first time, but it says so right there: access to Mount Ararat and to our records, and to the frozen surface—good luck to you if you're crazy enough to go out on it. But that's all. No access to Blowhole, *or to the liquid ocean*."

"I know. How do I get access to the local data files?"

"Don't ask me, lady. That's your problem." Buzz Sandstrom glared at Camille. "I've wasted as much time helping you as I'm going to. You know, you've got a bloody nerve. You come here to work on a disaster that could turn Europa from a scientific sanctuary to a hogs' trough for greedy developers, and you expect us to *help* you. You can stay—I can't make you leave, not when you have that permit—but I'm damned if I'll lift a finger for your convenience. And I'll make sure that everyone else on Mount Ararat knows why you're here, too."

Sandstrom glared at Camille for a moment before turning and heading out. At the doorway, he turned again.

"You know what I think? I think you should get the hell out of here, right now. Just bugger off."

Camille collapsed into the chair. *Welcome to Europa.*

She recalled David Lammerman's words: "What Mobarak's giving you is a vote of confidence . . . but don't think that means the solution will be easy."

Fair enough. But what was she supposed to do when the solution became *impossible?*

For the next twenty-four hours, Camille wandered the interior of Mount Ararat and found that her reputation had preceded her. Buzz Sandstrom had done exactly as he had threatened. What he said was anybody's guess, but people recoiled from Camille as though she carried the Great War plague. They were willing to tell her where she could obtain food, and that was all. Their faces told her to head back to the ship and return to Ganymede.

After hours of lonely effort, she managed to find the communications center and tried to contact Hilda Brandt. The research director was still away on Ganymede.

Camille placed the call. What did she have to lose? She was ready to try anything, and the worst that Brandt could do was to order her to leave Europa. She waited in the com center for six hours, until she had read every note and number in the place. Her call was never returned. That was a message all by itself.

She put on her suit and wandered back out to the deserted landing area. The ground cars sat in protected storage vaults. She examined a couple of them and found them in good working order, with plenty of fuel. Their controls were simple, too—nothing that she could not handle; but she had nowhere to go.

At last she went on foot up the gentle slope of the crater to its smoothed lip, then over and down the slope of Mount Ararat until the bare rock gave way to crumpled ice. She walked a few hundred yards out, trying to gauge how difficult it would be for a car to traverse what she saw. There were plenty of hills and valleys, but none of the jagged rifts and crevasses that marked most of Europa's surface.

Camille could feel the crunch of compressed materials beneath her boots. She bent low for a closer examination.

It was water-ice, but the upper inch or two had a strangely granular and spongy appearance. Millennia of sputtering by protons and heavier sulfur ions had riddled the top layers, to leave a porous slab that crunched and gave under Camille's weight. It was Europa's version of a regolith, a crumbled outer layer pounded by endless impact. The ice was relatively firm, enough so that she should be able to move across it to the steep-sided ice ridges and valleys. But what was the point of aimless rambling? She was interested in what lay *below* the ice, not on top of it.

It was hopeless. Camille was ready to give up.

Except that she couldn't stand the idea of Mobarak's cool acceptance of failure, or—perhaps worse—David's understanding smile.

She walked gloomily back to the inside of Mount Ararat and headed for the cafeteria, to eat a solitary meal there. The food tasted like ashes, although it was surely no worse than that served in DOS Center. She left her plate half-filled and set off again, wandering obsessively through the dimly lit interior corridors. The news of her movements somehow traveled ahead of her. There were two hundred in the research station, but she encountered only five of them in her travels.

At last she went to the computer center for the fourth time and logged on with no trouble. The conventions were the same system-wide. As before, she soon found herself at a dead end. She could not get to any of the information that she needed. She had no password of her own, no local knowledge, and access only to the most general data files. There were tantalizing hints that what she needed about Europan geography was available—*somewhere*. But where?

She began to skip around in the files, randomly browsing. Her breakthrough, when it came, looked like such a trifling advance that at first Camille did not know that she had something important.

A couple of the locked files did not simply reject her request for entry. Instead, they sent a message in return: "General access prohibited. If you are with user sites E-1 through E-4, press the override key to initiate data transfer." Camille liked the idea of an override key into the data banks. It was just what she needed. But how did a user obtain that privilege? Who were those lucky people, Mister E-1 and Miss E-4, who were allowed into locked files?

Camille had no idea. What she did have was a vague recollection of the same symbols being used somewhere in the communications center. She headed back there— another half-mile jaunt through the unfriendly corridors of Mount Ararat—and started to hunt.

She found them eventually, in an unlikely place. They were pinned to the wall, as part of a list of dedicated signal frequencies. Which meant that E-1 and the other three were not individual data-user identifications; they had to be *places*, to which signals were sent and from which signals were received using those assigned frequencies.

Which left only the question, where? Not anywhere on Mount Ararat, that was for sure. Yet not at some distant location in the Jovian system, either, since off-Europan communications were handled by the same nonlocal communication net that she had used to send her unsuccessful message to Hilda Brandt.

Camille made up a message that said nothing, and gave E-1 as its destination. It produced an unexpected result. A

Level-Two female Fax popped into view on Camille's screen.

"The geometry is unfavorable for transmission," it said politely. "Do you wish to send anyway, or wait and retransmit later?"

"I may have the wrong destination. Can you confirm the location?"

"In what form?"

A great question, since Camille had no idea of what the options were. "Place?"

"Place name, or coordinates?"

"Both."

"Your given message destination is named Sub-Jove. Its coordinates are one degree north, two degrees east. Do you wish to transmit?"

"I'll wait." Camille cut the connection. She now knew exactly where E-1 was located: on the other side of Europa, facing squarely at Jupiter. Messages would have to go through a couple of relay satellites, and apparently they were not at the moment in favorable orbit positions. And E-1 must be the Sub-Jove camp's access point to the computer systems, a node located outside the Mount Ararat base. It was Camille's first hint that off-base facilities even existed.

But it made sense. If scientists were in the habit of staying out on the ice for periods of weeks, even months, they would still need access to base data. And if the internal pointers were to be believed, users away from base could read *all* data, even if they couldn't write to any but their own files.

But reading data, and recording what she read, was all that Camille needed.

She sent the same message in rapid succession to the three other destinations. One good thing about a low-level Fax, it would never notice a repeating pattern of behavior and start to ask questions about it. E-2 was like E-1, over on the other side of Europa and far out of reach. Camille could fly there in her ship, but she would have no way of landing. E-3 was nearby, but it was right at Blowhole, where Camille's presence would be sure to arouse unwanted attention and interference. The fourth one, E-4, was out beyond Blowhole, nearly sixty kilometers from Mount Ararat. It would be hard to reach, even by ground car; but it was her only hope of progress. And—a big plus—according to the Fax, Skagerrak Station was currently unoccupied. If Camille could get there, she would be able to work without interruptions.

She had a toehold on her problem. But this time she was determined not to be impulsive. Too much was at stake. She signed off the communications system, returned to her hermit's cell, and went to bed. If the idea of taking a trip to an off-base facility still seemed worth a try in ten hours' time, she would make the attempt.

And if it did not?

She might go anyway.

Camille slept for five hours, woke up with her mind furiously active, tossed in her cot for another thirty minutes, and finally gave up.

Better admit it, she was committed.

On the walk to the ground vehicles she did not meet a soul. She was inclined to think of that as a good omen. She climbed aboard, checked power and supplies again—ample—and started the motor. The ground car purred its way up and over the lip of the crater, down the hillside, and out onto the ice on its combination of runners and wheels.

Sixty kilometers was not a long way for a normal surface trip, no more than an hour's jaunt; but she wanted to avoid Blowhole, and quite apart from that she had little hope of being able to follow a direct route. Europa's exterior was just too broken and jagged. Within the first ten minutes she found one crack too wide to cross and another too deep to see the bottom. Camille drove slowly and carefully, making detours around anything that looked steep enough to be dangerous.

She estimated that she would reach Skagerrak Station in maybe seven or eight hours. She felt really good: cool, calculating, and cautious; certainly not—banish the thought—*impulsive*.

It never occurred to Camille that impulsiveness is only one of many ways of being stupid.

15

Needle in an Icestack

The loss of the first baby tooth. The moment when you looked into a mirror and realized that was *you* in there.

The first serious date. First love, and first loss. That single, intrusive grey hair. There was a first time for everything.

With slow horror, Nell Cotter realized that she was going through another first.

"I knew it, you see, the moment I set eyes on her," Tristan Morgan was saying, his face as miserable as his chipmunk cheeks would permit. "I said to myself, that's the woman for me, the only one I'll ever want if I live to be ten thousand. I suppose in some ways it must have happened even before we met, because when I heard Wilsa's music, I felt that it spoke to me alone. And then I finally did meet her, and she seemed to like me, too. So to lose her, just like that, in a split second . . ."

He was pouring out his heart. But not, Nell realized, as he would have done to someone his own age.

No. He was opening up to Old Mother Cotter, a lady who was experienced and understanding, and ancient beyond belief. Peter Pan was consulting some wrinkled, antique crone who felt, for the first time in her life, "ever so much older than twenty."

She wanted to shake him and say, "Hey, Weepy Willie, wait a minute. What about *me*? I'm not *quite* past it, you know. Suppose I happen to feel the same way about Jon Perry?"

Instead, she nodded and said, "Don't give up. We've been jumping to conclusions, but we may be misunderstanding things. Wait until we see them again and hear their side of the story." Which meant, depressingly, that she was even older and more case-hardened than Tristan seemed to think. Because she didn't believe for one moment that there had been a misunderstanding. What they had witnessed was a classical lightning flash of mutual attraction, followed by a severing of former ties and an instant dumping of old ballast in the form of Nell and Tristan.

And when you admitted that fact, you had to face another one: If you needed a hot story about Cyrus Mobarak and the Europan fusion project, you wouldn't be able to piggyback on Jon Perry anymore to get it. You'd have to find your own way.

A new thought? Not at all. It had been banging around inside Nell's head long before Tristan Morgan started hustling around the Jovian system, trying to soothe his upset feelings by frantic action. She had traveled with him, because *something* was going to happen in the world of the Jupiter satellites, something big, something that would make a hell of a story. She was sure of it. The feeling had come to her before, half a dozen times, of forces converging to an unseen focus, and she had always been right. Maybe that was what Glyn Sefaris meant when he told Nell that she had a way of "being there."

She felt it now, the lines were drawing closer. But her sense of impending action could not tell her what would lie at the focal point. So far, she had found nothing worth reporting. There were small points of interest, such as the way that Von Neumanns were used throughout the Jovian system in situations where Earth workers would automatically do a genome boost to a natural form. But that would make at best a three-minute "Them and Us" comparison clip.

An Outward Bound robot mission to a nearby star had an even lower rating potential, but she had attached herself to Tristan because he was her only local contact. She had endured a couple more of the awful meetings of the Immaturity-of-the-Year awards ceremony that called itself Outward Bound, then leaped at the chance of a trip to the deuterium-separation facility on Ganymede. They had moved from there to the main plant, on a big ice fragment beyond Callisto, and then to an observers' visit to Hebe Station. During the Hebe landing, the price for Nell's ticket had at last been made clear: She was to serve Tristan as Mother Confessor.

Before that thought could emerge in full flower, it was pushed aside by another one.

"Tristan, we've flown to three different locations. But you've never once called through for permission to go anywhere, or permission to land."

"I know. It's because this ship and I are part of a *Starseed* troubleshooting group, and we have to go all sorts of places in a hurry. So we have a special deal where we act first, then fill out the paperwork afterward. Otherwise we'd never get anywhere in time to be useful."

It took a minute for his words to sink in; she must be getting as old as Tristan seemed to think she was. "Are you telling me that you have an automatic permit to go *anywhere* in the Jovian system?"

"Pretty much anywhere. I don't know what would happen if I tried to land someplace exclusive, like the General Assembly's private recsat."

The first rule of the business: *Go take a look.*

"Tristan, instead of standing around worrying about how Wilsa feels about you, why don't you *ask* her?"

"I'd love to. But she's on Europa."

"That's no more than three or four hours away. So why aren't *we* on Europa? You just told me that you can go there if you want to. Can you?"

He rubbed at a rounded cheek. "Well, I suppose so. Go talk to Wilsa directly, you mean? That's a pretty attractive idea. I guess I ought to put in a call to Hilda Brandt—we get on real well—just to make sure it's all right."

He was already reaching for the communication panel when Nell grabbed his hand. Damn it, she *was* experienced and understanding and ancient beyond belief—compared with some people she could mention.

"Tristan, don't you dare. *She might say no.* And then where would you be? Let's just up and *go*. It's a whole lot easier to get absolution than permission."

He was nodding, slowly. "Do you really think it's all been some sort of misunderstanding?"

I wouldn't take odds on it. "I can't say. But what I can say is that we'll know for sure—as soon as we arrive on Europa and talk to Wilsa and Jon."

To Nell, everything about Europa was no more strange than any totally new experience had to be. What made less sense to her was Tristan's obvious sense of uneasiness when the ship landed at Mount Ararat spaceport and a little robot car growled them along through a warren of underground tunnels.

"You said this is just a small outpost research station." Nell wondered when it would be safe to remove her suit; they ought to be far enough under the surface by now to be shielded, and there was already air around them. "And you told me not to expect a welcoming committee. So why does it worry you if we don't have one?"

"You've got it backwards." Tristan kept his gaze on the tunnel ahead. "I'm worried because there *will* be a bunch of people to meet us, as soon as we get off this car. You didn't see the answer to my last message. When I gave our ID and expected time of arrival, they fired back a reply saying they'd be here waiting. That never happened to me before. Makes me wonder if they checked and found out we're not approved to come here."

For once, Nell was forced to agree with Tristan. Attention from the Mount Ararat staff was the last thing she needed.

But they didn't have a choice. When the car finally halted, eight people came to surround it. By Europan standards, that was a crowd scene. A crowd, however, that did not include either Wilsa Sheer or Jon Perry. Nell climbed down and was suddenly glad that she and Tristan still wore their suits. If there were guilt on his face, it wouldn't be seen for another few minutes.

Except that quite enough guilt was already visible in the waiting group. Nell knew how to read body language. Without even thinking about it, she turned on her midget video camera.

"Welcome to Mount Ararat." The man standing at the middle of the group didn't sound welcoming at all. "I'm Buzz Sandstrom. I must say I didn't expect you'd be here so quickly. Now I'm wondering if we've dragged you all the way from Ganymede for nothing."

Tristan was silent. Shocked to silence? Nell nodded, encouraging the man to continue.

"We can't be sure," Sandstrom went on, "but we suspect that something bad must have happened to her. If anyone should get the blame for what happened," he added grudgingly, "I suppose that I'm the one."

Nell nodded again, still not speaking. Sandstrom was swallowing, obviously uncomfortable. Confession time was not yet over for the day.

"But I mean . . ." He gazed at Nell for absolution. "I didn't mean no harm. When she came here, out of the blue like that . . . well, I just got mad. Who wouldn't have? She didn't come here to *help* Europa, see? She came to ruin all our work. Or to try to. So I got mad, and I guess I got everyone else feeling the same way. And then—"

"What do you mean, *something bad* happened to her?" Tristan had seized and fixed on that one phrase, and he couldn't bear to wait any longer. "Is Wilsa in trouble?"

It was Sandstrom's turn for confusion. "Huh? Wilsa?"

"Wilsa Sheer. You said something bad happened—"

"Not Wilsa Sheer. She's fine, or I guess she is. She went down under the ice with Dr. Perry, and they're still there. I'm talking about Camille Hamilton."

The name registered with Nell, because she was still receiving briefings and updates on Mobarak's Jovian system activities. But she was willing to bet that it meant not a thing to Tristan Morgan. He had removed his suit helmet, and now he was gaping at Buzz Sandstrom, who seemed to mistake his popping eyes for strong disapproval.

"Hey, she may be just fine." Sandstrom was scowling but defensive. "We wouldn't have sent that emergency message at all, you know, except like I said, it *has* been over twenty-four hours. And we got no idea which way she went, or why her ground car isn't broadcasting an automatic positional signal. And we don't know how much experience she has—nothing about her in our records, no reply yet to our Ganymede inquiries. She could be dead already out there and we'd never know it. She shoulda' left a message where she was heading, but she didn't. And Dr. Brandt isn't on Europa, and we haven't been able to reach her."

Sandstrom was becoming increasingly tense, and so was Tristan. But Nell was finally relaxing. Hilda Brandt was far away, and the way things were going there was no danger that anyone on Europa was going to tell her and

Tristan to leave. Quite the contrary. The staff of Mount Ararat was desperate for someone—anyone—to take over and tell them what to do.

No problem at all.

Nell kept her video running, removed her helmet, scanned the group standing in front of her, and smiled pleasantly at Buzz Sandstrom.

"I'm Nell Cotter, and this is Tristan Morgan." She held out her hand. "Let's do introductions. But before that, let's go someplace where we can all sit down. I feel sure that we can help you—just as soon as you give us a few more facts."

Camille Hamilton was not dead. Not yet. But she was not sure how much longer she could remain alive. She was realizing, rather too late, that she was in over her head.

Literally.

The first twenty kilometers toward Skagerrak Station had been easy. The sun was up, reflecting from Europa's grainy surface with a bright but oddly cold light. After a few minutes Camille came across a group of tracks. She realized that they must be those of previous travelers who had been making their way toward Blowhole. The path ought to be the safest and the easiest. She followed the same route, and for three-quarters of an hour had nothing to worry about except boredom. She itched to get a look at the data from DOS, tucked away inside her pocket, but there was no way that she could drive and operate the car's computer at the same time.

A kilometer from Blowhole, the boredom ended. Camille could see through the car's front window, all the way to the open circle of water. The chances of being spotted by someone working at Blowhole were too high to risk. She waited until the car came to a smooth, shallow valley in the surface, then cut away along it to the left, on a path that ought to skirt Blowhole at a comfortable distance.

And at that point she realized how spoiled she had been for the first hour of her journey. She had traveled almost a third of the way to Skagerrak Station in smooth and carefree comfort. But the next kilometer taught her what most of Europa was really like. She followed her chosen valley, only to find that it grew steeper-sided and at last pinched down to a width too narrow for her car. She had to go into reverse—which meant tricky and slow progress—until she reached a place where she could head up the valley side and over to seek a better route. Ten minutes later, that route too was narrowing. She cut her losses while there was still enough room to turn the car around and decided on a new strategy. If the valleys were not obliging, she would try the hills.

At first it seemed an excellent decision. She could spy out the lay of the land far ahead, look for breaks and crevasses, and make her moves accordingly. Soon she was running along a broad arcuate ridge that stretched like a dark-backed snake as far as she could see. Her inertial guidance system told her that she was heading in just the right direction for Skagerrak. She ran on smoothly for over five kilometers.

It was the sound of the car's engine that finally told her something was wrong. Its higher-pitched tone and the increased power draw insisted that the car was moving uphill. Except that the car's instrument panel insisted, just as firmly, that it was traveling dead level.

Camille knew within a matter of seconds what must be happening. Under its own weight, the car was sinking a few inches into the spongy, sputtered ice cover; in moving forward, it was compressing the ice just in front of itself. Thus it was always climbing, but also always traveling level.

Solving the problem, though, was another matter. She had no idea if the surface was more or less firm down in the valleys to her left and right. For the moment, it made more sense to live with slower progress and increased power drain and just keep going as she was.

Except that option was about to disappear. A couple of hundred meters ahead, the smooth ridge ended in a murderously steep escarpment. Camille edged the car forward until she could see the severity of the slope, and decided at once that there was no way she would take a ride down that.

Which left three choices: go down to the valley on her right; go down to the left; or turn and go back the way she had come.

Camille stopped the car, climbed out, and examined the treads. They were embedded to a depth of a few inches, but there was no danger that they would lock permanently in the bubble-grained ice. She set off on foot down the left-hand slope and found that it easily held her weight. Behind her, the impression of her suit's boots left only a faint indentation, maybe a centimeter deep. She continued almost all the way to the valley floor and found it easy going. On the other side of the long depression there was an equally gentle slope, leading up to another powdery dark ridge.

She started back. It would do. And if she had to, she could always ascend the slope once more and try the right-hand side.

She started the car again, but instead of heading directly down the slope as she had done on foot, she angled it so that she would be making some forward progress at the same time.

It went easily for twenty meters. Then the car began canting to the left, and the tilt steadily became more pronounced. The weight on that side was driving the treads deeper. The farther the car inclined, the greater the imbalance of left and right.

But Camille was not greatly worried. If she had to, she would simply halt her forward progress and go into steady reverse. And if, in the worst possible case, the car became totally jammed in the ice, Blowhole was within walking distance of anyone with the protection of a suit.

The first inkling that there might be more to it than that came when the car began to descend into the ice, quite steadily and at a fixed angle. Camille realized that she had struck a patch of ultra-porous and weak surface, crumbling and soft enough for the whole car to sink into it as much as a meter.

Or two meters.

But still she did not realize the full extent of the trouble that she was in. Only when the view from the forward screen vanished, in favor of a dirty grey frost, did she wonder how far this could go.

She turned off the engine, and the only sounds in the car were those of the scrape and creak of ice, fracturing and failing beneath the car. That sound ended, but it was no relief. Camille was suddenly in free-fall for what felt like minutes; she later calculated that it was for just over three seconds.

The car landed with a final crunch, hard enough to jolt her but not to injure her. She was at last sitting level, and she heard and felt no sign of further settling.

Camille waited for a full minute to be completely sure. The car door slid open easily enough, but she was facing a wall of grey ice. In order to get out, she had to crawl to the rear and open the hatch that led through the roof.

She stared up at the rough-sided rectangular hole through which the car had entered. It was about six meters above her head, far out of reach. The pocket in the ice into which she had fallen was a good deal bigger than the entry hole, maybe eight meters long and four meters wide. It had been simple accident that the car had dropped in with its main door flush against one of the walls.

Camille lowered herself carefully over the rear of the car and tested the surface with one foot. It was quite solid, far more so than the friable upper crust. And although the floor of the pocket was nothing like level, she could move over its lumps and furrows and icy spikes with fair ease. Given Europa's low gravity, the top twenty or thirty meters of the moon's surface was probably honeycombed with caves like this, of all sizes.

She worked her way steadily around the base and found no place where the ice underfoot was not solid enough to bear her weight.

Which meant that she was safe.

For the moment.

And after that?

Camille swore. At herself, and at her own stupidity. (She refused even to *think* the word "impulsiveness.") It had seemed to make such good sense to go to Skagerrak Station for easy access to the Europa data that she needed. But how much sense did it make that she had not sent a message of any kind, saying what she was trying to do and where she was going? The outgoing messages from Mount Ararat did not seem to be closely monitored. She could have sent word to David, using the same communications link through which she had tried to reach Hilda Brandt.

But she hadn't done that. Nor had she left any sign at Mount Ararat to show where she was heading. The most that anyone who came to look for her would learn was that she had left in a ground car. They couldn't track her, either, since she had followed the well-worn trail of other cars almost all the way to Blowhole.

Camille went across to the wall of the ice pocket, started to climb it, and found that it was too smooth near the top. She could scramble up to within a tantalizing few feet of the aperture, but then the wall curved over and inward. Even a fly would have had trouble traversing the final stretch.

She allowed herself to slide back down to the floor and stared up. Damn it, in gravity this weak she ought to be able to *jump* right up and out of the hole. Except that there was no place on the floor to provide firm footing, and there was too much danger of landing on some sharp-edged ice spike.

Camille became conscious of the chill in her gloved hands. Her suit was designed more for protection from particle flux than for thermal insulation. Once outside the warm car, her arms and legs were beginning to feel cold. Her idea of walking back to Blowhole if she had to would not have worked. She would have frozen long before she got there.

There was one other way that someone might find her. The ground car had its own transmitter for emergencies, and she could send a distress signal. The big problem was the geometry. The signal beam from the transmitter would not pass through a layer of ice, so it could be received only by a vehicle that lay within an upward-pointing cone, with the transmitter as apex and the rectangular hole in the ice above as its defining outer boundary. In practice, that implied a spaceborne or an airborne search. And it was not clear to Camille that there was such a capability on Europa.

She climbed back inside the car and began to inspect its status indicators; and learned that she was in much worse shape than she had thought.

Air, her first worry, was no problem. She had enough for a week or more. The killer was heat. Or lack of it.

She had checked the car's power supply before she left Mount Ararat and confirmed that it was ample, enough to allow the car to be driven for hundreds of kilometers. But it was not power that could readily be converted to *warmth*. And heat, not mobility, was what she would need as the car's internal temperature dropped.

Even in an emergency Camille thought like a scientist, and the irony of the situation struck her clearly. With the old, primitive engines of a century ago, the energy that allowed a car to move came from coal or oil or uranium. That energy was first produced as *heat*; then heat was in turn converted—inefficiently—to forward motion. But today's propulsion systems were far more sophisticated, and they disdained the redundant intermediate step. Raw energy powered the rotation of wheels or produced linear motion *directly*. The engines were far more efficient, and in every way superior—except in the one-in-a-million case where a car could not move and heat was exactly what the passenger needed.

So what about the power source *designed* to warm the passenger compartment?

That was pathetically inadequate. The ground cars were intended for trips of, at most, a couple of hundred kilometers, which in turn meant that no one expected them to be occupied for days at a time. The heaters, fully charged when she left Mount Ararat, would keep the cabin tolerable for another twenty hours or so. That was for a car out on Europa's frigid surface, and Camille would gain a little more time than that because the ambient temperature in her ice cave was higher. So she had, say, thirty hours at the outside, and then the cabin would slowly go into a deep freeze, where no human could possibly survive.

Camille turned on the transmitter—its power draw was negligible—and began to send a distress signal. She turned her attention next to the food supply. It, too, was energy of a sort: chemical energy, whose slow release within her body would provide its own heat.

There was plenty of food, enough for several days. But long before it was exhausted, she would be a block of ice.

Water was also ample: twenty gallons of it. It could be heated. But that would draw from the same energy source that heated the cabin.

The car's spare suit? She could pull that on over the one she was wearing and improve the insulation. But that would not buy her more than another hour or two.

Camille was out of ideas. She leaned back in the seat and felt her mind drifting away from the problem. All she could do was to sit, and wait, and live for as long as she possibly could. Her salvation, if it came, depended on someone searching for her, locating the signal beacon, and finding the car in time.

She took out the storage unit for her DOS experimental data and inserted it into the car's computer. It was an act of deliberate folly, a recognition of the fact that she had given up hope of saving herself.

She watched the first data elements creep onto the screen in front of her and felt as though her mind were dividing into two parts. At one level, dark and primitive, she was desperately concerned with sheer survival. At another, higher level she had already retreated into the abstract, manageable world of astronomy and physics, where time and space were measured in billions of years and billions of light-years, where an individual was of no possible importance.

The data analysis continued, and Camille began to see patterns. At the same time, her hands and mouth were continuously at work. She was eating the food supplies, and without thinking about it, she kept on doing so long after her hunger was satisfied. And while she ate, she was drinking water, as hot as her mouth and throat could tolerate it.

Drinking, and drinking, and drinking. A gallon; a second whole gallon.

And then a third, as after many hours the cabin temperature began to fall . . . slowly, but steadily, dipping toward a level where the carbon dioxide and water vapor in Camille's exhaled breath would become no more than a puff of ice crystals. Except that long before that, there would be no breath.

Nell was changing her mind again about Tristan Morgan. Absurdly innocent and idealistic by video-show standards, yes; but put him in the right situation and he became a powerhouse.

He had said that he was no stranger to emergencies, and now he was proving it. Even before all of the facts were laid out for them, he had begun to take action.

"All right, let's look at what we *know*, as opposed to what we guess or wish were true." He cut off the babble that was starting up again around the long conference table deep inside Mount Ararat. "Camille Hamilton is in a ground car, and she's nowhere on Mount Ararat. Given the car's speed, by now she could be as far away as eight hundred kilometers. Every hour that goes by increases that upper limit by thirty."

"I don't believe that she could be anything like that far away," objected a redheaded woman engineer who possessed a lot of Tristan's own mannerisms, and for that reason seemed to disagree with him more than any of the others. "I bet I've spent more time in ground cars than anyone here, and I'm telling you, once you get off the standard routes it's *tough*. You often won't make a kilometer an hour."

"I'm sure you're right. But I'm setting limits on what we *know*, not on what we suspect or conjecture. And I think that's *all* we know." Tristan looked around the table. "Am I missing something?"

"We know that the car has a transmitter to send an emergency signal," said Sandstrom. "And we know that it's not in use."

Tristan frowned. "Not quite. We know that the car has a transmitter, I'll give you that. And we know that we haven't picked up a signal. But it could be operating with lousy geometry for ground reception." Tristan glanced around the table again. "Which brings me to my point. Based on what we *know*, Camille Hamilton could in principle be hundreds of kilometers away. In a case like this, you don't rely on ground search. You conduct search-and-rescue from orbit. The ship we came in can get us started, but it's not enough. It wasn't designed for high-resolution orbital survey. We need *reinforcements*."

"But we called already," said the redhead. "And we got nothing. You came here, but not to answer our call."

"So maybe you've been calling the wrong people." Nell spoke for the first time since the review of Camille Hamilton's situation had begun. "You said you called Hilda Brandt's office. But you already agreed that Hamilton doesn't work for Brandt, and never has. And you admitted that when you first found out who Hamilton *did* work for, you didn't much care what happened to her. Don't you think Brandt's staff on Ganymede might feel the same way you did? You know—some bimbo of Mobarak's arrives on Europa, and she's trying to cause nothing but trouble with her high-power fusion programs. So she gets herself into trouble? Poetic justice. The hell with her—let her find her own way out."

"But we don't feel that way anymore," said Sandstrom. He did not sound quite convincing.

"Maybe not. Because she's *here*, and you met her, and you know she's a real, living person. But I bet that to the staff of Ganymede, she's just a statistic. You won't change their views with a call or two."

There was the unhappy silence of agreement.

"So what can we do?" asked Sandstrom at last.

"Two things. Tristan, with help from a couple of your people, can use his ship to begin a scan from orbit. Even if we don't think it's likely to work, we have to try. And the rest of us can call for help to the only person in the Jovian system sure to want to provide it—the only person who *can* provide it. The man who sent her here: Cyrus Mobarak."

Cyrus Mobarak. It was one name able to unite Tristan Morgan and the Mount Ararat group completely. Nell might as well have said Beelzebub. Everyone agreed on Mobarak's power, and wealth, and influence everywhere in the system.

And no one wanted to face him.

They were, Nell decided as she placed the call to Mobarak's office, *scared* of him. And maybe they were right and she was the dummy. But she couldn't pull back now.

The connection was made in seconds, so quickly that Nell expected to find herself facing a Mobarak Fax. But the screen showed a human face, pleasant-featured and with a great shock of wiry, curled hair. His expression changed to a frown when he saw Nell, as though he had been hoping for someone else.

"I have a problem." Nell did not bother with an introduction. "One that I think Cyrus Mobarak will want to hear about."

"He is in a financial meeting and cannot be disturbed. I am David Lammerman. Can I help you?"

Lammerman. Nell knew that name, too. Like Camille Hamilton, he was a recent addition to the Mobarak retinue, recruited for work on the Europan fusion project. And according to the background material that Glyn Sefaris had been sending along, Lammerman and Hamilton were close. Nell had to be careful how she suggested that Camille was in trouble, but she also had to be sufficiently direct to guarantee Lammerman's total attention and cooperation.

"I'm calling from Europa. We need assistance from Cyrus Mobarak. We need high-performance orbital search equipment, able to perform automatic scans for something as small as a ground car, over a large part of the planetary surface. And we need it fast."

Lammerman eyes widened. He was opening his mouth, ready perhaps to point out that she was making an outrageous request.

"We need it *right now*," went on Nell, "because one of your people is lost out on the Europan surface. And if we don't find her *quickly*, she'll freeze. You said that Cyrus Mobarak could not be disturbed. Well, he has to be. You better get in there and disturb him, and get his approval to send the stuff."

The face on the screen no longer seemed easygoing and relaxed. Nell read an odd collection of emotions: shock, worry, disbelief, and a nervousness bordering on terror.

"I can't do that."

"Can't do what?"

"Disturb Cyrus Mobarak when he says he's not to be disturbed. No one does it."

"Well, someone had better start. Or that someone will have to explain to Mobarak that he killed a woman because he didn't have the nerve to break into a bean-counters' meeting." Nell nodded at Lammerman. "I'm going to get off the line now, so you don't have to waste more time talking to me. You know what we need. Go tell Mobarak that Camille Hamilton's life is in great danger."

"Camille!"

But Nell had cut the connection, though she was tempted to linger. The conflict of expressions on David Lammerman's face was still going on. She wanted to know which one would win.

Camille was alone, lost on the ice plains of Europa. She must be rescued, or she would freeze to a block of organic ice. And David Lammerman was like a block of ice himself as he walked through the long, echoing corridors of Ganymede.

Except that the legs of a block of ice did not tremble with each step. The heart of a block of ice did not pound and flutter and quiver within its chest. The fingers of a block of ice did not shake so much that they had to be curled into tight fists.

David raised one ice gauntlet and stood poised to knock on the door of gunmetal grey. At the last moment he changed his mind, slid both panels to one side, and walked straight in without knocking.

There were three men in the luxuriously appointed room. One of them, seated on a dark-blue sofa, was Cyrus Mobarak. He turned toward the door, annoyance written on his face. David would have turned and run, right then and there, but for two things. When Mobarak saw him, the irritated look was replaced by deep astonishment and David noticed, for the first time ever, a tiny bead of perspiration at Cyrus Mobarak's hairline. It said to David, more clearly than any words, he's *human*. He's having a tough time in here, and for once it shows.

"David?" Mobarak's single word contained many things. *How dare you intrude when you know I'm in the middle of a crucial meeting?* But behind that, stronger, *What happened, David? You've never in your life interrupted me before.* And, one layer deeper yet, *Bad news. It's written all over your face.*

David recognized the other two men. They were top wheelers and dealers of the Jovian system, fixits who supposedly held half of the General Assembly in their pockets. They were also men whose single frown could ruin a junior nothing such as David.

They were certainly frowning now.

David realized, in a rush of adrenalin, that he didn't give a damn what they thought or did. Concern for Camille's safety overrode everything, and if he could make it this far, he could keep going all the way. Anyway, his business was with Cyrus Mobarak, not with two overweight crooks.

"It's Camille. She's lost on the surface of Europa. If we don't get help there soon, she'll die."

Mobarak asked not a question. He seemed to understand everything, in the single lightning flash of comprehension that had intimidated David ever since he was a child. He nodded. "Go there yourself, as soon as you can. Take whatever resources you need. You know my personal credit number. Use it. I'll start work here at once, do whatever needs to be done at this end."

"Fuck that for a deal, Mobarak." The shorter and fatter of the men slapped his hand down furiously on the table of grained wood. To David, his red face was that of an outraged pig. "You fucking stay here. You promised us the whole fucking day, and we've hardly fucking started."

David felt a new and alien emotion: sympathy for his father. If this was what you had to put up with, to work with the money suppliers and influence peddlers of the system . . .

"I did promise you." Mobarak had a soft tone in his voice and a look in his eye that David had never encountered before. It would have turned his own heart to stone and his legs to jelly. But it was not, thank God, being directed at him, and the other two men did not seem able to read it.

"And I'm sorry to say that I can't keep that promise," went on Mobarak, just as mildly. "But it must be obvious to both of you gentlemen that this accident could not have been predicted. And if you know me at all, you realize that I'll make up whatever I owe you—and more—as soon as I return."

He turned back to David. "How long?"

David understood the question. *How long before Camille dies if she's not rescued?*

"No one knows. And there's no signal from her emergency beacon."

"Then go at once, as soon as you can pull together what you need. I'll make sure you have a Europan entry permit. Call me as soon as you get there. I'll be available, any time."

David nodded. As Mobarak turned back to the two men, David retreated without another word. He had interacted more significantly with his father in the past thirty seconds than in the whole of his previous life. Now he felt . . . what? Nervous? Overwhelmed? Relieved? Exhilarated?

Maybe all of those. More than anything, David felt like he had to throw up.

16

A Voice from the Grave

"Given sufficient ingenuity, no well-defined puzzle is insoluble."

Bat had encouraged himself with that dictum through days and weeks of fruitless analysis. Now perhaps he was about to receive his reward.

It was late, and his head ached with the accumulated toxins of fatigue. But he could not stop working. The end result of his labors might finally lie at his fingertips. He would have admitted to no emotion as he executed the access procedure, yet his body sat rigidly angled over the keyboard. Waiting. In a few more seconds, he would *know*.

The search had been time-consuming and hard. Everyone who had worked on the Pallas data banks at the end of the Great War was long dead. Bat had examined every file, every record, every data element, until finally even he could not justify more time for checking and rechecking. When it was over, he felt that he had learned nothing. And yet, a small curiosity about one of the senior computer technicians on Pallas had nagged at Bat's sense of the anomalous. Mordecai Perlman was certainly dead, and he had surely died of natural causes—Bat had seen the records. His body had been cremated, and his ashes sent, at his request, into the sun. His possessions and his credit had been distributed to his relatives, just as his will specified.

And yet not quite all of his credit had been disbursed. There remained a bank account on Ceres, with a modest balance. Every month the interest on that account was used to purchase access to a Ceres computer system. Every month new data were dumped into a certain set of files.

Bat had examined the information that was being entered, and found himself baffled. It was no more than general facts concerning what was happening in the Jovian system, throughout the Belt, and on Earth and Mars—a compressed version of the news of the period, much as it was sent out over the standard services. It was too general to have value within a well-organized data base. So why was it being entered at all?

Bat dug. And dug. And found his answer.

After the war, Mordecai Perlman had been involved in the early development of the Faxes. However, his published papers showed that he disagreed with the usual logic of simulation development. To most people, a Fax was no more than an expert system, a large body of rules and a neural network that allowed a computer, to a greater or lesser extent, to mimic the thought patterns and responses of a particular human being. A low-level Fax would simulate only the simplest of individual thought processes. A high-level Fax would approach the logical complexity of the human.

Wrong approach, said Mordecai Perlman. A human isn't a set of logical rules. What goes on in a person's subconscious mind and endocrine glands is far more important in deciding what a human being is like than any stupid set of conscious, logical rules.

Perlman had been ignored. Not because he was wrong,

but because the pressing need was for simple Faxes, those whose responses to a given situation would always be the same. The last thing that people wanted were Faxes with moods, off days, crying jags, and temper tantrums.

So Mordecai Perlman had lost the fight for general Fax development. Big business, and the conventional approach, had won. But he had not given up. Over the next ten years he had continued to specify the form of a computer model that would produce *his* kind of Fax. It would be far more flexible than the usual computer program, and it would display all of the quirks and illogicalities of a human being.

When Perlman's work had gone as far as he could take it, he gave the final proof that he believed in what he was doing. He implemented his design, constructing a Fax as he felt that it should be done.

He did not call it a Fax, because it was not one. He called it "Mord," because his software mimicked, as closely as he could make it do so, the unique world view, knowledge base, and gut reactions of Mordecai Perlman. And he must have regarded Mord as much more than a program, because he had arranged that after his death it would be kept up to date about system events. The data entries were the equivalent of news programs.

As soon as Bat realized the nature of Mord, he requested that a copy of the program be transferred to the Ganymede directory of Megachirops. His request was refused by the Ceres' computer facility. Mordecai Perlman, quirky as ever even after death, had not wanted himself—or Mord—cloned. The program could not be duplicated.

Bat pondered that refusal, and dug deeper. He learned that Mordecai Perlman had also filed for recognition of his program as a being, with all of the rights of a human. The general filing had been refused, but Mord had been granted certain limited rights. One of those rights was control of its own fate. If Mord *wanted*, the Fax could be copied, transferred to another system, or even totally purged from the program base.

Bat wondered if his own sanity were any greater than Mordecai Perlman's as he sent a request addressed directly to the computer program. Would Mord agree to being copied and sent to Ganymede?

The reply came quickly: *no copies*. Mord also did not want to be cloned. But the software would agree to be *transferred* to Ganymede, provided that the news-service data were transferred, too, and continued news-service inputs were guaranteed.

Bat agreed at once, although he had no interest in Mord's recent data acquisitions. He was seeking Mordecai Perlman's *past*. Everything depended on how much of the man had been fed into his creation.

And at any moment now, Bat was going to be in a position to find out. Program access was complete, and the screen and cameras in front of Bat were alive.

The face that appeared was of a balding, squint-eyed man in late middle age: Mordecai Perlman, presumably as he had been at the time when Mord was implemented.

The eyes narrowed and peered at Bat. "Hi. You the one who asked me to ship to Ganymede? Well, you're certainly a fatty, I'll say that for you."

Bat, used to Faxes, and subconsciously expecting the appearance of something close to one, revised his opinion. "I am indeed Megachirops, the one who brought you here. You are now in the Ganymede data banks."

"Sure am. I can tell. I wasn't sure at first that I wanted to come here, you know. Different planet, different computer systems, different access protocols. Then I changed my mind. I thought, what the hell. You're stuck in a rut, Mord. You been sitting in the same data banks for fifteen years. Get out there, live dangerously. The worst that can happen is they'll screw up and wipe you. And I was curious, too. Why'd you bring me here?"

"I changed my mind," Mord had just said. But a Fax *never* changed its mind. It couldn't. Bat came to an instant conclusion: Mordecai Perlman had been right. The usual way of building a Fax might be satisfactory for low-level behavior, but if you *really* wanted to simulate a human . . .

"I brought you here because I am puzzled by something that happened on Pallas a long time ago—back at the end of the Great War, when Mordecai Perlman was working there. I wonder if you"—Bat hesitated over the next word, but it was the right one—"remember it."

"Try me."

"Do you operate through key-word search and retrieval?"

"Damned if I know. Just *talk* to me, Mega-chops. That's what I'm used to."

It was easier if you ignored the fact that you were dealing with a machine and pretended that Mord was a human at some remote location. Bat settled into his seat, closed his eyes, and laid out the facts that he knew: the departure of the *Pelagic* from Mandrake and its destruction by a Seeker missile, the destruction of Mandrake itself, the subsequent purge from the Pallas data banks of everything about Mandrake.

"All sounds okay to me," said Mord when Bat finally opened his eyes again. "I'm disappointed. Seems you know everything there is to know already."

"I know very little. What was happening on Mandrake, and why was it destroyed? Why did the *Pelagic* have to flee? Why were the Pallas data banks purged? Can you answer any of those questions?"

"I can answer all of 'em. But what's in it for me?"

Ten minutes earlier that question would have thrown Bat; but he was adjusting to Mord. "I will make it worth your while to help me. But what I cannot do is to specify the inducements that you would find attractive. The usual pleasures of the flesh, if you will pardon my saying so, are unlikely to be items of strong prevailment in your case."

"Not like you, eh?" The image on the screen was grinning at Bat. "Mega-chomps is thinking, 'Mord ain't got no mouth, ain't got no dick. He don't eat, he don't drink, he don't screw. So what turns him on?' I'll tell you what. *Information.* You scratch my data bank and I'll scratch yours. But it has to be high-proof stuff, not garbage. Do you have anything that's not in the public files?"

"I have little else."

"Then that's what I want."

"But if it is provided to you, it must go no farther."

"'Course not. What do you think I am? Knowledge is power, but not if you spread it around."

Bat had his second revelation. Mord was more interesting—and more like Bat himself in many ways—than anyone in the Ganymede Transportation Department. Set aside the gross vulgarisms, which had obviously been imposed on Mord by his creator, and what remained was a kindred spirit. One, moreover, who could never intrude with a physical presence. Bat didn't *want* Mord to go back to Ceres. He liked him here, in Bat Cave. "Mord, I agree completely. We will trade information."

"Good enough." Mord nodded. "So I'll be a nice guy and go first. Let's see. Better start with the easy ones. Mandrake. You knew, did you, that it was an asteroid dedicated to Belt weapons development, right through the war? Naturally, what was being done there was a big secret. But at the end, I think a lot of high-ups in the Belt government got real nervous about whatever sort of horrors they'd been cooking up. When Mandrake was wiped out, I always wondered if mebbe our own side had done it. Too convenient otherwise. Couldn't prove that, mind you. The bosses were too clever to leave tracks.

"So Mandrake's colony and labs went bye-bye, nothing left but ash and hot rock. Official word, enemy attack. And next we got word to wipe out all references to Mandrake from the Pallas data banks. We did it, of course. It was that, or get wiped ourselves. But a few of us couldn't resist peeking as we purged, to see just what we were getting rid of. Far as I could see it was no big deal. Biological weapons of some kind, never found out what. But every one of them was destroyed during the Mandrake attacks."

"What about the *Pelagic*? It left Mandrake, and it was destroyed by a Seeker missile. A Belt missile."

"Never heard that name, *Pelagic*, before today. But if it made a run out of Mandrake near the end of the war, more than likely it was a bunch of the same experimenters running for cover—running from *their own side*, see, because I doubt that the Inner System even knew Mandrake was there. But they didn't run good enough, and they got zapped by a Seeker. Don't ever believe anyone who tells you that the Belt government was good during the war and the Inner System was bad. I was there, and far as I can tell they were *all* bastards. When they knew that peace was about to break out, they did anything they could to save their own rotten necks."

Mord scratched his nose thoughtfully, a gesture that made Bat wonder how much physical sensation could be built into a simulation. Did Mord itch? Did he—Bat could no longer think of the simulation as it—feel pain? Did he *dream*, in some cool swirl of maverick electrons?

"I think I've done my bit," Mord went on. "It's time for a little bit of the good old quid pro quo before you get more from me. You promised me some dirt. Remember?"

"It will be provided. But you must tell me the preferred form of input."

"Well, not like this, that's for sure. With all due respect to flesh—and you got a lot of it—when you have attosecond circuitry, like me, you chafe a bit when your data's fed to you at human speeds. Just give me a nice, broadband bus, and watch me guzzle. I'll help myself. Then we can talk some more about Pallas."

"At once." Bat reached for his control keyboard. "If you will permit one more thought before data transfer begins . . . I cannot help wondering if you have continuous consciousness. Or are there periods when you are turned off?"

"Getting a bit personal, aren't we?" Mord grinned. "No, I don't have continuous consciousness. What do you think I am? I need my beauty sleep, just like any other normal person." He raised his hand. "But right now I feel a data attack creeping up on me, so adios. See you in a while. And hey, Mega-chops, as one freak to another—lose some weight."

It was ridiculous to resent the insults of a mere simulation. The measure of Mordecai Perlman's success was the irritation that Bat felt at Mord's comment. But Bat knew that he should not be annoyed; Mordecai Perlman's success might be crucial to his own.

He crouched in his chair, his cowled robe pulled round his body. There had been definite progress: *biological weapons on Mandrake.*

And all destroyed? Bat might have accepted that were it not for Yarrow Gobel. The inspector-general was doing well, already advanced to maybe ten years old. He was extravert, bubbling over with rebellion and wild ideas, and physically fit. Bat wondered at what age Gobel had been when his personality changed from would-be explorer and soldier of fortune to the cautious, sober monitor of fiscal irregularities.

The attack on Gobel—on Bat himself—was proof that everything that had happened on Mandrake was *not* far off in the faded past. It was making a difference here and now, on Ganymede. Why, and how? Mandrake had been a center for biological experiments, intended to create new weapons for use in the Great War. Even, perhaps, Yarrow Gobel's "secret weapon." What relevance could that possibly have for today?

"*Most* of them were destroyed." Bat was muttering to himself. He had been awake for twenty-seven hours, and he was approaching exhaustion. "But what if an experiment, or its creator, *survived*?"

Then there would be a reason for that person to cut off any investigation likely to lead toward him—or her. Which raised the next question: Who in the Jovian system *today* could have been active on Mandrake at the time of the Great War?

Bat could not answer that. Not until he had slept. Tomorrow, with further help from Mord, he might find another angle of attack.

But the information he had already received was enough to set in train a new line of thought. The phrase "survival pod" carried its own psychological weight. A person hearing the term automatically thought "survival of people." But nothing required that a pod had to be used for such a purpose. Suppose that the pods had been used for something very different—say, as protected environments for something small, like microorganisms? Then the usual cutoff time beyond which the pod would be unable to support life was meaningless. The pod trajectories should have been examined not for the span of a mere month or two after the *Pelagic*'s destruction, but for their course over the years.

The programs to propagate those trajectories forward through time were already set up in Megachirops' file. Bat gave the command to execute them over an increased time range, and asked the same question as before: Were any survival pods picked up consistent with those orbital paths?

He did not have to watch the computations proceed. The results would be awaiting him when he awoke. He went to lie down, a mound of exhausted flesh pillowed and draped sybaritically in cushions and sheets of black silk.

His thoughts moved to Mord, to a Mordecai Perlman stripped of all material attributes, freed of all material needs, divested of all material pleasures. What was left? Thought, and the joys of pure intellect.

That would not suffice for Bat. Certainly not now, with thirty kilos of live lobster from Yarrow Gobel's sea farm still crawling in the Bat Cave tanks. To wait or not to wait? And for how long? Today's Gobel was disgusted at the very idea of eating something that he said looked like an enormous diseased insect. Yet it seemed unfair to feast on the gift without the participation of its donor . . .

Bat yawned, hugely.

Intellect was surely not everything. Not yet.

But someday, perhaps, when appetites waned and the burdens of aging flesh increased . . . well, then it might be enough . . . for Megachirops.

Bat slept, in curious contentment, while at the far end of Bat Cave tireless programs stepped a set of orbits forward through time from the destruction of the *Pelagic*. Possible fits were sought with the coordinates and velocities of pods recovered from space. And, at last, times and places of matches were recorded.

They were the simplest of routines, these programs, without the ability to be surprised or delighted at anything they found.

That pleasure would be reserved for Bat, upon his awakening.

17

De Profundis

Jon Perry and Wilsa Sheer returned to a different world.

They had left the surface of Europa and entered into the black pupil of Blowhole with the communications unit of the *Danae* set to maximum volume. They had not realized that it was even turned on, because Europa's ice blanket provided a quiet radio environment. The signal bands had been inactive when they were above the surface, and once beneath it all messages were damped to nothing by the surrounding water.

They had spent two days exploring the upper layers of the Europan ocean. Peaceful and productive days for Wilsa, frustrating days for Jon. It was galling to be confined to the "continental shelves" of Europa, above the ten-kilometer level, when he knew that the interesting part of the seabed, with its black and grey smokers, was dozens of kilometers deeper.

Yet he recognized the importance of this preliminary dive. He had to learn how well his experience gained on Earth applied to Europa; and he had to develop a feel for the important variables: the rate at which pressure increased with depth; the range of visibility through the clear, salt-free water; and the characteristic shape of submarine features. The last was surprisingly similar to Earth's. The undersea reefs and mountains of Terra, buoyed by surrounding water, often rose close to vertical from the deeps. Jon saw structures in the Europan ocean that he could swear he had met before on the PacAnt Ridge.

And then, at last, it was time to put surface suits on and ascend through Blowhole's narrow cylinder of warmed, open water to the icebound Europan surface. The final climb was made in total and uncanny silence. Neither Jon nor Wilsa felt like talking as the *Danae* rose under its own buoyancy, all of its engines off.

The blurt of sound that burst from the communications unit as the submersible rose the final few meters to the top of Blowhole and the antennae of the *Danae* cleared the waterline was enough to make Wilsa clap her hands over her ears. She was super-sensitive to sounds, and that loud, discordant noise *hurt*.

The monitor showed half a dozen messages, either being sent or in waiting mode on the emergency frequency. A man's voice, vaguely familiar but so grossly distorted by amplification that it could not be understood, was blaring from the speakers.

Wilsa turned and shouted to Jon in the pilot's seat, "What's going on?"

He shook his head and reached out to reduce the channel gain. As the *Danae* moved higher in the water and grapnels took hold to drag it up the smooth ascent ramp to open ice, a new, faint and far-off voice sounded from the speaker.

"Moving into fixed altitude, height twenty-four-fifty. We'll need a beacon direction before we can do a surface triangulation. Please confirm."

"Sorry, but we've lost it again," said the louder voice that they had first heard. "Hold on. It's the right distress signal, I'm sure of that. But it's being broadcast into a narrow solid-angle, and I think we've moved out of the cone. Maybe we have enough data anyway."

"That's Tristan!" said Wilsa. "Tristan Morgan. What can he possibly be doing on Europa?" *And am I somehow responsible for it?*

"Not on it. *Above* it." Jon pointed to the three-dimensional display that showed signal direction. "He's flying—in bound orbit, for a guess.'"

"We're picking it up now, too," said yet a third voice. "You're right, there's a sharp cut-in, from no signal to maximum strength. The car must be stuck in a steep-sided surface pocket, with the ice cutting off the beam. Stand by for range data."

"Receiving," said Tristan. And then, seconds later, "Hold on. We have a preliminary data reduction and a signal origin. It's much closer to Mount Ararat than we expected. We compute only twenty-five kilometers' linear distance—less than five from Blowhole. Is anyone at the station there?"

"No, damn it." The fourth voice was Buzz Sandstrom's, as angry as ever. "I sent everybody ranging way out, because we thought that's where the car was going to be found. Get an exact fix while I start bringing them back."

Jon glanced at Wilsa and flicked the transmission switch. "This is Jon Perry and Wilsa Sheer on the *Danae*. We don't know what's happening, because we've just come up Blowhole. But it sounds like you have a problem. Can we help?"

A wild babble emerged from the speaker. "One at a time." Tristan's voice cut through the rest. "Perry, we have an emergency on the surface just a few kilometers from you. Mount Ararat, is there a spare ground vehicle at Blowhole?"

"There are a couple." It was a fifth voice, and remarkable for its calm. "Dr. Perry, this is Hilda Brandt. Camille

Hamilton became stranded on the surface almost forty-two hours ago. We have finally determined her location, but her physical condition is unknown. The ground cars are straightforward to drive. You are closer than anyone else."

"Right. We're on our way." Jon was nodding to Wilsa and lifting the seal of the *Danae*. "Just tell us the direction. I'll call you as soon as we're inside a car."

"*No*. You will need more than the direction. Surface travel on Europa is always tricky, and it can be dangerous. Do not begin to drive until we provide you with detailed navigational data."

Her orders sounded like overprotection to Jon. The ground vehicle was as simple to drive as Hilda Brandt had promised. But within the first few minutes, he learned why she had insisted on providing navigation details. Travel through Europa's interior ocean called for no more than awareness of depth and pressure, plus avoidance of the upper and lower bounding surfaces of ice and seabed. Travel on the surface, though, was wholly controlled by gravity. Even on so small a world as Europa, it was not safe to plunge a car down near-vertical slopes or to risk being stuck in narrow-sided and bottomless crevices.

Jon did not try to second-guess the instructions coming through the communicator. He followed exactly as directed the sinuous lines of ice ridges and crept slowly along bleak and sheer-sided valleys. Five linear kilometers stretched to more than twice that in ground travel before Sandstrom's gruff voice was saying, "Slow now, and very cautious. We can't guide you beyond here. According to our data reduction, the distress signal from Camille Hamilton's car is coming from no more than a hundred meters ahead of you."

"Stay right there, Jon." Wilsa opened the door and stepped out onto the ice. She pointed at two parallel tracks, etched deep into the spongy surface and dark-shadowed under the slanting sunlight. "It's getting softer.

Don't move forward until I tell you that it's all right. This surface is strong enough for me, but I'm not sure about the car."

She walked cautiously forward. Already she could see something in the ice ahead, a rectangular block of darkness that reflected no light at all. The tracks of the ground car became deeper. She went more slowly, and in the final twenty meters to the hole she dropped to hands and knees to spread her weight. The terrible cold seemed to instantly suck away warmth through her suit. Half an hour of this and she would freeze.

She crept forward to the edge of the hole and found herself peering down into a gloomy cavern. She waited impatiently, until her eyes had partially adjusted. At the bottom of the cavern, five or six meters below her, she could at last make out the outline of a ground car. Nothing moved.

"I've found it." Wilsa began to wriggle her way back from the edge.

"I'll pass the word," said Jon. And then, "They ask, is she inside?"

They don't mean that. They mean, is she alive? "I can't tell." Wilsa paced cautiously back to the car. She could see her outgoing footprints in the grainy surface, but they were only a couple of centimeters deep.

"I'm going to take a look." Jon was climbing down to the surface to meet her, a towing cable over one shoulder and a portable communication unit in his hand. "If you'll come with me, and lower me down . . ."

"No." Wilsa turned and led the way. "You're twice my weight, and you've got Earth muscles. I go down. You stay on top and pull me out when I tell you."

He nodded, and they walked forward in silence to a point half a dozen paces from the hole. There he stopped and handed Wilsa the looped cable. "I'd love to see what's down there, but two of us might be more load than the rim can take. I'll step back a few meters for safety, then you go ahead. Keep me informed through your suit phone. I'll pass the word to the others."

Both of them knew what Wilsa was likely to find down there. But she did not think at all that Jon was shirking an unpleasant duty. He could have one of his own, just as distasteful. If they were right and Camille was dead, it would be Jon's task to inform the waiting searchers, in orbit and at Mount Ararat.

Wilsa noosed the cable around her waist and under her armpits, nodded to Jon, and walked steadily to the hole. She sat down, made sure that he had a firm hold on his end of the cable, then slid in one movement over the edge. The rough cable fibers scraped and cut into the ice, lowering her in a series of jerks until she landed a couple of feet from the car.

The light within the ice cavern was that of a pearly, blue-tinged twilight, quite enough to see by once she was used to it. Wilsa took a deep breath. She didn't like the thought of what came next, but there was no point in delay. She stepped over to the car, reached up for the roof hatch—the main door was blocked by the ice wall—and slid it back. As she had feared, the driver's seat was occupied. Slumped back in it was a still, human form wearing a surface suit.

Wilsa climbed inside, leaned close, and swore. The inside of the suit helmet carried a coating of ice crystals. She reached out and squeezed a forearm. It was as solid and unyielding as stone.

"She's here, Jon." Wilsa was amazed at the steadiness of her voice. "And I'm afraid that she is dead. Frozen. Tell them the bad news while I put the cable around her. When I give the word, lift her out."

"Put it around both of you. I can manage the load."

"I'm not sure you can." Wilsa had been making a closer inspection of the body. It was that of a hugely fat person, swollen and grotesquely misshapen as though it had been inflated like a balloon. The corpse did not appear to be that of a normal woman who had simply frozen to death. "Lift her up first, then we'll worry about me. The car can stay here until a party comes out for it from Mount Ararat."

She placed the looped cable gently around the body, making sure that nothing caught when Jon began to lift. He grunted with surprise at the weight, but pulled steadily. Wilsa watched the body rise, catch for a tricky moment on the underside of the hole, then roll like a ridiculous balloon clown up over the lip.

After it disappeared there was a long, long wait, which Wilsa passed by examining the status indicators of the car. It was ironic; there was enough power to take it back to Mount Ararat ten times over. But the energy for the heaters was totally exhausted. All of the car's food was gone, and most surprising, so was all of the water.

"Just a few moments more." Jon's voice sounded puzzled in her suit radio. "Is there anything in the car that might positively identify the body as Camille Hamilton?"

Wilsa found that question baffling. One person had been lost out on Europa, one person had been found—who the devil else could it be? "I don't see anything." She stared at the control panel. "The computer is still turned on, and there are data modules in place. But I can't see any form of individual identification. Why do you ask?"

"I just described her appearance to Mount Ararat. They say it sounds all wrong. Camille Hamilton was *thin*, thin and blond and fragile. I can't see her hair color, because of the ice inside the helmet. But you saw the body, and nobody could say it was thin. It's huge."

"I'm ready to come up." Wilsa did not want to talk anymore. She did not know Camille Hamilton, but the *identity* of the body was not the important thing. The touch of marble limbs, which only one day ago had been part of a living, breathing woman . . . that was too much, whoever she had been.

The drive back to Mount Ararat was dreadful. All of the pleasure and contentment that Wilsa had experienced while cruising the deep ocean had vanished. She sat close to Jon, aware at every moment of the journey that a bloated, icy tragedy lay only a few feet behind them. Jon had wanted to open the suit helmet, to look at the face within and try to confirm the corpse's identity. Wilsa would not allow it. The idea that the woman's face, even in death, should be exposed to the sleeting downpour of ions was too much. Wilsa kept thinking of Mozart's funeral, Mozart dead at thirty-five, of the dreary ride to the pauper's grave, the lid-slipped coffin, the endless December rain driving into the open, mute mouth.

Wilsa kept the cabin temperature sweltering hot, as though further cold could do more harm to those rigid limbs. And still she shivered.

If the journey was bad, the arrival at Mount Ararat was worse. Wilsa wanted solitude; but when Jon halted the ground car, it seemed that the whole population of Europa had come to mourn.

There was Tristan, returned from orbit and staring at Wilsa with an awful kick-me expression that was totally out of place on his cheerful face. There was Nell Cotter, regarding Wilsa and Jon with a cold, speculative eye. And worst of all, there was a towering stranger, David Lammerman, whose face lit up with joy when he saw the size of the bulky figure being carried from the car. But when Camille Hamilton's helmet was opened and her frozen, lifeless face was revealed, he gasped and stood motionless while tears ran down his cheeks.

"Can you identify her?" asked Hilda Brandt.

Lammerman nodded numbly.

"Very well." The older woman took charge. She had seemed on their arrival as upset as anyone, but after her first close inspection of Camille's face she became calm and businesslike. "We can't let her stay here. Let's go to my rooms, where it's warmer. We all need warmth. Four of you, give a hand with the stretcher."

"It's all right. I'll take her." Lammerman lifted the body alone, cradling it tenderly in his arms, and moved off after Hilda Brandt. The others followed, heading for Brandt's private quarters. Jon Perry fell into step with Nell Cotter and began talking to her, while Tristan lagged behind with Wilsa, last in the group.

"I didn't expect to see you here." Wilsa knew how stilted and awkward her words sounded. "I thought it was really difficult to get permission to visit Europa. So when I got the chance to come—a chance I thought I'd never have again . . ."

It wasn't an apology. Not quite. But Tristan seized it gratefully. "It's almost impossible to get here usually, because Hilda Brandt likes to keep the wrong people out. But when she learned that Camille Hamilton was lost out on the surface, she threw all the rules overboard. She let Lammerman in. And Cyrus Mobarak provided the ships for the high-resolution search. Otherwise . . ."

He stopped abruptly and closed his eyes.

Otherwise? Otherwise, Tristan had been about to say, we would have been too late. (And I thought at first that it was *you*.)

But we were *too late*. Wilsa reached out and squeezed Tristan's hand. He clung to it desperately, like a lifeline, and did not let go even when they entered Hilda Brandt's suite.

Everyone was present except David Lammerman. He must have taken Camille's body somewhere else. To a morgue? wondered Wilsa. She took a seat near the door. *A morgue, on Europa. But the whole world was a morgue. Its frigid, kilometers-deep crust was a natural tomb, a sarcopha-*

gus big enough to hold everyone in the solar system, past or present.

At that thought, Wilsa's traitorous mind created a roll of muffled drums, followed by a mournful *sordino* phrase deep in the cellos and basses.

A requiem mass for Camille Hamilton, whom she had never met in life? There were stranger things. Wilsa allowed Tristan to hold her hand while she retreated into the one place that she knew sorrows could not reach. She realized that the others in the room were talking, gesturing, arguing, but she could not hear them. Normal speech did not get through when composition seized her.

Disturbance, when it came, was physical.

And urgent.

A great hand gripped her arm. She looked up to find a big, wild-eyed face staring into hers. It was David Lammerman, dragging her to her feet. He seemed as unable to speak as she had been unable to listen. He hustled her outside, with Tristan following. Nell Cotter, obeying her natural instinct, quietly rose, turned on her camera, and went after them.

Lammerman had placed the body of Camille Hamilton on a long trestle table in the next room. Her suit helmet was off, and the double suit that she was wearing was peeled away from her arms and torso. Wilsa saw a bloated, neckless head and pale, swollen limbs, each as thick as her own thighs. The skin of the upper arms was translucent and tight-stretched, like milky latex film.

Lammerman drew Wilsa closer to the table. She stared down at Camille Hamilton and realized that the stony rigidity of the corpse was disappearing in the warm air. The bulging forearms were sagging, their stretched skin dimpling as body liquids pooled under Europa's gentle gravity.

"Look!" David Lammerman's grip on Wilsa's arm was strong enough to bruise. She gazed down, saw nothing, and tried to pull away. Then the mouth of the corpse moved in a tiny, near-invisible spasm.

Escaping body gases? But the sodden eyelashes were quivering.

"Oh, my God. She's *alive!*" Wilsa touched the swollen cheek. The skin was clammy, but it had warmed to more than room temperature. She turned to Tristan. "She *is.* We need a doctor."

He hesitated for a second, fighting the urge to stay and watch. Then he nodded and was gone. Nell Cotter moved forward, bending low over the body.

"She's breathing now. Lift her head."

But the words were unnecessary. Blue eyes flickered open for a split second, while the puffed hands began to scrabble at the tabletop. There was a faint grunt of discomfort and effort.

"Help her," said Wilsa. "She's trying to sit up."

The two women raised the body carefully to a sitting position. David Lammerman leaned close. "Camille. Can you hear me?"

The eyes remained closed, but a whimper came from the parted lips.

"She's hurting," he said. "Camille, how can we help you?"

There was a silence. "She can't hear you," said Nell. But Camille's eyes were opening again, to wander vaguely around the room and to at last return to focus on Wilsa and Nell. The swollen cheeks puffed in and out. And the slack mouth spoke. "Bathroom. Need . . . go bathroom."

Wilsa and Nell stared at each other in confusion. But the gross body was trying to stand up.

"Take one arm." Nell gripped and lifted. Wilsa grabbed hold, and in a moment Camille Hamilton stood teetering between the two women. She was huge, twice as wide as either of them.

"Bathroom," she said again. "Donkey-headed and . . . impulsive. Gotta pee."

"She knows what she wants," said Nell. "Better do it."

"It's this way," said Wilsa. Between them they guided Camille slowly along the corridor, with David Lammerman drifting helplessly behind. Before they reached the bathroom, everyone else came hurrying out of Hilda Brandt's rooms.

"Stay clear," said Nell firmly. What she and Wilsa were doing was tricky enough without half a dozen others crowding around. "She's alive. We're going in here."

"Gotta pee," said Camille urgently.

They eased the rest of the double suit off her. The body revealed was lumpy and grotesque, hard islands of flesh sitting amid distended bulges of liquid flab, and all within that pale skin stretched to breaking. As soon as she was free of the suit, Camille staggered single-mindedly into a stall.

"What's happening?" David Lammerman poked his head in. "Gabriel Shumi is here—the Europan chief medical officer."

"She's going to the bathroom," said Nell. "Get the hell away, and tell the others to stay out, too. The doctor can look at her as soon as she's done." Then to Wilsa, when he had vanished, "If she's *ever* done. This is ridiculous. It's been *minutes*. How long can she keep it up?"

Wilsa surveyed the still-swollen body, and listened to the steady and apparently endless expulsion of liquid. "Quite a while. She probably masses fifty kilos normally. I'd guess that she's over a hundred and fifty at the moment. I think it's all just extra water. When she was out on the ice, she must have drunk twenty gallons of it."

"Why, for God's sake?"

But Camille was trying to stand up. "Think I'm done," she said in a slurred voice. "For the moment. Have to stay near here, though. More where that came from."

They helped her into her suit. Once dressed and on her feet, she was able to move unaided into the corridor. A gurney was waiting, and the physician standing next to it did not give Camille the option of walking. He had her on it and ready to be wheeled away within seconds.

Dr. Shumi waved aside the others when they tried to follow. He was a tall, elegant man, with a great air of authority. *Be a big hit*, thought Nell, *among the Inner Circle back on Earth*. But she sensed a deep-seated unease behind that professional poise, and she could make a guess at the cause. Any physician who chose to practice on a small research station like Mount Ararat must be *avoiding* medical problems, not seeking them out. Minor ailments were cured on site, major ones shipped at once to Ganymede's superior facilities. Gabriel Shumi had it easy. He must be profoundly uncomfortable with an anomaly like Camille Hamilton suddenly dropped in his lap.

"I promise to return and give you a report as soon as I can," the doctor was saying. "But I cannot allow spectators."

"Will she be all right?" asked David Lammerman.

"Well, it's too soon for me to give you an opinion on that."

His halfhearted tone confirmed Nell's impression. Gabriel Shumi was out of his depth, and he didn't like it. Dead people who came back to life were not in his casebook.

"I've never in my life seen so much edema," he went on. "Fluid retention and swelling. Her body seems to be taking care of that problem in the . . . er, the natural way. As far as I can tell, she's doing well. But I need to do a thorough examination."

He waved off further questions and hustled the gurney away along the corridor. With the removal of Camille's presence, the group spun away into small clusters to talk about what they had seen; and then, when that phenomenon did not yield to analysis, to discuss other things. Tristan and Wilsa locked themselves into an intense personal conversation. David Lammerman listened in silence to Buzz Sandstrom, who was denying that he had forced Camille out onto the ice. But David heard hardly a word. His face glowed with joy, not with accusation. He did not understand how Camille had survived. He did not care. *She was alive!*

Nell stood alone. She had not merely *seen*, she had recorded. Every element of the resurrection was on video, even Camille's amazing bladder action, but Nell wasn't sure of what to do with the film. There was surely a place in Earth's junk-sport programs for a clip of the solar system's longest continuous pee, but that was a branch of the business that Nell was happy to avoid. What did it all *mean*? Until she knew that, her footage was a mere curiosity.

She scanned the group. When she came to Hilda Brandt, the research director met her eye and jerked her head for Nell to come over to her. She went reluctantly.

"Isn't it nice to have a happy ending for a change?" Brandt was apparently as pleasant and unassuming as ever. "But I think this particular party is over. I know that you, at least, are wondering what comes next. I'm afraid that it has to be an anticlimax. Jon Perry stays here and does the job for which he came to Europa. But everyone else must leave. This is a protected environment. Although I must say, it hasn't looked anything like that for the past twenty-four hours."

Her eyes, bright and innocent, gazed into Nell's. "I need help. Will you give a hand getting everyone out of here without a fuss? If you do, I give my word that you'll be in the front row when Jon Perry comes back next time from the Europan seabed."

Hilda Brandt was behaving as though nothing out of the ordinary had happened. Her casual manner reduced Camille's revival from the impossible to the commonplace. Nell nodded, even as she subvocalized: *What does she really think of all this? And why me? Why has Hilda Brandt singled me out to help her?*

She could think of only one answer. Brandt understood, like no one else in the group, the advantage of a friendly press. Comparing that understanding with the adolescent naiveté of Outward Bound, Nell again sensed an incongruity. Outward Bound members and sophistication lived in different universes. But somehow Hilda Brandt inhabited both.

Nell tried to shepherd people along the corridor. They would not budge. It would take physical violence to move them until they received another report from Dr. Shumi on Camille's condition. She caught Hilda Brandt's eye and shrugged. The older woman smiled sympathetically, as though she had *expected* Nell to be unsuccessful. She did not seem upset by the failure.

Nell's mind continued to spin with puzzling questions. *So why did she ask me, if she knew it wouldn't work?* And an answer, a flash of inspiration: *She wanted to give me a job that would isolate me from talking to the others. But why?* And finally, a warning to herself: *Be careful. Pawns never get to see much of the board. There is more to the Outer System, Nell Cotter, than is dreamed of in your philosophy. If you want to get to the bottom of all this, you'd better not forget it. And if you want to stay out of trouble, you'd better not confuse Hilda Brandt's statements with her motives.*

18

Deep Discovery

Jon Perry was thoroughly miserable. He had never been good at understanding emotions, his own or anybody else's. He had watched Nell Cotter as she wandered through the group urging everyone back toward Hilda Brandt's quarters, and he had tried without success to read her facial expression. Finally he went over to her. She greeted him with a small, distant nod. She accepted his offer of assistance, and she even talked to him freely enough; but it was the bright, impersonal chatter of a stranger in an elevator.

Until, without warning, she turned and whispered in a low, savage voice: "*Why did you do it?* And *don't* say, 'Do what?'"

Jon had wondered the same thing himself. He liked Wilsa, and he felt totally at ease with her. But that was not the reason he had headed for Europa with her after as good as promising that he would take Nell with him. And he had *wanted* to go with Nell.

He shook his head. "I don't know. I'm sorry, but I really don't. I don't know why I did it."

She stared at him for two seconds, standing motionless

in her characteristic cocked-head stance. "You just saved your face, Jon Perry. Not to mention some other bits. You gave me the only answer I can believe. All right, then."

He followed her eyes as she surveyed the others. They were moving, slowly but steadily, toward Hilda Brandt's suite of rooms.

"They can go the rest of the way without us." Nell linked her arm in his. "We'll stay outside. I have to talk to you."

"I've been wanting to talk to you for days."

"So you get your chance. But first, you listen. Hilda Brandt wants me and the rest of us off Europa within the next few hours. Everybody except you. But Wilsa says that she's been invited to come back after her next set of concerts. Did you arrange that?"

"No. Honest. Nell, I didn't even know about it. I don't feel that way about Wilsa."

"Then how *do* you feel about her? Oh, hell, I'm not going to start that again. But I'm damned if I'll go back to Ganymede to stew over you without knowing where I stand. Make up your mind, Jon Perry. Are you and I going to be an item, or aren't we?"

"Well . . ."

"No stalling." She reached up to grab him by the ears, hard enough to hurt. "Yes or no?"

"Yes. *Definitely* yes. I wasn't stalling. I want you, want to be with you. It's what I've thought about ever since we got to Arenas. You're so-m-mm—"

The rest of his sentence was smothered by an urgent kiss on the lips from Nell. "Tell me the good stuff some other time," she said as she released him. "We'll have to postpone everything else, because they're coming. Don't think I'm a patient woman, though."

Jon glanced toward Hilda Brandt's suite, then realized that Nell was not looking in that direction. He turned to scan the main corridor. Dr. Gabriel Shumi approached—

and with him, barely recognizable, was a plump, fair-haired woman. The corpse from the ice tomb. Her face was patchy with broken veins and blotches of pink, and the doctor had his hand ready at her arm; but as they entered Brandt's suite, she was walking steadily and without assistance.

"Camille Hamilton," said Nell. "Come on. I have to cover this."

She and Jon hurried into the room just as Shumi was beginning to talk. Camille, a little bewildered-looking to Jon now that he could see her eyes, sat on a broad, cloth-covered armchair in the middle of the chamber.

"I promised a report for Dr. Brandt as soon as possible, otherwise I'd not be here now." The physician's fine-featured face wore an unhappy expression. His own words were repugnant to him. "And if I hadn't been assured by everyone in this room that Camille Hamilton was frozen solid and apparently dead an hour ago, I'd ask you to stop playing games and wasting the time of overworked doctors. Miss Hamilton, please stand up. And turn around."

Camille did so, wobble-legged and bowing her head in embarrassment. "I feel like the prize exhibit in an old-fashioned animal show. A turkey, maybe." She glanced at everyone in turn. "Where are Jon Perry and Wilsa Sheer? I want to thank them for saving my life."

"As you can see," went on Shumi, "she appears to be recovering, and she's functioning almost normally. But please don't ask me, or anyone else in the medical facility, *how*. There are two or three ways of taking a human being's body temperature all the way down below freezing point and back up, safely, and we do it often enough in tricky operations. But it doesn't just *happen* because someone is exposed to extreme cold."

"People who fall through ice," volunteered Tristan, "into freezing water . . ."

"All of their systems switch off and their body temper-

ature drops in a few seconds. The brain's oxygen require-
ment drops, too. That's how they can survive." Gabriel
Shumi gestured to Camille to sit down again. "But that's
not what happened here, according to everything that was
told to me. The temperature in her car would have gone
down slowly, over a period of time. That's a killer. And
stranger than that, you have the retained water . . . and
the ice."

"*Ice*?" Hilda Brandt had been smiling at Camille with a
proprietary air.

"Solid ice, Dr. Brandt. When we got Miss Hamilton to
the X-ray department, there were lumps of water-ice
scattered over her body, close to the skin. Anything from
a few grams to a couple of kilos. As they melted she got rid
of the excess water in the natural way—sixty kilograms
from the time she stepped into my lab to the time she
stepped out of it. A wonderful flushing job for the
kidneys, you might say. I estimate that there are still about
fifteen to twenty kilos to go before she reaches her usual
body weight. But it's all liquid."

"No hurry *now*," said Camille. She smiled. "You're all
quite safe, I won't disgrace myself."

"Wouldn't the formation of ice *help*?" asked David
Lammerman. He wore a nonstop grin. "I mean, when
water turns to ice, it gives up its latent heat. That heat
would keep the temperature up in the rest of the body."

"Indeed it would. And it did." Shumi nodded at David
in a patronizing way. "But I challenge you to tell me *how*
it could help in this case. If I drank ten or twenty gallons
of water—assuming I could swallow that much, which I'm
sure I couldn't—and you started to freeze me, I might
begin to form lumps of ice all through my body . . . but
they certainly wouldn't show up in just the places to keep
the rest of me from freezing."

"*Did* you do that?" David Lammerman had been edging

closer to Camille. He wanted to grab her. "Drink twenty gallons of water?"

"David, I don't know *what* I did." Camille moved forward and slipped her arm through his. "As far as I'm concerned, it all happened just the way I told it to Dr. Shumi. I was sitting in the car, knowing that I didn't have enough heat and convinced that I'd freeze to death before anyone noticed my beacon or realized that I was missing. Then I started analyzing new data I'd received from DOS—I guess that was my form of mental escape. The last thing I remember, I was in the middle of doing calculations and they were getting really interesting. And then I woke up. Woke up *here*. I don't recall drinking water, or becoming unconscious, or *anything*. Maybe something about being frozen affected my brain, though I feel normal enough now."

"It didn't affect you," said Shumi. "Not in any of the usual ways. I pulled in your brain-scan profile from Ganymede. Your performance is exactly the same as always."

"So what *did* happen to me?"

"That's the point where we came in." Gabriel Shumi glanced across at Hilda Brandt. "I can't answer that question. Although I admit that Miss Hamilton has every reason to ask it. Maybe in a few days . . ."

"Do you have a recommendation for me, Dr. Shumi?"

"Well, she certainly shouldn't leave Europa until she is physically back to normal. That might be as soon as three days from now if she keeps up this rate of progress. But of course I'd like to make a closer examination—"

"If she consents. She is a *patient* with us, you know, not a test animal."

"Of course." Shumi was taken aback at the unexpected edge in Hilda Brandt's voice.

"Very well." The director moved to stand in front of Camille and gazed into her eyes. She seemed pleased by what she saw. "So that's the deal, my dear. Even if Dr. Shumi hadn't insisted on it, I was going to refuse to let you go for at least a couple of days."

She straightened up. "And for the rest of you, I'm afraid the party's over. This is a research facility, though you might find that hard to believe from present operations. We'll find someone to make arrangements to take all of you over to Ganymede."

There was a casual certainty to her manner that discouraged argument. Nell, seeing her now, was doubly convinced that Hilda Brandt's earlier request for assistance had been made for other reasons. The director could have cleared the other room *alone*, and in just a couple of minutes, had she chosen to do so.

"But I have to stay, Nell," Jon whispered. "I'll be heading for the *Spindrift* in an hour or two. If you want me to have another try at persuading Dr. Brandt for you—"

"Waste of time. Look at her."

Jon stared at Hilda Brandt's relaxed, kindly face. "She looks approachable enough to me."

"That's because you don't know her. She's *approachable*, but she won't say yes."

"Well, if you want to take a few minutes with me, right now—"

"Why, Jon! You want a quickie? Lovely idea, but I don't think so. I gave those up ten years ago. Now I really like to *wallow*." Nell reached out to pat his cheek. "There, I've shocked you."

"I didn't mean *that*!"

"I know you didn't. You're Mister Innocent. It's just my lewd mind, and I must say that I'm tempted. I want to see you *bare*." Nell hesitated, and finally shook her head. "No. You go do your thing in the *Spindrift*, and keep those sexy hands on the controls. But remember, I'll be back—as soon as I can find a way to wangle it. Europa is where the action is."

* * *

Just my lewd mind. Jon decided he liked that. He had never known a woman who talked so, at least not to him. He thought about Nell all the way to Blowhole. How had he been smart enough to catch her? And why did *she* call *him* "Mister Innocent?" He was quite experienced, not innocent at all.

When at last he was on Blowhole's descending ramp of ice, he realized that Hilda Brandt had been wiser than he knew. The preliminary descent that he and Wilsa Sheer had made in the *Danae*, at the time unnecessary in Jon's mind, allowed him now to concentrate on the *Spindrift* rather than worry about what came later.

And he *needed* to concentrate. By Europan standards he was an experienced operator of the Blowhole system, so no one had been sent to help him with the ice-to-water launch. But part of his mind was still with Nell.

They were going to be with each other for a long time. They were going to share many wonderful years.

Unless thinking about her killed him first.

He looked up from the ice and found the *Spindrift* moving away from him. But its balance was quite different from the *Danae's*, and as a result he had placed the towing grapnels in the wrong place. The rounded, transparent vessel was tilting far forward. Chasing after it and correcting the list, he misjudged the amount of time left to him. When he looked up again the submersible was halfway along the ice ramp, its hatch wide open. He had to hop aboard and batten down when the submersible was on its last thirty meters of the inclined runway. Even then the seals did not seat cleanly. They finally came into alignment when water was already lapping at the vessel's base.

Then at last the *Spindrift* was balanced and free, gliding smoothly off the ice slipway and into the calm waters of Blowhole. For the first five minutes Jon allowed the submersible to fall uncontrolled, down through the thick-ribbed ice shield that girded Europa. Not until he passed the frozen lower boundary, where the pressure was already up to fifteen Earth atmospheres, did he lift his eyes from the gauges and monitors.

The only thing to strike him as out of place was the unfamiliar green of the pressure/depth indicator. That display had been modified, to change from the tenth of an atmosphere per meter pressure increase of Earth to the puny eightieth of an atmosphere increase per meter appropriate to Europa.

Puny—except that Jon was heading for black depths unheard of in Earth's oceans. More from habit than need (he knew by instinct where he was, and where he was going) he checked the inertial navigation system. Satisfied, he set an unhurried course for Scaldino: forty-seven kilometers down, water pressure six hundred Earth atmospheres. A high-pressure region even by Earth's standards.

He glanced at the new gauge. *Present depth: five and a half kilometers. Pressure: eighty-six atmospheres.*

He sent one of the free-swimmers ahead of the vessel and turned on its lights. The water was less clear than he remembered it from his last trip. Either the level of upwelling here was higher, or debris was melting out and falling from the bottom of the ice layer far above. That happened on Earth, too, in the Arctic Ocean. There was one huge difference here. The cloudiness in the Europan water could be from any sort of inorganic compound, but it could not be from the fascinating assorted detritus of living things, the miscellany that made every scoop of Earth water an experiment, a sample that might contain a previously unclassified species of life.

Jon wanted to examine as much of the seabed as possible on the way to Scaldino. He allowed the *Spindrift* to fall until he was within thirty meters of the bottom and could see the floor's jagged contours easily in the clear water.

Spikes of rock like blue and black sharks'-teeth jutted dangerously up toward the transparent hull of his vessel. The route was taking him past a northern underwater continuation of Mount Ararat. He skirted the flat, rocky table, which according to his charts rose in places all the way through the ice layer to within a couple of hundred meters of the surface of Europa.

Melt the blanket of ice and it would turn to water, with only nine-tenths of its original volume. The surface level would fall, perhaps far enough to leave this rock table exposed.

Jon thought of the Mobarak fusion project. Its success would turn near-surface submarine shelves like this one into prime candidates for life, abundant life like the coral colonies that populated the underwater shelves of Earth.

And if that happened, could native life compete? Given even minimal warmth and light, Earth's life was vigorous, tenacious, uncompromising. Europa's life might survive only if it were protected by inaccessibility, isolated by fifty kilometers of ocean.

Depth: nineteen kilometers. Pressure: two hundred and sixty atmospheres.

Thinking of the fusion project, Jon's thoughts moved to Camille. Her arrival at Europa on Mobarak's behalf, and her odd disappearance and reappearance, had drawn the others to the moon. They had now retreated to Ganymede, leaving Jon with the uncomfortable feeling that he had missed something important.

He was reminded of another experience, two years earlier. While working the slopes of the PacAnt Ridge in the *Spindrift* he had been following the glowing, yellow-green lights of a great colony of *Spirula* squid, all the way from a kilometer's depth up to within a couple of hundred meters of the ocean's surface. Because he had been below for two days without surface communication, he had not heard about the soliton. A gigantic isolated wave, over fifty meters high and a thousand kilometers long, had been sweeping across the whole southern Pacific, its course uninterrupted by land masses. While Jon was observing *Spirula*, the main crest of the soliton had moved right above him.

Although the solitary wave carried within it uncountable gigawatts of energy, Jon and the *Spindrift* were quite safe. The soliton was so broad that even the floating bases, out on the open surface, had been lifted effortlessly, up and up, and just as easily lowered.

But now Jon's built-in sense of absolute location caught the inexplicable lift and settling of the *Spindrift*. Even before his instruments confirmed the movement and the pressure change, the hair on the nape of his neck stood on end. Here was something profoundly unsettling: an unseen force that could arrive unannounced, quietly do its powerful work, and vanish just as silently and mysteriously.

But why did he think of that *now*, with reference not to the Europan ocean, but to the events on Mount Ararat? Because, momentarily, he had been filled with the same sense of great forces, poised to produce great effects. But like the soliton, those forces had moved on, their energies undissipated, leaving no sign behind that they had ever been. Leaving nothing but that sense of unease, of uncanny powers beyond control . . .

Depth: forty-five kilometers. Pressure: five hundred and seventy atmospheres.

The jagged rock spears were gone, replaced by a smooth, powdery surface, a snowfield of pale blue that ran on as far as the *Spindrift*'s lights could follow. No human had ever penetrated so deep into the pure liquid globe of Europa's ocean. Scaldino was supposed to be two kilometers deeper, and according to Jon's data readout the vent was less than one kilometer ahead. But the blue plain in front of him was uniformly flat.

Something had to change. Jon switched to ultrasonic imaging and caught a first glimpse of it. Not far ahead of the submersible the plain showed a crack, as straight and clean and narrow as a ruled line. He reduced speed and eased the *Spindrift* forward.

Two minutes later he was hovering on the brink of a sharp-edged crevasse, less than three hundred meters wide. The external water temperature was an extraordinary twenty degrees Celsius. Room temperature. This was the top of Scaldino, Europa's warmest known vent. The bottom must be even hotter.

Jon set the swimmers for pulsed laser production and moved to high-resolution imaging mode. Brief flashes of light provided him with snapshot glimpses of stark, vertical walls that plunged toward an unseen floor. He set the *Spindrift* to hold at a constant fifteen meters from the cliff face and began to cruise back and forth in five-kilometer sweeps, slowly descending.

He saw nothing of note. After the first hour he began to feel that the search was ridiculous. He was attempting the impossible. To hope to find an isolated pinpoint of life in the twenty-five million square kilometers of Europan seabed . . .

Except that the *Spindrift* was being vectored by an invisible pointer of heat flow. The submersible followed the temperature gradient, along and down the fissure. The external readings rose steadily. To thirty degrees Celsius. To forty. By Europan standards the heat within this rocky cleft was incredible, above blood heat. And Jon's instruments showed that the composition of the ambient water and of the sea cliff was perfect for the development of life: carbonates, sulfur, phosphorites, magnesium. The ingredients were all here, in abundance.

But, of course, life was far more than the right ingredients. Had Shelley Solbourne found merely the components, and mistakenly assumed that their presence and proportions automatically established the existence of living organisms?

He moved on, timing the blinking of his eyes to avoid missing the regular flashes of illumination.

Quite suddenly, at the end of the third hour, the evidence appeared.

Jon brought the submersible to a halt. In one pulse of light from the free-swimmers, he glimpsed a granular cluster of nodules clinging to the wall of the cliff. They were pale blue and rounded. Hair-thin tendrils emerging from their centers floated in the warm water, gently waving as they winnowed the upward current.

Shelley Solbourne had not been mistaken.

Life!

The nodules were tiny, the biggest one less than half a centimeter across. Jon did not worry about that. Size was meaningless. Back on Earth, humans happened to be giants, but almost all of the other forms on the planet were at the millimeter level and smaller.

He used the *Spindrift*'s remote handlers to detach, clip free, and store half a dozen of the little rounded shells. That was more than enough to provide the data he had come for, and he did not want to disturb a possibly delicate local balance.

He continued down, until upwelling material turned the water around the *Spindrift* to a murky soup through which the swimmers' lights could penetrate only a meter or two. The ultrasonics showed that the cleft was narrowing, to the point where the submersible could go no farther. The water temperature had stabilized at close to forty-three degrees Celsius. It was rich in minerals.

Jon took the *Spindrift* across the few meters to the other wall and increased the buoyancy a fraction. The submersible began to drift upward. Halfway to the lip of the pale-blue plain, he paused again. The smooth cliff face had given way to multiple broken strata whose uneven edges created a series of horizontal cracks. Each of the ledges thus formed was covered by a mass of fat, stubby worms, the biggest of which was as thick as Jon's forearm. The creatures were banded with vivid blue and yellow, like colorful leeches, and they pulsed in a lazy, rhythmic pattern of expansion and contraction, so slowly that it was necessary to watch for minutes to detect movement.

So Europa had its own giants. Jon used the waldoes to tease the writhing bundles delicately apart and placed half a dozen of the monster annelids into the *Spindrift*'s pressurized storage units. They would be safe there, even when he returned to the surface and began to analyze them.

Maybe that had been the problem when Shelley Solbourne discovered the Europan life forms. Without pressure storage, the finds would disintegrate and be lost when they were raised. But why hadn't she tried again, making her own sealed containers? That's certainly what he would have done.

Jon stopped trying to second-guess Shelley's motives. He already knew that she was a badly screwed-up lady. Anyway, he was moving up onto his own plane of exultation. *Life on Europa!* There might be a hundred, a thousand, other hydrothermal vents here, each with its own living forms. There might also be hidden-away, far-off life lurking inside the icy snowballs of the Oort Cloud, or on the Earthlike worlds that orbited the suns of Eta Cassiopeiae. There might even be free-space lifeforms, unattached to any parent world.

But Jon was the first human to prove that there was native life on another world and to observe it at close range. He would be the first to return those forms for scientific examination, the first to name them, to establish their taxonomy, to *study* them.

And suddenly his time in the deep ocean was no longer a pleasure. He wanted to begin his investigations. The

Spindrift was a wonderful vehicle, but the powers of analysis that it offered were limited. They did not allow him to determine cell structure, or to explore cell chemistry. He could not map major organic functions, from digestion to reproduction. He could not look at growth rates, or heat balance, or energy-production mechanisms. For those, he needed microscopes, genomers, low-energy lasers, restriction enzymes. He needed Mount Ararat, and the controlled and precise environment of a pressure lab.

But before he began that detailed analysis, announcement must be made of his discovery. Jon set the *Spindrift* onto an automated maximum-speed return path to Blowhole, while he, in his adrenalin high, settled down to decide the message that he would send when he reached the station and could get his hands on a wide-open communication channel.

It had to be something intriguing, something powerful. Something with a headline that would grab people who normally cared nothing for scientific results.

"Discovery: We Are Not Alone." That was not specific enough.

"Discovery: Existence of Alien Life Forms Confirmed in Europan Ocean." That, according to Nell, was just the sort of thing that made millions of people turn off their sets without waiting for details. "What people want, Jon, is horror and sex and violence. And if they can't get those in their own lives, video is the next best thing."

All right. How about, "The Terrifying Giant Striped Leeches of Europa. Pictures Follow."

Jon grinned as he imagined that one burning its way across the solar system information channels. Then he thought of something else that Nell had told him, and the grin vanished. During her review of his taped show back on Earth, she had nodded to the screen at one point and said, "You're all right, mostly. You come across like a sober, serious scientist, the sort people trust and believe.

But now and again I see a great big lump of ham in you, struggling to get out. Don't let it."

He could think of a dozen bizarre or striking ways to announce the confirmation of Europan life. But Nell was right, they would not do. No ham today. This was too important for cuteness, too big for self-aggrandizement, too profound for trivialities.

The message that he finally sent to Mount Ararat was addressed not to the whole solar system, but to Hilda Brandt alone. It read: "The existence of Europan native life is confirmed. I am now beginning detailed analysis. Jon Perry."

19

The Touch of Torquemada

Sometimes a beautiful theory must bend in submission to an ugly fact. Bat was ready to admit that the point had been reached.

Almost.

He scowled at the screen. "Do you have physical proof?"

"Of course I don't have *physical proof*." Mord scowled right back at him. "I don't have physical *anything*. I'm a disembodied entity, remember, the ghost of the machine. I can't carry around a bag of documents and pictures and diaries, the way you carry a bag of doughnuts. But I'm sure I'm right, sure as you're sitting there feeding your fat face."

"And it was true for the whole period of the war?"

"Except maybe for a week of two when he had to travel to Ceres. I saw him in the cafeteria just about every day. He must have been twenty or so, but he already had a head full of wild ideas about fusion. He'd talk your ear off if you let him."

"No trips to Mandrake?"

"Hell, I don't know. So what if there were? Mobarak

wasn't masterminding bio weapons development, that's for sure. We were all so damned busy, we hardly had time to take a leak. Anyway, far as I know he didn't understand any more biology than I did. And I can tell you for a fact that he was right there with us on Pallas at the end of the war. I remember talking to him. We were all wondering if we were going to be blown to blazes in one last big flare-up of the fighting."

The cameras that served as Mord's eyes zoomed in for a close-up of Bat's face. Mord's image sniffed. "I don't get this at all. You told me Mobarak's one of the few people allowed to come in here to see you without a big hassle. I thought he was your *buddy*."

"He is in many ways a kindred spirit. And just as certainly he is also my long-time adversary. For he is Torquemada, and as such, he is many things." Bat sighed. "So once again it will be necessary to meet with him. In person. Do you wish to remain?"

"Me? You're out of your tiny mind. Sit and listen to you two again, telling each other your daft riddles? I'd rather die. If I hadn't already." Mord reached out a simulated hand and switched himself off.

"You have heard the recent news of Europa?" Usually the conversation would begin far from its central concerns and spiral toward that axis through infinite whorls of digression. But today Bat appeared unwilling to display the subtle touch of Megachirops.

Cyrus Mobarak shrugged. As always in his meetings with Bat he showed no signs of his public flamboyance.

"Which I take to be an affirmative," went on Bat. "And so I ask my next question. Have you seen today's pronouncement by the members of Outward Bound?"

"I skimmed it. They're predictable. I could have written their reaction myself."

"But you would not. They are confident that they have the votes in the General Assembly to ban your fusion project on Europa. The reputed confirmation of native life forms has tilted the balance in their favor."

"So they say. We shall see." Mobarak stirred in his seat, as though infected by Bat's directness and eager to move on. "I don't think they will win."

"Indeed? The work of Dr. Perry has dealt them a powerful card, and they have long been your sworn enemies. It is tempting to identify them as the secret and inimical presence whom you detect in the Jovian system." Bat's eyes were invisible, hidden by the dark cowl around his head. His voice was distant, almost dreamy. "Of course, I cannot bring myself to offer such an identification, for two reasons well known to you. First, the members of Outward Bound could hardly be your *secret* enemy. They make no attempt to disguise their feelings about you."

"And the second reason?" After twenty years of interaction through the Puzzle Network, Mobarak knew the mind of Megachirops. The opening gambit was on its way, but it would not be the main purpose of the meeting. An onlooker would have seen no more than two men sitting in civilized conversation. The other levels of communication—or combat—four or five layers deep, remained hidden.

"They do not qualify as your enemy, Cyrus Mobarak, because you are no enemy of theirs. On the contrary, you, as Torquemada, are their *principal financial supporter*, and have been so for years."

"A strange thought." But Mobarak was smiling the urbane, guarded smile that so annoyed Nell Cotter. "Why would I give money to people who hate me, and who fight against everything that I want to do?"

"You ask me to conjecture? It would surely be quicker and more certain if you were to explain. Unless you propose to dispute my statements?"

"Not at all." Mobarak gave a quick chopping movement of his hand to suggest that what Bat had said was self-evident. "Where do you want to begin? I'm assuming that you already know the 'big secret' of Outward Bound."

"That the real objective of Project *Starseed* is not an unmanned ship to the nearer stars, but a *manned* ship that will carry a selected few to explore the Oort Cloud? That is obvious, but it does not enlighten."

"Ah, but a ship with a human crew has other needs." Mobarak appeared to be scanning Bat Cave, never meeting Bat's eyes. "Why does Outward Bound insist on a helium-3/deuterium drive? Because such a drive produces only charged-fusion products, *magnetically controllable* fusion products, which can be diverted from the crew's living area. So there is a need for far less shielding. And why do they care about *that*? Only because shielding is heavy. They wish to minimize *travel time*. That's why they avoid the use of the Mobies, and that is why they say that I am the enemy."

"And you are not?"

"I am their single best hope. They do not know—because I have not yet told them—that I now have Mobies that produce only charged-fusion products. There will be a time for that revelation, when *Starseed* is almost ready to fly. Meanwhile, their dislike of the Mobarak fusion drives serves one central function. It *unites* Outward Bound. It is one of their few points of total agreement."

"And you need that unity."

"I do. I'm sure that you can tell me why, since it is a point amenable to the process of pure deduction. Unless you have been too busy *sitting there feeding your fat face.*" Mobarak repeated Mord's words with no trace of expression, and they produced no reaction from Bat. But the unspoken exchange was clear to both men.

I have a data tap that tells me what goes on in your very own Bat Cave.

I am well aware of that. And you know that I know, or you would not have revealed your knowledge to me. But as you are also aware, more goes on in Bat Cave than you can discover from your data tap.

More goes on in Bat Cave, and more goes on inside the head of Rustum Battachariya. That is why I am here.

"If you heard those words," replied Bat, "you also realize that my suspicions of you as far as Mandrake are concerned have been completely banished."

"I could have given you an assurance long ago."

"You could have indeed. But would I have believed it?"

"Let me say it, and you can decide: I have never visited Mandrake, not ever. And I cannot tell you who conducted those biological experiments at the time of the Great War."

There was a tiny pause, a moment of suspense so short that no onlooker would have caught it. It said to both men; *"This is the crux, the central moment of the meeting."*

"Oddly enough, I believe that each of those statements is true." Bat was smiling at some secret joke. "Language is a wonderfully flexible tool, is it not? It allows so many statements to be made, literally true ones, yet whose meaning depends wholly on interpretation. So let us return to the mystery of Outward Bound."

"Shall I say it, or will you? There is no mystery. The Outward Bound members are fanatics. Their hearts are set on the Outer System, on Saturn and beyond. They oppose *anything*—such as the large-scale changes that the devil incarnate, Cyrus Mobarak, proposes for Europa—that might focus solar system attention and resources on the Jovian system. They like to think that they are winning, and that Europa will remain undeveloped. But the issue is far from settled. The crucial Assembly votes will soon take place. Now suppose that at this critical moment, native life were to be discovered on Europa by Dr. Jon Perry, Earth's top expert on hydrothermal-vent life forms."

Bat was nodding, his eyes half closed. "That result has not been officially confirmed."

"But your sources have already picked it up, and so have many others. The word was leaked to Outward Bound, and not by me. Using all of the financial resources that they can lay their hands on—let us not waste time asking where those resources come from—Outward Bound is trumpeting the news of that discovery from every media outlet, together with the message: 'Europan life must be protected.' They are doing it now, as we sit here. Within the next few days, every person in the system will have heard their pronouncement."

"And your Europan development will be thwarted."

"For the moment. But suppose that Outward Bound were then to be discredited and forced to admit that they were *wrong*? That there is no native life on Europa? With such an admission, Outward Bound's credibility would collapse. All *moderate* opposition to the Europan fusion project would vanish with it. A vote in the project's favor by the General Assembly would be a foregone conclusion. The battle would be over."

Mobarak raised bushy grey eyebrows at Bat and leaned back in his seat. He gave every impression of a man who had said all that needed to be said.

As indeed he had. Bat could see the picture, more of it than he was meant to see. He could fill in every blank on Torquemada's canvas. Except one crucial element.

"*When* do you expect a second announcement?"

Cyrus Mobarak shrugged. "There I can only guess. That element of timing is beyond my control. But I will be surprised if it takes more than a few days."

20

Storm on Europa

Mount Ararat was a small research base, designed to accommodate only a couple of hundred scientists, but nothing had been skimped in the way of equipment. Jon compared his working tools with those available on the PacAnt floating bases, and decided again and again in favor of Europa. For Hilda Brandt's researchers, it was nothing but the best.

The Mount Ararat equipment was so good that the trickiest part of Jon's work had been the first task; the transfer of specimens from the pressurized storage units of the *Spindrift* to High-P tanks in the base's lab. He had done that himself, unwilling to allow anyone else to touch the containers. His official reason was that he did not want others exposed to the risk should one of the *Spindrift*'s pressure tanks fail; their contents, still at six hundred atmospheres, had the stored energy of bombs. But the real reason had nothing to do with safety: Jon was simply fascinated by what he had found. Until his analysis was complete, he wanted the Europan life forms all to himself.

The first few hours were spent in separating the specimens into discrete chambers, each only a foot across. Then he could change the internal pressure of any chosen tank to see how individual organisms were affected by pressure reduction. Jon had done the same thing many times on Earth. General behavior changed first, and ultimately damage came in the form of cellular disruption.

If, that is, Europan forms *had* cellular structure. Jon had to remind himself, again and again: *This is alien life.* To assume that it had a resemblance to *anything* on Earth would be to run the risk of committing a major blunder.

Remember the Burgess Shale. The history of Earth biology was full of cases like that famous one, where a worker had shoehorned new discoveries into existing classes and phyla and led the field astray for decades.

Jon had that example in his head when he began with an analysis of the general structure and anatomy of his specimens. If he were to play the role of a new Linnaeus, a whole taxonomy for Europan life had to be created. But he had tools of which Carl von Linné, back in the eighteenth century, could not have dreamed. Low-intensity radiation and particles provided three-dimensional tomographic plots of internal structure. Tuned frequency lasers offered the chemical composition of every organ, at submillimeter resolution. Quantum interference devices delicately mapped minute magnetic fields, along with the tiny currents that created them.

The work went slowly, but there was never a moment of tedium. By the end of the second day, Jon was ready to move to the next stage: cytology, the detail of individual cells. He was increasingly eager to see that cell structure, because during the final stages of preliminary analysis an awful suspicion had been creeping into his mind.

It had begun as a pleasant surprise: The Europan life forms might be grossly different in appearance and function from the organisms found on Earth's surface, and even from the chemosynthetic sulfur-based life supported by Earth's oceanic vents; but there were enough similarities that his descriptions could be made with existing notations. He would not be driven to devise a whole new taxonomy for Europan life.

And then it began to dawn on him: There were not merely *enough* similarities; for the big leechlike creatures, there were *too many*.

He listed them: multicellular structure, with cellular differentiation. Internal body cavity, with digestive tube and mouth. Tough outer integument, an ectoderm with nervous and sensory capacities. Two-sex reproductive organs.

Jon had never seen anything like the creatures that he was examining; but he could well imagine a hybrid of mollusk and annelid worm that would fit their description.

And at the cellular level?

He did the analysis, already afraid of what he would find.

The results ticked in. True eukaryotic cells, with well-defined nuclei. Twenty familiar amino acids. Mitochondria, and ATP for energy production within them. And then, the final coffin nail: the cell scans were unambiguous. A DNA-based system was used for the coding of genetic material, with RNA as messenger.

Jon stared with a sinking feeling at the listing of bases produced by the first part of the genome scan. Even the RNA codons for the amino acids were the same; CGU produced arginine, ACG gave threonine, UAC coded for tyrosine . . .

At the most basic molecular level, the organisms that he had dredged up from the depths of Scaldino were not just *like* Earth organisms—they *were* Earth organisms. Parallel evolution might lead to DNA and RNA as the most efficient method for the transfer of genetic material, but the odds were impossibly long that the very same amino acids would be used and that the same symbiosis of cell and mitochondria would have taken place.

Far more likely—overwhelmingly likely—was a much simpler explanation: Europan quarantine, designed so carefully to protect that pristine ocean environment, had failed. Sometime, perhaps as long ago as the original prewar Europan expeditions, Earth life had found its way through the shield of ice and drifted down to the warm hydrothermal vents. And there, without competition, that same Earth life—vigorous, tenacious, uncompromising— had established a toehold. It had grown, mutated, and multiplied into riotous profusion.

Jon was filled with a colossal, soul-wounding gloom. He slumped at the terminal and laid his head on his forearms. A new living biosphere? No way. Instead of discovering a whole different world, he had found *nothing*, not one thing of value, only careless contamination. He did not need to travel all the way to Jupiter to find *that*. It was common enough on Earth.

The dreadful feeling of disappointment lasted for less than a minute. It was swept away by an even stronger emotion: *relief*.

He had come so close—so close to the absolute brink! He had, thank God, sent word of the confirmation of native Europan life to Hilda Brandt alone. Suppose he had followed his first inclination, and blazed a message out through the news media? Then he, Jon Perry, would have become the laughingstock of the whole solar system.

Jon wandered out of the lab with a copy of his results, convinced that he was a coward first and a scientist a poor second. Sure, it would be nice to become the new Linnaeus and live in the glow of fame. But suppose he had made his announcement at a big public press conference *before* he made his detailed analysis? That had been the temptation. Then he would be remembered all right— remembered as another Lamarck, a great and once-distinguished scientist now famous to most people only as the creator of a discredited theory.

Jon could point to half a dozen other cases of bogus "great discoveries," from Blondlot's N-rays early in the twentieth century to polywater and cold fusion. His skin ran with goose bumps at the thought of joining that select leper colony of scientific pariahs.

Another thought suddenly made things worse: *Suppose he was too late?* Suppose that Hilda Brandt had already presented his earlier message to the Jovian General Assembly?

He had to talk to her. At once. Jon found himself racing through the white corridors of Mount Ararat, stared at by the few people he passed.

Hilda Brandt was in a meeting with half a dozen of her senior staff. Fortunately, Europa possessed none of the multiple layers of bureaucracy that plagued Earth. Jon hammered on her door and blundered through. She took one look at his face and turned to the others.

"You can manage this well enough without me. Buzz, I'd like you to carry on in your own office." And as Sandstrom and the rest left, staring at Jon with annoyance and undisguised curiosity, "Cheer up, Jon Perry. Whatever it is, it can't be that bad."

"It's worse." How was he going to tell her? Straight. There was no other way. "What I said to you about Europan life—it's all wrong. It's not native life forms. There's been *contamination* of the Europan ocean. The life down there developed from *Earth forms*. Look at this."

He laid the summary of his results in front of her. The kindly, concerned expression did not change. Only a flicker of bright brown eyes showed that she heard him, and understood the significance of his statements.

"Are you *sure*?"

"Absolutely. It was tricky to take the deep-ocean specimens and move them into the *Spindrift*, but once I got back to Mount Ararat the whole analysis was straightforward. Your staff can confirm the results."

"Have you mentioned this to anyone else?"

"Nobody. I came straight here."

"That's good. Will you do me a favor and keep it that way for the moment? Your discovery has big implications for Europa. I need to decide how I'm going to break this to my staff, and then I have to make a trip to Ganymede as soon as I get a ship in to take me."

Jon's own problems began to seem minor. A contaminated Europan ocean could make nonsense of the decades of work done at Mount Ararat. Every one of Hilda Brandt's programs might be in jeopardy. "I won't say a word until you tell me to. But what about Wilsa Sheer? She gave her final Ganymede concert yesterday, and she's supposed to be arriving here at any time. She's sure to ask me how things are going."

"She's already here. She landed an hour ago. You had a Do-Not-Disturb sign on your lab terminals, so I didn't interrupt. Wilsa's in Guest Suite Four, tell her as much as you like." Hilda Brandt was rapidly gathering papers and closing file-cabinet drawers. "But I don't want either of you using the communications systems until I get back. I'm going to tell Buzz Sandstrom to put the whole Mount Ararat base into isolation mode until we have a strategy worked out. A lot of careers are at stake."

Hilda Brandt's plump and aging body could move with speed and economy. Before Jon could ask more questions she had swept a final stack of files into her case, nodded, and headed for the door. "I have a few other things to take care of before I can leave. Better make sure your results look nice and tidy. When this goes public you're going to be hit with a million questions."

She was gone before Jon had a chance to mention a new worry. When he had spoken the word *contamination*, another idea with different and more ominous overtones had flickered across the back of his mind.

It was one that he should be able to confirm with a few

more minutes of work. He rushed out of Brandt's office, almost colliding with Buzz Sandstrom in the doorway. The muscular deputy glared at him in surprised annoyance. "What the devil have you been doing in there?" Jon took no notice and headed back to the lab.

The genome scans that he had performed on the Europan organisms were still available in rapid-access files. He searched for and loaded the appropriate matching programs, those that would take his new genetic data and use it to seek segment-by-segment matches with the stored genomes of existing forms.

And at once he ran into a snag. Jon had a good idea of which Earth forms he needed: selected annelid worms, and some form of mollusk, probably a gastropod. But those genomes were missing from the files.

Accident, or design? His suspicions were growing. Europan research workers had little interest in the organisms of Earth; perhaps it was not too surprising then that the genomes he required were not to be found in the data bank. But the fact that genomes for so many other Earth organisms *were* in the files was surely significant.

He swore under his breath. If only he were back on the *Spindrift*. He knew that its onboard computer files held just what he needed.

Jon called up the display of the Europan genomes anyway and began to examine them visually, segment after segment. It was slow, painstaking work, and it depended too much on his memory. He could never be *sure*, not as a computer match using the *Spindrift*'s stored data would have provided certainty. But what he saw was familiar enough to convince him at a deep interior level that he was right.

Contamination, yes. But not the natural contamination of a random drift of Earth life into Europa's deep ocean. That could certainly have happened. But it would not—could not—have produced in less than a century mutations so exquisitely suited to the chemistry and temperatures of the Europan black smoker.

Deliberate contamination, *constructed* contamination; and then—

Use the right words. *A setup.*

The leeches, and probably all of the other life forms he had found, were not the product of natural evolution. They were genetic hybrids, designed organisms crafted from existing Earth forms to thrive and multiply in the Europan deep ocean. And Jon did not have to look far to find their maker.

He stared at the genetic sequences and cursed his blindness. *Shelley Solbourne.* Manuel Posada had given Jon all the clues that he needed when he was still in Arenas. Shelley had left PacAnt 9 and headed out for the Jovian system. She had come up with "indirect" evidence of Europan life. But then, instead of staying to confirm its nature, as any mortal scientist would have done—lasting fame within reach for the discoverer of the first alien life form—she had returned to Earth. That had not amazed Posada, a nonscientist; but it should have raised a million red flags with Jon. He recalled Posada's words: ". . . did well for herself and came back to Earth a wealthy woman."

And Jon, in his innocence, had never thought to ask where that wealth had come from!

He did not need to ask now. Someone had paid Shelley, and paid her well, to develop chemosynthetic hybrids that could flourish in Europa's hydrothermal vents. She had done her job competently, as she did everything she touched. Then she had seeded the results in the deep ocean, "discovered" their existence—but not, of course, produced specimens for inspection—and returned quietly, and wealthily, to Earth.

Why hadn't Jon followed up his own first thought back in Arenas? He had wanted to go over to see Shelley in her Dunedin villa and discuss the discovery. Instead he had been kept constantly busy, hustled off Earth at maximum speed and shipped to Ganymede within three days. No reason had ever been offered for all the rush.

And it had not ended when Jon left Earth. Surely, whoever had paid Shelley Solbourne to seed the ocean of Europa had also *intended* for Jon to discover the deception. He had been manipulated, from first to last.

But his manipulation was over now. Enough was enough. He would confirm his suspicions directly, using the data banks on the *Spindrift*. And then, with proof in hand, he would act.

He grimly transferred the evidence of the Europan genomes to a portable data-storage device, slipped it into his pocket, and headed for Hilda Brandt's quarters. He didn't want to trust anyone, but she had to be the exception. She, and she alone, could not be in on the fraud. It made no sense for her to hire someone to plant imported life in the Europan ocean, and then permit Jon to come in and prove that her own effort was a fake.

Brandt was not there. But Buzz Sandstrom was. He was sitting at the desk, his cropped head bowed in concentration.

"Has Dr. Brandt left yet?" Jon blurted out the question as he realized that Sandstrom was reading the work summary left behind during Jon's previous visit.

Sandstrom lifted his head, and Jon had never seen such anger on any face.

"Dr. Brandt has gone to Ganymede." Sandstrom stood up, muscles flexing. "I'm in charge. She told me that there was bad news on the way, but I had no idea of *how* bad 'til I saw *this*."

He tapped the summary sheets. "Everybody's work here depends on an *uncontaminated environment*. I don't know why Dr. Brandt allowed you and that Sheer woman to come here at all, messing things up. You've destroyed all we've been doing."

Jon stared at him in disbelief. "Me? I didn't contaminate anything. All I proved is that the deep ocean was *already* spoiled, long ago."

"You expect me to believe that? Until you got here, Europa was fine. If the ocean is spoiled now, it's because you came. You and your Earth ship, and your Earth filth, you ruined us. I always said it was too risky, bringing you. And now you've opened the door for Mobarak and his whole lousy fusion project."

It was tempting to pick up Sandstrom's furious mood and reply in kind. But it would accomplish nothing. Jon swallowed his irritation. "You're right about one thing, but you're wrong about another. Someone *did* come here from Earth and spoil this ocean. It wasn't me and my submersible. It was Shelley Solbourne."

That stopped Sandstrom. Jon looked for any sign of guilt on the man's face, and saw only surprise and anger. If Shelley had worked with accomplices on Europa, Sandstrom was not one of them.

"And it's worse than you think," Jon went on. "The report that you've been reading says *contamination*, because I assumed that it was accidental. Now I know that it wasn't. It was done *deliberately*."

"Nonsense! Why would anyone ruin a world on purpose?"

"I can't tell you that. All I'm saying is that the contamination of the Europan ocean was *intentional*. Modified forms of Earth life were planted here, specially designed forms. I can prove it."

Sandstrom had been reaching across the desk to flip a switch on a panel. Now he sat down again. "Do it." His expression had moved from anger to glacial coldness. "I liked Shelley Solbourne. She'd had a hard life, and she liked to grumble about it. But she did good, solid work, and I won't see her slandered when she's not here to defend herself. You say you can prove what you said. Go on, then. I'll give you five minutes."

Jon took the data storage unit out of his pocket. "This contains the scanned genomes of the Europan-vent life forms. I've inspected them, and I'm sure that they're not naturally evolved organisms. They're hybrids, gene-supplied from existing Earth forms for adaptation to the Europan deep-ocean environment. Shelley Solbourne planted them here. And I *can* prove it. All I have to do is to match their DNA against the appropriate Earth forms."

"So why haven't you done it?"

"The genome maps for the organisms I need aren't in the Europa data banks. But they *are* in my data storage bank on board the *Spindrift*. We can just go back to Blowhole—"

"Are you out of your mind? Mount Ararat has been placed in *isolation mode*. Dr. Brandt told me to put us there. You can't go to Blowhole now."

"She was referring to *off-world* communications—so no one could leak word of what's going on until she decides how to handle it. I'm sure she didn't mean it to apply to trips out onto the surface. I'm saying, one quick visit to the *Spindrift*—"

"And I'm saying, forget it. You have the nerve to stand there and ask me to give you *another* chance to take a submersible and mess up the inside of Europa even worse than you have already? I wouldn't do that, even if I didn't have specific instructions not to. *Isolation is isolation.* You've had your five minutes."

"I've not had half that!"

"It doesn't matter. It's over, Perry. We won't let Europa be destroyed." Sandstrom was staring past him. Jon turned and found three men in the doorway, each as muscular as the deputy.

"See? So don't try anything." Sandstrom nodded to the newcomers. "All right, take him to Suite Four, with the new arrival. Don't say nothing to nobody. And make sure it's *secure* there, until I figure out what comes next."

Jon was almost to the point of deciding that he must be guilty of *something*; he wasn't sure of what, but if the way he was being treated was anything to go by, it had to be a major offense.

Because Wilsa Sheer was even angrier than Buzz Sandstrom. She had been pleasant for maybe thirty seconds, until she realized that the door was being closed—and locked—behind Jon. Then she had swelled with fury, all five feet of her, and looked around for someone to thunder at. There was only one candidate.

Jon waited for a break in the weather, then explained the whole thing as carefully and systematically as her outraged interruptions would allow. It went slowly, but by the time he came to the contents of the data storage unit, still clutched in his sweaty hand, and his need to compare that with files held on the *Spindrift*, Wilsa's lightning flashes had gone. There was still an occasional rumble, but it was not directed at him.

"Buzz Sandstrom's going to keep us here until Hilda Brandt returns?" She was eyeing the walls and the door of the suite.

"That's not quite what he told me. Until he decides 'what comes *next*,' he said."

"And Hilda Brandt asked you who else you told, and you said nobody?"

"Right. What of it?"

"Maybe nothing. Or maybe I've been exposed to too many opera librettos. But I can't help recalling the look on their faces when they stuffed you in through the door. Those goons follow orders. You and Sandstrom—and now me—are the only ones who know that the Europa life forms aren't native. We're the only ones who can ruin

Europa's official status of an off-limits, untouchable world."

"Hilda Brandt knows, too."

"You take comfort from that if you like." Wilsa's face was calm now, but she was sitting barefoot, and her long, modified toes were curling and uncurling. "Me, I'm thinking of how convenient it would be if you and I weren't around to explain your findings. Wouldn't it be nice for the Europan administration if your new analysis disappeared, and you and me with it?"

"Nonsense. Brandt wouldn't go along with that."

"Why would she have to know? Sandstrom's in charge until she gets back."

Wilsa began to wander from room to room, although Guest Suite Four was too small for effective prowling. A main living area, furnished with a table and three soft chairs, led to a small kitchen. Wilsa went into it and began opening drawers, banging cupboards, and muttering to herself. Beyond the living room, separated from it by a sliding door, lay the bedroom and a compact bathroom. There was just one external door, leading to the outside corridor. When Wilsa finished her inspection, she returned to stare at it.

"Locked. There's no other exit." Jon could read her thoughts. "Come and sit down, you're making *me* nervous."

"We *have* to find a way out." She swung around to glare at him. "I'm not going to stay locked up. I *won't*. It's different for you. You were raised on Earth. Earth people are used to physical restraint."

"That's not true! Where did you get that idea?"

"You still have *jails* on Earth, don't you? But I was raised in the Belt. Belters must have freedom to move, or they suffocate."

"You were happy in a submersible. That's a lot more like a jail than this apartment."

"It's totally different. I was in a submersible because I *wanted* to be there. It's the principle of the thing."

"Suppose we could get out of here." Jon wasn't sure of how seriously to take Wilsa. "We couldn't escape from Europa. There's no ship available, for one thing—Hilda Brandt had to call one in to take her to Ganymede."

"I'll settle for getting away from Mount Ararat. How about the *Spindrift*. Is it working?"

"It should be. But it's over at Blowhole."

"So we escape from here and we go to Blowhole and the *Spindrift*."

"Yeah. Sure. We escape. Like to tell me *how*?"

"There's no food in this kitchen. I just checked. They have to come and feed us, unless they've decided to starve us to death. When they bring food, you overpower the guards."

She had to be joking.

"Sure. All three of 'em. Then I grab their weapons, right?"

"That's it. Then we run away through the corridors. We put on suits, we take a ground car—" But Wilsa was grinning.

"You're right, you *have* been reading too many opera librettos. You saw those muscles. If you can take their weapons away, be my guest."

"Maybe I can't." Wilsa came to sit down again. "But I'm dead serious about one thing. I won't stay cooped up here if there's any way at all to get out."

"So do you have any *real* ideas?"

"Not a thing. Not yet. But you're the scientist. I'm the artist. It's *your* job to think of something."

"Prison escapes aren't science. They're *engineering*." Now it was Jon's turn to prowl the suite. "The ceiling's solid. Same with the walls and the floor. The air ducts are only a few centimeters wide."

"Door?"

"Honeycombed graphite matrix. Harder than steel. It would be easier to break the walls. I give up."

Wilsa shook her head. "Not me. I don't give up. I told you how I feel about lockups." She stood up again and wandered through to inspect the kitchen cooking utensils. "Nice sharp knives."

"Forget it. Unless you're going to be the one to use 'em."

"How about this thing? It's a pressure cooker, isn't it? If we block the safety valve, fill it with water, and set the heat high enough–"

"You'd have a bomb, of unknown strength. Do you like that sort of gadget? Because I don't. It wouldn't destroy the apartment, but it would blow superheated water all over. Make a hell of a mess of the kitchen. Of us, too, if we were anywhere near it."

"We could hide in the bedroom. And if we could make it explode near the door—"

"It wouldn't make more than a scratch." But the challenge was raising Jon's interest; he was hunched over the stove. "Even if you blocked the safety valve, there'd be no way of getting it to the door at the exact moment it blew up. You'd have to keep the heat underneath the pot right 'til it exploded. Nice try, but you'll never blow your way free with a pressure-cooker bomb."

"So we need something different."

"I never said that." Jon was bending over the pot of glossy black ceramic, studying the safety valve. "It *would* be easy enough to block this—see, right here. That's a start. Let me try it."

"You have an idea?"

"Not an *idea*, exactly . . . call it a thought. We've got one thing going for us. Sandstrom expects us to behave the way *I* would behave if you hadn't been pestering me. He doesn't realize that you're a lunatic, so he doesn't *expect* us to go all-out to escape. That gives us a shot—*one* shot—at surprising him."

"But we have no surprise."

"I didn't say that, either. Come sit down, and let's talk about cooperation. You have to find a way of buying me five minutes after they get here."

21

Out and Down
on Europa

By the time that the door to the suite was finally unlocked from outside, Jon Perry had begun to take seriously the idea that he and Wilsa Sheer could be left to starve to death. He had sat by the stove, ready for action, for six endless hours. The pressure cooker had boiled low and been refilled eight times. All feeling of tension had long since given way to hunger, and he was drifting off into an uneasy half-sleep when Wilsa, kneeling with her ear to the door, suddenly whispered, "Now!"

He jerked awake, forced the improvised safety-valve baffle into position, turned the heat to its maximum setting, and hurried after her into the bedroom.

The next big question was whether their captors would follow. They might prefer to drop off food in the living room or the kitchen and leave. Jon already knew that they were carrying dinner—the smell was making him salivate.

"We're in here," called Wilsa as the outer door swung wide. "In the bedroom. Bring it in. We thought you were going to leave us hungry forever!"

They had agreed that as far as possible she should do the

talking—"Because you're not *used* to public performance," as she put it.

Quite right. Jon was not. And even though he knew that as a keyboard performer she was a consummate master, he was still amazed that she could now make her *voice* project such a plausible mixture of worry, relief, and irritation.

The same muscle-bound trio of males came in, and their actions ruined at once the idea that they were not expecting an attempt at escape. The first one came through to the bedroom and peered around suspiciously on the threshold before he entered. He saw Jon and Wilsa seated on the bed, but even so he made a tour of the whole room before summoning the others.

"Put them down on the side table." Wilsa pointed, but she did not move. "And tell us when we'll get *out* of here. I'm sick and tired of doing nothing. I didn't come all the way to Europa to be locked up. And I need to practice for my next concert."

"It depends on Buzz," said the first man in the room, as the others placed two plastic trays on the table. He was almost apologetic. "Buzz is the boss. Though of course"—as an afterthought—"we all report to Dr. Brandt."

Jon decided that the men had no idea of why he and Wilsa were locked away. But Wilsa was right; they followed orders, and it was enough that Sandstrom said so. *Dump these two out on the ice. Yes, sir. No, I've changed my mind; stick them down Blowhole and drown them. Yes, sir.*

And all the while a pulse inside Jon's head was ticking away like a manic metronome. He had tried to make estimates of the cooker's blowing point, but he had been forced in his experiments to err on the side of safety, stopping before he could be sure. His final best guess was between four and five minutes. But it might be anything from two seconds to never. Suppose that the material was just too strong and nothing happened?

Wilsa was performing miracles of casual self-control.

She had stood up very slowly, and somehow she was ushering one of the men with her toward the loaded trays.

"Neither Dr. Perry nor I are used to the Jovian food, you know," she said. "I'm not sure that we will even know what it is, or how to eat it. If you would just explain to me what you have brought, and how it was prepared . . ."

The man was bemused—he knew that Wilsa had been to Europa before—but he did not seem worried. With his two companions standing against the wall and monitoring Jon's every move, there was no reason for alarm. Jon and Wilsa were unarmed. He allowed Wilsa to remove the covers of the dishes on the tray and bent over them with her.

As he did so, it came.

Jon had been expecting it, willing it to happen, steeling himself for the shock. He thought he was prepared for anything, from the mild pop of a loosened lid to a God-hurled thunderbolt. Even so, the sound that hit his ears was so loud that it *hurt*. His head rang and his heart froze. Knowing what was happening, he was nevertheless shocked and disoriented.

Everything slowed to a tenth of its usual speed. *Primary explosion* . . . (still going on, an erupting volcano a few feet away) . . . *thump* . . . (that had to be the disintegration of the whole pressurized container) . . . *shiver* . . . (the resonance shook the interior of the suite) . . . *roar* . . . (long-sustained, shattering) . . .

Jon watched shards of black ceramic, propelled by a shock wave of superheated steam, fly and splinter against the walls of the living room and kitchen. Hundreds more of them, small and as sharp as needles, flew into the bedroom through the open door.

It was like the signal of an immense starting gun. Before the reverberations were over, Jon and Wilsa were through the bedroom door and racing out into the living room.

Speed was the only thing that mattered now. The three men had been lucky; none of the fragments had touched them. But when Jon turned as he left the bedroom, he saw that they had not moved a millimeter.

Stunned with surprise? Let's hope so. Surprise was all that he and Wilsa had going for them.

But it was enough. They were through and out. When he turned to slam the door, still not one of the three men had moved. He spun the ciphers, tugged to make sure that the door was locked, and followed Wilsa along the corridor.

As they turned the first corner a couple of people were approaching with confusion on their faces. Jon and Wilsa flashed past before any blocking move could be made. Once around the corner Jon grabbed Wilsa to slow her to a walking pace. But his own feet would not cooperate. They insisted on running at maximum speed, regardless of his efforts to act casual.

This part of the escape was something over which they had no control. But it was also the part about which Jon had been least worried. Anyone drawn by the explosion *could* try to stop them. But unless Jon and Wilsa were unlucky enough to run into Buzz Sandstrom himself, no one would have any reason to try. Buzz's orders for them to say nothing to anyone were working in their favor.

Fortunately, Mount Ararat was as deserted as usual. Once clear of the corridor leading to the guest suites Jon forced himself to a more moderate pace. It made no difference, since they met no one on their way to the exit leading up to the spaceport.

"I know you think there's no ship available," said Wilsa as they scrambled into surface suits. "But it would be stupid not to take just a *peek*. We might get lucky and make it clear off Europa."

But luck, for the moment, had run out. The saucer of the Mount Ararat spaceport was bare of ships. They hurried over to the covered area that housed the ground cars and found that it, too, was a disappointment. Most of the cars were being recharged, and only one was present in the garage. Fortunately, it had ample power to take them to Blowhole.

"Think positive," said Wilsa as they climbed aboard. "Once we grab this one, nobody can follow until they can get their hands on a recharged car. I was worried that we'd be caught before we reached the *Spindrift*, because we daren't drive as fast as an experienced Europan. But now we'll be all right."

All right? Jon wondered. It depended on how you defined the expression. It was probably not worth mentioning the fact that Buzz Sandstrom, angry before, would be foaming at the mouth when he learned about their escape and run for Europa's surface. He would be after them in minutes, and it was hard to believe that he would not catch them.

"How long before you'll be missed on Ganymede and someone comes after you?"

"I have a concert on Callisto in five days. If Magnus Klein doesn't hear from me in three, he'll stage a personal Europan invasion. And Tristan will lead the landing party, because I promised to call him when I arrived here, and I didn't. How about you?"

"Just Nell Cotter." He laughed. "I shouldn't say 'just.' You know Nell. She'll eat Sandstrom alive if he tells her we've been lost."

As he spoke, he kept peering at the path ahead of the car. They were beelining for Blowhole at top speed. Then it occurred to Jon that rather than instigating a pursuit, it would be far more logical for Sandstrom to call ahead and arrange for somebody to block their path. Now, too late, Jon wished that he had not been so explicit about his wish to consult the onboard data bank of the *Spindrift*.

He had plenty of opportunity for brooding. Once over the lip of the Mount Ararat spaceport, the car seemed to drive itself. The path ahead was clearly illuminated by

Ganymede and Callisto, high in the sky, and the sparkling ice-road was marked by the old imprints of other ground cars making their way to and from Blowhole. Jon had only to keep an eye on the power supply, follow the powdery grooves across the gently rolling ice, and worry about a welcoming committee at the end of the road.

"Problem," said Wilsa suddenly. She must have been doing her own share of nail-biting, because while Jon was driving, she had been scanning the horizon in front of them at high magnification.

"Cars?"

"No. But we're close enough to Blowhole that I ought to be able to see the *Spindrift*. I can't."

"Maybe it's partway down the ice ramp." But Jon did not believe it. The *Spindrift* held the rest of the evidence, with its log showing just what life forms had been collected at the Europan hydrothermal vent. Destroy those records, and destroy Jon himself, and who could prove that the Europan life forms were not native to this world? To provide a proof, someone would have to make another trip down into the depths and collect more samples. And Mount Ararat controlled all such access.

Wilsa was peering at the display on its highest magnification. "There *is* something at the top of the ramp. I don't think it's the *Spindrift*, though. It looks like the *Danae*. Same outline, same color."

"Any sign of people or cars?"

"Don't see them. Want to slow down until I'm sure?"

"Nah." Jon grunted, shook his head, and held the car at maximum speed. No matter what was waiting at Blowhole, he and Wilsa had nowhere else to go. He had seen what had happened to Camille Hamilton when she went wandering off to unfamiliar Europan ground.

A couple of minutes later he could confirm Wilsa's suggestion. It was indeed the *Danae*, sitting deserted on the open ice. He took a minute to stare around the

Blowhole buildings for any sign of the *Spindrift*. No trace. But he fancied that he saw a dark dot far back along the icy road that led from Mount Ararat.

The decision to stick to maximum speed had been the right one. And forget any ideas of wandering around to find the *Spindrift*.

"Come on. We may soon have company." Jon stopped the car, jumped out, and ran across to attach the launch grapples to the *Danae*.

"If they've destroyed the *Spindrift* to get rid of evidence, that's good," said Wilsa. She was climbing aboard. "They won't be able to follow us down."

"Good for *you*," said Jon as he climbed after her. "The *Spindrift* isn't your ship. But it's been a home to me for the past seven years."

And never will be again. Jon knew that, as clearly as he knew anything. Whatever happened next, his future did not hold another seven years on PacAnt 14. As for what it did hold—if he had any future for longer than a few hours . . .

He allowed Wilsa to occupy the pilot's seat while he checked the seals on the *Danae*. As they moved down the ramp he glanced up. Ganymede was in full phase, directly overhead. *That* was real safety, not the murky depths of the Europan ocean. But for the next day or two, he and Wilsa had no choice.

There was a slapping of small waves on the submersible's sides. Then they were under, drifting deeper through cold, clear water. Down, down, down. The familiar ambience of a deep-ocean vessel at once began to provide Jon with a sense of security. A *false* sense. He knew how dangerous that could be. Anyone who had been pursuing them knew that they were heading down Blowhole. Sonic detectors would track the *Danae* easily by its engine noise.

As the submersible approached the bottom edge of the Europan ice blanket, Jon held out a warning hand.

"No deeper. Hold us right here."

"Why?"

"Suppose they have the *Spindrift* in one of the hangars close to Blowhole? They'll follow right after us."

"So what? We can't stop them."

"I think we can—if we hurry."

He didn't have to ask her to change seats. With the unspoken understanding that they had shared since their first meeting, she was already moving aside. Jon took the controls, switched on all the vessel's lights, and inched toward the wall of Blowhole. On each trip to the deeps he had seen the massive heating units that kept the water column of Blowhole liquid, but he had not taken much notice of them. Now he had to make a close inspection.

There were three of them, secured to the lower edge of the ice blanket and forming a horizontal equilateral triangle. Jon homed in on the first one and saw that it was a set of nested black cylinders. The interior one was presumably the power unit, and he could see it vibrating slightly. The others were heat exchangers and pumps, used to provide an upward current of warmed water. The outermost cylinder, ten meters across, was crusted black with mineral deposits.

"There has to be a way to turn these things on and off from down here." Jon maneuvered the *Danae* delicately around the power unit. "And I'll bet it's direct, not through an electronic signal, because water cuts off radio signals. Do you see a switch or a lever or something?"

"Can't see much of anything at all. Too much crud." Wilsa, ignoring the display screens, had her nose pressed to the submersible's transparent window. "But that lump could be a switch. Can you knock off some of the muck?"

"I can try." Jon longed for the multipurpose remote handlers of the *Spindrift*, strong enough to cut metal, yet sensitive enough to thread a needle. All of the handling tools on the *Danae* were crude by comparison. He reached out with one of the two-fingered waldoes and scraped at the bottom of the power unit. Black flakes drifted away into the depths, and the formless lump took on a cleaner, knoblike shape. "I think you're right. It's some sort of key, or switch. Looks as though it ought to pull out when we get more scale off it."

But Wilsa's attention was elsewhere. Bigger flakes had been loosened, and the blue belly of the cylinder was now revealed. "Look at that!" She was pointing at a niche in the underside. "I think I'm seeing things."

Jon looked to where she was pointing. Cut deep into the metal of the inner cylinder, clearly visible now that the deposits were gone, was a stylized letter M.

"If you're seeing things, I'm seeing them, too. It's the Mobarak emblem. That's a Moby!"

"It sure is." Wilsa snorted. "How's that for irony? Everyone on Europa curses Mobarak's name, talks like he's the very devil—and they rely on the Mobies to keep Blowhole open!"

"It makes sense, though. Mobies are the best."

"Makes sense to *you*, Jon Perry, because you're logical. But anyone else in the system would agree with me that it's bizarre. I wonder if Buzz Sandstrom knows about this Moby."

"You can ask him yourself—after I'm safely away from Europa." Jon had returned to scraping at the switch. When he had cleared away as much scale as he could, he reached out with the clumsy two-fingered manipulator and tugged. There was no sound, but the vibration of the innermost cylinder ceased. "Success, I think. Two more to go."

"And then what?"

"And then, given a decent delay at the top before they can bring the *Spindrift* to Blowhole and launch it, we'll be snug where they can't reach us. The warm water from these power units is the only thing that keeps Blowhole open. The higher-up units are just circulating pumps. The temperature at the surface is down around seventy Kelvin. Water freezes while you watch. A few feet of hard ice is as good a barrier as steel. We'll have enough time to get far away, and we'll be safe enough when we come back, because it won't freeze at this depth for weeks."

As Jon spoke, he was maneuvering the ship to the other two power units in turn and repeating the procedure. They were also Mobies. While he did so, Wilsa was reexamining the *Danae*'s control board.

"I didn't take much notice earlier, but some of these gauges have been changed."

"That's because the submersible has been changed, too." Jon, his task complete, set the *Danae* to descend at its maximum rate. "I knew they were doing this. The sensors and handlers are still primitive, but the hull has supposedly been strengthened enough to take the pressure at any depth in Europa's ocean. And that's good—because that's where we're heading."

"For the hydrothermal vents?"

"No. That's where Sandstrom's little helpers will be most likely to look for us if they enter Blowhole. I'm going to find us a hidey-hole as far away from the vents as we can get. Somewhere nobody has ever been."

In spite of his assurance that the *Danae* could now take any necessary pressure, Jon was watching the feedback from smart sensors scattered throughout the outer and inner hulls. As they plunged deeper, he was reassured by what he saw. At twenty kilometers and two hundred and seventy atmospheres of outside pressure, the strain gauges showed negligible hull deformation. The measured stresses were exactly what he expected.

The only trouble was that where the *Danae* could go, the *Spindrift* could follow—*if* Sandstrom could find a Europan who would be willing to pilot a ship down to a hundred kilometers and more. Because that's where Jon was going.

He smiled. Buzz would love to see them chased and caught. But would any Europan be willing to plunge into the deepest ocean? No one ever had, not in a century of exploration.

He angled the vessel away from a direct descent. If Sandstrom or anyone else from Mount Ararat did come looking, there was no point in making the search easier for them. The deepest known point of the Europan sea was far away on the other side of the planet, near the Sub-Jovian point, but according to the charts the *Danae* could reach places one hundred and eighteen kilometers below the ice layer by traveling no more than a couple of hundred great-circle kilometers. Jon felt sure that no one had ever even been anywhere near that region. It made an equation that he liked: Greater uneasiness in a pursuer = greater security for the pursued. Jon was starting to enjoy himself.

And so was Wilsa, for quite a different reason. She was eating . . . at last. The boxes of rations on board the *Danae* contained simple fare, but that was what she was used to when a concert was coming up. Magnus Klein, that tyrant masquerading as an agent, would never let her eat rich food. Her diet here was no worse than it would have been on Ganymede.

She passed crackers, dried apricots, and a citrus drink to Jon, watched the depth and pressure indicators move steadily higher, and after a while gave that up in favor of studying bottom return signals from the sonic imager. Since there was nothing of interest to her on the seabed she went into a quiet trance, humming Schubert songs and accompanying herself on an invisible set of keyboards.

She came back to the world, quite abruptly, when the depth monitor showed a hundred and seventeen kilometers. She stared around, then realized that she had responded not to sight, but to sound. The noise that had caught her attention came from the sonic echo-location system. It was providing a wincingly flattened minor third in place of its earlier monotone. Its signal indicated that the seabed was no longer a uniform surface. Wilsa stared, and stared again.

"Jon." She jabbed at the screen with her finger. "What is *that*?"

"Huh?" Jon was expecting to see nothing, and his attention had been on the pressure gauges.

"There, on the seafloor. *There.* Can't you see them?"

The Europan ocean bed, a kilometer below, appeared close enough to touch under the imaging system's high magnification. Its former bland plain had turned into a pattern of lines, as evenly spaced as a plowed field. The space between furrows was only a few tens of meters, but as the *Danae* came closer, each one was seen to stretch like a ruled grid from horizon to seabed horizon. The water above the furrows was slightly blurred and clouded as if by small-scale turbulence.

Wilsa, who regarded Jon as the ultimate expert on everything to do with oceans and submersibles, expected a casual answer. It was disturbing to turn and find him gaping at the screen with an expression that reflected her own confusion.

"I don't know what it is." He was already cautiously guiding the ship lower, meter by careful meter. "Don't even know what it *could* be. But I know that we have to find out. Hold tight. I'm taking us all the way down."

22

The Bat Takes Flight

Bat's special chair, planted in the middle of Bat Cave, was his most treasured possession. He had owned it for nearly twenty years. Well-padded and covered with the softest of velvet, custom-shaped to accommodate the great balloons of his buttocks, it permitted him to sit in motionless comfort for days at a time. When he was drifting and dreaming, or deep into a tough problem, he did just that: *sat*. He would move for food intake or elimination, and that was all; certainly he would not stir, as Magrit Knudsen had long ago learned, for something as irrelevant as personal hygiene.

But now, for the first time, Bat's comfort seat had failed him. He had tried to relax into it and had found that he could not sit still. Soon he was standing up to prowl the cave from one end to the other, monitoring his message center, eyeing the displays or glancing hopefully at the door, while he examined treasured and delicate war relics, or fingered fragile, yellowed documents that should never have been touched by human hands.

He thought he was busy, but he was merely waiting.

Waiting for the improbable event: for a visit from a man

who, if he came to Bat Cave at this time, would be arriving in response to Bat's *own request*—an abrupt request, an unprecedented request, a quite unreasonable request made with no shred of explanation.

The door announced in its soft voice that someone stood outside. Bat started and dropped what he was holding: a Hidalgan Olfact, an inorganic device surpassing all living forms in sensitivity to odors. It had been developed in the later days of the Great War and improved continuously until its makers and its production factory were annihilated in an unrelated reprisal raid. All work records had been lost. Twenty years of intense postwar effort had gone into studying the Olfact, and finally to making a new device that could match its performance.

But the object that Bat had dropped was the original prototype. It was *priceless*.

Bat regained his self-control, caught the spidery Olfact in its slow fall under Ganymedean gravity, and placed it carefully back in position before turning to the opening door. He breathed a sigh of self-condemnation. If it had broken . . .

"I want you to know what it took me to get here." Cyrus Mobarak came bustling in, showing rare signs of impatience. "This is the second time in two weeks that I've left a meeting with my top backers. One more walkout and I'll have a Jovian reputation that I'll never live down."

"I am honored that you took my request for a meeting so seriously." Mobarak might be upset, but now Bat could relax a little. He had estimated seventy-thirty odds that Mobarak would not respond to his message.

"Only because your reputation says that you *never* ask for a meeting with *anyone.*" Mobarak sat down uninvited, his grey mop of hair falling over his eyes. "This had better be damned good."

"I fear that it may be damned bad." Bat settled into his chair. Still, he was not sitting easy. A personal visit—even one from Gobel, bearing lobsters—remained a personal visit, with the unsettling presence of a second individual in Bat's private living quarters. "The fact that I asked you to come here shows that I have a need, and I suspect that my need may be urgent."

"Equipment?"

"Nothing so simple. Something much more precious. Information." Bat had played through this meeting a dozen times while waiting for Mobarak's arrival. He had not liked most of the outcomes. The other man enjoyed intellectual subtleties as much as Bat did, but there was no time now for those multilayered and pleasurable complexities of subterfuge and evasion. The best approach was probably crudity: shock tactics, hitting Mobarak with something so out of the usual that both men would be forced to operate at a new level of directness. Today it must be Rustum Battachariya confronting Cyrus Mobarak, not the complex maneuvering of Megachirops versus Torquemada.

"I want to tell you things that I am not supposed to know." Bat broke his own rules of politeness and offered nothing for refreshment before beginning the conversation. "I tell you these things not as the basis of a proposed quid pro quo for information that you may provide, but rather to prove the serious level of my worries. And I assure you at the outset that I am rarely a *dispenser* of information. If you give me what I need today, it will go no further without your permission."

"Fine." Cyrus Mobarak looked interested but wary. "Surprise me. If you can."

"I will try. Let me begin with small things. Long before you arrived on Ganymede, Cyrus Mobarak had a reputation as someone of great power and influence, both on Earth and through the whole Inner System. The Mobarak fusion units had made you a very rich man, but Mobies were only a small part of the story. And simple wealth was never your goal. You *used* wealth, to buy influence and to steer events."

"Just like every other man or woman who ever had money. If you don't use it, why bother to acquire it?" Mobarak shrugged. "No secrets so far. I'm listening, but I've heard nothing either to surprise or inform me."

"I have scarcely begun. Wealth can *start* many things. It can also, just as often, be used to *stop* them. For example, a moderate amount of money by your standards—great wealth to most people—has been used to publicize and promote the cause of Outward Bound. Part of that effort, quite naturally, is the search for habitable planets around other stars. Now, to most people it would seem equally reasonable that the Distributed Observation System, with its unrivaled power to probe beyond the solar system, should be diverted to aid in the search.

"But you and I know better, do we not? *We* know that DOS is ill-suited to survey the heavens only a few tens of lightyears away, rather than the millions or billions for which it was designed. And we know that the change in emphasis of DOS activities, with its associated curtailment of deep-space experiments, was made for a quite different reason. Specifically, it was done so that David Lammerman and Camille Hamilton would lose their research positions at DOS Center, and could thus be persuaded to come to the Jovian system and work for Cyrus Mobarak."

"An amazing suggestion." Mobarak, now that he had settled in, was quite relaxed. One bushy eyebrow had gone up, and there was a crooked smile on his face. "I'm surprised that you would even consider something so preposterous, still less suggest it to me."

"When you have been forced to accept the improbable, as I have been, it is one short step to the preposterous. I notice that you have not denied it."

"Did you bring me here just so you could listen to denials?"

"No. I cite the case of David Lammerman and Camille Hamilton only to point out to you that I have unusual sources of information—"

"I never doubted it. I originally came to you for assistance for that very reason."

"We will return to that subject later. Before then, I want to prove to you that I am, for the first time, willing to reveal to another living being many of my sources, and also many of my conclusions. Your diversion of the use of DOS to serve your own purposes was my initial, and quite unimportant, example. Let me offer another, closer to my real concern. I know the name of your adversary in the Jovian system."

Both eyebrows raised this time. Mobarak sat bolt upright. "*What?*"

"Thank you. You have told me all that I needed to know. You *are* surprised, genuinely surprised."

"I am." Mobarak leaned back. "I never expected you to find out so quickly."

"No, that will not do." Bat pushed the black hood away from his head, to reveal his close-cropped scalp and dark, thoughtful eyes. "You *were* surprised, and now you are shrewd enough to admit it at once. But you were surprised for a different reason. Because there is, you see, *no adversary*. You invented that person.

"When you first came to see me, I took your request at face value. Who in the Jovian system might seek to harm you, you asked, or to sabotage the cause of the Europan fusion project?

"I looked. And I found no one. Less than no one. Your efforts in the Jovian system were going remarkably well. Surely you must have known that, too. Then why ask me for help? And so I was led at last to another thought. Who had made this odd request of me? Not some innocent to intrigue, but *Torquemada*, scourge of the unwary problem-solver, bane of the incompetent puzzler, my old and infinitely devious rival. Wasn't it likely that he would *test* me, as he had always tested me? And that if he did, surely he would also practice misdirection, as he and I had always practiced it.

"So then I had to ask a different question: *Why* would you come here and task me with a pointless inquiry? For simple intellectual sport? Most unlikely. You could obtain that over the Puzzle Network. You would come, I decided, only to further some agenda of your own.

"What agenda? And now I had to invert the problem, as Torquemada himself loves to invert. Thus: Suppose that you had no hidden enemy in the Jovian system, but, rather, a secret *ally*. If you would like that relationship to remain hidden, you would also worry that it might be revealed. You were confident of *your* discretion, but what of the other party? Suppose that person was a weak link, or that the connection was not sufficiently hidden?

"So now comes the first twist of Torquemada. You approach your old rival in the Puzzle Network, and you invite Megachirops to discover the existence of a linkage between your affairs and those of some other person in the Jovian system. If I fail, that is the best possible answer for you. Because where I fail—I will not pretend to false modesty—no one else will succeed.

"Ah, but suppose that I *succeed*? This is the nicest point, the *second* twist of Torquemada. For you had told me to find an adversary. Yet since there was none, I could at most find a *relationship*. And if I discovered that, you would then say, 'Aha, there's my enemy, that's all I needed to know. Thank you. I can handle the problem from this point.' The only way that I could truly surprise you was to claim that I had *discovered the identity of your adversary*. Because there is, of course, no such person."

Bat, monitoring his own performance, was dissatisfied with it. It was too cerebral, too much like an interaction on the Puzzle Network. He had wanted to be brutal and direct, pushing the Sun King off his legendary balance. It was cause for amazement and relief when Mobarak brushed the hair out of his eyes, leaned forward, and said casually, "All right, I'll call you. Who is this hidden ally?"

Bat released a long, sighing breath. "It is the director of Europan science activities: Dr. Hilda Brandt."

The little nod of the other man's head should have filled Bat with delight. His long shot, built up from meager scraps of information and a lot of guesswork, had paid off. But in that very moment of success, the worries that had led him to make his call to Cyrus Mobarak came back. Bat found himself rushing on, breaking in his urgency every rule of gaming.

"She has been your insider with Outward Bound— although you knew her long before that organization became important to you. I suspect that you understand her better than any of the rest of us in the Jovian system. I *hope* you do, for now I must ask two life-and-death questions. You said in our last meeting that evidence would soon appear showing that the Europan native life forms are not genuine. I must know, will that denial of native life be provided by Dr. Jon Perry, who has been exploring the Europan ocean for the very purpose of *confirming* the existence of such life? And second, will those negative conclusions be provided by Jon Perry *directly* to Hilda Brandt?"

Mobarak was staring at him, finally perhaps off balance—but not as far off balance as Bat, who could feel himself quivering. He was ashamed of his emotion and loss of objectivity.

"Suppose the answers to both your questions are yes. So what?"

"So—*this*." Bat pulled out from his robe the list of calls that he had made over the past day. "To confirm some of my thoughts and suspicions, I have tried again and again to reach Jon Perry. And I have failed, a dozen times.

Observe these replies: Ararat Base admits that Jon Perry and Wilsa Sheer are on Europa, but they insist that they are 'unavailable.' Europa itself is in isolation mode. Mount Ararat will not permit me to communicate with Perry and Sheer in any way."

"What about it? They're probably in the submersible again, wandering around."

"Then why am I not offered that information? But regardless of where they are, I believe that they may be in terrible personal danger."

"I don't see why. They've been there before. They're both experienced."

"The danger does not come from the planet. It comes from Hilda Brandt."

"Nonsense. I know Hilda . . . and you're the one who insists that I know her better than anyone else in this system."

"That is true. Yet I think that perhaps you do not know her at all. She is a complex personality."

"So is anyone worth knowing."

"I mean unusually complex. More so than you . . . or me. And far more dangerous. I wish I could find a way to prove to you how dangerous."

"Oh, rubbish." Mobarak rose from his seat and went striding away toward Bat Cave's communications center. "Give me a fast line, and I'll settle this in a minute. Camille Hamilton is still at Ararat Base, too, and David has an open connection to her. I'll find out exactly where Jon Perry and Wilsa Sheer are, and what's been happening on Europa."

"You are proposing to call David Lammerman?" Bat rose from his seat also, and padded across to stand at Mobarak's side.

"Right now."

"You seek his assistance?"

"I sure do." Mobarak was keying in access codes. "I'll

tell him to sort this out. If necessary, I'll tell him to head right over to Europa and to call us from there."

"Then permit me to intrude where I have no right to." Bat placed his hand next to Mobarak's on the console, preventing the completion of the call sequence. It was the closest that Bat had come to physical contact with anyone in years, and far beyond his comfort level. He forced himself to keep his hand there, and went on: "You asked me to discover your enemy in the Jovian system. In exploring that question, I naturally considered many people, and reviewed many private files. Including David Lammerman's."

Mobarak pulled his hand away from the console as though it had stung him. "You investigated David? You thought that *David*—"

"I looked at everyone. And I learned much of personal relationships that did not concern me. But they should concern you."

"Are you telling me that *David*—I can't believe it." Cyrus Mobarak looked sick, and his face aged fifteen years. "I can't *believe* . . ."

"That he is your enemy, and would betray you?" Bat was filled with conflicting emotions. He was confronting naked misery, just the sort of situation that he had designed his whole life to avoid. He should retreat, and remain aloof. Or at the very least, he should *use* Mobarak's misunderstanding to further his own purposes. Emotion was a weakness that should be exploited.

Except that the man bent-headed in front of him was, in a curious but real sense, Bat's *best friend*—an alien thought! They had jousted over the Puzzle Network since Bat's youth: Torquemada and Megachirops, Megachirops versus Torquemada, aware of each other always, head and shoulders above the rest, knowing that they were each other's only real competition. They had spent twenty years in teasing and challenging, devising special problems intended for one other remote and invisible person. Bat's most diabolical brain teasers had been constructed with Torquemada alone in mind.

Friendship? Did not such intellectual contact mean *more* than the carnal contacts, mindless camaraderie, or inebriated revelry that most of humanity was forced to describe as friendship? And did not the higher form of friendship impose its own duties and constraints?

Bat sighed again, this time for opportunity foregone. "I am sorry. You mistake my meaning. David Lammerman is no enemy of yours, although many would say that he has ample reason to be. Tell me, are you"—Bat had to force the alien word out—"*fond* of your son?"

"Am I fond—" Mobarak cleared his throat. "My God. David is my only child. We've seen too little of each other over the years, but not because I wanted it that way. Of course I'm fond of him. I would give him *anything*. But he avoids me."

"He does." Bat was committed now, to discussion of the kind he most hated. There was no way out of it, even though he wriggled in horror at the waves of raw emotion filling the air around him. "And I know why he avoids you. I have seen tapes made when he was talking to you, or preparing to do so. He thinks that his father is the greatest man in history, but he is terrified of him. He becomes tongue-tied in your presence. You crush him with your personality."

"I don't mean to. He's the apple of my eye."

"You do it without thinking. Cyrus Mobarak overwhelms David Lammerman. If you want to be close to him, you must let him *breathe*."

"How? I'm just being myself with him."

"Then you must be someone different, someone more like the Cyrus Mobarak who meets with me. I have seen you on tape also, many times. Do you think I am unaware that with me your personality has been *damped down*, for my benefit?" Bat lifted his hand at last from the control console. "Call David now, if you wish. But *ask* him for what you need. Do not *tell* him. Say that you would like his assistance, that there is a special task that you dare not entrust to anyone else in the system. Can you do that?"

"I can try." Mobarak at last made the connection, while Bat drifted back to his special comfort seat. He was exhausted. He had taken all that he could stand, and *hated* it. How did Magrit Knudsen handle this sort of thing, day after day? Yet she seemed to *thrive* on such personal confrontation, such emotional intertwining.

"David." The line was open. Mobarak's voice was gruff and oddly tentative. "David, are you busy?"

"I'm pretty busy." David Lammerman's face was on the screen, guarded and uncertain. "I'm in a meeting with Tristan Morgan and Nell Cotter. We're discussing the ways that Mobies might help Outward Bound."

"David, I hate to interrupt. But I need your help with a . . . a special task that I dare not entrust to anyone else. I am in a meeting with Rustum Battachariya. Jon Perry and Wilsa Sheer are on Europa, and we have reason to think that they are in great danger. Would you try to reach them through Camille, and make sure they are safe?"

"Of course." David Lammerman's face was puzzled. "The last time I spoke to Camille, everything was going well. But I'll call Europa right now. Are *you* all right?"

"I'm fine."

"And if there *are* problems on Europa . . ."

"Use your best judgment. You can call me if you want a second opinion—but you certainly don't have to. Go to Europa yourself, if you think it's necessary. Use my credit, my name, anything else you need. I know you'll do the intelligent thing. But please hurry. This is urgent."

"I'll sure do my best." David glanced away from the camera for a moment. "I'll have help here if I need it. I'd better get on with it. Are you *sure* you are all right."

"I am certain of it. I'm . . . better than I've ever been."

There was a long, self-conscious moment, when neither man spoke. They finally nodded at each other and simultaneously broke contact.

"Well." Cyrus Mobarak stared blindly at the blank screen. "I tried. He's very competent, you know. Did you notice that he didn't ask me one unnecessary question? But I have a thousand questions. About Europa, about Hilda Brandt. About how you connected me with her. About why you think she's dangerous. When will you be ready to give me answers?"

"Very soon." Bat was more than happy to change back to factual discussions. "There is one thing I must do first."

He rose and lumbered over to Mobarak's side, where he set up his own instruction sequence.

"You're ordering a *ship*?" Mobarak could not quite follow the abbreviated command codes, shortened for Bat's personal use.

"Indeed I am. A ship, and also suits."

"For me?" Mobarak had seen his own name flash across the display.

"Yes. And for me also. I am going with you."

Mobarak stared in amazement at the screen, where the complete mission profile was appearing. His name was there, along with that of Rustum Battachariya.

Rustum Battachariya. Passenger!

A few minutes earlier, Bat had wished for a way to prove to Mobarak just how dangerous he believed Hilda Brandt to be. He had found one now, without saying a word.

Proof enough for anyone: For the first time in uncounted years, the Great Bat was about to abandon his cave on Ganymede. He would endure the chaos and crowded discomfort of a high-gee flight through the open space of the Jovian system, his destination the barren, naked surface of Europa.

23

Too Late

The communication channel offered only one reply to all inquiries: "*Europa is in isolation mode until further notice. Your approach request has been noted, but permission to land cannot be provided.*"

Three of those anonymous rejections were quite enough. David Lammerman's fourth message was not a request; it was a notice of intention to land, with a well-defined arrival time.

And that produced results. In rapid succession there appeared on the ship's screen a confused, low-level Fax of Buzz Sandstrom; a less polite but equally confused high-level Fax; a Mount Ararat mid-level live official who changed in a few seconds from calm obnoxious superiority to shock, anger, and disbelief; and, at last, Sandstrom himself.

"You've heard it six times." His nostrils were dilated, and he was leaning far forward so that his distorted face filled the screen. "*Go away.* We're in *isolation mode.* You can't land at Mount Ararat, no matter who you are."

"I'm afraid we must, unless you let me talk at once to Camille Hamilton, Jon Perry, or Wilsa Sheer." Lammerman's voice remained as mild and reasonable as ever. "Actually, we're already in final approach. I called as a courtesy, to make sure that nothing in the spaceport will be damaged by our ship's exhaust when we come down."

"Touch down and you'll be under arrest the minute you step out of your ship."

"Then that's the way it will have to be."

"Buzz is going through the ceiling," said Tristan Morgan softly. He and Nell Cotter were sitting tucked away in the rear of the cabin, where they could watch Sandstrom but not be seen or heard by him. "I've met him a dozen times, and he's not really such a bad guy. A bit dim, maybe. But I've never seen him like this before."

"I don't think it's all anger." Nell had been watching every muscle-twitch on Sandstrom's face, and recording it. "He may be annoyed, but there's more to it than that. Seems like he's battle-scarred. Nearly ready to weep. Somebody's been giving him a prize chewing-out. A little more shove, and I think he'll break completely."

"You have to be wrong. He's deputy director on Europa. He dishes it out, he doesn't take it."

"All the more reason why he doesn't like it. But that limits the choice of chewer: Hilda Brandt or nobody. Let me past. I want to try something."

She edged around Tristan and moved forward, to a point where Sandstrom could see her. "If you say we can't talk to the others, then I demand to speak with Dr Brandt. Immediately. And I will tell her how you have been behaving toward us."

"And who the hell are you?" Buzz Sandstrom had met Nell on her previous visit to Europa, but he did not seem to recognize her. He hesitated, then went on in quieter tones: "I really don't see why Dr. Brandt would want to talk with you."

"Well, you can't say that about me, Buzz." Tristan had followed Nell and was standing beside her. "I talk to Hilda all the time. And we're *entitled* to land on Mount Ararat. We have a permit from Rustum Battachariya, the head of Passenger Transport for the Outer System—including Europa."

"That doesn't overrule an isolation-mode notice."

"I don't agree. But that's something for the lawyers to argue over. We'll be touching down at Mount Ararat in five minutes. We need a landing slot. And we want to talk to Hilda, or to Perry and the others. Better cooperate, Buzz, or you'll get yourself in *real* trouble."

"Cooperate!" But Buzz Sandstrom was wilting. His muscles had lost a lot of their tightness, and the line of his jaw no longer had its pugnacious jut. "Even if you do land, you can't talk to Dr. Brandt. She's not here."

"According to the system transit manifests, she is. She arrived on Europa a couple of hours ago, and there's no record of her leaving."

"I didn't mean she's not on Europa." Buzz was actually starting to sound placating. "I mean she's not *here*, not at Ararat Base."

"So where is she?"

"On the surface. Camille Hamilton is with her, so you can't talk to her either. They're out at Blowhole. It's iced over, and they're trying to clear it." Sandstrom lost the last shred of belligerence. "Look, Tristan, it's not my fault. I was just following Dr. Brandt's orders. There was no *reason* for her to get so angry with me. She was the one told me to put Europa in isolation mode, and she was the one told me to keep Perry and Sheer from talking to others. How was I supposed to know the two of 'em would go out and commit suicide?"

"They're *dead*?"

"No. Yes. I mean—I don't know. They may be. I mean, it happened over two days ago. They escaped from Ararat Base and went out onto the surface. They took a submersible down below the ice without permission."

"So they're safe."

"*No*. You see, they took the *Danae*, a ship that was being modified and wasn't ready for full use. And they're not just under the ice, exploring; they're *stuck* under there, with no way back and not enough oxygen. They closed Blowhole *themselves*; it iced over when .they cut off the power below. And I had nothing to do with *any* of that." Sandstrom's voice rose to a wail just as the signal for the final descent phase sounded through the ship. "But I'm being blamed for the whole stupid thing!"

Blowhole had vanished. To Nell and the others approaching in the ground cars, its former location was signaled only by a circle of buildings and a long, shallow-sloping ramp that ran down to end in a blank wall of new ice. A glittering submersible—the *Spindrift*, or its identical twin—sat at the top of the ramp, surrounded by half a dozen cars.

"See, water-ice is different from most ices. When it freezes, it *expands*." Buzz Sandstrom was in the same ground car as Nell. He had been enormously relieved when Hilda Brandt did not accuse him of permitting an unauthorized ship to land at Mount Ararat. As soon as she found out who the three newcomers were, she had actually told him to bring them along to help. Now Buzz was explaining to Nell—and to her insatiable unseen recorders—the problem of recovering the bodies of Jon Perry and Wilsa Sheer from underneath the ice.

"So Blowhole doesn't just fill with ice if the heat is turned off," he went on, "because the column of water wants to expand when it freezes. The only way it can go is *up*. It squeezes higher in the cylinder. See the ramp? It used to lead down to open water, when the water level was down below the ice level. Now you could drive this car right out where Blowhole used to be."

"How thick is the ice? It's not solid all the way down the hole, surely?"

"No. It hasn't had time to freeze that much. But it's maybe thirty meters, according to sonar readings. They might as well be digging at it with toothpicks. Maybe that's just as well. If they broke through, they'd fall into the water."

"They" were a dozen suited figures, working with mobile construction equipment on the ice over Blowhole. As Nell's car approached on its caterpillar tracks, closely followed by the car holding David Lammerman and Tristan Morgan, all excavation work stopped. Two of the suited people came hurrying across to meet the arriving cars.

"Waste of time digging." Hilda Brandt nodded to the new arrivals. She was easily recognizable by the high-level insignia on her suit. "We need a fresh idea. I was hoping that one of you might think of something."

Nell was impressed again by the other woman's self-confidence and concentration. She offered no explanation of why she had put Europa in isolation mode, and made no comment as to why she had now chosen to change her mind and accept help. Just the statement: We have a problem that needs a solution.

A problem? Nell couldn't make herself see it that objectively. The death of Jon Perry wouldn't be a problem, it would be the worst thing in the world. But Hilda Brandt remained so damned *calm*.

Don't let yourself brood on it. Be a reporter—ask questions. "Why did they seal themselves down under the ice if they knew it might kill them?"

"They didn't." Camille was at Hilda Brandt's side. It was clear that she knew nothing of the recent embargo of Europa and regarded the arrival of Nell and the others simply as extra help. "They thought they were quite safe. They would have been, under normal circumstances, because the *Danae* can carry a fourteen-day oxygen supply, and more than that of food and water. But when the hull was strengthened to withstand greater pressure, most of the air tanks were temporarily removed. They hadn't been replaced when Jon Perry stole the submersible. The gauges *show* a fourteen-day supply, but that's totally misleading. The air will last less than two days for two people. Jon Perry and Wilsa Sheer have been down for over two and a half days. If they've spent most of their time asleep, or sitting very still, it's possible that they are still alive. But time's against us. And we're farther from getting them out than we've ever been. The layer of ice covering Blowhole gets thicker by the hour."

Nell found herself staring at Tristan. There it was, the explicit statement that neither Buzz Sandstrom nor Hilda Brandt had been willing to provide. Jon and Wilsa, according to Camille's numbers, were surely dead. This was no rescue mission. It was the doleful recovery of corpses.

Yet Hilda Brandt still seemed to be denying it, acting as though every minute counted. She had moved to stand by David Lammerman and was listening intently. He was pointing at Blowhole and then back toward Mount Ararat. After a few seconds, she began to nod. She waved.

"Come here, would you? I want you to hear this, then tell me what you think."

Her call and gesture were to Camille Hamilton, but of course everyone else crowded around as well.

"Actually, it's not just my idea." David Lammerman had been confident and in command since leaving Ganymede. Now he showed, just for a moment, a trace of his old diffidence. It vanished as he went on: "When we first landed at Ararat Base and learned what had happened at Blowhole, I wondered about ways to open up the ice. I didn't know that you were trying to excavate, but I'd decided straightaway that excavation couldn't work. It seemed to me that only something really powerful would do the job fast enough and yet keep the ice open long enough for us to find . . . whatever's down there."

David glanced from Nell to Tristan, then away. "So I asked myself, what's the most powerful energy source that I know of on Europa? And it became obvious: *the drive on the ship that brought us here*. It's powered by a Moby. I called Cyrus Mobarak—" He caught Camille's shocked expression and gave her an embarrassed smile. "I know, Camille. But I really did. On my own. I spoke to him, and by now he should have landed and be on his way to Blowhole. But I didn't want to wait until he arrived, so I asked him, could a ship's Moby be modified to melt a path down into Blowhole without destroying itself and anything down there in its way?"

"And his reply?" Hilda Brandt spoke for everyone.

"He said he didn't see why not. But it would be very tricky, because a ship's fusion drive was never designed to interact directly with water and ice. It's an unstable situation, he's pretty sure of that. But he says he's not the real expert on Moby stability." He pointed at Camille. "She is. He says we must ask her. That was Cyrus Mobarak's opinion, and it's mine as well. Camille?"

Camille hardly seemed to be listening. She was staring all around at the grey-white, lifeless ice-world, then up into the black, star-swarmed sky; everywhere except at the waiting circle of people. At last she shook her head.

"I'm not an expert. Not on Mobies. I'm still learning."

"We're all learning," said Hilda Brandt. "All our lives. That's not the point. The point is, can the ship's Moby do it? If it can, someone at Ararat Base will fly it over here as soon as I give the order."

"You don't understand." Camille sensed what they were going to ask her to do. It sounded like the only way that Jon Perry and Wilsa Sheer might be saved . . . except that she knew it was impossible. "The Moby has the *power* to do it; it has raw energy to spare. That's not the question. It's the stability. A stability analysis, even a first-order one, for a ship's Moby sitting in Blowhole—that would need a huge amount of computation."

She took a couple of steps backward, distancing herself from the group.

"But you can do that!" said David. He and the whole party were following Camille, drifting across the spongy ice. He took her arm. "You've done a hundred calculations like it. And I could have the Moby out of our ship in five minutes."

"I might be able to do the calculation—given enough time. But you need an answer *now*. I'd have to go back to Mount Ararat, get on the computer, and enter all the parameters for the ship's Moby. *And* the Blowhole geometry, and then the surface-material properties, and radiation rates, and ambient temperatures." Camille shook herself free of David's grip. "You're talking about a monster computation, about something that might run for days before it converged."

"And we don't have days, do we?" murmured Hilda Brandt thoughtfully. "Or even hours." She lowered her head as though studying the mottled patterns of ice at her feet. Finally she said, as though to herself, "That's it, then. Damned, aren't we, either way? But really, what is the choice?"

She sighed, walked up to Camille, and reached out to take her by the shoulders. She stared in through the visor of the suit, oblivious to the ground car that was grinding its way across the ice from Mount Ararat, and unaware of the strange-looking figure that emerged from it.

Rustum Battachariya, an exception to the "one-size-fits-all" rule of surface superconductor suits, had been stripped to his shoes and underwear and stuffed into a translucent container of green shielding plastic designed to hold large flux-intolerant equipment.

It was big enough . . . barely. Bat could walk, after a fashion, by shuffling his feet a few inches at a time while he held his arms close to his sides. But it was freezing cold; the radio of his improvised suit was not working right; and while the green plastic was not opaque, it was far from transparent. Bat could see little and hear only the scuffle of boots across the surface. At his side, guiding him along, walked Cyrus Mobarak.

Hilda Brandt ignored the waddling green-clad figure with its penguin gait. She had been staring at Camille steadily, eye to eye. "Camille Hamilton," she said at last, "look at me, and listen. The ship will be here in ten minutes. I already sent the order to fly it over. The Moby can be taken out of it and made ready for use in fifteen minutes. At the end of that period, we need to know how to position the Moby, and what settings to use with it. There will be no opportunity to return to Ararat Base, or to sit at a computer. You must decide the settings *yourself*. Fifteen minutes. You hear me? You will have fifteen minutes. No more."

"I can't do that!" Camille was trying to pull free. David Lammerman made an instinctive gesture to help her, then controlled himself and turned away. Everyone else stood motionless, as frozen as the Europan ice crystals beneath their triple-insulated boots. Nell, not understanding what she was seeing, knowing only that it was dramatic and somehow important, prayed that her hidden recorder was working.

"I *can't*," repeated Camille. "Without my models, and without a computer and all the parameters—"

"You *can*. I know you better than you know yourself. Look inside, Camille. Don't you realize that you can *always* feel the answers, even before the computers come back with theirs? You understand fusion stability, even in complicated situations, without having to think about it.

You've studied it and studied it until it's part of your deep subconscious. *Look inside.*"

"No." Camille was shivering. Hilda Brandt's eyes were enormous twin moons that filled the sky. Camille could not look away. "You're wrong, quite wrong. I calculate *everything.*"

"You do. But you don't need to calculate everything *with the computers*, because you are already doing it in your head. The computer solutions are just your security. If you don't like the look of their answers, what do you do? You run them again, *until they are the way you feel they ought to be.* You've talked to a lot of people about the 'shortcuts' that you use to get quick results. Use them *now*—when we need them."

Camille could not escape. She could not even move. A terrible force, hot and imperative, was holding her to those luminous eyes. A voice, far away, was saying, "Fifteen minutes. You will have fifteen minutes."

It said it again. A third time. On the fourth repetition, the Europan sky and landscape vanished. Camille slipped away into that strange interior domain of rippling plasma, hers alone, where no one else could ever follow.

The Moby, stripped of its accessories, was surprisingly small for its fifty-gigawatt output. A bright-blue rounded cylinder, two meters long and no more than half that across, it sat cradled in an upright frame, its broad end down. The open lattice of the supports, held in exact alignment by twin gyroscopes at its top, had been carefully placed in the center of Blowhole.

David Lammerman was checking the Moby's power settings and nozzle diameters for the third time. He really needed to consult Camille on a fine point or two, but she had been led away, pale and close to fainting, as soon as her listing of Moby parameters was complete. She had stood motionless for twenty-five agonizing minutes—twenty-five, not fifteen—and not even Hilda Brandt had dared to interrupt her concentration. Finally she had called for an audio link and begun to define Moby settings as fast as she could speak.

It was left to David to make those settings, and to worry that Camille's answers might be disastrously wrong. Suppose that the unknowns of local gravity or temperature proved more important than anyone realized? Had anyone, ever, examined such a direct plasma/water-ice interaction? He wanted to ask Camille about the effects on the Moby of the ambient high-energy particle flux, about latent heats, about conductivities, about radiation losses to the open space above Europa's surface. About *everything*.

But time had run out. Somewhere beneath his feet—he wished he knew how far; if the Moby performed as planned, that depth was a crucial variable—somewhere down there, anything from fifty meters to a hundred kilometers below, Jon Perry and Wilsa Sheer were either dead or dying, from oxygen starvation.

There could be no delays.

David prepared to switch on. At his side, Cyrus Mobarak had observed his son in his task of calibration. Three times he had held out a hand to interrupt, three times drawn it back. He resisted the urge to take over and make his own check of Moby settings. The only exception was at the end, when he realized that David was within seconds of switching on. Mobarak began to urge everyone away from Blowhole.

Hilda Brandt refused to move. She stood at the very edge of the circle of ice until David himself, his task complete, came across, grabbed her arm, and pulled her far from the perimeter.

They watched and waited for fifteen endless seconds. David, sure that something must be wrong with one of his settings, started forward across the ice. Cyrus Mobarak's hand, suddenly firm on his arm, held him in place.

"No," murmured a gruff, mesmerizing voice. "Low-order transients. Delaying the fusion cycle."

David did not reply. He did not need to. For although there was nothing to see on the Moby itself, the ice in a fifteen-meter circle around it suddenly began to sputter and fume. A second later, a thick hemisphere of water vapor was forming. The Moby at its center became invisible in a cloud of white.

"Is it working?" The voice over the suit radio was Tristan Morgan's, but it was barely audible above half a dozen others that were exclaiming as the vapor cloud turned blue at its spreading base.

Everyone instinctively stepped farther back. The ice beneath their feet had begun to tremble, responding to an immense energy release. The Moby reappeared for a moment, lifted on a plume of violet flame. Then it began moving down, descending at a measured couple of meters a second.

David strained forward, counting, waiting. He did not have Camille's quantitative understanding of processes, but he knew in general terms what was happening. The first critical point would come after seventeen seconds. Four concentric zones of activity must be stably established around the Moby. In the innermost one, the Moby plasma jets, hell fires at temperatures of hundreds of millions of degrees, impinged directly on the frozen surface of Blowhole. The ice beneath them did not melt or boil. It dissociated into monomolecular hydrogen and monomolecular oxygen. Those elements spread outward and recombined in the second zone with a violence more powerful than an ordinary chemical reaction. Ice at that point also dissociated, this time into ordinary oxygen and hydrogen, which burned in turn at a temperature of a few thousand degrees. The heat from this converted the next zone of Blowhole to superheated steam. It was this steam that in the fourth zone finally melted the outer perimeter of the column.

Fifteen, sixteen, seventeen. The hole in the ice, if Camille were right, was now close to its maximum diameter. The Moby was beginning to drop at a constant rate, slicing a thirty-meter-wide core through the upper level of Europa's ice blanket.

Twenty-three, twenty-four, twenty-five. An immense conical cloud, bursting almost straight up out of Blowhole, was lit from within by the infernal fires of stellar-temperature plasma. To an orbiting observer directly above, Blowhole would appear as a pinpoint hard X-ray source.

Twenty-eight, twenty-nine, thirty. Precisely on that count there came a sudden change. The cloud blew out and away in a fraction of a second. David took a couple of steps forward. It could not be that the Moby had switched itself off—that would not happen for another ten seconds. So it must have reached open water and was falling free through the original and unfrozen center of Blowhole.

That was bad news. The ice was less thick than they had estimated. If the Moby, working at full power, had encountered the *Danae* close to the bottom of the ice . . .

David had set forty seconds as the lower limit of safety, and he was determined to wait that long. Tristan Morgan, sitting inside the *Spindrift*, lacked such self-control. As soon as the vapor cloud blew away he sent the submersible rolling down the ramp. It hovered for a moment on the edge, tipped crazily, then entered Blowhole with a gigantic splash.

Tristan was piloting the *Spindrift* with Hilda Brandt's consent and approval. Nell, sitting at his side, had asked and received no such blessing. She had invited herself and scrambled aboard when everyone else was preoccupied with the Moby's fiery descent into Blowhole.

This time the soft restraining arms that enclosed her as the ship's tilt angle exceeded tolerance were no surprise. She peered into the turbulent water ahead, trying to see their course as the *Spindrift* bucked and yawed and rolled in the violent up-currents. Less than a hundred meters below, the Moby was turning ice-cold water into its component elements.

It did its job. Now if only—for God's sake—it would turn itself—off.

Nell was recording, but the water around the transparent submersible was a meaningless chaos of blue-lit, bubbling updrafts, as wild as those of any Earth seaquake.

She turned to Tristan. He lacked Jon Perry's unnatural calm in an emergency. His mouth was gaping, and his eyes started out of his head as he struggled to hold the *Spindrift* on a steady downward course. Above all else, he was trying to avoid the solid wall of Blowhole.

And failing.

The ship shivered and creaked as it was thrown against an invisible and unmoving barrier of ice. The hull at Nell's side rang like a bell. Stress indicators all across the control panel flickered to danger levels, and back again. A second collision, moments after the first, wrenched a shrill scream from twisting braces.

The ship rolled a hundred and twenty degrees. Nell was suddenly hanging facedown and peering into bubbling darkness. She caught a glimpse of a brilliant pinpoint of violet-blue, far beneath.

"Can't hold it!" But just as Tristan was gasping out those words, the tumult ended. The *Spindrift* steadied, rolled back to an even keel, and was all at once descending peacefully through a dark, endless chimney.

Nell stared down through the transparent floor. The ship's lights showed nothing beneath but clear, subsiding water. Beyond their range of visibility, the now-quiescent Moby would be heading down, down, down, toward the remote seafloor. Long before it got there, its internal chambers would collapse under the monstrous pressure. It would be crushed into a compact, useless mass, something for future Europan generations to recover, and perhaps to wonder at.

Nell and Tristan did not give the vanished Moby another thought. The *Spindrift*'s ultrasonic imager had been turned on, and now its shape-detection programs were raking the dark interior ocean for objects whose external profile matched that of the *Danae*'s.

The submersible fell and fell, until it was close to the lower edge of the ice blanket. The scanning imager remained silent.

Tristan angled the descent. "Feels like a waste of time, but Hilda says we gotta do this—or topside will start freezing over again."

He took the *Spindrift* across to Blowhole's wall and approached the first of the three heating units attached to the ice face. Two flexible mechanical arms reached forward from their external mooring, moving under Tristan's control.

Grasping the switch with the submersible's waldoes looked easy, but it seemed to Nell to take forever. She itched to have a go at it herself. Tristan was an experienced pilot in the Jovian atmosphere, but he was unfamiliar with both the *Spindrift* and the Europan environment.

And so am I. Less used to them than he is. Nell forced herself to sit back and be quiet. Tristan was doing his best. Distractions and offers of help would only slow him down.

It took a couple of minutes—hours to Nell, until she checked the clock—to turn on the first heating unit. The other two went more quickly. Tristan grunted in satisfaction as the third unit vibrated into action.

"At least we're sure of a way back," he said. "Now we can stay down for as long as we like and go as far as we want."

He had pumped ballast and they were dropping fast, into the quiet dark. But *where* were they going? Nell peered down. With the whole of Europa's ocean empty beneath them, how would they ever find the speck of a submersible, even with the *Spindrift*'s superior equipment to help them?

Answer: They wouldn't. Rather than face the reality of Jon and Wilsa's death, she and Tristan had charged off on a pointless search. Millions of cubic miles of ocean would take months to survey. *Years.*

Nell, sick at heart, was telling herself to turn off her recorder, to give up hope, when a loud beep came from the ultrasonic imager.

"Got something," said Tristan. "Moving target. Holding steady."

Which was more than his voice was doing.

"Is it them?" asked Nell. *Listen to me. I sound like an old frog.*

Tristan did not answer. There was only one other submersible in the Europan ocean. What she was really asking was something quite different: "Are they alive?"

That question could not be answered with the information from the imager. The *Danae* appeared to be intact, floating quietly, its power off, about three kilometers below them. It must have been heading back toward Blowhole. But that said nothing about the condition of its passengers.

Tristan sent a sonic signal to the *Danae* and they waited breathlessly for a reply. For a word from a human voice—any word.

There was nothing. Only a fixed message from the onboard computer of the *Danae*, returning its own status signal: *Functioning normally.*

Tristan put the *Spindrift* into a reckless descent, plunging at the image on the screen until Nell was sure that the two ships would collide. At the last moment he pulled out, to place the submersible directly ahead of the *Danae*. The *Spindrift*'s free-swimmer lights went straight for the forward window of the other submersible, shining in to illuminate what lay behind it. Nell saw two suited figures, lolling against each other. Their heads were tilted back, their faces invisible.

"It's them," said Tristan. "They're unconscious."

Or dead. Nell did not need the other possibility spelled out to her. "How fast can we get them to the surface?"

"Few minutes. I can get underneath, do a direct lift. It's going to be uncomfortable, though. We'll have to go up flat on our backs and feet-first."

He was not asking her consent. As the *Spindrift* dropped, tilted vertically, grabbed, and began the upward run to Blowhole and the surface, Nell was tempted to query the *Danae*'s computer. It could report the internal oxygen and carbon-dioxide levels, information that might tell her if the interior could still support life.

She reached toward the console . . . and changed her mind. She was no expert on life-support requirements. She would know for sure soon enough.

Or not soon enough. She stared out of the forward window. They seemed to have been heading upward for ages, but still they were only just at the bottom of the ice shield. She closed her eyes and willed the *Spindrift* onward with its burden. *Faster!*

The upper end of Blowhole's cylinder of liquid water, violently created just a few minutes earlier, was barely wide enough for the unwieldy combination of *Danae* and *Spindrift*. Tristan was making things worse by taking the upward run far too fast. Nell felt the shudder and scrape of the submersibles' hulls against ice, and then a bigger and final jolt as the ships rammed through something solid. As the *Spindrift* crunched its way above the surface and began to push the other ship toward the ramp, Nell understood for the first time the deadly cold of Europa.

The area where the ships now floated had been subjected to million-degree temperatures no more than half an hour earlier; already it had crusted with a new layer of ice. The heating units, in operation again but over a kilometer below them, were not yet having an effect here.

Nell had somehow imagined that the group around Blowhole would still be standing there, exactly as she and Tristan had left them. After all, knowing what might be found below the ice, how could anyone bear to tear himself away?

But the area seemed deserted. The *Danae* and *Spindrift* crept steadily along the ramp. Only when the first submersible approached the lumpy Europan surface did Nell realize her mistake. Not far from the end of the ramp— and so large that when she had scanned the area, she had mistaken it for one of the surrounding buildings—the biggest ground car that she had ever seen loomed over the *Danae*. It was at least thirty meters long and twenty meters across. While she watched, one end slid open. The *Danae* was grabbed from within and pulled through into a monstrous cargo hold. The end closed. Less than a minute later it opened again.

"Europan mobile lab," said Tristan as the *Spindrift* was taken in turn and pulled into the hold. The great door slid closed again, sealing itself. "Particle-flux protected, breathable air once you're past the inner lock. Shirt-sleeve environment. They can get their suits off and put a medical team to work right away. Good thinking by somebody—Hilda, for a bet."

The *Danae* had disappeared. Tristan already had his suit halfway off, waiting impatiently for the lock to cycle them through and the outside pressure to equalize. As soon as the *Spindrift*'s hatch could be opened, he jumped out and headed for the inner door.

Nell followed, a lot more slowly. She was afraid of what she might see on the other side. Only Glyn Sefaris's imagined voice spurred her on; "Do your job, Nell. You're a *reporter*. You didn't come all this way to back off now."

The *Danae* was sitting in the middle of the next room, hatch open and people swarming over it. Rustum Batta-chariya sat hunched on a long workbench on the far left. In spite of the biting cold he had ripped open his makeshift suit. Now, like a nightmare parody of an exotic dancer, his black, bulging body was partially visible through folds of billowing and translucent green plastic. Hilda Brandt flanked him on one side, Cyrus Mobarak on the other. Gabriel Shumi stood a couple of paces in front of them. There was no sign of David Lammerman or Camille Hamilton.

Tristan was struggling to get to the *Danae*'s open hatch. He was held back by three people dressed in the uniform of the Europan general support staff, and they were gently pushing him away from the submersible. Instead of going across to join him, Nell headed for the tall, angular form of Gabriel Shumi.

"Are they alive, doctor?" That was the only question that mattered.

Europa's chief medical officer stared right through her and went across to sit on the bench next to Cyrus Mobarak. He put his hands to his head and rubbed his temples until his carefully styled hair was a rumpled mess.

"I think it is time," he said quietly, "that I retired to Callisto. I own a deep farm there, you know. A big one." Shumi wasn't replying to Nell's question. She realized that he wasn't talking to Mobarak either, or to anyone else on the bench. He was babbling.

Nell went to stand directly in front of him and placed her face close to his. "How are Jon Perry and Wilsa Sheer? The people in the submersible—*are they alive?*"

He glared back at her. "Alive? Why, don't you know you can't kill a visitor to the Europan ocean just by freezing her body solid, or by cutting off his air supply?

I'm beginning to wonder if you can do it by chopping somebody to bits. But if you're going to ask me *how* anyone can possibly be alive, when every rule in the medical book says they must have died over a day ago . . ." He stared mournfully across at the *Danae*.

Shumi had chosen the worst possible time to lose his grip. "You *are* saying they're alive, aren't you?" Nell grabbed him by the shoulders and shook him, as he again stared right through her. "Doctor Shumi! You must answer."

He was nodding absentmindedly. "They were dead, you know, when I opened the hatch. Both of them. No pulse, no heartbeat, stone dead. The air inside was poison. Too low in oxygen, too high in carbon dioxide, quite unbreathable. I declared them dead. They *were* dead. We began to pick them up, so we could move them out. And the second we lifted them they both gave a little body twitch, and then they started to breathe. First the man, then the woman. And now—"

Nell didn't wait to hear any more. She ran around the submersible to the side away from Tristan, found a toehold on one of the *Danae*'s free-swimmer supports, and hoisted herself high enough to reach the front window. One of the men holding Tristan started after her. She climbed higher, up onto the roof, where it was difficult for him to reach her, and hung headdown to peer into the cabin and to allow her handheld minicamera a view of the interior.

Jon and Wilsa were still in their seats. Their faces had a curious purple-red tinge, and their eyes were half-closed. Upside down, Nell could not read their expressions, but she could see that they were breathing. And they were laboriously moving their hands and feet at the medical team's urging.

"Get *off* there—right now." The man following Nell had reached the roof and grabbed her arm. She meekly allowed herself to be helped down and led back to the group sitting on the bench. It now included Tristan.

Nell went to his side and gripped his hand. "I saw them. They're alive and moving. They're going to be fine. That's all that matters."

She spoke softly, but Gabriel Shumi somehow heard her. "All that matters to *you*," he said mournfully. "But I will be asked to produce reports detailing just what happened. I will be called upon to provide explanations for all this. When no explanation is possible."

"Ah. *Explanations*. A most timely word." Bat had been sitting motionless, staring straight ahead. He had seemed as far out of things as Shumi was. Now he roused himself. "With Wilsa Sheer and Jon Perry rescued and recovering, it is time to think of explanations. They are surely overdue. But this is not the place for them."

He turned to Hilda Brandt. "If you would be so kind as to make available a warmer compartment within this vehicle, and find for me some alternative and less revealing form of body covering, both would be much appreciated. For although I am now ready to admit that I have misjudged you"—his glance included Cyrus Mobarak as well as Hilda Brandt—"I believe that we have much to say to each other. It is time . . . to talk."

24

Monsters

The biggest unoccupied room that the Europan mobile lab offered was a data-review station, about three meters square—roughly the size of Bat's bed.

He stared at the six people crowding in on him—sitting on *top* of him, by Bat standards—and decided that this was the worst day of his life.

It was not his departure from the treasures and safety of Bat Cave, although he had missed them before he was three paces from his front door. It was not the ride from Ganymede to Europa, although he had been shoehorned for seven hours into a seat designed for some human shrimp one-third his size. It was not the ignominy of being led—near-naked, chilled, purblind, and encased like a monstrous green sausage—across the bleak prospect of Europa's surface. It was not even the presence, normally intolerable to him, of so many other humans close enough to touch, nor the narrow, uncomfortable seat on which he was now perched.

It was something worse than all of those. It was knowledge that he had been guilty of basic error.

He had obtained the first hint of a problem in his logic

when the arrival at Europa went unquestioned and unimpeded; he had suspected a major blunder when he peered through the insulating green plastic of his improvised suit and noted the composition of the group assembled around the frozen-over circle of Blowhole. He had confirmed his error when he saw Hilda Brandt commanding Camille Hamilton, and observed the latter's dreamlike trance.

And yet—he tried to comfort himself—he must also be at least *partially* right. Surely there were limits to how far logic, strictly applied, could have led him astray.

He glanced around at the people crowding in on him: David Lammerman and Camille Hamilton, close together physically and, he suspected, now closer than ever mentally; Nell Cotter, her eyes noting everything; Tristan Morgan, impatience written on his face, fidgeting, on the point of speech; Cyrus Mobarak, staring steadily at Bat and quite impassive—but still Torquemada, and therefore neither to be underestimated nor taken for granted.

And finally, Hilda Brandt. She nodded to him. *Go ahead, it's your move.*

She was right. This was Bat's show. And he was not sure where to begin. He might never be able to restore his self-esteem, but if he botched this he could certainly make himself feel even worse.

Then go slowly. The desperate run from Ganymede was over. No one was going anywhere, and there was no need for haste.

"I would like to tell you a story." His dark eyes flickered from person to person, and his voice was little more than a whisper. "To at least one of you, it will already be familiar. To others, it may be incomprehensible. Still others among you may even find it boring. For this is not merely a story, it is a story of long ago. A *war* story, in fact. A tale of the last days of the Great War."

Bat stirred in his hard chair. He had been provided with adequate clothing: a vast cylinder of cloth with holes cut through for his arms and head. But there was nothing to eat; he was still cold; and he yearned for his kitchen, his own robes, and the comfort of the padded seat deep in Bat Cave.

"Both sides performed weapons development throughout the war," he went on. "That is well-known. And new weapons, almost by definition, are *secret* weapons. Full advantage cannot be gained from their use if the enemy knows of their existence, since then they can build defenses against them.

"One such secret weapon had been in development on a small asteroid called Mandrake." Bat scanned the group. Every face wore a look of mild interest or polite incomprehension. No information there. "From its designer's point of view, the weapon was almost perfected. But when it was described to the Belt leaders, they decided that it had two big problems. The first—a minor point to them—was that it involved a form of biological experimentation strictly forbidden by all military and civilian codes. The second, and from the leaders' point of view much the more important, was that the weapon would be of no *practical* use for years. With the war going badly for the Belt, this could not be the secret weapon to snatch victory from defeat.

"Now permit me one general observation: In the Great War, Earth and Mars were the big losers in terms of casualties, but it was the other side—the Belt colonies—that was forced to surrender unconditionally. The Belt lost the war. Its production facilities were shattered, its people starved to submission, its leaders in danger of postwar trial as war criminals. After the war, popular sentiment said that the Belt leaders were human monsters. They deserved their fate of annihilation in the final battles. The only pity was that they were not available to be put on trial.

"That is a typical postwar attitude of victors. War history is written by the *winners*. But suppose that in this case, the written history were true? Suppose that the Belt leaders were truly cold, ruthless, and self-serving?"

Cyrus Mobarak was nodding. "They were. I was there, and I remember the situation clearly. You did what you were told, or that was the end of you."

"Very well. So those leaders would not have hesitated to employ an awful weapon, or been averse to destroying a useless one—especially a weapon that after the war might cause them more trouble. Of course, the Belt leaders did not alert anyone on Mandrake to their plans. They simply arranged for a full-scale attack on the asteroid, one that would reduce all evidence of experiments to ash and lifeless rock.

"But somehow, almost too late, the science chief of those biological experiments—who happened to be away from Mandrake at the time—learned of the plan to destroy the asteroid. Word was sent secretly to Mandrake. A few of the scientists managed to find a ship, a converted ore-carrier named the *Pelagic*. They fled, taking some of their experiments with them. But they were too late. A Seeker missile had already been commanded to destroy anything that tried to escape from Mandrake. It followed the *Pelagic* and blew it apart. Everyone on board perished.

"That should be the end of the story. All of the Belt political and military leaders died in the final days of the war. Good riddance, surely, for everyone in the system. The labs on Mandrake were destroyed. Records of the work, stored on Pallas, had already been purged. The *Pelagic* had been vaporized. The developer of the destroyed biological weapons was still alive, but no more eager than any other human to be offered as a scapegoat for war crimes. It was better by far to leave the Belt, lie low, and later build a new career somewhere else.

"And that is exactly what happened. It was as though the experiments on Mandrake had never been. The past vanished, for a full twenty-four years. And then, two years ago, a routine search of Belt debris came across the flight recorder of the *Pelagic*.

"The recorder showed that although nineteen people had embarked on the ship at Mandrake, only ten were on board when the *Pelagic* was annihilated. Where were the other nine? They must have been jettisoned, dead or alive, into space.

"All that would mean nothing to almost anyone in the system. It meant little to me, when I first learned of it a few months ago, even though I am far more interested than most people in relics of the Great War. I am *very* interested.

"Ah, but then why was I so delinquent? Only because I could find no record of the recovery of a life-support pod within a reasonable time of the *Pelagic*'s destruction, and at a place consistent with the ship's final position. I concluded, quite reasonably, that anyone in a survival pod was long dead.

"The information from the remnant of the *Pelagic* might mean something more to just one person—to someone who had waited for a quarter of a century for new information about that ship, without any real hope that it would ever be forthcoming. That person did not conclude, as I did, that those in the pods must be dead. Why not? Because there was another relevant fact."

Bat was interrupted. The door of the room opened in a blast of cold air. Jon Perry and Wilsa Sheer, pale-faced but otherwise apparently normal, were ushered in by Buzz Sandstrom. He glanced questioningly at Hilda Brandt.

She nodded. "Sit down. Not you, Buzz. You go and make sure that Blowhole is opening up all right. Apply heat from on top if you have to. And close this door behind you. It's too cold in here already."

She turned back to Bat as Nell and Tristan squeezed room between them for the two new arrivals. "Very well, Rustum Battachariya. There is no need for you to continue. I am ready to end this charade. I admit my guilt. After what I did with Camille out there on the surface, in front of witnesses, it would be pointless to deny it. I led certain biological research projects in the Belt during the Great War." She ignored Cyrus Mobarak's head-jerk of surprise. "If I also tell you that I had to cooperate with the Belt government or die, and that I opposed the whole war, it does not alter the facts. Now tell me what you propose to do with this information."

"I, personally? Very little." Bat stared sadly down at his rolling belly. "Not now. One day ago—one *hour* ago—I believed that murder would soon be committed on Europa. I thought that Jon Perry's life was in danger, and from something far more inimical than an accidental oxygen shortage. I rushed here from Ganymede for that reason. And I learned, within minutes of my arrival at Blowhole, that I had made a gross error. To save Jon Perry and Wilsa Sheer, you proved willing to risk exposure. That was not the action of my war crimes perpetrator. I had been wrong in thinking you *dangerous* simply because you are *devious*.

"I could and should return at once to Ganymede. But I must satisfy my own curiosity. Be assured, I will take your answers no farther. I cannot, of course, say the same for others here, or ask their silence. What you say to me may have direct relevance to them."

"It does indeed. But ask on. The time for silence is past."

"The survival pods. Nine were launched. What happened to the rest of them? I found evidence of only three having been recovered."

"So did I." Hilda Brandt was visibly troubled for the first time since the *Danae* had bobbed to the surface of Blowhole. "We have to assume that the other six were lost, and the children with them. Of the nineteen people on the

Pelagic when it left Mandrake, only three have survived: Jon Perry, Wilsa Sheer, and Camille Hamilton."

The rest of the people in the room had been sitting quietly, aware that they were eavesdroppers on a private dialogue. But Hilda Brandt's final words were too much for them. Everyone began to talk at once. They stopped only when they realized that she was continuing, quietly and conversationally.

"—and survived *then*, of course, only because of what they were. They floated free in space for many months—and lived. Just as they survived experiences in and below the Europan ice that would have been fatal to anyone else. I had my hopes that Camille would revive, you see, even when everyone swore that she was frozen and dead. And recover she did. After that, although I wanted Jon and Wilsa returned to the surface as fast as possible, I had less worry that their experience would prove fatal. I even allowed myself to gloat a little bit at how well I had done my work so long ago. And although I have no desire to learn by experiment, I cannot help but wonder how far their survival abilities might extend."

Cyrus Mobarak had been uncharacteristically silent. More than anyone else in the room, he understood the personalities of Battachariya and Hilda Brandt. And he had been forming his own odd conclusion. "Are you two saying what I *think* you're saying? That these three"—he swept his arm past Jon Perry, Wilsa Sheer, and Camille Hamilton—"are the result of those biological experiments on Mandrake twenty-five years ago? But you didn't know until just one year ago that they were still alive?"

"Dr. Brandt knew it more than a year ago," said Bat. "She tracked the pod trajectories long before I did. I learned it myself only very recently."

"Why didn't she know it a *generation* ago, when the pods were first found? Didn't it show up in the news media each time one was discovered?"

Bat raised dark eyebrows, as severe a criticism of naiveté as he would ever offer to Cyrus Mobarak. "In a solar system still reeling and staggering after the greatest disaster in human history? We all know better than that. For years after the end of the Great War, information systems were a blind chaos. The discoveries were *recorded*, certainly, but they were not *publicized*. And I suspect that at the time, Dr. Brandt had certain other postwar priorities."

"Maybe at that time." Mobarak turned on Brandt accusingly. "But if you knew they had survived a full year ago, why didn't you say something then? You owed it to them."

"Say what, and to whom?" Hilda Brandt snapped back at him. "Think about it, Cyrus, and tell me what good it could do. I knew that I would probably tell them eventually, but only after I'd had a chance to take a good look at them and convince myself that it was the right thing to do. They've been living happy, healthy, normal lives for a quarter of a century. Are you telling me that I ought to have had them labeled as biological experiments, so that people could start treating them as freaks and monsters?"

Understanding had been dawning slowly on Jon, Wilsa, and Camille. They had heard, but they could not *believe*.

Camille, sitting in the meeting from the beginning, was the first to react. "Are you agreeing with Mobarak . . . that we are just *experiments*? Human freaks, that you made on Mandrake?"

"*No!* I'm saying anything but that. You see, Cyrus, that's *exactly* the sort of thing I was afraid of." Hilda Brandt swung back to Camille and spoke with great emphasis. "You are *not* monsters or freaks, any one of you, and I should have my tongue cut out for using those words. You are human beings—*superior* human beings."

"But what did you *do* to us?" asked Wilsa.

"*Improved* you. You were modified before you were born, to give you control over your autonomic nervous system and a better interface between conscious and unconscious thought. If necessary, you three can slow or speed up your metabolic rate and reaction times. You can modify all bodily functions. You can achieve levels of muscle control impossible for anyone else. You can also—with sufficient urging—integrate data in ways that the rest of us find hard to even imagine. It's mental superiority, as well as physical. Camille, you are like other people—only you are *better*."

Nell Cotter thought suddenly of Jon Perry, with his absolute sense of position, coolly guiding the *Spindrift* through the seaquake while his fingers rippled across the submersible's controls too fast to follow. Of Wilsa at her keyboards, her fingers and toes performing as twenty independent instruments of impossible coordination and precision. And of Camille, her attention turned totally inward, performing under Hilda Brandt's direction the feats of computation that everyone—including Camille herself—had believed could never be done without a computer.

Then Nell had another vision, of ice blocks bulging beneath fair skin bloated with liquid. "You mean that when Camille was trapped and frozen—"

"—her body did what it had to." Hilda Brandt nodded. "She drank all the water that she could find. As that water froze near the surface of her body, she used the released latent heat to keep her core temperature up and allow her to remain alive. It was a form of hibernation, but Camille never knew *consciously* what was happening. Her built-in survival mechanisms took over." She turned to Jon and Wilsa. "And the same with you two. You managed with too little air, for far longer than Gabriel Shumi said was possible."

"We just sat in the ship," said Wilsa. "We fell asleep, but we didn't do anything special."

"Not special for *you*." Hilda Brandt was looking at the

three fondly. "Just impossible for anyone else—until there are more people like you. And there will be—my God, what now?"

Brandt's question was not to Camille and the other two, but to Buzz Sandstrom, who had come barreling through the door as though he were trying to knock it down.

"It's Ganymede. Bad news." Sandstrom had been recovering his cockiness after Jon and Wilsa's rescue, but now he seemed out of his depth again. "We got a call from our staff there. It's all over the news media. They say the life forms in the ocean here aren't native! Somebody leaked that they're Earth forms, changed and imported."

"Hmm. I wonder who might have done *that*." Hilda Brandt stared at Bat, who shook his head. "All right, I believe you. What did you tell them, Buzz?"

"Nothing."

"Why not?"

"I'd nothing to say. Anyway, they won't talk to me. They say they'll only talk to you."

"They're feeling insecure. Go and assure them that I'm on my way." Hilda Brandt sighed and stood up, but she did not leave the room. Instead she turned to Battachariya. "Do you know what upsets me more than anything else about all this?"

"I do. It is the fear that your children may now be regarded by the ignorant as monsters and freaks."

"My *children*. They are not . . ." Brandt paused. "Well, we learn something every day. You are a phenomenon, Rustum Battachariya, did you know that? You deny emotion, yet at *understanding* emotion . . ."

She turned to Jon, Wilsa, and Camille. "He is right, of course. That is exactly how I think of you. You *are* my children, in an emotional if not in a genetic sense. I would never do anything to harm you."

And again to Bat. "You see, *that's* what hurts and upsets me, more than anything. That you, an intelligent man whom Magrit Knudsen describes as sensitive and perceptive, could be convinced that I would kill to protect the Europan environment. So convinced that you had to come rushing here to stop me from killing not a *stranger*, but someone whom I had known since birth—since *before* birth. What sort of animal do you think I am?"

"I was in error. I have already admitted that. I had not interacted with you sufficiently at the time. Also, I could not forget the assault on Yarrow Gobel."

"Which was never intended, and you should have known it!" Hilda Brandt chided Bat, like a teacher disappointed by a slow pupil. "When someone of body mass less than sixty kilos, like Inspector-General Gobel, intercepts a dose designed for someone of body mass of . . . two hundred and fifty kilos?"

"Two hundred and ninety."

"You see my point. Your memory loss would have been temporary and partial. It would have applied only to events of recent months, and you would have been back to normal long ago."

She finally went to the open door. "However, that is no excuse. I accept full responsibility for Yarrow Gobel's mishap. As I accept full responsibility for all of my actions. When I return, you will tell me what you propose to do about it. But first I must reassure the members of my staff. They think that the universe is ending. Which, of course, it is not."

She turned to Cyrus Mobarak. "It may be impossible to preserve Europa, now that word is out that our ocean is contaminated with Earth forms. So you win, Cyrus, and I lose. But winners and losers often switch. I won't give up. And I have won, too, in other ways."

She was gone before Mobarak or anyone else could comment.

25

Winners and Losers

Nell Cotter had been trained to hold her mind and her camera on the main action. When Hilda Brandt left the room, that wasn't easy. Nell sensed a change in group focus, but she was not sure of the new center.

Jon Perry and Wilsa Sheer were sitting between Nell and Tristan. Just beyond Tristan was Camille, and next to her, David Lammerman. The six were eyeing each other uneasily, ignoring Battachariya and Mobarak, who sat facing them. Nell felt Jon Perry inch away from her a fraction as she turned to look along the line of people.

She split the camera field to record the facial expressions of the three refugees from the *Pelagic*, and sought to guess their thoughts. *Together at birth, even before birth, raised for the first year or two as a unit, breathing in each other's sight and sounds and smells. No wonder Jon and Wilsa responded so strongly and immediately to each other. Then thrown out as babies into open space, alone and abandoned, to live or to die.*

Six had not survived. The other three had been found one by one in the post-war chaos and raised in the totally different environments of Earth, Mars, and the Belt. They had followed separate careers, unaware of each other's existence until Hilda Brandt brought them together. But now they would begin to see themselves as like each other—and as unlike any other human beings who ever lived.

And how will others see them? Nell realized that she had already started to think differently about Jon Perry. Would she dare a close relationship with a man who had an absolute and unnatural control over his mind and body? She recalled the report from Arenas of Jon's impossibly fast run after the carnival float. Now it was believable.

And then she felt fascination, anger at herself, and a strong affection. Jon was still Jon. *He* hadn't changed, if she had not.

Hilda Brandt is right, we are all human beings.

She forced herself to reach out and grip Jon's thigh. The muscle trembled and tightened beneath her touch, then slowly relaxed. He leaned toward her, placing his hand on hers.

No Ice Man here. I'll believe absolute body control when I feel it for myself. And if it's real, I'll bet it can be a load of fun.

But how typical am I?

Nell glanced along the line to Tristan Morgan. For perhaps the first time in his life, he was not fidgeting in his seat. He had taken Wilsa's hand in his, and he was talking quietly into her ear. She wore a lonely, wistful smile. But at least it *was* a smile. Camille and David, at the far end, were staring back at Nell, observing her and Jon as calmly as she was observing them. Perhaps one side effect of a modified nervous system was an ability to resist shocks that would stupefy ordinary people. And maybe it was catching. Nell felt fine.

She turned her attention to her camera, which was covering Cyrus Mobarak and Rustum Battachariya. For the past half hour Mobarak had said little. He was less on-stage than Nell had ever seen him. But with Hilda Brandt out of the room he was coming to life.

"Well, then. This is apparently a time for general revelation and confession." Mobarak's tone to Bat was conversational, even casual. If he were shocked or ruffled, no one would ever know it. "All secrets are to be revealed—and you never did tell me how you decided that Hilda Brandt and I had been working together. Are you willing to discuss it? Or does that remain privileged information?"

Out of the corner of her eye, Nell saw Tristan Morgan jerk forward. But she had no time to look at him, because Battachariya was already answering.

"Not at all privileged. And I fear that there was no deep insight, only a rather pedestrian chain of logic." Nell thought she detected a trace of satisfaction on Bat's face, the first that she had seen since he had joined the group at Blowhole. But he continued serenely. "After several false starts, I at last came up with identifiers for the three children of the *Pelagic* who had been found in survival pods and revived: Jon Perry, Wilsa Sheer, and Camille Hamilton. Those names shocked me beyond belief— because I learned that each of them, now grown to adulthood, *was presently in the Jovian system.* More than that, each had recently appeared here for the first time, from widely separated locations.

"By then I also suspected that all three had been the subject of biological experiments at the end of the Great War. So it was natural to conclude that someone else, a full year before me, had read the message in the *Pelagic*'s flight recorder and been led to those same three names. The most logical person was surely one who had been involved in the original experiments.

"Very good so far, and very simple. But I was missing one key piece of information: *Who?* Who could have worked on Mandrake during the war, and twenty-five years later have been instrumental in bringing those three here at this time?

"I had one prime candidate: *you*."

This time Bat actually smiled at Mobarak's rising eyebrows. "That's right. Cyrus Mobarak, the Sun King himself. Who else? Consider the facts. You were in the Belt at the end of the Great War, a young man in your twenties. You have since become an individual of great wealth and influence, well able to pull wires behind the scenes on Earth. You could and did have Jon Perry sent to Europa. You could and did reorder DOS priorities, so that Camille Hamilton and David Lammerman had little choice but to come here and work for you. You could and did bring Wilsa Sheer to the Jovian system. All it took was substantial concert funding, with a fat commission for a major new work. You had enough money to make the offer irresistible. Her agent would do the rest.

"And then my beautiful, logical structure crumbled apart. Because it was not logical at all.

"If you were eager to see the present condition of your long-ago experiments, why not send Camille Hamilton and Wilsa Sheer to *Earth*, where you and Jon Perry were already located? That was surely easier than a rendezvous at Jupiter. Just as fatal for my argument, I learned that you had other, very plausible reasons for wanting Jon Perry on Europa. The 'native' Europan life forms that you had planted needed to be exposed for what they are, *designed* forms imported from Earth, in order to destroy the opposition to your Europan fusion project. You needed Camille for much the same reason, to help your plans for Europan development.

"Finally, my friend Mord delivered the death blow: You had worked with Mordecai Perlman himself on Pallas at the end of the war. You were madly developing your new fusion ideas. Mord swore that you could not also have worked on the biological projects on Mandrake.

"That was the end. A nice theory, ruined by facts. But as any Puzzle Network enthusiast knows, even wrong theories can lead to new insights. I no longer had a *name*, for that of Cyrus Mobarak would not do. But I did have a *place:* Europa. Everything converged here. Even Wilsa Sheer, for no reason obvious to me, had come to Europa. And in Europan affairs, there is just one dominant figure. I could find no suspicious elements in Hilda Brandt's past—I think that she could give both of us lessons in concealment—but she had spent the war in the Belt, coming here only long after it was over. She had also requested that Jon Perry be sent to Europa, to examine supposed native life.

"Yet Hilda Brandt would not do, either. She has great influence in the Jovian system, and she might well have performed secret wartime work in the Belt. If so, she surely would have longed to see how that work turned out, so long after. But her power did not extend, as Cyrus Mobarak's does, to the Inner System. *She* could not have directed Camille Hamilton here from DOS, nor guaranteed that it was Jon Perry, and not some other submersible expert, who came from Earth. Could not—*unless she were given assistance.*

"Finally, the pieces fit. Not one name. *Two.* And two people, each manipulating the other, each *using* the other, to achieve their separate objectives."

"My esteemed adversary, I am disappointed." Mobarak was shaking his head. "You and I have explored each other's minds for twenty years. Yet you suspected that I might stoop to murder?"

"No, I did not. I felt—right or wrong—that I understood the mind of Torquemada. What I did *not* know was the mind and nature of Hilda Brandt. And I could not trust you to know it, either. Might she be a person who would examine her experiments, evaluate their present status, and then cold-bloodedly destroy them to serve other objectives of her own? I could not take that risk."

"You ought to have consulted me. Hilda Brandt isn't that sort of person. But she asked the right question before she left: What are you going to do about all this?"

"About Brandt's past, and her experiments? I personally will do nothing. It is not my prerogative or my concern. But what they"—Bat gestured to Wilsa and the others—"may choose to do is another matter. Most of the events that we are talking about occurred a quarter of a century ago, and although there is no statute of limitation for war crimes, there is certainly a statute of limitation for *interest* in war crimes. Particularly ones that were arguably never committed. I doubt that anyone not in this room cares one jot about what happened on Mandrake."

Bat turned to Nell. "Do they, Miss Cotter? I feel sure that you are recording everything, as always. But is there really a *public* interest in any of this?"

I wonder if he knows about the subvocal, too. Nell shook her head and managed to avoid glancing at her hidden camera. "People care only if it makes an interesting show. They will love to see the Moby burning down into Blowhole, and then the submersible rescue. That's exciting, and visual, and near real-time. But you'd have to *pay* them to make them watch a program about a twenty-five-year-old crime that maybe didn't happen."

"And the results of the experiments?"

"People won't believe there's anything different about Jon and the others unless they can *see* it. And they can't. Video audiences believe *pictures*, not statements."

"A sound philosophy. I can only applaud its wisdom."

Bat began to lift himself laboriously from his narrow seat. As well-padded as he was, he could feel the ribbed seams of the chair's narrow sides cutting into tender flesh. "So Hilda Brandt was right. The universe is not ending, and the story of the *Pelagic* will again fade into history. But there is a lesson to be learned from this, for all of us." Bat rubbed at his sore behind. He was weary and hungry and feeling dangerously pontifical. It was time to go home. He turned to Cyrus Mobarak.

"Winners and losers, as Hilda Brandt said. You manipulated events and people, and won the fight for the development of Europa. But everyone, saint or sinner, pursues his or her personal objectives, and those are rarely the same for any two people, no matter how much they pretend collaboration. Before you feel too much satisfaction in your victory, remember that you were *yourself* manipulated for Hilda Brandt's benefit. You brought her the three individuals whom she wanted—and you never realized that you were doing so.

"It is time for the two of us to recognize that not every subtle mind of the solar system moves within the circle of the Puzzle Network. Hilda Brandt proved the master of us both. You won this time, but perhaps you will not always win."

"No, he *didn't*." The voice was Wilsa Sheer's, breaking in unexpectedly on Bat's ruminations. He looked at her in annoyance. He had not finished.

"Didn't win, I mean." She ignored Bat's glare. "Can we show them, Jon? I know you want to wait for confirmation, but this is important."

"You want me to do it *twice*? I thought that once in a lifetime was more than enough." But Jon Perry was standing up, walking across to the data station and peering at the back of it. "All right. Anyone know how to work this thing?"

"I do." Tristan was already out of his seat. "Let me." He grabbed the data unit from Jon's hand. "Which segment?"

"There's only one. Don't look for sound, it's just video." Jon turned back to face the others while Tristan was mounting the unit. "I hate to stick my neck out again. So the only thing I'll say is that this recording was made less than three days ago, that you'll be looking at the deep ocean floor of Europa—one hundred and eighteen kilometers below the ice—and that the ambient temperature is nine degrees above freezing."

The light in the little room dimmed. The data-station screen flickered and steadied to the black-and-white, low-contrast presentation of a typical ultrasonics image. The sensor was scanning across the seabed from the far horizon. There was nothing to see but a uniform, soft-edged floor laid down by a billion years of faint tidal motion.

Tristan opened his mouth—and before he could speak, a set of sawtoothed structures jumped into view, as straight as ruled lines. Greater detail emerged as the submersible steadily descended; each furrow changed from its sharp-edged outline to reveal a dividing set of sandwich wafers.

"And here's where we added visible wavelengths to the ultrasonics." Jon Perry was commenting in spite of himself. A free-swimmer could be seen, moving ahead of the *Danae*. The picture on the screen was sharper, and in glowing false color. A glittering line of faceted beads was revealed along the edge of each sandwich.

"Just silicon and ferrite crystals, most people would say. But I wanted to take a better look. Watch now, as we send the swimmer in."

The light source was no more than a couple of feet from one of the edged ridges. As it came closer yet and the beam increased in intensity, the ridge *moved*. It began flattening out, flowing downward, sluggishly heading away from the light.

"Photophobic, or heat sensitive. We'll know which when we've had a chance to examine what's in the *Danae*'s hold. We had lots of time down there, so I stowed away plenty of samples. But even without that analysis, it's easy to make some guesses. You are looking at a stable structure that repairs itself and replicates itself—you'll see that happening on the edges of the wafers if you watch for a while. The structures also operate at a higher temperature than the ambient seabed, and they use chemical energy to make that possible. You've already seen them avoiding stimuli that might do them harm."

Tristan had stayed close to the data unit, and he was staring at the screen from just a few centimeters away. "Those things are *alive.*"

"If you accept most definitions of alive. The furrows are acting as only living things are supposed to be able to act. They even seem to be evolving as they spread. But I was burned once before. This time I'd rather not say too much until I'm *sure.*"

But Jon is sure. He just doesn't want to come right out and say it. Nell glanced across at Cyrus Mobarak. *And he's sure, too. Look at his face. Winners and losers. He's under tight control again, but he knows he didn't win at all. These are the real native life forms. With them, Europa is protected. It won't be developed for a long time.*

"How do you know these weren't brought from Earth, too, and planted here?" Tristan was still squinting at the screen.

"Because they're not DNA-based, like every living thing on Earth. They're aperiodic crystal structures in *clays*—but still, they can reproduce. We've wondered about this sort of thing for a long time. Cairns-Smith suggested the idea over a century ago, but it's the first time we've encountered it."

"But couldn't these have been made *artificially,* like the other ones you found and said were native Europan?"

Jon grimaced. "Don't remind me. But I'm sure that these are not constructs. Even if it could be done—which I don't believe—it wouldn't make any sense. Wilsa and I visited a place on the Europan seabed where no one had ever been. No one would normally go there. Why put something where the chances are it wouldn't be found for decades?"

Cyrus Mobarak stood up suddenly. "Outmaneuvered—by Nature. Winners and losers, eh? Damnation. Was it Margaret Fuller who said, 'I accept the universe'? Well, so do I."

Nell looked at him and marveled at the resilience of the man. It would be easy to believe that Cyrus Mobarak was blessed naturally with the super nervous system that Hilda Brandt had sought to create. In the past hour he had seen years of planning apparently succeed and then, in just a few minutes, seen it thwarted—by the very person he himself had brought to Europa to help him win.

Yet already Mobarak was recovering. There was no sign on his face of defeat or resignation. Like Hilda Brandt, he would take endless shocks and still come up for another round.

"I think we must assume that the Europan fusion project will have to be put on hold," Mobarak went on briskly. "That affects you, Camille, and you too, David, at least as much as it affects me. Naturally, I hope that both of you will go on working with me. But if you want to accept other positions—"

"I want to go back to DOS," Camille blurted. "I want you to arrange it and get me observing time."

She could see that Mobarak was surprised and David was hurt. And she wasn't really ready, either, but Mobarak himself had said that it was the time for revelations. If Jon Perry were willing to stick his neck out, so was she.

Camille waved a puny slip of printout. It was all she had to show. "This is from my DOS experiment—the one I left running in background mode when we came to the Jovian system. Results started to come in just before I left Abacus. But I couldn't understand them, and I didn't have my computer models available. Now, after Blowhole and the Moby, that doesn't seem to matter so much. I think I know what I'm seeing, even without my computer to confirm it. But I still need the best images that DOS can give me . . . because if I'm right, seven billion light-years out, halfway to infinite red shift, there's a uniform thermally radiating surface bigger than a galaxy."

Her words had no effect on Cyrus Mobarak, she could see that. But they certainly did on David.

"My God. A Stapledon! You think you're seeing evidence of a Stapledon-Dyson construct?" He turned to Mobarak. "Camille's saying that DOS has located an artificial structure, a monstrous one, surrounding a whole galaxy to capture its energy. That can only mean an intelligent civilization."

Still it produced no reaction from Mobarak. "Seven billion light-years," he said slowly. "So whatever you saw, it happened seven billion years ago. Before the solar system even existed. If it was there, it must be long gone by now. Maybe I'm missing something, but that doesn't strike me as being very important—not compared with modifying the surface of Europa, or sending Tristan off on *Starseed* to explore the Oort Cloud." He paused, until Bat prompted him with a curious throat-clearing sound. "But maybe I'm wrong. David, you understand this better than I do. And I trust your judgment. If you tell me that you want to leave here and go back to DOS with Camille, and follow up on what she's found . . . I'll find a way to arrange it."

Nell's camera must have caught the uncertainty on David Lammerman's face, because Nell saw it herself. He was staring intently at Camille Hamilton, waiting, questioning. *Is it all right?* At last she gave a little nod, and he turned to face Cyrus Mobarak.

"I *do* think that Camille's discovery is enormously important," he said quietly. "She ought to be given access to DOS at once, with as much observing time as she needs. And I'd like to return to DOS, too, and work with her. But not at once. Right now, if you'll let me—" he looked

Mobarak directly in the eyes "—I think it's time that I started to learn the family business."

Nell's camera was still running. And finally she had her own experience of winners and losers. She was a first-time winner, because for the one and only time in her life, her camera was capturing the soul of Cyrus Mobarak.

But she was a loser, too, and a lousy reporter; because she knew that she would never bring herself to use the shot.

26

End Game

Home. At last.

Bat opened the door and ambled the length of Bat Cave, picking up old, defanged weapons, opening the tiny—and empty—cases for multimegaton bombs, and shuffling files at the same time that he admired their studied disorder.

The communications unit was spilling over with messages, buzzing and chirping at him as he progressed along the room. He padded across to it. Half a dozen problems and solutions from members of the Puzzle Network; four Call Me signals from Magrit Knudsen, one from Mord, electronically itching to know what had happened; and five No Reply Needed messages from the staff of the Passenger Transport Department.

Bat frowned at the final arriving line, still visible on the screen—*"You did it! Today Europa, tomorrow the stars!"*—as he headed for the kitchen. He paused on the threshold. All the way from Europa to Ganymede he had been promising himself a five-cheese, five-liter fondue, made in his special cook pot. But in his absence, Bat Cave had been invaded. The main kitchen work surface was occupied by a long, decorated cake that read "Welcome Home, Bat" in red marzipan.

He leaned over and sniffed. The aroma was pleasant, but not quite right. He cut a small piece, popped it into his mouth, and revised his opinion. It was ghastly: oily and heavy, and sickly sweet.

Bat carried the cake over to the recycling unit. But even as he poised it on the edge of the chute, that great head-to-toe weariness swept through him again. After all the talk and all the stirring of emotion at Mount Ararat, he had not been able to sleep for one moment on the return trip. Now he didn't have the energy to read his messages, or to call Magrit Knudsen, or to chat with Mord. He didn't even have the energy to *eat*. Everything would have to wait until tomorrow.

He headed for the great bed, yawning, stripping off his clothes as he went, rubbing and scratching his smooth black belly. The silky sheets were as soft and cool and thoroughly delightful as he remembered them. He turned back the top one, climbed in naked, and slid his feet down.

About a meter in, they stuck and would go no farther. Someone had turned the sheets back halfway to make an apple-pie bed.

Yarrow Gobel. Progressed to a twelve-year-old, with an adolescent boy's ideas of what was funny. Bat sighed, climbed out, and patiently remade his bed.

He climbed back in and closed his eyes. He was exhausted. But now, unbelievably, when all of his worries were gone and he was snug in the depths of Bat Cave, sleep still would not come. He blinked his eyes open and stared at the grainy ceiling. What was the problem?

Not the events in the mobile lab at Blowhole, even though he had suffered the ignominy of being *wrong*.

Had it come after that, at Ararat Base? Bat had observed the duos and trios, forming before his astonished eyes and establishing themselves in real-time. Cyrus Mobarak and

Tristan Morgan, feeling their way toward the use of a Moby in Project *Starseed*, with David Lammerman as the accepted intermediary. A David Lammerman who was also working out, with Camille's blessing and assistance, a new father-son relationship. And a Tristan Morgan who had half his mind on Wilsa Sheer—while she, Camille, and Jon Perry puzzled their way toward the structure of their own relationship. They might pursue their separate careers, but they would always share a unique heritage. Naturally they were fascinated by each other, and also by Hilda Brandt. They did not seem to resent what she had done. To children who had never known parents, perhaps she was the nearest thing to a mother that they would ever have.

And then there was Brandt herself. She had not accepted that Europa might lose its restricted status, even when she thought that the life forms there were synthetic. She could protect it now, with a far better chance of success than before.

Except that Cyrus Mobarak, too, did not give up easily. There would be a gigantic battle over the Europan fusion project, fought at every public and private level of science, politics, and skullduggery. As to who might win, Mobarak or Brandt . . . that was a real problem, worthy of the top brains in the Puzzle Network.

And yet none of that was Bat's concern. What afflicted him was a worry far more *personal*.

He clambered wearily out of bed again and went to the message unit. He ignored the Puzzle Network entries, but he read all of the others. Not one of them had anything to do with work. They were inquiries about his journey to Europa, and announcements of forthcoming meetings—*social*, not professional. Two were simply invitations to dinner!

Bat returned to bed. People were misinterpreting his trip to Europa. They seemed to think it signaled a complete change in his personality. He knew what they were after. They wanted a sign that read—in their own distorted terms—"Happy Ending."

They were wrong, of course. Life was not a video show. And yet, maybe that was not the real message . . .

Bat closed his eyes. But he could not close his ears and his mind. Around Bat Cave, in every direction, the interior of Ganymede pulsed with activity. Humans, as busy as termites, bored and built and ran and fetched and carried; thousand after thousand of them, eternally awake, endlessly bustling. He imagined that he could actually *hear* them.

And it could only get worse. The population of Ganymede was increasing. The change was obvious in the transportation manifests, which showed more and more flights in and out every year, bigger and bigger ships carrying larger numbers of passengers and heavier cargoes. Where would it end? With Ganymede the natural nexus between the Inner and Outer Systems, how long would it be before it was groaning under the burden of too many people, like Earth before the Great War?

Bat opened his eyes again. His trip away from the cave had allowed him to see the problem. Perhaps it had also provided a solution—the only solution that he could imagine, anywhere within the whole solar system.

He climbed out of bed for one last time and returned to the message terminal.

"Mord." Bat spoke to the skeptical face that appeared at last on the screen. He had made a decision. He was willing to put his money on Hilda Brandt. "What do you think of the idea of permanent relocation to Europa?"

POSTLUDE

A quarter of a century; a hundred major radiation storms and the random buffeting of solar winds; half a dozen passages through the jumble of the Asteroid Belt. The original orbits had been twisted and tugged and turned, until no trajectory analysis could ever track their chaos.

First year: *As the limits of conventional survival were reached and passed, second-stage techniques took over. Tissue resorption began. Arms and legs vanished; internal organs modified their functions. Hearts and livers and lungs atrophied, while each small body shrank and rounded to a smooth, featureless ovoid.*

Five years: *The pod interiors hovered at the temperature of liquid nitrogen. Within them, vital functions had long since slowed and stopped. Brains became fixed crystalline matrices, through whose frozen networks the minimal signals flickered like uneasy dreams.*

Decades: *The end of the Great War was distant history, but the infants would not die. Time and survival had lost meaning. It was unimportant to say that discovery might come today, tomorrow, or in the far future.*

* * *

At long last, the six pods had converged close to their original tight grouping, floating from alien skies once more into the busy routes of commerce. From its vantage point far above the ecliptic, a broad-beam survey unit bathed the potential menaces to shipping in a ghostly glimmer of pale violet. The beam moved away. Half a minute later it swung back for a puzzled second look.

In their icy wombs the children waited. Time stretched on, toward the hour of second birth.

MORE SCIENCE FICTION
BESTSELLERS FROM TOR

☐	53676-2	ARSLAN	$3.95
☐	53677-0	M.J. Engh	Canada $4.95
☐	54333-5	CV	$2.95
☐	54334-3	Damon Knight	Canada $3.50
☐	54622-9	THE FALLING WOMAN	$3.95
☐	54623-7	Pat Murphy	Canada $4.95
☐	53327-5	THE INFINITY LINK	$4.95
☐	53328-3	Jeffrey A. Carver	Canada $5.95
☐	50984-6	KILLER	$3.95
☐		David Drake & Karl Edward Wagner	Canada $4.95
☐	50024-5	LAND'S END	$4.95
☐	50026-1	Frederik Pohl & Jack Williamson	Canada $5.95
☐	54564-8	NIGHTFLYERS	$3.50
☐	54565-6	George R.R. Martin	Canada $4.50
☐	55716-6	PHANTOMS ON THE WIND	$3.50
☐	55717-4	Robert E. Vardeman	Canada $4.50
☐	55259-8	SUBTERRANEAN GALLERY	$3.95
☐	55258-X	Richard Paul Russo	Canada $4.95
☐	54425-0	THE WANDERER	$2.95
☐	54426-9	Fritz Leiber	Canada $3.25
☐	55711-5	WORLD'S END	$2.95
☐	55712-3	Joan D. Vinge	Canada $3.50

Buy them at your local bookstore or use this handy coupon:
Clip and mail this page with your order.

Publishers Book and Audio Mailing Service
P.O. Box 120159, Staten Island, NY 10312-0004

Please send me the book(s) I have checked above. I am enclosing $ _____
(Please add $1.25 for the first book, and $.25 for each additional book to cover postage and handling.
Send check or money order only—no CODs.)

Name _____
Address _____
City _____ State/Zip _____
Please allow six weeks for delivery. Prices subject to change without notice.

AWARD-WINNING SF FROM MIKE RESNICK

☐ ☐	51192-1	ALTERNATE PRESIDENTS	$4.99 Canada $5.99
☐ ☐	51246-4	BWANA/BULLY	$3.99 Canada $4.99
☐ ☐	50042-3	IVORY: A LEGEND OF PAST AND FUTURE	$4.95 Canada $5.95
☐ ☐	50716-9	PARADISE: A CHRONICLE OF A DISTANT WORLD	$4.95 Canada $5.95
☐ ☐	55112-5	SANTIAGO: A MYTH OF THE FAR FUTURE	$3.50 Canada $3.95
☐ ☐	51113-1	SECOND CONTACT	$3.95 Canada $4.95
☐ ☐	50985-4	STALKING THE UNICORN: A FABLE OF TONIGHT	$3.95 Canada $4.95